WHEN THE TIDES HELD THE MOON

WHEN THE TIDES HELD THE MOON

Venessa Vida Kelley

EREWHON

an imprint of Kensington Publishing Corp.
erewhonbooks.com

EREWHON BOOKS are published by:
Kensington Publishing Corp.
900 Third Avenue
New York, NY 10022
erewhonbooks.com

ISBN 978-1-64566-153-5 (hardcover)

First Erewhon hardcover printing: May 2025

10 9 8 7 6 5 4 3 2 1

Printed in the United States of America

Library of Congress Control Number: 2024944362

Electronic edition: ISBN 978-1-64566-157-3

Edited by Diana Pho
Cover design/illustration and interior illustrations by Venessa Vida Kelley
Interior design by Leah Marsh
Additional interior art courtesy of Ann Lou/Adobe Stock (seaweed ornaments)

The authorized representative in the EU for product safety and compliance is eucomply OU, Parnu mnt 139b-14, Apt 123
Tallinn, Berlin 11317, hello@eucompliancepartner.com

For Sonny and Roger and all who hold their breath.

El día de San Ciriaco

Humacao, Puerto Rico
8 de agosto 1899

On the night I lose my memories, I learn the sky can mimic
metal. The hurricane is a dark blue-green gray. A storm of
oxidized pewter.

And my ears can hardly stand the noise.

"¡Auxilio!"

"¡Ayúdano', Señor!"

A hundred screams—a thousand—drown in squalls as the world
tips sideways and the river runs thick with debris and the dead.

I'm in here with them, my hands raking across rocks for an
anchor that won't get torn upstream with me. I figure out quick

there's no resisting the current, so I let it tow me under, and as the roar deadens to a growl, I think: *Better.*

Only when my scrapes start stinging and I can't taste salt does danger finally come for me—in a wave that knocks me chest-first into the exposed roots of a Flamboyan tree.

I can't breathe. But before the world goes black, a voice— maybe God's—speaks:

"¡SÁLVALO!"

Here, in the rapids, I can see it. A face that matches the sky.

Fierce. Pewter.

Then, gone.

ONE

Red Hook District, Brooklyn, New York
February 15, 1911

Tití Luz used to tell me, "No hay mal que por bien no venga," which was a timeworn proverb for saying every cloud has a silver lining, hurricanes notwithstanding.

She was the reason I'd sailed sixteen hundred miles to get here, a promise she'd pressed out of me on her deathbed. The way she saw it, Nueva York was a stockpile of the freedom America had pledged to Puerto Rico, and she couldn't rest in peace if I didn't vow to claim my share. There wasn't really a choice; Tití Luz could out-stubborn even the tuberculosis that was killing her, and would have kept breathing just to guilt me. So I agreed. Sailing away from the solitude that had hung around me my whole life seemed a decent enough silver lining once she was gone.

Bueno, the joke was on me. Because, in a city of almost ten million people, being boricua in a dingy Brooklyn foundry gets you nothing *but* solitude.

Speaking nothing but Puerto Rican Spanish, it's not like I got off the boat expecting to share nightly drinks with the entire

Sixth Ward. But ironwork always takes a crew, and English wasn't so hard for a malleable mouth like mine to learn. I didn't think I'd be stripping ingots four years later with a bunch of Irish extranjeros who'd never bothered to learn my real name, still hunting for silver linings.

Then again, the way my life turned on its head when I volunteered to build that maldito tank, maybe I just hadn't gotten the right commission.

"All right ya useless cabbages, who wants a crack at a head-smelter?"

From his perch on the stairs overlooking the molding floor of the Structural Ironworks Department, Paddy McCoy was a wobbly-jowled guard in his watchtower, scouring for inmates. My coworkers and I nearly fit the bill; we were busy sweating buckets at the blast furnaces below him, prepping beams for another millionaire's monument to himself: the Woolworth Building.

At our station next to the cooling beds, Farty Walsh shuffled away from me and into the foreman's line of sight holding up two sooty palms like he was facing arrest. "Wasn't it you sayin' beam rollers' hands is too thick for smelters, chief? Or did the gombeens in Ornamental waste 'emselves makin' pretty gates for the Vanderbilts now?"

Two dozen snorts and snickers blended with the furnaces' roar as I turned back to my work. Farty was better at wagging his lips than helping me strip iron bars fresh from the crucibles, but I hated to admit the malcriado had a point. Head-smelter commissions were troublesome, technical puzzles—so named for being a legitimate dolor de cabeza to deliver on time. They usually fell to the twiggy, smooth-fingered craftsmen in the Ornamental Ironwork Department the next building over, not the rough nuts in Structural, most of whom were built broader and only slightly fleshier than the metal we pounded.

Don't ask how a flaquito like me wound up in here.

"One day, you'll get that smart mouth o' yours caught in the forge, Mr. Walsh," McCoy snarked on his way down to the shop floor. "The Ornamental lads is all tied up with the Woolworth, same as you."

Across from Farty and me, Innis scoffed around the pipe between his teeth. "Meanin' it's a shite job."

"Meaning it's an opportunity," McCoy countered. "It's headed to one o' them Coney Island parks. Might be a good time, if you've had your fill of rivets and beam rollin'."

Farty spat, the only wet thing in this building that wasn't petroleum. "Aye, if it's so much fun, I bet Wheezy'll do it. He's havin' a bad dose."

Just to be clear, my name's Benny, not Wheezy—a nickname Farty invented for two reasons: the first being the busted lungs God saw fit to give me, and the second being Farty's need for a pithy way to remind everyone that, sure as I was shorter than him, I'd always be lower too.

No one called Marty Walsh "Farty" but me, the only reason being that anyone who talked out of his ass as much as he did deserved a name to match. Not that I'd ever said it to him out loud.

"Ah, lay offa Wheezy!" Farty's cogging partner and drinking buddy Dan sidled up next to us with a black stripe drawn thickly across his forehead from wiping sweat. In the reddish glow of the furnaces, we all looked brown . . .

"He's just mopey 'cause Long Island's got no palm trees!"

. . . but I was the one who got it rubbed in his face.

I knelt over the mold and tugged my cap down over the scene of heckling coworkers, taking smaller sips of air to ward off the whistle rising in my chest. If I started coughing, I'd never stop, and the day was long enough without these pendejos cracking wise about my shitty breathing.

I was still staring at the ground when McCoy's shoes shuffled into view followed by a leaf of folded stationery.

"You interested, Caldera?"

Farty leaned leisurely on one leg to watch his influence play out. I would deliver the apology he owed me on his behalf in the mirror later; if he knew how good my impression of his voice was, it would wipe that self-satisfied smirk clean off his grimy face. Standing up, I stripped my leather gloves, wiped my sweaty palms on my corduroys, and took the order.

The "blueprint" was just an artist's sketch. Drawn in black ink was an iron-and-glass cage balanced on a steel undercarriage, albeit the bars wrapped around only three sides leaving an unobstructed viewing pane on the fourth. It looked fit to hold a small lake, with a drainage hatch by the bottom and another in the lattice roof reachable by a set of iron rungs built onto the side. Tiny script cluttered the drawing—stuff like "Panes must be impervious to rupture" and "Padlock or rim lock? You decide."

I smoothed my expression in case anyone was looking for a crack in it to stick a fingernail through. "On wheels?" I asked.

McCoy lifted his bowler hat to scratch at the patch of thinning cabello underneath. "Just the rims. As for the tempered panes, Bushwick Glass Works will take care of 'em sure. But the gentleman did say the asset must be transportable."

That wasn't so bad. The wagons that ran coffee between the plantations and piers in Puerto Rico had needed rims too. At my old foundry, I'd forged everything from shipping vessel parts to mill machinery to ornamented ceiling tiles for la Casa de la Alcaldía de San Juan by the time I was fifteen. It was fascinating work, easy to disappear into if you had a brain full of noise like mine.

"By when?" I asked.

Pink-faced, he stepped around the paper and pointed to the corner of it. I had to read the words aloud to make sure I didn't misinterpret them.

"'Asset needed before next'—" My voice shrank. "'*Full moon*'?"

Sniggers spread around us like a rash as I did the math. The last full moon was two nights ago, which left only nineteen working days to finish this head-smelter unless I came in on weekends.

More to the point, what the hell sort of customer sets deadlines by the moon?

"Mangy gobshites," McCoy muttered. "Let's take a walk, Benny."

He steered me by the shoulders away from those cabrones, toward the stairs leading up to his office. "You know I had my reservations four years ago, hiring a kid who didn't speak a lick o' English," he said. "But you've always had a surprising aptitude for metalwork. Most of these lads ain't made for labor what needs sharp eyes and imagination, but I don't mind sayin' you got plenty of both."

What McCoy called "aptitude" was what got my coworkers resenting me in the first place. Right off the steamship, I'd walked into his office and sold him a thumper in broken English about how the Humacao sugar mill at el Centro Pasto Viejo had sent me as their Spanish-speaking envoy. A factory full of grim, sweaty smithies watched me hammer on the gears they'd cast for the production plant to prove they had been improperly made, and though McCoy knew I was lying about who sent me, he also knew I wasn't lying about the gears. I was on the payroll by lunch.

Maybe he'd always known what I was worth, but he'd never said it aloud.

"Thanks."

Near the foot of the stairs, he stuck his thumbs under his too-tight suspenders and leaned toward my ear, a tang of stout beer and café on his breath. "Ever fancy yourself working in our Ornamental Department, Caldera?"

I stopped walking. "Beg your pardon, chief?"

"I'd give you the lead. Dan, Innis, and Elmer'll be your crew. Who knows—" He gave my filthy striped shirt a tap. "Could be this head-smelter's your ticket away from the furnaces, hm?"

Like every other smithy in Structural, fantasizing about a desk in the clean, well-lit Ornamental building next door was an unspoken part of the job description, and he knew it. But unlike my coworkers, I wasn't so thirsty for the pay raise or the white-starched shirt. The only thing less tolerable than being brown and spare in a sea of burly Irishmen was my asthma.

And no one in Ornamental had to breathe black air.

A moment of mute disbelief passed before the furnace heat on my teeth told me I was smiling. "All right. I'll do it."

"Good lad!"

McCoy clapped me on the shoulder and swung us around to face a dozen sooty ears cocked in our direction. "Back to the boilers, ya nosy eejits," he hollered, giving me a light shove back toward the ingots. "Woolworth Building ain't gonna reach the sky by itself!"

I resumed my spot next to Farty where a new mold glowed like a small sun, and tucked my smile away before he could see it. That lambón had gotten his wish; I'd expected his standard smirk waiting for me, smug and sour like a lemon peel was permanently wedged between his molars.

No smirk, though. Rather, his expression gave off a chill that cut through the heat like an ice pick. I looked away before it could stick me in the neck.

Farty Walsh was always a bigger hazard when he wasn't smiling.

The month rattled past like a subway car. Busting a lung to meet a batty deadline with second-rate help would have slowed down any other smithy, but nothing motivated me like having the freedom to run my own project. McCoy had said I could do as I pleased if I thought I could improve the design, so I gave myself permission to speculate. What kind of person would pay to visit a big, metal box by the ocean when the ocean was right there— *for free?*

I sought inspiration closer to the equator. From the dusty recesses of my brain, Caribbean lines spilled onto the blueprint: whiplash ocean wave panels, sea spray membranes, cast-iron clamshells. While my team rolled bars and hinges, I molded frames and panels with San Juan sabor.

Once the cage was constructed and the glass installed, what assembly remained fell to me alone, which I far preferred to negotiating tasks with my cranky coworkers. At some point through lunches, overtime, and weekends, I'd begun assembling a dream instead of a tank, and I wasn't keen to share it. I'd glance daily out the window at the building next door, too impatient for a future inside it to mind the dots of blood that started showing up on my handkerchief when I coughed.

I'd begun to believe what Tití Luz had said. That in America, "todo es posible." Because on the second Sunday evening in March, less than a month after the head-smelter arrived, it sat finished in the moonlit delivery bay, polished, sealed, and mounted on six burnished steel wheels I'd hammered myself.

I stood back to survey my work like an artist who'd mixed the powdered pigment of his hope with linseed oil and painted with it. Then, I draped the tarp over the tank for the last time and punched out.

Walking down Second Street toward Gowanus Bay the night before pickup day, neither my exhaustion nor the sting of New York winter could douse my excitement for what tomorrow might bring. My favorite spot on the dock was out there waiting, a row of crusty pilings where the barges lined up hull-to-hull like oversized sardine cans to frame a clear view of the water that wrapped around Brooklyn and beyond. It was pretty in its way, though a far cry from the waterfront I missed.

La Bahía de San Juan was blue. The kind that smelled of salt and seaweed and made you forget your island was still bloody from a war it couldn't win. Even after the San Ciriaco hurricane blew the dream of Puerto Rican liberation away with the gunpowder, the sea did as the sea does and made it like nothing had changed. Had I known I would never see that shade of blue again, I would have paid better attention.

The Gowanus Canal looked like spilled wood stain and stank of piss and horseshit. If you felt brave enough to stick your hand in it, it would disappear into the silt, then probably fall clean off your arm once the infections set in. But at this hour, it was easy to imagine a different waterfront if you squinted. Night turned the steamship soup colorless, emptied it of commerce, and left you in the peaceful company of a waxing moon, an island wind, and musical currents lapping their rhythm against the hulls of lonely barges. Out here, even a guy with busted lungs could breathe.

I took the necklace Tití Luz gave me out of my pocket and ran a chilly thumb over the San Cristóbal embossed on the pewter medallion. Across the bay, a different patron saint of travelers guarded the Iron City with her back to Manhattan, Lady Liberty's glowing torch held high like a promise. I'd made a promise too, to Tití Luz. Maybe I'd finally make good on it. Find the liberty America never gave us tucked somewhere between the tenements and brownstones.

Until then, I hung San Cristóbal back around my neck and blew on my fingers, grateful for a place where I could forget I was a man without a country.

Pickup day was the sort of Monday you hated punching in for. Gray and cold, with factory-smoke skies shedding dirty snow-flakes too sparse to make a home on the pavement. My coworkers dragged themselves in by the neck with their usual torpor, half rat-assed on whatever they drank the night before.

I was sober enough to dry up the canal, and twitchier than un gato estresa'o waiting for the tank to meet its new owner. While Farty, Dan, Innis, and I took up our next assignment at the furnace—rivets for the Woolworth—I pictured a stiff, whis-kered jefe in winter wools and starched whites, fragrant with leather.

Maybe everyone else did too, because as soon as the musta-chioed man swaggered unannounced onto the foundry floor in his faded fur-trimmed cape and bright green suit, productivity ground to a halt.

"Sir! It's a mite dangerous in here for visitors!" Our illustri-ous foreman rushed out of his office and down the stairs with a fresh coffee stain on his shirt, one hand snatching off his wayward bowler hat and the other held out in greeting. "Patrick McCoy, at your service! Mr. Samuel Morgan, is it?"

This threadbare dandy commissioned the tank? He looked like an avocado stuck in a bird's nest in his rubber boots, mat-ted cuffs, and missing waistcoat buttons comically at odds with his lime-colored clothes. Floating next to him was a young lady—pretty, with large eyes and creamy skin flushed from the chill. She wasn't shopworn like her compañero; in her fancy woolen winter coat, tight coils of apple-red hair poking out from under a hat that matched her crimson skirt, she looked like she'd stepped off the December cover of *The Delineator.*

Mr. Morgan removed his top hat, revealing slick waves of neatly parted brown locks. "My apologies for letting myself in. It appears your receptionist is out to lunch, and I couldn't wait."

My ears fastened on his voice. The Avocado Man had no accent I could trace beyond Long Island Sound, no telltale bump or angle in his features pertaining to coordinates beyond the spot where he stood. No one in the foundry qualified as American by most of America's standards, least of all me, but this guy sure *sounded* like the real deal.

"Right this way, sir," McCoy said amiably. As our visitors walked ahead of him toward the delivery bay, McCoy spun back to wave a frantic hand at Dan, Elmer, Innis, and me. We threw off our leather gloves to join them outside.

Halfway out the barn doors, I almost walked right into McCoy's backside.

"Jesus, Mary, and Joseph," whispered McCoy as I looked over his shoulder and said, "Madre de Dios."

Beyond the tarp, four white horses stood in a neat line hitched to a brightly painted stagecoach, giant rhinestone-encrusted plumes sprouting like palm fronds from their green bridles. On the coach's endgate and side panels, the words "Morgan's Menagerie of Human Oddities" shone in gilded red letters.

The tank was headed to a *sideshow.*

"Tell me I did not come all the way out here to freeze my beans off, Sam," a deep, tetchy voice called from the driver's seat. "I'm shivering fit to shake the coach to pieces!"

By now, all the smithies were congregating to watch, and our eyes blinked wide as a Black man made entirely of muscles swung out onto the gravel with a hefty *thud.* He strode over, his thick neck, thick arms, and thick calves bulging through his clothing like a sneeze would provide all the force necessary to make his sleeves explode. This guy didn't have the manicured air of his compañeros—too busy was he with rubbing warmth into his massive hands and burrowing his head into a scarf that barely reached around his neck.

"Strongest man in the world, weak against a little chill," Mr. Morgan muttered before he remembered we were there. "Ah, where are my manners? Introductions, yes?"

He gestured to the pelirroja first. "May I present Miss Sonia Kutzler, our own Flexible Fräulein."

She cut in front of Mr. Morgan with a dainty outstretched hand and a greeting that sounded like German words forced through a Brooklyn sieve. "Guten Tag."

"And this"—Mr. Morgan gestured to his freezing friend—"is Matthias Martin."

Mr. Martin cleared his throat. The Avocado Man rolled his eyes and added, "That is, the *Mighty* Matthias."

"Great Galahad!" cried Dan, who elbowed past me to snatch the hand the Mighty Matthias had offered McCoy. "You're the strongest man in the world! Marty, c'mere and meet the strongest man in the world!"

"Shut your flatter-trap, I know who he is!" Farty tore off his cap and sidled up to Dan. "I say, it's a real treat, Mr. Matthias, sir! I've still got your flyer from my last jaunt to Luna Park! Got to see you lift two thousand pounds!"

My eyes bulged. Never in my life had I seen Irishmen fawn over a colored man. Was this what it took to get respect in America? A body like Hércules?

Mr. Martin's mighty head gave a restrained nod. "Ain't that nice."

"Well now, can you really lift two thousand pounds?" McCoy asked breathlessly before Mr. Morgan smoothly inserted himself between them.

"Fifteen cents for a ticket to find out, my good man! The asset, if you please?"

Everything above my neck went weightless as McCoy motioned for my coworkers and me to remove the tarp. It seemed to take an age to fall away, but suddenly, there it was, the effort of the longest month of my life on six wheels, towering fourteen feet above the ground. I swayed on my feet like I'd exposed my guts instead of a tank.

Mr. Morgan's face was unreadable. "This . . . is not what I illustrated."

I reached for San Cristóbal, my heart beating like my blood had gone thick. McCoy had allowed me liberties with the design— had I taken too many?

The foreman's mouth drew a thin line between his jowls as he removed his hat. "If it don't meet your requir—"

"It's better."

McCoy and I both stood up straighter.

"Good heavens . . ." Mr. Morgan ran a finger along a seashell I'd improvised into the design. "Are you an artist as well as a blacksmith? This . . . is astounding!"

"Well, I certainly do my best to exceed expectations, sir! Very glad you're pleased with my design," McCoy said.

Though my chest hadn't stopped hardening to concrete, the rest of me unraveled with relief—

Wait.

"If exceeding expectations was your goal, then it's no wonder the tallest building in New York City is in the care of such a discerning craftsman," Mr. Morgan gushed.

Had I heard wrong? The chief's eyes shifted in my direction, then snapped away like an elastic. "That's mighty kind of you to say, sir."

Two feet away from where McCoy was taking credit for *my work*, I thought maybe that thumper had slipped out by accident— only my stomach knew better, slowly souring like I'd swallowed something rotten. Before I could pretend the feeling away, I felt my breath tangle somewhere below my throat and blanched.

Not. Now.

A cough scorched a painful path out of my chest. I threw an arm across my face and backed toward the nearest shadow, but on the way I bumped into Innis and his pipe, breath whistling out of me like I'd soldered a boiling kettle to my neck. Innis adjusted his cap so his wide eyes could telegraph a discreet warning at me, but every muscle was already taut with the pointless effort of holding in what had already decided to escape. My next cough was a loud *hack.*

That's when I felt the familiar prickle of someone watching. I looked up, and there was the Mighty Matthias. *Frowning* at me.

He tipped his head toward the dandy's ear, whispered something into it, and then *Mr. Morgan's* gaze met mine too, before he quickly looked away.

I flapped out my handkerchief and stuffed it over my mouth.

"My good man," Mr. Morgan said amiably to McCoy, "seeing as this marvelous structure is the product of your own ingenuity, I'm very interested to know your opinion on a particular matter of concern. What would happen if someone were to attempt to break this enclosure from the outside? Say"—he knocked his gloved knuckles on the glass where iron bars didn't protect it—"with the force of a heavy blow?"

"Well now," McCoy laughed uncomfortably, "I'd say those are the very four-inch-thick tempered panels you ordered, sir. Reckon it'd take a cannon to break that glass sure."

"Fascinating. Matthias"—he turned to the strongman—"would you do us the honor of a quality test?"

Mr. Martin shrugged. "If you say so."

He strolled over to the glass wall, pulled his fist out of his pocket, and shook it out. He drew back his arm to strike—

"*Don't!*"

I hardly knew where the air for that shout came from, but somehow it came out of me.

"The glass is as good as he says," I wheezed as embarrassment chased the blood from my fingertips. "But the seals . . . need more time to set. If you strike it . . . it'll loosen the glass from the brackets."

Next to McCoy's warning expression, Mr. Morgan's gaze was inscrutable. I grimaced. Tití Luz had often warned me "el pez muere por la boca," and here I was about to become the fish snared by its own mouth. "And when will the seals be set?"

"Tomorrow." It was the date on the calendar I'd prepared for—the full moon.

Morgan's mustache twitched, then widened over a genteel smile as he stepped toward me with his hand held out. I took it and matched the man's hard grip with my own because, when you're an extranjero, people will size you up with whatever measuring stick you give them, and Tití Luz always said I should give them no less than a yard.

"Have you a name, son?"

"Benny, sir. Benny Caldera."

He leaned back on a leg and scratched his chin. "Caldera. That Italian?"

My accent almost climbed into my mouth before I gulped it back and answered the way I knew would make the most sense to him. "Porto Rican, sir."

"*Porto Rican*," said Mr. Morgan conspiratorially in Mr. Martin's direction, as if that guy should've recognized me from somewhere because he's Black and I'm brown. "Mr. Caldera, say you were in my shoes. That you absolutely had to make use of this asset tonight or else its entire function would be rendered completely and irrevocably obsolete. What would you do?"

I tried to ignore how far down McCoy's frown had dragged his jowls while this green-suited gringo waited for me to make spontaneous liquid volume calculations.

"A fast coat of pitch could help," I croaked. "It'd be a day before it's cured. But just . . . don't fill the tank all the way at first. If there's less pressure on the joints"—I coughed—"the seal should hold."

I'd be damned before I saw a month of late nights and missed lunches crumble in the Brooklyn winter because this fuzzy aguacate couldn't wait for tar to set.

"'Course it'll be fine to fill all the way eventually," McCoy chimed in, as if he'd known these vulnerabilities all along.

"Capital!" Mr. Morgan turned and whispered something at the pelirroja, who nodded once at whatever he'd said. Then he pulled an envelope out of his coat containing the banknote that would pay for the job. McCoy and I both sagged with relief as Mr. Morgan flipped his top hat back on his head, bid us an extravagant farewell, and spun back toward the carriage. "Let's get on with it, Matthias."

Every smithy's jaw slackened as the Mighty Matthias looped an arm under each side of the yoke and heaved the massive iron tongue over his shoulders like it was no heavier than a couple of potato sacks. Then he hauled the entire thing over to the wagon *by himself* and hitched it. The sight had stunned me so stupid, I hadn't noticed the Flexible Fraülein had quietly slid into my periphery.

"Dropped my hankie," she said in a breathy Bushwick voice. We both looked down. It was hanging off my shoe.

"I'll get it!" cried Elmer, nearly upending Dan in his rush to aid the señorita.

Her Gibson Girl mouth curled in a coy sonrisa. "That's all right. Mr. Caldera will get it for me."

Elmer squeaked as I picked it up and shook it out. It was already smeared with grime. "Sorry about the dirt. Here ya go."

"On second thought"—she gently pushed my hand back toward me—"you keep it. 'Til we meet again, mein Freund." With a wink and a brush of red skirt against my shoes, she turned back toward the stagecoach.

To the crack of the reins, the caravan creaked its way out of the delivery bay. And in the same slippery way strange dreams vanish with the night when you wake, the Mighty Matthias, the Flexible Fraülein, and the Avocado Man were gone.

At first, I didn't understand why the other smithies were giving me a wide berth as we shuffled back through the barn doors toward our workstations. But when McCoy strode over to me, jowls quivering like an angry vieja, I started to figure it out.

"Mr. Caldera! What in Jesus's name did you think you was doin', speaking to the gentleman like that?"

It was involuntary, the wave of shame that rose up my throat and rinsed all the thoughts from my head. "I-I answered his question—"

"Made a fool of me in front of customer, is what you did," he snapped. "How do you think it looks when the foreman don't know his own design well enough to defend it?"

"I'm sorry, I—"

"The next time you talk over me"—he stuck a calloused finger in my face—"I'll make sure you're tending stoves 'til Judgment Day, and that's if I don't boot your arse out the door first!"

"I thought that . . . cómo se dice . . . that . . ." English words were disappearing faster than I could hold on to them, leaking through the hundreds of cracks all those late nights had left behind.

McCoy started to walk away, and a withering vision of the clean, bright drafting room next door snapped me back into focus.

"Wait!"

I rushed over and, against all my practice and better judgment, let the desperation show on my face. "That was my design," I reminded him—quietly, so he wouldn't think I was out to embarrass him further. "And Mr. Morgan called it 'astounding.' Ain't that worth something?"

He squinted at me like I'd gone batty. "That design came outta my department. Which makes it *my* design. Who the hell do you think you are, Caldera?"

I fell back on my heels. He got me with that question.

Because I really didn't know.

"Back to your rivets. *Now*."

Watching my foreman stride off into the smoke with my ground-up dignity under his soles, I choked back the bile in my throat. That balding *chayote*. I didn't know if I was madder at him or myself for buying his sweet talk when it was always just a setup to put his name on work he didn't have the chops to do himself.

Caramba, I couldn't even let myself stay mad. The workday schedule made no allowances for anger or grief or any kind of hurt, really; and anyway, letting myself seethe over losing the chance to work in Ornamental meant accepting that McCoy had never meant to give me the chance to begin with.

"Get a load o' that Friday face, now."

My head turned slowly to find Farty slouched against a pillar biting off a greasy fingernail. His other hand was tucked behind his back, like maybe he could have been a gentleman if only he'd had the proper motivation.

"Lay off, Marty," I muttered, striding away from him toward the rivet rounds.

He jogged cheerfully along behind me. "You could always catch up with that Morgan chap, Wheezy. The way they took a shining to you, I thought they was gonna do the charitable thing and take you with 'em. Put you on a stage for the Coney crowds."

I bit back a cough and looked around for my leather gloves. Where the hell had I put them?

"Then again, they probably didn't want a cur like you slobberin' all over that pretty little ginger . . ."

Tití Luz's voice was in my head again. *No digas nada. Dogs tame easier than people. It is why there will always be yanquis trying to convince you you're a mutt instead of a man. Don't you believe them, Benigno.*

Suddenly, Farty's breath was next to my ear.

"Or was it the strongman you liked best?"

I stuck my forearm under his collar and shoved him off. "I'll weld your goddamn mouth shut!"

"What in hell's goin' on?" shouted McCoy from his office window.

"Nothin', chief," I called back in a barbed voice. Beside me, Farty sucked innocently on his teeth, then held up a sooty brown bundle.

"Lookin' for these?"

My leather gloves. I rolled my shoulders and yanked them out of his grip, loaded the dolly with rivet stock, and carted it away from his lemon-peel smile.

Back at the furnace, the stock felt heavier than usual. I drove it into the flames and watched it turn red through scratchy eyes before pulling it out and onto the anvil. By the factory clock, it would be four relentless hours before I could leave behind the rivets and the ache in my chest, fill my acid belly with something flavorless, and fall into my cot. Didn't much feel like walking to the pier tonight anyway.

"Look at this peaky bugger," I heard Farty say to Dan. "You oughta be more careful with that temper, Wheezy. You're apt to get *burnt*."

I was about to tell him to "get burnt" himself when I realized: something *was* burning.

I looked down. I'd wrapped my palm around the glowing round—without noticing the freshly sliced *hole* in my glove.

"¡Coño!" The round clanged to the floor.

Three more Spanish obscenities flew out of my mouth in the time it took to shake off my gloves and run to the spigot, smithies dodging as I rushed past. I stuck my crackling skin under the water, grateful to stand where my shock and mortification could face the wall.

Quick feet scuffled in my direction.

"Lad, let me see it."

"It's nothing—"

Innis snatched my hand out of the water by the wrist and pocketed his pipe at the sight of the sizzling stripe across my palm. "There's a pure mess. Come on, you need patchin'."

The first-aid tin sat coated in black ash at the end of a long row of tongs. Inside it was a half-empty jar of camphorated Vaseline, an empty aspirin bottle, and a pilled roll of gauze, a humiliating testament to how infrequently beam rollers ever needed first-aid. I reached for the Vaseline.

"Don't be daft." He snatched the jar away and pointed at my burn. "Give it here."

He dabbed on the goop while I hissed through my teeth. "You can't let 'em get the better of you, you know," he said. "Marty's a vulture lookin' for carrion, and you just gave 'im a feast."

I stared at the floor with my uninjured hand in my pocket squeezing the pewter out of San Cristóbal. "Just finish so's I can throw on a new set of gloves."

He shook his head. "You're no good with a burnt flapper."

"Think I can't handle the pain?"

"Pain ain't the problem," he muttered and reached for the gauze. "You'll need time."

I felt myself pale. Beam rollers didn't get time off work for burned hands. They got fired.

As Innis wrapped my palm, I noticed the brass ring on his hand and remembered this guy had a family of his own: five chiquitines with his coal-black hair and translucent skin. I wondered how many of their scrapes he'd patched up just like this.

"Why are you helpin' me?" I mumbled.

"Welp, you're a lad in your twenties with no family," he said flatly. "Your lungs is broke. And like it or not, you're out of a job. With no hand, you'll be a dead man walking—though if you ask me, you look halfway there."

"You give great sermons."

He wound the gauze around my palm and shrugged. "Might not be so bad gettin' outta here. Give you a chance to sort out how to stop survivin' and live for a change. Hankie?"

I reached around my waist with my good hand and tried not to flinch as he looped it around the dressing for extra cushioning.

Given the choice, I'd let Farty change my name from Wheezy to Worthless over losing the only job I'd ever had in New York, but as I'd run out of choices, I dragged myself to McCoy's office. I was great at impressions, but Paddy McCoy had me beat with his impersonation of a beneficent boss who regretted firing his best smithy.

It wouldn't be the last time I regretted building that maldito tank.

The Merman

A welcome crust of ice has formed around the estuary overnight. It dissuades the smaller vessels from haunting the embankments, freeing us to venture closer to the shores where human flotsam settles and my mother and I can sift through it unseen. Among the scattered broken glass, rotting bulkheads, and iron sheaths, she discovers a treasure grown rare in the many moons since steamships soured the waters: the emptied dwelling of an eastern oyster.

"It is a splendid shell," I hum when she delivers her gift to my ladled hands. "What new delight are you planning for it?"

"A carving of the moon over the reef that delighted you so as a merling," she answers with sea spray in her eyes as she stretches brazenly out over a mossy rock. "The one in the Tailfin Sea."

The sun has yet to douse behind the human-made mountains they call the City, but I know better than to remind her what

risks baring her tail to daylight above the surface may inflict
upon her welfare. Her skin and scales conceal her better than
mine do me, she would argue. I inherited her tidal hues—blue
and green and pearl—but lack the flecks of age that mimic the
rocks along the estuary's shores. Even her hair, a subtle brown
compared to my reef-tone red, more closely imitates the
indigenous kelp.

She also knows no fear of the humans who abide less than
a league from the small island where she hunts for shells,
abandoned though it may be.

"The Tailfin Sea," I repeat. "What turns your thoughts to so
distant a place?"

"It lives in my thoughts, not as a place, but as the time when
last I saw your spirit untroubled," she sings softly to my mind.
"Would you not like a remembrance of peaceful nights under the
moon until we may again journey to warmer deeps?"

Though her question drops anchor on my heart, her intentions
are blameless. We once were voyagers, my mother more traveled
than any mer in the harmony, until our migrations ceased in a
billow of smoke, and I was . . . altered.

I return the shell to her palm. "I would like it, Mother, but
when can you expect me to return to the Tailfin Sea?" I ask.
"Without our kin, our songs are sunk in a thunder of engines and
propellers fit to wake the giant oarfish. Neptune Himself would
turn His fins on this estuary were we not here to Keep it."

Her face dims as the stars do when the human city lights its
night-lamps. She slides off the rock to rejoin me in the water

and, bringing her hand to my cheek, wades deeper into the
trench of things I will not sing about.

"Keep the estuary? Or keep humans from drowning in it?"

I give no answer, for she is my mother and has charted my mind
as thoroughly as she has charted the Atlantic.

Her smile restored, she unwinds a rope of seaweed from her braided
tresses, ties it around the hinge of the oyster's shell, and swims a circle
around me to fasten it behind my neck. It settles lightly over my heart.

"You have not carved it yet," I protest as she turns me by my
shoulders to face her.

Mother's fingers dance over the braids that frame my face,
admiring once more the cowrie shells she has woven into my
hair, each engraved by her skilled hand. "Perhaps you might carve
it yourself one day. For Neptune would never turn His fins on
the estuary. Nor would the Currents abandon to silence the souls
who dwell—or die—in it. Do you believe me?"

Her voice is as soft and melodious as a rolling wave, the better
to assure me my soul is included in her appraisal. Though the
water's chill is no matter to merskin, I feel her gaze glowing with
the warmth of the Tailfin Sea she longs to see again if only I
could bear to leave the estuary with her.

I decide I must. Someday. For her. "I believe you."

"I am glad of it. Though the Currents' call may sound distant at times,
you are a Son of Neptune and my beloved starfish." She touches her
forehead to mine. "Keep this shell, that you might never forget it."

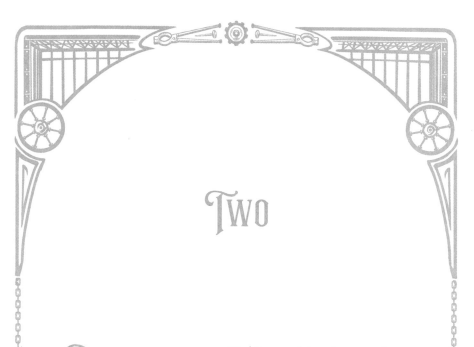

Two

Once, ten years ago, as Tití Luz and I rode our solitary wagon away from her bankrupted tobacco hacienda in Caguas, she'd given me a stern order to never look back, not even if you'd forgotten your keys. *Dios tiene su plan*, she'd said. If God had wanted you to have your keys, He would've made sure you remembered them when you left.

When the only things behind you are the sneering faces of a couple of malicious pendejos like Farty and Dan, that advice feels especially practical.

I'd never been idle a day in my life, and as I stood outside the ironworks without so much as a flea in my ear for what to do with myself, I knew I hated it. Another cough was brewing; not finding my handkerchief where I usually kept it, I reached into the other pocket and pulled it out.

'Pérate. If my handkerchief was wrapped around the gauze, then what was it doing in my pocket?

I inspected my bandage more closely. I'd been too distracted by my cooked meat to notice a monogram embroidered on the knot, two letters tucked into the folds on either side of a black *M*. The hankie I'd given Innis wasn't mine, but that redheaded Kutzler lady's.

My burn was weeping through the fabric; it seemed a shame to ruin Miss Kutzler's fancy thing with the effects of my mistakes, whether or not her German was an act (as I strongly suspected it was). I shoved my handkerchief—my real one—between my teeth and bit down as I undid the knot in the other one. Slowly, it came free and fell open into my good hand.

"Pero, ¿qué?"

There was charcoal on the linen, smudged. What I'd mistaken for soot earlier was handwriting:

Fulton St. Ferry Term. 5 p.m.

I looked around, expecting to find the Fraülein's poofy sleeves tucked behind a lamppost, but there was only the usual noisy exhibition of longshoremen and merchants swarming the docks like foulmouthed ants.

This couldn't be an invitation, could it? I wasn't the guy pretty German señoritas wanted to meet under the Brooklyn Bridge—I was the guy they pretended not to notice, then crossed the street to escape from. I pried more information from my memory of our brief encounter: Miss Kutzler only dropped her handkerchief on my foot after the Avocado Man had whispered into her ear. And that made me think.

Maybe the invitation wasn't from her.

The Fulton Ferry station sat in the shadow of the Brooklyn Bridge, on the edge of brick tenements, boardwalk, and cobblestones. Right across from it stood the Menagerie's plumed team and caravan, bright and colorful against the faded relic of steamship transit. I pulled my cap down and hid under the awning of the windbeaten hotel across the street to look for Mr. Morgan when the Avocado Man himself emerged from the Water Street market swinging a bucket of pitch.

"You're early."

"¡Cristo!" I jumped back and nearly landed my ass in a pickle barrel before the Mighty Matthias reached out a thick hand to steady me, his friendly smile tipped in amusement.

Suddenly next to Mr. Martin—though *under* him might be more accurate—I had an up-close view of the Strongest Man in the World and was a little thrown to see him in a delicate pair of wire-framed glasses. His earlier complaints about the cold made a lot more sense now that I saw how thin the layers were that insulated him from the March chill. Maybe clothiers didn't make garments for physiques like his if he had to rely on an overcoat that barely buttoned and ended well above his knees.

"Sorry," I said. "I wasn't spyin' or nothin', I was just—"

"Hey, Sam!" he yelled over my head. "The smithy made it!"

Mr. Morgan paused in his steps. Miss Kutzler poked her face out of the carriage window, beaming with the satisfaction of knowing her little hankie trick had worked.

"Come on." The strongman thumped me on the shoulder and steered me into the street. "You don't want a room at a flophouse like this, trust me."

I fought to keep upright under the weight of Mr. Martin's grip as Miss Kutzler stepped onto the street with a different skirt under her wool coat—a modest charcoal gray one that, against her bright red hair, gave her the look of an iron right out of the fire.

Mr. Morgan put down the bucket to greet me. "Delighted and, if I may say, surprised to see you here so soon, Mr. Caldera," he said. "I do hope you didn't skive off work for our sake."

"No, uh, I tangled with a hot round and, well . . ."

Four sets of eyes looked down at my bandaged hand, and the pelirroja clasped her hands over her heart in dramatic sympathy. "That looks abso-tively awful! You ain't gonna lose that hand, are ya?"

"It's a burn, Sonia," Mr. Martin said dully, "not the plague."

"Still," said Mr. Morgan with a knitted brow, "a burn may impede his usefulness for tonight's engagements."

I paled. A vision of my muddy, lifeless body stuffed into a burlap sack at the bottom of the Hudson invaded my thoughts with the meticulous detail of a blueprint. "'E-engagements,' sir?"

"No formalities, please. It's Sam," he said, to which Mr. Martin added, "Matthias for me," and Miss Kutzler finished, "Sonia on the offseason!"

"Thanks, um, Sam. Mr. Morgan—sir. It's just I'm not really an engagements kind of guy. I'm more the *dis*engagement type."

The straight line of his brows tilted. "And yet, here you are."

He walked backward and lifted a corner of the tarp, revealing one of the ornamentation panels I'd wrought. "It didn't take a scholar to figure out your foreman wasn't the craftsman behind our commission—"

"Excuse me, no, not a scholar," interrupted Matthias, glaring sourly over his folded arms at Mr. Morgan. He bent his head in my direction. "I told him if McSaggy-Face *really* designed this tank, I'd eat my hat."

"Yeah, yeah, everyone's a genius," Sonia grumbled. "I'm the one who got him to come—"

"And *that* is why," Mr. Morgan plowed on, "we can use your hand. Burned or not." He dug into the folds of his cape and produced a folded bit of paper which he held out to me.

I took it and read aloud, "'Sober men wanted for perilous aquatic excursion. Generous wages, swimmers preferred. Risk of injury and possible death. Inquiries to Samuel T. Morgan, 1200 Surf Avenue, Brooklyn.'"

He plucked the paper out of my grip and restored it to his cape. "The papers refused to run it. For the best, I suppose. Goodness knows thrill-seekers at Coney Island are a dime a dozen. We'd have a line around the park," he declared, as if drowning for your wages was so tempting. "But that's where you come in."

My brain was still stuck on *aquatic*. "Me? But I can't swim."

All three of them stepped back.

"Can't swim?" Mr. Morgan repeated, aghast. "Are you not from an island?"

"I was a smithy on the coast, but I grew up in the mountains. Couldn't really swim in those rivers." Not after the hurricane, anyway. Whether I'd known how to swim before the storm trapped me in tree roots and turned off the lights in my memory was anyone's guess.

"So, he can't swim." Sonia waved a dainty hand by way of dismissing this skill's relevance to my valuable qualities. "'Swimmers preferred' don't mean 'swimmers required,' does it?"

"Of course, not," Mr. Morgan agreed, sounding slightly less enthusiastic. "More important to the cause is the tank's integrity, and as Mr. Caldera is the most knowledgeable person here on that count, his presence would safeguard against any unplanned setbacks while we procure its"—he cleared his throat—"inhabitant."

My gaze drifted nervously back to the house-sized cargo as the words "risk of injury and possible death" came back to mind. "What kind of inhabitant?"

Mr. Morgan looped an arm around my shoulder and a mix of pipe smoke, brandy, and tangy cologne wafted up my nose, coaxing a cough from my throat.

"Secrecy is key, but it may be safe enough to tell you this," he murmured. "Not even P. T. Barnum, that colossal goldbrick, could gaff so rare and astounding an exhibit. No one alive—no one but

I—has ever seen the like of it. But you"—he gave my shoulder a squeeze—"would be among the very first in human history to do so without having to pay a dime for the honor. All I'd need is your promise not to tell a soul what we are catching."

Ave María. I wondered how many suckers this Morgan guy had hooked with that slick voice of his, peddling excitement and intrigue for a jitney per ticket.

I glanced down at his bucket. "And?"

"And a second coat of pitch."

Always a catch.

"In exchange for . . ." Mr. Morgan produced a small clip of banknotes. He tugged one out and handed it to me.

I nearly choked at the number on it. "Twenty dollars?!"

His face fell. "Is that not sufficient?"

"Gosh, no, jeez, it's plenty," I sputtered through numb lips. "It's—it's too much!"

Morgan shook his head decisively. "I should say not. Something you need for something I want is how agreements are made. Now then." He adjusted his top hat. "Do we have one?"

This guy's mouth was obviously well-practiced in manipulating the average Juan Bobo. On a day when my hopes got stuffed in the blast furnace, I wasn't keen to make the same mistake I'd made the day McCoy hooked me with that head-smelter. I was about to return his banknote when a strong wind off the East River turned my head toward the water.

The Fulton Ferry was set to depart. As the last Manhattan-bound workmen stepped aboard, the operator shouted to the street, "Final call for New York Schemers and Dreamers! Last chance to wave at Lady Liberty! Alll aboooard!"

I got a funny feeling hearing him say that. A niggle that made me pocket the banknote.

Keeping secrets was easy. *Lo que no se dice, no se sabe,* Tití Luz often said, and no one was better at keeping their mouth shut than me. Anyway, earning some extra cash sure beat all the nothing I'd originally planned for the evening.

"Sure," I said. "So long as I don't get wet."

Before I had traded my Caribbean island for one coated in soot, the only excitement I'd ever had was with my boyhood pal Ramón. That kid was a professional at roping me into dicey schemes, which always ended in me getting my ears boxed while Ramón got off like the sneaky sinvergüenza he was. Something about this little side job had the familiar whiff of a momentary thrill that would end up blunting my hearing.

Mr. Morgan said we were riding out to someplace in Queens called Lawrence Point. With time to burn until we reached our destination, Matthias and I made like a couple of fish and climbed into the tank through the bottom hatch with two paintbrushes, the bucket of pitch, and a greasy paper bag of Gage & Tollner's fried oysters to split as we rode north.

This guy loved small talk almost as much as I hated it. He asked so many ironworking questions, I wondered if he wasn't fixing to open his own foundry; stuff like whether steel was stronger than heavy iron and if I'd ever met a Skywalker. I was impressed Matthias even knew what the Native Mohawk ironworkers called themselves, but as Skywalkers usually worked off-site (and hundreds of feet in the air), I'd only ever talked to one once. We had breaked for lunch at the same outside table, and when I'd asked where he was from—"Uptown, midtown, downtown, out-of-town?"—he'd laughed, pointed at the clouds, and said, "Look up."

Less than halfway through the bucket of pitch, right about when Matthias switched to talking about the weather, I started thinking the strongman's name should have been *Metido* instead.

"Sure beats a Porto Rican winter, doesn't it?"

I cut a look at him mid-brushstroke. "That a joke?"

"It's a fact. Two jitneys says you never saw a snowflake in your whole life before you came here, and now you can't get enough of 'em."

The first time I saw snow, I lost an entire night's sleep watching it fall in thick cottony clumps from the sky.

"Lucky guess," I said.

Matthias laughed so heartily, the metal under us vibrated. "Brother, if it were me, I'd've stayed in Porto Rico just so's I didn't have to freeze my ass off five months out of the year."

That wasn't likely. Staying in Puerto Rico for the temperature was like choosing purgatory over heaven because you had an aversion to white robes and trumpets. Not that Nueva York was such an improvement.

"What?" Matthias asked when he noticed me scowling at my paintbrush.

"Nah, nothing. I just . . ." I rolled my eyes at myself. "I built a tank bigger than my room in the tenement, and I don't even get to live in it."

"Ha! The poetry of the peasant class," he remarked, reloading his brush. "Mind if I use that little anecdote?"

"For what?"

"My autobiography," he said proudly. "*The Heaviest Weight: A Mighty Memoir.* Catchy title, right?"

"I guess. Does that mean I'll be in it?"

"Depends on whether you gonna be a main character," he said in the manner of issuing a challenge. "So, tell me. How does a Porto Rican join up with a bunch of Ulstermen in Red Hook, instead of the rest of his compadres in East Harlem?"

The question stunned the words right out of my head.

Matthias pushed up his glasses to sharpen his already sharp focus on me. "You do know you ain't the only Porto Rican in New York City, don't you?"

I looked away. "I know."

Two weeks before I'd sailed into the Atlantic Basin, Tití Luz gave me her San Cristóbal necklace with an address to a rooming house on Second Avenue. She had connections with an unobtrusive society of revolutionary exiles in East Harlem who rolled tobacco to the beat of the latest socialist essay just like the tabaqueros back home—except they made plans and propaganda for Puerto Rican liberation from the seclusion of cigar factories sixteen hundred miles away. Tití Luz was a revolutionary herself; she'd had no reason to doubt I'd fit in with a community so like the one that had helped raise me. "They will greet you like family," she'd said.

But after what happened between Ramón and me, I wasn't much inclined to believe in Tití Luz's idea of family with New York borinqueños. I disembarked in Red Hook, and though the address said to go west, I stayed put.

Until today, I supposed. "How do you know so much about my people, anyway? You're a strongman."

"I am a *writer*," he clarified. "I know everything about this city. Hell, I know everything about every other place I've been, and I've been places. If it's where I make my bed and earn my bread, I make it my business to know where my feet stand. Don't you?"

"I stopped feeling my feet back on Flatbush Avenue."

With one hand, he unwound his red woolen scarf and tossed it to me. The residual ache of workplace disappointments eased in my chest as I wrapped it around my neck. "Thanks."

"You're welcome," Matthias said, resuming his brushstrokes. "So, what you gonna do with that bum hand now you ain't got a job?"

"You always ask this many questions when you first meet someone?"

"Just passing the time," he said innocently. "All right, how 'bout you ask me something?"

You'd think I would have been prepared for this opportunity, brimming as I was with questions like "What sort of guy was Samuel Morgan who'd run a sideshow but speak like a gentleman?" and "Is it true that Coney Island pleasure-seekers ditch the rules of civilized society on the southbound Brooklyn Rapid Transit train?" and, more intriguingly, "What *exactly* will this tank hold that required me to make it so indestructible?"

What I asked instead: "Can you really lift two thousand pounds?"

Matthias barked another laugh. "Do I look like John Henry to you?"

"Who's John Henry?"

"Jesus, Benny, never mind. The point is, do you *believe* I can lift two thousand pounds?"

That one was easy. I'd watched this guy lift a solid metal tongue with his bare hands and drag an apartment-sized iron tank without breaking a sweat, much less his bones. Had I not stopped him, I was willing to bet the San Cristóbal in my pocket there would be a Mighty fist-sized hole in the glass where he would have punched it.

I nodded.

"Then brother"—he flicked his cap—"that's all you need to know."

Daylight changed shifts with the night, and we spilled out the hatch at a bare stretch of road that dead-ended at a patch of rocky riverbank beside the East River. For the first time, I could see the pancake-flat outline of Rikers Island, a distant stretch of fuzz beside two dark lumps that Matthias informed me were the Brother Islands. He said the larger lump played host to a hospital for contagious diseases and a small lighthouse that guided ships through the dicey waters of Hell Gate.

"Speaking of Hell Gate"—Matthias nudged my shoulder—
"looks like a couple o' devils escaped."

I followed the strongman's gaze to a dusty Hudson motorcar
by the shore where two men were hitching a rowboat to the back
fender in matching light-brown duffle coats, though neither of
them could pass for Navy men. One wore a peg leg from the right
knee down and didn't seem to notice us; the other lumbered over,
teetering a bit on the shifting pebbles like his shoes had never
stood on unstable ground before.

"Hey, Emmett, bring your walnut limb over here and get a load
o' this cargo," the approaching man said, prompting the guy with
the peg leg to abandon the rope for a look. "We bringin' Moby
Dick home in this thing, or what!"

Sonia was at my side in an instant and hooked her arm
through mine. "Stick with me, kiddo. I'll introduce you to the
gang," she murmured, then gently pulled me along.

Stood together, the two men were taller than me by a few
inches, not quite middle-aged, and similarly dressed, their
matching blond hair glinting gold under their flat caps. In the
dim lamplight, they looked like two of the same person, peg leg
notwithstanding.

"Meet Benny Caldera," Sonia announced, "the craftsman behind this bee-yoo-tiful tank. Benny, meet Eli and Emmett Rhodes
and Madam Navya."

That was three names. Where was the third person?

A light tug on my coat made me look down. At my feet, in
women's winter furs over what looked like brightly colored,
loose-fitting trousers, stood a woman of proportions so impossible, I rubbed my eyes in case they were fooling me. This lady they
called madam couldn't have been taller than two feet.

"Navya Attwal. Pleased to make your acquaintance, Mr.
Benny," she said in a cadence that tickled my eardrums. I took her
hand with three fingers and promptly forgot how not to gawp.

"You . . . You're a—"

"A *madam*." Her air of authority seemed even more pronounced in a voice like a slightly sped-up gramophone record. "'Midget' is a hateful word. I find nothing more accurately expresses my sovereignty—and intolerance for ignoramuses—than does my actual title."

"Madam it is," I said quickly. "Nice to meet you."

"I'm Eli," announced one of the rubios, "and this one-legged lunkhead to my right is Emmett."

Eli saw my bandaged meat hook and clapped me on the shoulder in lieu of a handshake while Emmett made the sort of face I was used to seeing from guys who wondered what shade of trouble I was. He leaned toward Mr. Morgan, who was hassling a wad of fish netting by the motorcar. "What's with the outsider, Sam? I thought we all agreed we was keepin' this a secret!"

With a soft grunt, Morgan heaved the heavy net over his shoulder and wheeled around. "I am buying his discretion and expertise," he whispered impatiently, "and if you all don't quiet down and give me a hand with this confounded netting, I'll pay him out of your earnings!"

Matthias strolled over, plucked the netting off Mr. Morgan's shoulder, and laid it quietly in the small boat with an eye roll that well conveyed his disdain for being the only capable person here. Eli clapped my shoulder again before turning back to the motorcar, prompting a small glare in my direction from the less friendly Rhodes before he walked off too.

"Don't mind Emmett," Sonia said. "He's just overprotective of his twin nincompoop."

Twins, then. That didn't seem so odd for a sideshow, but then again, neither did Sonia. And anyway, I was hardly an expert on the topic of seaside entertainment if it didn't involve perching on a pier to stare at Lady Liberty.

"Pardon me, Mr. Benny." My eyes dipped to find Madam Navya shivering at my feet. "If you could please assist me into the carriage. God did not make me for standing outside in this relentless cold—on Holi of all days! We should be celebrating around a bonfire instead of freezing to death in this late-night inanity!"

"Oh! Yes, ma'am—uh, madam."

What etiquette had Tití Luz given me for assisting women no taller than my knee? I haltingly reached toward her waist to pick her up before she slapped my fingers away and gasped, "Ghanta! What are you doing?!"

"I-I don't know!"

Behind me, Sonia was cackling into her gloves. "Aw, Navya, go easy on him!"

"Presumptuous boy," the madam snapped. "I simply need the stepstool, which is inside the carriage and should be placed on the ground so I may ascend it! Dur fitteh muh!"

Spluttering apologies, I rushed to the coach, reached through the window for the stool, and froze when my hand grazed against cold metal instead. I peeked in. Lying in the footwell of the carriage was a small pistol.

I snatched up the stepstool like it might set off the trigger and placed it before Madam Navya's feet. "Uh, there's something. On the floor. Maybe just . . . be careful."

Madam Navya eyed me like I was dimmer than a candlestick when she slipped into the coach and emerged a moment later with the pistol. In her hands, it looked like a full-sized rifle.

"Your derringer, Mr. Morgan," she called out. Morgan felt his pockets, then strode over and plucked the gun from her fingers.

His gaze caught my alarm as he tucked it into his waistcoat. "Not to worry," he said, smiling. "For emergencies only."

The alarm bells going off between my ears were finally too loud to ignore. He headed to the motorcar. I jogged after him.

"Sir, would it be all right to ask what we're catching now?"

"Please, *stop* with the 'sirs.' I'm not a hundred-year-old man." Morgan threw his cape into the back of the car, dipped into the footwell, and came back out with a stack of buckets. "All right. What do you know about sirens? And I don't mean fire engines."

To say his question had broadsided me was an understatement. In the split second he waited for me to answer, I worried I'd forgotten all my English words. All my Spanish ones too. Because there wasn't a translation for his question that made any sense—not if he really intended to say "sirenas."

"You mean the half bird–half ladies that lure sailors to their deaths with a song," I half answered, half asked. "'Fields of bones,' and all that?"

His eyebrows rose to his hairline. "You know *The Odyssey*?"

Tití Luz was a seasoned lectora who had taught me to read so I could take over reciting texts to entertain the tabaqueros on days when she felt too hoarse, though I suspected it was actually so I'd have a leg up on the other morenos looking for work during the job famine. I wasn't much a fan of delivering socialist essays, but as far as books went, I'd devour anything that wasn't la Sagrada Biblia. "I'm familiar."

Recovered from the shock of discovering I wasn't as simple as I looked, Morgan leaned in. "Then, what if I told you the succubus of the sea exists—right here in our own waters—and that the beast is not half bird, but half *fish*?"

I stared at his armful of buckets. "You mean . . ."

"Yes," he said, his eyes glittering. "After tonight, Morgan's Menagerie will finally have its very own mermaid!" He pushed the buckets into my arms. "Now, fill 'er up!"

And he marched off.

Bueno. I didn't know anything else about Sam Morgan, but I was the only other person in Lawrence Point who knew exactly how much he'd paid McCoy today. As disappointing as my day had been, I knew his would be a hundred times worse when he rode back to Coney Island in the morning with an empty tank.

With the dory now bobbing amidst a broken crust of ice along the riverbank, Eli, Emmett, and I filled the tank, the extra handkerchief back around my bandage in case I needed my right hand for anything beyond this maldito Jack-and-Jill business. I couldn't be the only skeptic hanging out in the cold with the Avocado Man, but as no one said anything, I just kept quiet and hoped for a ride home later.

Once the tank was full enough to submerge a man up to his waist, we rejoined the rest of the crew to hear Mr. Morgan whisper through his plan. Everyone had a job—even Madam Navya, whose size apparently made her "singularly well-suited for a lookout"—but Sonia's cheerful air evaporated in the icy breeze as soon as she heard her part in this locura.

She was the bait.

"Nope. Uh-uh," Sonia said in a trembling whisper. "What if it starts workin' us over with its voice or somethin'?"

"Relax, Sonia," drawled Emmett with a wry smile. "It don't even know the lyrics to 'Shine On, Harvest Moon.'"

Sonia's frigid glare made the ice-encrusted river look like a tepid bath.

"Ah, thank you for reminding me." Morgan reached into his trouser pockets and produced a small mound of dark, fluffy wads. "Earplugs. Courtesy of Lulu for blocking sounds of sinister intent. Everyone, take two."

"I know what I'll be wearing when Emmett starts snoring—Ow!" Eli yelped as Emmett elbowed him in the ribs.

"Be quiet, you pair of congenital numbskulls," Morgan hissed. "Their hearing is exceptional! Do you want to run them off?" Eli hid his eye roll and gave Emmett a stealthy shove while Morgan put his telescope to his eye and pointed it at the sky. "The moon is in position," he said breathlessly. "Now. You must go *now*."

"Jesus Christmas, this is where the *General Slocum* sank," Sonia whispered, staring woefully at the dory. "If the boat goes under—"

"Matthias will keep you perfectly safe." Morgan tacked on a cavalier smile. "Would I ever endanger Coney Island's favorite Fräulein for a mermaid?"

"Nobody answer that," grumbled Matthias. "Let's go, Sonia."

Muttering about "the toes 'bout to break clean off" inside his rubber boots, Matthias looped one arm around Sonia's waist, another behind her leg, and lifted her off the ground as if she weighed no more than the combined mass of her clothes, her lips trembling as he placed her gently in the boat. Then, in wide strokes that hewed through the ice, the strongman rowed away from us until both he and Sonia were just another shadow on the water.

We moved to a set of logs by the bank, me sandwiched under a wool blanket between Morgan and Eli, Emmett huddled against Eli's other side trying to rub warmth into his brother's shoulder.

And we waited.

An hour later, and moments from becoming the world's first human piragua, Mr. Morgan seized my arm so roughly I almost fell off the log. Wordlessly, he pointed at a glittery spot on the water we all squinted at.

Sonia was in the boat, upright, untouched, and alone. Per Morgan's earlier instructions, Matthias had hidden himself.

But just ahead of the dory—against all logic and reason—a shadow dipped in and out of the water.

Madre de Dios.

Something was pulling the boat to shore.

THREE

We scrambled noiselessly to our feet—and peg leg—but in the shock of Morgan's vindication, we'd all completely forgotten where the hell to put ourselves. Morgan grabbed Eli's sleeve and shoved him toward a length of embankment thick with brittle grass where Eli and Emmett quickly hid themselves. He then produced a small bottle from his pocket, uncorked it with his teeth, and dumped its contents over both his gloves.

I knew that acid smell like I knew the taste of sugar. In ironwork, chloroform was a solvent we used sparingly, but Morgan had just saturated his gloves with enough to polish a floor—or knock out a horse.

He whapped me in the chest. *Get down!* he mouthed.

I dove behind the log and watched. Sonia was suddenly much closer, pale as a ghost with both hands cupped over her ears, terror in the set of her trembling lips, and a Matthias-sized lump in front of her legs. Below them, cutting a V-shaped path through the water, was the moonlit outline of a head.

No puede ser, I thought for all of a split second before my imagination fired off, flipping between visions of a rosy fair-haired maiden and a scaly sea snake with sharklike rows of teeth—until the shadow in the water turned back toward the boat and my head emptied. Two wet, lustrous arms slid out of the surf and gripped a cleat to bring the boat in broadside, revealing a steely back and long, dark waves of hair flowing down it like spilled paint. My breath caught at the sight.

And the thing *heard* me.

I shoved Matthias's scarf into my mouth, but it was too late; the figure went still and cocked its ear in my direction. Morgan glared at me like maybe *I* should get a face full of chloroform.

"NOW!" Matthias's shout fuzzed through my earplugs.

The net flew out over the water, and Matthias vaulted over the hull, falling on the creature in a giant splash. Eli, Emmett, and Morgan rushed out of their hiding places to help him while Sonia shrieked, clinging to the dinghy for dear life as it pitched and swayed.

My feet went one way, then back, before I realized I had no idea what to do. The men were all wrestling with it, falling over each other and spraying water like alley cats caught in an open hydrant, every sound blunted by the little wads of leather and cotton I'd stuffed in my ears. Suddenly unconcerned with keeping quiet, Morgan roared, "Matthias, hold it down! I can't get my glove under its nose!"

"Too . . . damn . . . slippery!" came Matthias's strained reply.

With a yelp, Eli fell backward into the water—just zipped out of view like he'd got sucked into a whirlpool.

"Eli!" howled Emmett. "Something's got him!"

"Benny, for Christ's sake, do something helpful!" Morgan shouted.

I shook out of my stupor and bungled my way into the shallows, lungs closing and shins screaming at getting unceremoniously baptized in ice water. I could hardly see anything but flying spray, fishnet, and quick flashes of whatever slick and shining thing was writhing inside it. Emmett had ditched wrangling the net to jump on his brother's flailing feet, so when I saw an arm whip out of the water, I lunged for it and yanked.

No sooner had Eli's head resurfaced than I felt something snake around my ankle. In a blink, my own foot went out, and I flopped backward onto the pebbled bank, river water rushing up my chest like a frosty curtain.

A hand shot out from between my knees. With the force of a hammer, it made a fist in my coat and dragged the rest of itself onto my chest, soaking the last dry fibers of my clothes and filling my nose with brine. Ropes of long, dark hair draped like seaweed over glistening gray shoulders and the curve of breasts.

¡Una sirena!

Its free hand grabbed my bandaged one so firmly the rest of me went limp with agony. My mouth fell open in a shout that couldn't squeeze past my asthma.

That's when I heard it: a word, both song and shriek, that blared in my mind like the bells of Visitation Church.

¡SÁLVALO! it cried.

"S-save it?" I gasped.

An audible *crack* halted the mayhem. The creature jolted, then slumped face-first against my chest, leaving me an unobstructed view of the derringer's smoking barrel glinting in the moonlight. Morgan held it, wild-eyed, wet, and heaving in his green suit.

"D-Dios m-misericordioso . . ."

Something else was happening.

La sirena's body. It was *melting.* In seconds, it withered and fizzed down until everything from my coat to the bandage on my hand was coated in pearly froth. I didn't move in case the stuff might make *me* dissolve like baking soda in vinegar, but then, just as quickly, a gentle tide rose up my chest and carried the foam away.

For a fleeting moment, it seemed everything had gone still except my shaking. I whipped my head around, searching for eyes that had seen what I'd just seen, but every face was hidden, backlit by moonlight.

Except one.

My blood cooled to river water as I realized I'd locked gazes with *the thing in the net.* Its face was carved in an expression that mirrored my own undiluted shock—eyes wide with horror, mouth open mid-gasp.

Por Dios, it looked *human.*

The next sound blasted past our earplugs at a volume that sent us cowering where we stood. It came from the creature, an almost musical wail that ripped from its throat and echoed back from every corner of the East River—and deadened the instant Morgan's glove closed over its nose and mouth.

There was more splashing. Grunts from Matthias. Sonia's muffled sobs. Then quiet.

We all stood in mute shock; even Sam Morgan looked like a man who, for all his planning, sure as hell hadn't planned for this.

"Mr. Morgan! Mr. Morgan!" Madam Navya's high voice pierced the stillness. "Up the road! A light approaches!"

Morgan's head snapped up. He threw off his gloves, dug the plugs out of his ears, and flung them into the river. "Matthias, get Sonia and stow the boat! Emmett, Eli, Benny—help me move this *thing* to the tank!"

"M-Matthias," whimpered Sonia, circling her arms around his neck so he could swing her carefully onto the embankment.

Body shaking apart and chest humming like a busted accordion, I staggered on feet I couldn't feel toward Morgan, who was roughly maneuvering his hands around the beast's limp torso in the net.

I'd gotten only the briefest glimpse before Morgan had knocked it out. The way it looked at me—I had to know if my fear had filled in human features where there weren't any, but the netting was hiding its face. When its head rolled backward, I slipped an arm behind its neck and touched warm skin. How could anything with so little insulation survive a winter out here without dying from exposure, much less generate its own heat?

"Guys . . ." Eli, pale and gaping, held up a long, glittering tail. Santa María, the body must have been nine feet long, head to fin!

"Stop gawking at it and move!" Morgan jerked his head toward the tank, and as one, we shuffled our soaked and shivering bodies over the rough sand.

"Benny, climb up there and open the hatch," Morgan ordered, shifting the weight I'd been carrying onto himself. I let go and hastily climbed the rungs, crawled over to open the lattice hatch, then lowered halfway back down to resume my position at the creature's head.

We hauled it off the ground. It was so heavy and awkward, I thought it made a lot more sense for the strongman to be up here instead of me, but one good pull and three pushes from below sent me onto my back with its dripping head in my lap. The face was colorless in the moonlight and still mostly hidden under hair, but something dark and syrupy dribbling across its forehead made my gut twist.

"Mr. Morgan," I whisper-wheezed, "I think it's bleeding!"

Morgan's face poked out from behind Emmett and Eli on their way up the rungs. "It's still breathing, isn't it?"

I checked. Its chest neither rose nor fell.

"I— I can't tell . . ."

"It'll be fine," he said. "Just get it in the tank!"

We rushed to rearrange the ropes, rolling the body up in the net so we could unroll it into the water. As I did, the hair fell away from its face . . .

Against its shimmering skin was a pair of thick eyebrows—one of them split and bleeding into its hairline—knitted together in humanlike misery. Long eyelashes rested on either side of a straight nose that sloped toward dark gunmetal lips parted over a set of squared-off teeth. Farther down, I couldn't find gills or other sharklike traits. No breasts like la sirena. Just a lean, muscled torso that blended into scales at the hips.

Every hair on my neck stood at attention. "Un tritón," I whispered.

A merman.

"Everything copacetic, kid?" Eli's worried voice nudged me out of my trance. "You look like the gravity train's about to take you downtown."

"Nah, no, I'm fine . . ."

I blew on my freezing hands and repositioned myself for the final move. As soon as the tail was in, we shifted onto our stomachs and brought the rest of the netting down as far as we could until Morgan gave the signal to let go. The merman splashed in sideways, spraying our kneecaps with water.

"There'll be no line for the bath tonight, right, Em?" Eli joked, for his twin's obvious benefit. Emmett looked like someone had hit him with a hundred volts of the creeps.

We resituated the tarp over the tank, offering me another opportunity to look through the bars. Blood ribboned from the merman's forehead like smoke from an ember, the sinewy arms and barbed fins motionless while its long hair swirled then settled gently around its shoulders. The creature's chest had just risen in a breath when I finally understood something.

Sálvalo. That didn't mean "save it."

It meant "save *him*."

Morgan ordered Matthias to drive ahead with Eli and Emmett in the motorcar. Back by the coach, Madam Navya paced in a tiny circle, muttering in a language I'd never heard before. Sonia greeted me on the ground with a towel and a blanket, which she wrapped around my shoulders. I wasn't sure if I was grateful to have something dry to hold, or miffed that, foreseeing nothing else, Morgan's retinue had known how stinking wet we'd all get.

"Take these too. Emmett won't miss 'em." Sonia pushed a pair of gray stockings into my hand. "You gotta get out of those shoes before your piggies never live to see another market."

She was trying valiantly to recover her charm, but the tremor in her voice couldn't sell it. "Hey." I tried to meet her eyes. "*Hey.* You all right?"

Sonia nodded and smiled at the ground. "Jake as cake."

In short order, Morgan corralled us into the carriage where I was all too glad to go. Remembering I owed Madam Navya a bit of chivalry after accidentally trying to manhandle her earlier, I offered her my hand and helped her up the stepstool into the seat beside Sam, then sat in the back next to Sonia. The Fraülein charitably looked away as my boots came loose and exposed all the holes I hadn't the skill to darn.

With a snap of the whip, the horses moved and Morgan started laughing—softly at first, then explosively. "I did it, I've done it!" he bellowed. "Take *that*, Reynolds, you highfalutin louse!"

"Dash Mr. Reynolds," Madam Navya snapped angrily from behind her tightly clasped fingers. "What do you think our fate will be in this life—or the next, for that matter—now that we have stolen a god from the river?"

"Aw, quit it, will ya?" Sonia's shaking hands dropped her glove. "You're spookin' the hell outta me!"

I turned and squinted past the endgate through the gap in the tarp where, incredibly, a merman drifted in the silt. It had turned around, lending me a partial view of its lower half: dark, striped, and glinting like textured chrome, with a sharp crest of fin that began at the small of its back and ended where the crease of knees might be if God had given it legs.

Then again, if the madam was right, maybe God as I knew Him had had nothing to do with it.

"Shame about the mermaid," Morgan went on as if no one had said anything at all. "We might have had *two* of them on display for fifty cents a head. But this will do splendidly! I never would have believed it. How many decades of my life had I wasted studying the beasts only to find out the moon was the key all along?"

Was he talking to us or himself? "Key to what, sir?"

Morgan chuckled and snapped the reins. "Fame, wealth, the longevity of my hard-won enterprise." Another snap. "Redemption."

I didn't know what to say. My vision was still branded with the afterimage of the merman's horrorstruck face.

América, la tierra de oportunidad, I thought. A homeland for "Schemers and Dreamers" who dared to change their fates. But if this was what it took for Morgan to change his, then I wasn't sure I had what it took to change mine.

The Merman

I drift in shadow. Gauze and a helmsman's grate veil the moon's consoling light. My body, a sudden stranger, spurns my commands.

What affliction is this? I cannot move. I cannot fight,
nor strike, nor weep!

Never have I felt water so confounding and strange. It thrums with the ocean's remnant call, but just as scales shed are not tail-skin, this is not Ocean. Though my bond to the estuary strains the farther this alien vessel carries me away, it is not yet severed. I am, lamentably, still here.

My wrists feel bound. With effort, I drag my fingers
to my chest . . .

No. The shell. The eastern oyster's dwelling you meant for me to carve, Mother. It is gone.

You are gone.

I watched as your voice joined the Currents, my deadly errors to blame. Would that my heart had borne that fatal blow instead of yours!

Now that I am torn from Neptune's robes, shall I ever hear your song again?

FOUR

I asked Mr. Morgan to drop me off at the ironworks. Goodness knows a giant tarp-covered cage couldn't just roll down the Cobble Hill main drag near my neighborhood without drawing the kind of attention Morgan especially wanted to avoid.

The coach rocked as I stepped off, jolting Madam Navya awake. "Arey, kya? Are we home yet?"

"We're dropping off Benny," whispered Sonia, and the madam promptly nodded off again.

Morgan followed me onto the gravel. "As promised," he said, digging into his pocket and producing a clip of wet banknotes. "Twenty for the labor and an additional ten for your secrecy."

Cristo, this was more than I made in two *weeks*. I glanced at the notes, then at the gap in the tarp where el tritón was still out cold, and said, "Twenty's more than enough."

He side-eyed me like I'd left my good sense in the river, put away his clip and touched his top hat brim. "Suit yourself.

Messrs. Thompson and Dundy appreciate your services, Mr. Caldera. Fare thee well," he said and turned back toward the driver's seat.

Before I could leave, Sonia draped her elegant hand out the window for me to kiss. I shook it instead, and her grip was so limp it was practically undetectable.

"Perhaps one day you shall come to see us at Luna Park, ja?" she said, smiling through that fake German accent.

"Perhaps."

Twenty minutes and several blocks later, I turned the corner of Verandah Place ready to take up permanent residence next to my shitty coal stove, even if the smoke it leaked made my lungs stick. It might have been a simple enough plan, seeing as my tub, stove, and bed all occupied the same thirteen square feet.

Except when I arrived at my tenement, my tub, stove, and bed were out on the corner with the trash.

"No me digas . . ."

I ran up the steps. Crammed my key in the lock and jiggled it. But the door stayed shut. Knocking was pointless when I knew my landlady could hear me; that woman slept so light, she practically levitated over her bed at night. Changed locks and my stuff on the curb could only mean she'd found out I'd lost my job—and my belongings were too cruddy to keep.

Two guesses who told her I was newly unemployed.

"Coño carajo, that's what I get for turning down those last ten bucks!"

By some small miracle, no one had taken my cuatro, which I found lodged under the mattress in its crumbling leatherette case and thrown out of tune. But most of my clothes were missing and my bedsheets too, no doubt pilfered by any number of the down-on-their-luck bums in this neighborhood. And now I was one of them, because I wound up doing the same.

There was just enough feeling left in my limbs to climb the Rosenblums' fence and steal some dry clothes off their line. Then I dumped what belongings I could salvage onto the mattress and dragged it behind me to the alley that ran alongside the Unitarian church across the street.

Sonia's blanket slid off my shoulders. I started shucking my boots on the only clean lamplit spot on the pavement before something bright in the church window caught my attention. I looked again.

As my eyes took in my reflection—and the dark red stain that stretched across my stomach and lap—all the wind rushed out of me.

I was *covered* in merman blood.

My coat came off so fast it might as well have been on fire. I shed my shirt next, then my trousers, until I was standing in the alley in nothing but my union suit and Emmett's stockings, vibrating like a hammered round.

An especially icy breeze skated over my palm when I noticed my bandage had slipped off, too.

"Pero, ¿qué *demonio* . . . ?"

Where was my burn?

In case getting my ass poached in ice-cold river water had made me forget which hand I'd scalded, I checked my other palm, but both were clean. There wasn't so much as a scar left!

I was panting now. My heart batted at my ribs. Memories of the day's events were already blurring at the edges. When I tried to remember anything that might have altered the state of my injury after taking off Sonia's hankie, the only thing that came to mind was how my burn screamed at me when that thing grabbed my hand.

No, not "that thing."

She.

As soon as I thought it, the reasoning fell into place. La sirena had healed me. She must have done it in the trickle of seconds it took her to wash my palm in salty water and wring the life out of it—as she was shouting "sálvalo" into my mind knowing I'd understand it. And didn't that fit Morgan's definition of an agreement? "Something you need for something I want"?

Of course, thanks to Morgan, she hadn't stayed alive long enough to ensure I kept up my end of the deal.

I stared at my patched-up lifeline, and for a long, unnerving moment wondered if healing an enemy's wound in a trade for their compañero's salvation meant the mermaid had a soul. Because if so, then . . . *Jesucristo*.

No one had to know. I had my hand back; in a couple hours, I could beg McCoy to rehire me and go right back to sweating ashes, stripping molds, and hacking up blood until New York City was lousy with skyscrapers for every sucker who believed there was a place uptown with their name on it. All I'd have to do is never let my leather gloves out of my sight again. I'd seal the mermaid's murder in the same vault where I kept all my painful memories and make good on my promise to Tití Luz—as soon as I found a new place to live.

I laid down, pulled Sonia's blanket over me and dragged in a shivery breath. Only my eyes wouldn't close. My thoughts kept drifting to the creature in the tank; his horrified gaze and his echoing cry—like the whole *river* was in agony with him.

After the dozenth inspection of my pristine palms, I sat up and pressed them together.

I didn't know if I still believed in God, and praying for myself was a lost cause, but maybe the universe could spare some favor for someone else's pain.

"Dale consuelo al tritón, Señor," I whispered. "Amén."

The effort didn't cost me anything. I just figured the merman needed solace more than I needed God to exist.

The wind carries my name.

Benigno . . . Milagrito mío . . .

The sand of Playa del Condado is rough and gritty under my toes. Soft breezes loosen my hair and sweep my black curls into my eyes. I breathe in salty air—deeply, for once—and instantly recognize the warm embrace of a Caribbean night. Overhead is a moon so large, the waves swell vertically in a bid to touch it.

On the water stands a figure I'd recognize anywhere: Tití Luz, dressed in the same lacy pink traje she'd worn in her casket. Her gloved hand reaches out to me. Her mouth doesn't open when she speaks.

Ven . . . Ven a la isla, milagrito.

"¿La isla?" I repeat.

Ven conmigo, mi luna.

"No puedo," I whisper back.

Ven . . . Sálvalo, Benigno . . .

My bare feet step into the waves. They walk and walk, but Tití Luz remains a small figure on the water. I look back over my shoulder where the shore is disappearing behind me. I should be sinking.

"I can't reach you," I call out, but she turns her head, distracted. Like she's being called away herself.

"¿Tití?"

With the deafening crescendo of an arriving subway train, a gale blows in from the sea. Behind Tití Luz, the ocean waves suddenly ascend, moving like a living thing, rising like skyscrapers to block out the moon. They crest over her head . . .

When I start running to reach her, the water gives out under my feet. My arms flail for an anchor to the air, but there's nothing to hold on to.

A spray of foam swallows us alive—

"¡Tití Luz!"

I woke up wheezing her name. Quaking with cold and coughing wisps of steam. I searched the alley like a ghost had followed me back from Lawrence Point, and either it was out to save me from dying of exposure in my sleep or it wanted me to get off my mattress and go to "la isla."

To the merman in Coney Island.

Twenty clams and a week's pay. After buying clothes and something hot to pour down my throat, I wondered how much I'd have left.

Enough for a train ticket, I hoped.

FIVE

eing a superstitious lady in life, Tití Luz would have either enthusiastically endorsed this impromptu trip, or else told me to pray for San Miguel's protection from whatever evil influence had lured me out of Red Hook. Either way, I was on the BRT from Knickerbocker station bound for the Devil's Playground with an emergency wardrobe, my cuatro, and a duffel of my rescued belongings on my back.

The trip was long enough for a light nap, but when my eyes creaked back open an hour later, nearly every passenger had migrated to the righthand windows where the sun poured in, and a strange skyline grew larger in the distance. I crushed my nose against the glass for a better look.

Sloping roller coasters cut into the horizon like small mountains alongside a scattering of Ferris wheels, bathhouses, and white, gilded towers. They stood against the beachfront like monuments to American pleasure-seeking as we approached, but the effect seemed less impressive once I took in the view behind it: the Atlantic Ocean.

Maybe Innis was right about getting out of the factory.

The Culver Depot for Brooklyn Rapid Transit sat at Surf Avenue and West Fifth Street beside gigantic billboards for Cloverleaf Salmon and the *Galveston Flood*. The latter depicted a natural disaster of San Ciriaco proportions, except a large outdoor venue had been illustrated around it filled with a horde of smiling gentry. Not an actual flood, then; it was a *show*.

I shook my head. "Yanquis."

Wandering off the unloading platform, a flutter of streamers down the block caught my eye. I quickened my pace toward a guy who looked like he knew the place.

"Pardon, sir, is that Luna Park?"

The man tracked my finger behind him to a tall white archway where a wooden roller coaster peeked out from between the pillars. "Nah," he said. "This here's Steeplechase. Don't you recognize the Funny Face?"

He walked off before I could press him for directions, distracted as I was by the clownish mask mounted to the wall with droopy eyes, red lips, and too many teeth for a human mouth. I wouldn't have called it funny; over sun-bleached gates shuttered to an empty street, it made Steeplechase Park look like a ruin from a lost civilization.

Was Luna Park shuttered too? What if Samuel Morgan wasn't even there?

I was beginning to wish I'd held onto Mr. Morgan's batty help-wanted ad when a flyer tumbled in on an ocean breeze and attached itself to my trousers. I peeled it off my leg.

"Morgan's Menagerie of Human Oddities." The address was displayed conveniently on the back, too.

Barco que no anda no llega a puerto.

I followed Surf Avenue farther east and finally came upon the gilded entrance I was looking for. Between two enormous rainbow spires lined with enough electric bulbs to light a small city was "Luna Park" spelled in yet more light bulbs. A large red heart bore the words "The Heart of Coney Island" below it, sending a pleasant shiver of excitement through me.

This place had to shine like the sun on a summer evening.

"Hello?" I took out my old key ring and banged it on the iron post. "Anybody here?"

I kept it up until a portly fellow in painter's coveralls with a mousey *bigote* on his upper lip jogged out of a bend in the promenade with New York–brand exasperation. "Aw-right, aw-right, I'm comin'. Jeez, whatsamattawitchoo?"

This guy's Brooklyn accent was thick enough to insulate a house. I couldn't *wait* to try it out later.

"Sorry, I was hoping you could help me find someone." I passed him the flyer. "Do you know Samuel Morgan?"

The overalls man thumbed at his runny nose with a hankie. "Who's askin'?"

"Benny." I held out my mended meat hook. "Benny Caldera."

"Caldera, Caldera," he murmured as he shook it. "Lemme guess, that's Portuguese?"

"Porto Rican, actually."

"Yeah, 'course, that's what I meant." He felt around his coveralls, then pulled out keys to unlock the gate. "I'm Oscar Barnes, the distinguished gatekeeper they don't pay enough to keep around on the offseason. Sam expecting you?"

"Uh, not exactly. I built him, uh—an *asset* and decided to come check on it."

"An *asset*, says you! I tell ya, that guy's always movin' dough around," he remarked as the gate swung open. "All righty, Mr. Caldera. Follow me."

I waited for him to mention it, the creature Morgan had brought in during the night. Then again, maybe this guy had made the same agreement with the showman that I had, another crisp banknote exchanged for silence in Oscar's pocket. But a sidelong glance at Oscar's tepid expression changed my mind.

This guy clearly had no idea Morgan had a tank, much less a merman.

Oscar led me through a wide vein of boardwalk lined with empty storefronts and hibernating attractions. On the way, we passed a drained lake, a building-sized slide, and other mechanical wonders that towered overhead with goofy names like "The Teaser," "The Tickler," and "Whirl the Whirl." The smithy in me recognized a patchwork of influences in the architecture—European, Oriental, Ancient Roman—with swag molding and acanthus scrolls all over the place looking like someone had slicked plaster over flowers at the height of their bloom.

"First time here, eh?" asked Oscar when he caught me with my head on a swivel.

"Yeah," I said breathlessly.

He dug a cigar and matchbook out of his coveralls. "I can tell you ain't seen Dreamland yet by that moony look on your face. Good thing too if you're here to see Sam."

"Why's that?"

Oscar stopped walking. "Gee whiz, kid. Ain't you heard of the Amusement War?"

I shook my head.

He hooted like I'd just made all this extra walking worth his trouble. "Well, lemme educate you on account of Sam Morgan being real keen to win it," he said, wiping his nose on a paint-splattered sleeve before it could run onto his mustache.

"Obviously, George Tilyou's baby came first—Steeplechase Park—and everyone went wild for it. But then came Thompson and Dundy with plans for a bigger park the likes o' nothin' nobody ain't never seen before. And boy did they deliver," he said proudly. "Luna Park was the biggest, prettiest thirty-nine acres of Brooklyn seaside amusement, and for a whole year after they built it, nothing on Surf Avenue could top our attractions—or our crowds."

He lit up his stogie. I held my face away from it. "But *then*," Oscar continued dramatically, "in comes William H. Reynolds with *Dreamland*. Now, it'd be one thing if he did something different. Made something new. But nah, that louse just took everything we got here and made it *more*. We got a tower? He built two. He found out we got a midget in the sideshow, so he bought himself a whole midget city. More thrills, more chills, more dollar bills, know what I mean?"

Oscar picked a new key off the ring and stopped in front of a green awning that read "Morgan's Menagerie of Human Oddities" in the same bold letters I'd seen on the coach last night.

"Do me a favor. When you see Sam," he said, adjusting his cap, "make sure you're still wearin' that doofy smile. He'll be pleased as punch to see someone fawning over Luna Park again."

I let out a short laugh as he unlocked the door. "That shouldn't be too hard. Thanks."

Oscar directed me inside where a mildew-scented draft met me at the entrance. Then he closed the door and shut the daylight out, leaving me in the dark. I reached for San Cristóbal.

"Mr. Morgan?"

My eyes were adjusting. A few steps into a room as chilly and dimly lit as my tenement at night, I felt my arm brush against something cold, turned to look, then practically leapt out of my union suit.

A dilapidated, sour-smelling creature with clubbed, taxidermic limbs sat on a table display next to me. Under it, the word "Chimera" was printed on a small panel in a distinguished-looking font. When I backed away from it, I nearly landed in the balding lap of a yeti.

This was a whole *room* of weird monstruos. I pulled myself together and kept walking past more beasts of horror and fancy, each christened with some mythological name or other. Not that I thought the Menagerie was going for authenticity, what with the Hydra's mismatched heads being obviously stitched onto a salvaged alligator skin steamer trunk.

Caramba. Luna Park patrons were suckers.

A stripe of light under a set of double doors lured me out of the creature room and into a slim hallway. The path was lit by a series of small electric lamps, each hung over a large painted particle board of "fantastic freaks." Weirder than the freaks themselves was the realization that I *recognized* some of them.

Matthias's was first. "Mighty" wasn't the word that came to mind as I examined this painted jungle-man depiction in which he wore nothing but an animal print leotard that bared his thick, tattooed chest, arms, and legs. Sure enough, stretched over the dumbbells he held aloft were the words "Watch Him Lift 2,000 Pounds!"

Beside that poster was the Flexible Fraülein's. I paused to gape at Sonia's likeness, balanced on one leg in a skimpy yellow costume with ruffled sleeves, her other leg draped unnaturally over her shoulder as if it had broken off the hinge of her hip.

Every poster left more clues about Morgan's odd crew as I went. Next was Madam Navya, the "smallest woman in the world," followed by Eli and Emmett, whose illustration addressed all my questions about what made two brothers with a missing leg between them qualify as curiosities. The answer, I now understood: they performed not merely as twins, but as *conjoined* twins!

There were posters for people I hadn't met yet too. The Menagerie included a fire-breathing phoenix, a twelve-foot-tall giant, and a woman so fat "It Takes Seven Men to Hug Her!" My excitement whittled into discomfort at the ruses the posters advertised.

If Eli and Emmett's act was fake, were they *all* embusteros? Matthias's words revisited my thoughts.

Do you believe *I can lift two thousand pounds?*

At the end of the hall, an electric lamp hung with nothing beneath it but the ghost of an outline where a painting had once been. I pulled my coat tighter around me, feeling like that Oscar guy had stranded me in a haunted house.

The hallway led to a theater. Two electric chandeliers glowed warm over a large room striped with benches facing a red-curtained proscenium stage, the round apron of which was accessible by a set of steps built into one side and a ramp built into the other. Red, green, and yellow bunting hung over plaster friezes depicting gods and beasts I knew from Homero's stories.

"Zeus, Atena, cíclope," I whispered, "Pegaso, Poseidón..."

A burble of water from behind the curtain cut me off mid-pantheon.

Now, a smarter person would've turned around and taken the straightest path out of Luna Park toward the BRT—chalked the whole thing up to a New York snipe hunt that Tití Luz would have thumped me for if she were still alive.

Shame I wasn't smart. I took one last glance around to make sure I was alone and snuck closer to the stage, toward a sliver of blue light shining through the gap in the crushed red velvet. I fit my hand in it and with a deep breath, stepped through.

There it was in the center of the stage, propped on a wooden and steel platform just like it had been in the sketch, but with the springs and wheels stripped and the water filled to the top. Someone must have cleaned it because the grass and silt were gone. Near the ceiling, a hopper window let in daylight, which reflected fluid patterns off the water that danced on the walls like the whole stage had been dropped in the Hudson.

In the tank's farthest corner was a spot the sunlight didn't touch. I squinted at it, then froze.

The last time our eyes met, el tritón's face was a cast of horror. But he'd apparently gotten over last night's shock. His narrow glare was the East River's deadly chill personified, and it held me in place like a finger pointed at my chest.

"Mr. Caldera?"

I spun around. My duffel slipped off my shoulder, sending my cuatro case tumbling to the floor before I could catch it. Samuel

Morgan was standing stock still to my left in the wing of the stage managing to look surprised, confused, and agitated all at once—before a heavy splash turned my head and everything else I was holding crashed to the floor.

From liquid stillness, the water started churning and swirling until it became a roiling, frothy maelstrom.

"Budge up, son." Morgan strode toward me and pulled his pistol from the inside pocket of his waistcoat.

"M-Mr. Morgan?" I squeaked.

He stepped around me. "It's not for you."

A thunderclap exploded in my ears, vibrating the stage under my feet, only Morgan's gun hadn't fired. Rather, el tritón had flung himself at the glass, sending a spray of water over the top that slapped the ground at our feet, soaked my duffle, and nearly made me tap a kidney all over my only clean undergarments.

"There's no sense exhausting yourself!" Morgan shouted at the swirling fizz over our heads. He banged the pistol repeatedly against an iron corner bracket. "Can you understand me? That—glass—can't—be—broken!"

The churning subsided.

There, pressed into the high corner like a fox in a hole, was the merman. His face was hidden under an eddy of long copper-colored hair with seashell beads woven into braids that ran along his temples. As his locks settled around his shoulders, I made out the dark gash across his brow where he'd gotten hurt last night, no longer bleeding, but still raised and raw. I watched, stunned silent, as he slid slowly down the wall into a heap. He landed in partial sunlight where I could see the rest of him better.

From the waist up, his skin was like blue- and green-tinted metal, a shade darker than the Statue of Liberty, with a lean, chiseled chest and shoulders made for cleaving through currents.

Compared to his upper half, his tail was a deeper blue, with a silvery turquoise stripe and a dense arrangement of scales that glittered like sapphires and pearls. At the end of it, long flowing fronds set between sharp spines wafted gently; they caught the light as they moved, reflecting a rainbow iridescence like kerosene on water.

A warning flickered in the petrified corners of my mind that I was seeing something I shouldn't be seeing. When I peered at his face again, I shrank back. Once more, his clear eyes fastened on mine like he was telegraphing his plans for my murder right into my head.

Morgan was the one who killed the mermaid and captured him; why was he staring daggers at *me*?

"We're still getting used to each other," grumbled Morgan, rubbing at his temple.

"Shouldn't we be wearing earplugs right now?" I whispered.

"I'd say that awful noise it made last night debunked conventional wisdom regarding the dangers of its voice." Turning to look upon me as a parent would upon un nene who'd just knocked over la cafetera, he added, "I didn't realize we'd be seeing you so soon, Benny. To what do I owe this pleasure?"

"Well, you said—or Miss Kutzler said, I guess—to come and visit."

"In the offseason?"

"Well, you know, I just figured I'd check on the commission. Make sure it was holding up with a full tank plus the, uh . . ." I pursed my lips toward the bars without looking at them.

Morgan cut his eyes toward the tank, then back at me, like my presence was a riddle he wasn't awake enough to solve. "With a guitar?"

I cleared my throat. "I'm between apartments at the moment."

"What in the Bill Bailey is all the racket out here?" a familiar voice offstage said over the impatient clack of heels up wooden steps. Sonia's ruby head popped out from behind the curtain, and catching sight of me, her dainty features flipped from confusion to delight.

"Kiddo!" she cried, hoisting her tweed skirt hem to dash toward us. I hadn't said a word before her arms were squeezing the blood out of my neck. "Sam, why didn't you mention Benny was here? Oh, I honestly didn't think you was gonna make the journey, what with you being the industrious type and all, but you're just full of surprises, ain't ya! I'll bet you didn't know we kept busy in the offseason even though the seaside's a ghost town—"

"Miss Kutzler, button up before you wear our ears off," Morgan groaned as he slipped his roscoe back into his pocket.

Sonia rolled her eyes. "In a minute. Benny, how's your hand?"

She reached for it to look, but I crammed it back into my pocket. "It's jake! I'm, uh—a fast healer."

"Ain't that lucky!" She hooked me by the arm and steered me toward the stairs. "Let's get out of this drafty old box, and you can tell us all about what you think of our dear Luna Park!"

"At last, a topic worth discussing," Morgan drawled, and led the way to an exit tucked between the stage and the audience seating while Sonia latched herself to my arm.

"Wait!" I backed out of her grip. "My stuff . . ."

I knelt to pick up my things by the tank and hazarded one last look into the water.

El tritón no longer faced us, exposing a set of diagonal stripes across his back, ribbed and red where the net had held him. He was curled tightly into the corner now, with one webbed hand wrapped around his bruised arm and the other fisted in his hair.

I got to my feet and ran to catch up with Sonia, trying not to dwell on what I'd just learned.

Pain looks the same in merpeople as it does in humans.

Mr. Morgan guided us through a door tucked in the stage's right wing. It led outside to a gravel path at the end of which stood a shabby midway tent. As we walked, Sonia gabbed, describing in mouthwatering detail the scents of hot dogs and friedcakes, manic scenes of patrons tugging each other from one attraction to the next amidst clacking coasters and noisy calliopes playing "Hands Across the Sea." Morgan opened the canvas flap so she could escort me inside.

The tent was chillier than a butcher shop, with pipe smoke–stained canvas walls. It housed a sort of makeshift office, with a maple table in the middle of an oriental rug and a matching maple writing desk against the corner where a folding partition wall stuck out of the canvas.

Sonia sat me down at the table and dragged the corner chair over so she could keep chewing my ear off from a seated position.

"The gentry, the sweat shoppers, immigrants, sailors, families, sweethearts—everyone who's anyone is here in the summer. Sad and lonely goops come too, but you just put 'em on the Canals of Venice ride next to a pretty face, and voilà—"

"My dear Miss Kutzler, you asked for his opinion." Mr. Morgan reached into his desk drawer, pulled out a pipe, and slumped into the chair across from us. "Will you stop flapping your tongue and let him give it?"

Sonia flushed and closed her mouth, leaving me rummaging for an opinion. Truth was, I hadn't managed a complete thought since the merman had skewered me with his eyes.

"This place is really something," I said. "Never seen anything like it."

Smiling, Morgan lit his pipe and blew several puffs into the air above our faces. "Of course you haven't," he said loftily. "Luna

Park is the standard-bearer of seaside entertainment, however much Reynolds thinks he can put us out of business."

There was that name again, only now I knew why it kept coming up. "Mr. Barnes mentioned something about that. Dreamland—or Reynolds—copying Luna Park, I mean."

Morgan harrumphed and took another pull from the pipe. "That pretentious skunk thinks he can outclass our establishment," he said in a billow of smoke. "Capable though he may be at smearing white glaze on someone else's art and calling it original, he can't copy a live merman, can he?"

I couldn't argue with that. This Reynolds guy would be hard-pressed to find anything on earth that could compete with the merman in the tank without catching one himself—and, unlike Morgan, *that* guy probably hadn't spent a lifetime figuring out how.

"I happen to agree with your appraisal of Luna," Morgan remarked, blowing a hoop of smoke for us to admire, "but what of *our* corner of it?"

"It's great," I said. "Really great. Except . . ." Questions like this always felt like a trick. In a contest between hearing an unhappy truth and being lied to, folks would almost always rather get snowed. I shot a nervous glance at Sonia, who waited for my answer with large green eyes that didn't blink.

Morgan leaned in. "Except?"

"It does seem a little, I dunno . . ." I remembered those decomposing creatures in the museo de monstruos and winced. "Run-down?"

Morgan smacked the table, and I jumped. "Of course it is! Sonia, didn't I tell you this place was run down?"

Her pout was back. "Actually, I believe it was *me* who told—"

"Mr. Caldera," he interrupted. "Between now and our May reopening, we face an uphill climb. As you've already noticed, our little production here is showing its age. The oddity museum is positively decrepit, the theater needs a complete renovation—we've got quite a lot on our plates now, and as you came such a long way to check on your handiwork, I'm curious to know just how attached are you to your current occupation?"

For better or worse I was, as of yesterday, unattached. But between telepathic mermaids and my Tití Luz, I'd been so concerned with taking orders from the deceased that I hadn't given any real thought to what might happen once I got here. Well out of character for a guy who ran calculations just to cross Van Brunt Street in rush hour.

Morgan noticed my hesitation. "Fate favors a bold spirit," he said, "and a lad who can make art from metal and be relied upon in a pinch to help pull off the greatest acquisition in sideshow history is a bold spirit indeed. Our friend Oscar is a hardworking fellow, but he is neither discreet nor an artist, and I need both to make this production worthy of its new star."

This man was absolutely full of shit. But he'd also called me a bold spirit.

And that was a damn sight better than being called Wheezy.

"Guess I could make the commute."

"No commute. The exhibits share a house on West Twelfth Street called the Albemarle. You'll live with them, just a stroll down the street." His words rolled out quickly, leaving no room for sensible reservations to intrude. "How does fifty cents an hour sound in exchange for maintaining the tank and putting a fresh coat of paint on our establishment?"

Fifty cents an hour? That was more chavo than even a job in Ornamental would have earned! How could he justify the expense when this place was only open six months out of the year?

Olvídate, it wasn't my place to sort that out for him. "Sounds like a deal," I said.

"Capital!" Morgan stood and held out his hand. I stood up into a cloud of pipe smoke and shook it, careful to match his grip.

Sonia leapt up as well. "Oh, just you wait 'til you meet the rest of the gang, Benny," she said, pulling me by the arm with strength that hadn't been there yesterday. "They'll be over the moon when they hear you're joining us!"

As we reached the tent flap, Morgan cleared his throat. We both looked back.

"Our conversation continues tomorrow, all right, Sonia?"

I might have imagined it, but the Fraülein's sparkle seemed to lose some luster. "Sure, Sam. Tomorrow."

"Splendid." He set the pipe back between his teeth. "Welcome to the Menagerie, Benny."

SIX

onia met me under the awning in her winter coat and
muff ready to lead us back down Surf Avenue. Between
asking me questions she immediately answered herself,
complaining about being the youngest person in the Menagerie,
and vowing to spit in Dreamland's man-made lake, the Fraülein's
company was a lot like the train ride down. I didn't have to do
anything but take it in.

Before I knew it, we had arrived at the long porch of a
red-gabled mansion three stories tall with a large sign hanging
over the sidewalk that read "ALBEMARLE HOTEL, L. M. Porter
Prop."

"A hotel?" I asked.

"Don't worry, we got our own place in back. A necessary amen-
ity for us curious types." She pulled me past the front gate into
a tight, earthy-smelling alleyway between the Albemarle and
Moxie's Cigar Shoppe.

The narrow path eventually widened to a wooden staircase that led to a second-floor entrance. Following Sonia up the

creaking steps, I kept thinking about that empty spot in the Menagerie's hallway—whether I'd find out whose act had darkened the wallpaper before the poster disappeared.

Sonia pounded on the storm door. "Ich bin zuhause, mein Lieben! Open up, we got company!"

The inside door swung open, bringing me eye level with an enormous silver belt buckle.

My gaze slowly lifted. "*Santa María*."

The belt of said buckle was holding up the trousers of a man so tall the door frame cut off his whole head from view. I backed up until I nearly fell over the guardrail.

"This is making third day this week without keys," the man grumbled, his voice so deep it could have come from the hotel basement. "Perhaps is lost?"

"I know where they are," Sonia muttered with an eye roll. "I just can't seem to remember to move them out of my purse ever since Sam turned my dressing room into a shrine to Morton's salt and changed the locks."

She reached back, grabbed my coat sleeve, and yanked me forward.

"This is Mr. Benny Caldera," Sonia announced proudly, sidling around the screen door to steer me inside. "He built the new exhibit, and wouldn't you know, he's gonna be one of us now!"

An airless noise came out of my mouth as I craned my neck to make eye contact with a real-life giant.

"Ah, you is iron man, yes?" boomed el gigante. "I am Igor Rybakov of Moscow."

From my vantage point five feet below his face, I made out black hair streaked with gray, a low brow, and a chin curtain that made him look like Abraham Lincoln's distant Russian relative. When we shook hands, his fist ate up the bottom third of my forearm.

"Where are you lazy good-for-nothings?" Sonia yelled into the hall, maneuvering me into a parlor where the window looked out on the scenic railway ride.

"Miss Vera, Eli, Emmett, and Matthias are gone to market. I get it the coffee," said Igor, ducking under the rafter and around the corner.

She blew him a kiss and started taking off my coat.

"Oh, you don't have to—"

Sonia tutted and wrenched it off me in stark contrast to yesterday's flimsy handshake. "Put away your charm school manners. They won't do you no good here."

She marched off in Igor's direction with everything I had, except my cuatro and a dim sense that the last eighteen hours of my life had been one very long dream. The light aroma of cigarettes and kerosene lured me farther into the room where my eyes took in rose-colored damask walls, cherrywood furniture, a clean oriental rug, and a Tiffany lamp, which sat on an end table between me and a modest brick fireplace.

On either side of a bureau, two bookshelves were stocked like someone had raided a Coney Island souvenir shop and brought home the loot, overrun with carnival trinkets, postcards, mugs, souvenir dishes, and ships in bottles. In the center of the chaise, an embroidered pillow read: "With It. For It. Never Against It."

Jesucristo, this place made the tenement look like a hovel—

"So, you're the Porto Rican Sonia's been gabbing about," came a soft voice to my right.

I turned around to find a woman smirking at me. She had been so quiet, I'd thought I was alone, which just went to show how distracted I was.

What God had given Igor in length, he had given this woman in weight.

"Louisa Porter, resident fat lady," she introduced, lifting her dimpled hand toward me. "But you can call me Lulu."

I took it and smiled. "Benny."

"You look like you just turned up at a rodeo with no horse, Benny," she said wryly. "As most of the men Sonia brings home tend to do."

I peeled my hat off my head. "Sorry—what's a rodeo?"

She giggled, a sound so easy and warm that I laughed along. "Take a load off. No one here's gonna bite you."

"Right. Thanks." I sat in the nearest chair, twisted my fingers in my necklace, and didn't know where to put my eyes. Her poster had said it took seven men to hug her—an obvious miscalculation—but she was certainly the heaviest woman I'd ever seen, though I supposed everyone looks heavy to a guy who'd grown up during a famine. In lieu of a chair, she sat on an upholstered bench beside a walking cane; with her wavy brown hair swept up in a stylish knot and delicately rouged face, she couldn't have been older than thirty.

Lulu cleared her throat. "You're allowed to look at me, you know."

"Hm? Oh. Sorry, I didn't wanna be—" My turn to clear my throat. "So, the sign out there says you own this place? It's nice!"

"Thanks. My husband Charlie, God rest 'im, was the original proprietor. Before his buggy met the front end of an Oldsmobile roadster at twenty miles per hour, that is."

"Aw, gosh, I'm *really* sorry," I repeated.

"Hey, you weren't driving the car, were you? These things happen, and it's a good thing being fat turns a nice profit," she said without irony. "Speaking of, I'm also the company costumer, which gives me the unique leverage of knowing too much about the dimensions of everyone else in this house. Now, what's this Sonia's saying about you joining the Menagerie?"

"*Mama!*" A flash of yellow curls darted past my legs attached to a kid who threw himself at Lulu's skirt and hid his face. Maybe he was part of the show too—he looked like a live cherub.

"Shararti ladka! That little terror is going to destroy my library!" cried a high-pitched voice I instantly recognized as Madam Navya's. She stomped into the room, a torn sheet of paper in her fist.

"Timothy Franklin Porter, what did you do?" Lulu groaned.

"Just wookin'," came the muffled voice from Lulu's skirts.

"Looking indeed! Look at *this*!" The madam thrust the shard of paper up at Lulu. "This boy has no respect for the Holy Puranas!"

Lulu shot her son a withering glare. "What have I told you about digging through the madam's books?"

"I wanted to see the ewo-phant," he whined.

"*Ganesha*, you simple boy," Navya snapped. "If this goblin could sit still for a minute of his life, I would teach him about the deities, but instead he prefers to desecrate my sacred texts!"

Lulu pinched the spot between her eyebrows and drew a calming breath. "Look, I'm sorry, and so is Timmy, *right*?" she said pointedly at her son. He wagged his head so rigorously, curls bounced around his face. "I will replace your Puranas, Navya, I promise," Lulu said sincerely. "In the meantime, perhaps both of you want to greet our guest?"

"Hi," I said with a weak wave.

Timmy's greeting involved burrowing his face into his mother's skirt again. Madam Navya folded her arms across her chest.

"I have already met Mr. Benny," she said in a tired voice. "Last night, he tried to pick me up with his hands."

So much for first impressions.

Sonia arrived just as Navya left muttering complaints in her other language. "What's got her garters in a knot?"

Lulu's face drooped with the exhaustion of every mother whose nene caused more problems than she had fixes for. "One guess."

"Aw, not this little *angel*," Sonia cooed, scooping the boy up into her arms to tickle him.

"He is a demon!" Navya corrected from across the house.

The screen door's groan ended the debate. "There weren't nothing but flounder at the market today, so I won't hear no bellyaching," shouted a coarser voice than I'd heard so far, with an Irish accent, though not from Ulster. A tall woman stepped into view. Her charcoal overcoat swept the floor, and from under a feathered hat, tawny ringlets poked out over freckles and an unpainted face. A cigarillo hung from her lips.

She halted in the entryway at the sight of me. "Oi! No one said I were feedin' an extra mouth!"

Matthias's head stuck out from behind her. "That ain't a mouth, that's Benny!" He squeezed his formidable self past the woman to deliver a friendly smack that knocked the tension right out of my shoulders. "Vera, this here's the Porto Rican prodigy from Red Hook," he said, while the lady took one more drag, then laid the cigarillo in an ashtray for safekeeping. "Benny, meet Ms. Vera Campbell."

"You're, the, uh . . . fire-breather?" I asked, putting the clues together.

"And you're the accomplice," she said, grinning with her hand outstretched. "Hope you like flambéed flounder."

As I shook her hand, Matthias's brow lifted. "Say, ain't that the hand you barbecued yesterday?"

I snatched it back. "Uh, yeah, turns out it wasn't as bad as I thought."

Thankfully, he pondered me for only a moment before asking what northern wind had brought me south. I told him I'd come to check on the tank and see whether I might still be useful to the Menagerie after humiliating myself at the Ironworks the other day, prompting Matthias to give me another congratulatory golpetazo on the shoulder. "So you went to Luna Park," he sniggered, "and you came out alive?"

"Yeah, the merman wasn't too happy to see me."

Matthias's thick hand slid his glasses down his nose and snorted. "I wasn't talking about the merman."

"Stop it, you're gonna spook 'im," said Sonia, smacking him on the arm. "Where're the twins?"

"Here," grumbled another familiar voice from the foyer. "We need a new place for hooch, fellas. Those goldbricks over on Eighth ain't got nothing but piss water and absinthe—hey now, look who it is!"

Striding into the room was Eli who seemed pleased to see me, followed soon after by Emmett, who very much didn't. I blinked; beyond their matching blond hair, they didn't look nearly as alike in the daylight as they had last night.

"C'mere, Emmett, it's the hero of the hour, Benny!" he said, clapping me on the shoulder as I gave an awkward left-handed wave.

"You have my socks," Emmett said coolly.

"Oh." I looked down at my feet. "Sorry, I . . . I'm still wearing them, actually. Sonia said you wouldn't mind."

Emmett swung his glare on her.

"Well, you *shouldn't* mind," she huffed. "With only one foot, you've got one too many of every pair anyway."

Emmett and I both gawped at her before a tea tray descended from the sky and settled between our faces. Igor's bass voice rippled down into my boots.

"Is ready, the coffee."

Dinner was burned fish, blackened peas, and charred mashed potatoes. By way of an explanation, Eli was quick to tell me that sharing the house required sharing cooking duty—and that Vera incinerated every item on the menu whenever it was her turn in the kitchen.

The company, as they referred to themselves, carried on with an easy blend of warmth and hostility, teasing and poking at each other like siblings without a parent between them—unless you counted Lulu, who volleyed between managing Timmy's table manners and managing everyone else's. With so many accents competing to be heard, their dynamic was a toss-up between a brood of misfits and an international alliance.

We had something in common, though. We all cleaned our plates despite Vera's culinary deficiencies, which told me more about my new housemates than their posters in the Menagerie ever could.

You only swallow ashes if you know what it's like to go hungry.

Eli passed around absinthe at dessert with pieces of sweet rugelach from the local Jewish bakery to help cut the burn of licorice-flavored lava. It wasn't long before the booze had settled pleasantly in the tips of my ears—and loosened my tongue.

"I couldn't help noticing you all seem a little . . . *different* from the posters of you hanging in the park," I said. "The stuff they say about you—is any of it real?"

"I think our new friend here is having some trouble telling truth from fiction," Matthias observed. He leaned back in his chair and held up a finger. "Sideshow Rule Number One: Real is whatever's in your head."

"Now, now," Vera said, blowing a new ring of smoke into the cloud over her head, "I were a tried and true fire-breather."

"You could try keeping your act out of the kitchen for once." Emmett sat slack in his chair, rubbing his stomach queasily. "I'll be belchin' smoke for a— Hey! What'd you do that for!"

Vera had dropped her cigarillo in his drink like she'd just dropped a coin in the church collection plate. "There's the rest of your dessert, ya New Jersey git."

"Speakin' of smoke"—Sonia stood up from the table and began unlacing her boots—"Vera, hand me one, will you?"

The fire-breather shot her a look of extreme inconvenience before handing over a new cigarillo, which Sonia set between her lips. Sonia then gestured to Emmett, who sulkily dug a match out of his pocket and flicked it across the table where she caught it—then wedged it between her black-stockinged toes.

"Now it's a party," Eli declared. "Don't blink, Benny."

Blink? But where was I supposed to look?

I forgot to bite into my rugelach as Sonia folded over by the waist like saltwater taffy and laid her forearms flat against the floor. Slowly, her spine stacked on top of itself until rolls of tweed skirt were balanced on her bright red bun like whipped cream on a cupcake.

From there, her legs lifted smoothly over her head, toes still gripping the match angled sharply toward the ground. Her limbs didn't so much as tremble as she raised a hand to the matchstick and, with a scratch of her fingernail, brought a flame to life.

Then with the casual air of a lady enjoying an evening smoke, Sonia lit the cigarillo . . . *with her foot.*

My dessert thunked back onto my plate.

Claps and laughter erupted around me. Even Emmett condescended to raise his glass in Sonia's honor, and as soon as my brain caught up, I joined him. Madam Navya alone looked morally outraged.

The Fraülein took a smug drag on Vera's rompepecho. "Real enough for ya, Benny?"

"I'm sold!"

Sonia unknotted her appendages. With a demure curtsey, she plucked the cigarillo from her lips and offered it to me. "This one's on the house."

I leaned away from it and laughed. "No, thanks. My lungs and cigarettes ain't on good terms."

Vera leaned over the table and snatched it out of Sonia's fingers. "I'll take that."

"I gotta hand it to you, Sonia," Matthias said, still clapping. "You're the only one who passes for normal, but you're probably the oddest carny in this company."

"Being a carny don't require being odd on the outside," she remarked, shaking her skirt out. "It's a state of mind."

"Yeah, the state of desperation," Eli snorted.

I leaned forward in my chair. "How'd you guys wind up in a sideshow anyway?"

Emmett thumbed at his nose and cracked his first smile of the evening, though I wouldn't call it pleasant. "We'd tell you, but then we'd have to kill you."

"Shut up, Em," Matthias muttered.

"We are here by the ineffable movements of fate," said Madam Navya with liquored-up authority. "I've long believed we were all of us warring kinsmen in a past life, brought back together in this life that we might yet learn how not to kill each other."

Igor dabbed his mouth with his absurdly small handkerchief. "Is also much more pleasant for to be famous than feared. Is not so loud, the screaming."

Madam Navya hiccupped. "That too."

"Speak for yerselves," Vera remarked, unbuttoning the lace around her collar. "I came here to strike terror into the heart of every eejit who confuses me for some starchy mot in skirts. I been beggin' Lulu here to make me britches ever since the season ended so's I can stop stealing Eli's."

Lulu snatched the fork from Timmy's hand before he could finish gouging a stick figure into the arm of his high chair, then pointed it at Vera. "I don't see you offering to watch Timmy so I can make 'em."

"Jesus, *I'll* watch Timmy," groaned Eli. "I'm running out of pants."

Sonia leaned forward and propped her head on her hand. "It's *your* story I wanna hear," she said. "What tale of intrigue brought a Porto Rican blacksmith to the Empire City?"

I pushed my cup away. "It ain't that intriguing."

"I don't believe that for a second. Spill it."

My usual reflex to interrogations was withdrawal, so I was surprised when I realized I *wanted* to spill it. Maybe the absinthe had primed me with a brash impulse to entertain the entertainers. Or maybe, with so little left to lose, I thought I'd try my hand at being the sort of guy who opens up to strangers without worrying they'll stick a knife through the gap.

"I snuck aboard a steamer."

Everyone seemed to sit up straighter. Sonia's eyes flashed in anticipation of a juicy story. "You were a *stowaway*?"

"Is that what you'd call it?"

"Sneaking aboard ships is very risky behavior indeed," Madam Navya said, though she'd directed it at Timmy.

I licked my finger and dabbed up the crumbs off my plate. "Not that risky. I was eighteen. I had no family left, no future, so I climbed aboard the *USS Carolina* in the middle of the night. Hid under some dirty sheets in the linen room."

Emmett's eyes were on me as he poured himself and Eli another shot. "And you weren't caught?"

"Oh, I got caught," I laughed. "I was only on the ship three hours when a camarero—that is, a guy on the waitstaff—found me. Dragged me and my cuatro to the chief steward, but by then my lungs had already started making trouble. And I guess he felt sorry for me 'cause next thing I know, he's telling the seaman who'd found me to get me a mop and a bed in steerage."

"I'll be damned," Matthias murmured.

"Yeah. Would've been nicer waiting tables instead, but I didn't know English yet."

"This kid's sellin' us a thumper," said Emmett. He leaned back in his chair and folded his arms over his chest. "You stowed away on a steamship. Didn't speak no English. And you expect us to believe you landed a job in a Red Hook ironworks right off the boat?"

"Good English don't build cities," I said curtly. "Good smithies do."

"And yet Benny here speaks it like he been livin' in Brooklyn since before it became a borough," Matthias observed as he took a pencil and notebook out of his pocket. "How long did that take? Anyone teach you?"

"You're writing this down?" Emmett balked.

"'Bout a year," I said, taking Matthias's cue to ignore Eli's brother. "I dunno, it's not too different from learning music. My ears are good at picking up sounds and my mouth's good at spitting 'em back out. I used to do impressions of my old coworkers."

"Ooh, I wanna hear an impression!" cried Vera.

"Me too!" Sonia seconded, prompting thirds from others around the table.

"Good idea," Emmett said, with a bite that made me wonder if his beef with me had nothing to do with socks. "How's about you do one of old Igor here?"

Igor's face brightened. "To hear that, I would be truly eager!"

By now, it sure looked like I'd left Farty behind only to replace him with the Coney Island model. Fine. If Emmett wanted proof so badly, I'd let him have it.

I examined Igor's face—the broad lips over his Abe Lincoln beard—and imagined the boom that rumbled from his long neck. The words would be easy enough; I wrapped my tongue around them and pulled them into the back of my mouth where my ears told me Igor talked.

Finally, I imagined my throat twice as long and felt it open.

"*To hear that, I would be truly eager*," I said in my very best Russian Giant.

Gasps chorused around the table.

"Aye Haye! This man is possessed!" Madam Navya gasped.

Laughter burst out of me in a way it hadn't since I was un nene. Matthias smacked the table so hard I thought the oak might buckle. "Holy shit, the guy's a Leonardo!"

"You're in the wrong line of work, kiddo," Sonia gushed, eyes wide. "With a skill like that, why the hell aren't you on stage with the rest of us?"

"Well, the stage is occupied right now, ain't it?" I snorted, taking another sip from my cup.

A subtle shift in the air put out our levity like one of Vera's rompepechos. Everyone suddenly seemed very interested in the contents of their cups. Igor got up and lumbered to the kitchen.

"I say something wrong?"

Eli shifted uneasily in his chair. "Nah. We just ain't as keen on the new exhibit as Sam is."

"Merman's a feckin' tinderbox," Vera slurred. "An' everyone knows you don't mix fire-breathers with tinderboxes."

"*You* weren't the one Sam hung out there like a worm on a hook," Sonia said indignantly. "Stranded out there like a couple o' schmucks . . . If Matthias hadn't been there, I'd've died of fright thinking I was gonna be dragged overboard by some slippery sea savage."

"Morgan's choices . . . s'will visit punishment upon us all," Madam Navya hiccupped gravely. "S'what happens when you imprison a deity."

"It ain't a *deity*," Matthias scoffed. "But I'll tell you what. Once the merman starts raking in dough, I'll eat my hat if Morgan still remembers our names in a month."

"Would he? Forget your names?" I'd known these folks for less than a day and already knew I'd never forget them.

"It's like this. We got a credo in our line of work," Lulu explained. "It goes: With it, for it, never against it."

"That was on the pillow in the parlor," I said, "but what exactly is 'it'?"

"'It' is the sideshow," Matthias replied. "But it's also the sideshow *life*. Being 'with it, for it, and never against it' means being tied to this here family. Devoted to it. Ready to die to protect it."

"And Sam ain't never been the type," Eli said, shaking his head. "It's why he goes home to Queens every night, 'stead of hanging with us freaks in Nightmare Alley."

"You were at the theater today, right?" Lulu asked when she saw I was still confundido. "Notice that empty spot at the end of the posters? His name was Saul Spencer, the Living Skeleton. He couldn't help being thin like I can't help being fat, so we'd go on stage together as a bit—make the audience guess our weights, then step on the scale to wow the crowd when they guessed wrong. Saul was the oldest Menagerie member since the days when Jack Morgan ran it as a traveling show. He was Timmy's godfather too, and the man who put me back together after Charlie died."

Her eyes went soft with the recollection. "When scarlet fever took him at the end of the season last year, we was all in rough shape. But not Sam. He just pulled down the poster. Like Saul was never here."

"It's 'cause Sam's got his own bloody credo," Vera clarified. "He's with, for, and never against *hisself*."

My stomach sank. This was the same guy who had charmed me into kidnapping a merman and buttered me up to renovate his theater. What if his good faith only lasted if he saw an advantage to having me around?

"Hey. Don't worry about ol' Sam," Lulu said, reading the worry on my face. "Now that you're here, you'll be family too. And we take care of each other."

"Family," I snorted. "You don't even know if you like me."

Sonia looped her arm through mine. "Of course we like you!"

"I don't," Emmett muttered.

"Emmett's opinion don't matter on account o' his oddity being the gigantic stick up his arse," Vera deadpanned.

"All right," I said slowly, "but what happens to my job when I'm done fixing the theater?"

Matthias chuckled. "Just do your Igor impression for the boss man and *boom*"—he snapped his fingers—"job security."

Igor poked his head back in. "If Benny is good cook, I give him my spot in show, no problem."

"But . . ."

But I don't belong here, I almost said, as if I'd ever belonged anywhere. The only family I'd ever had before was a well-to-do tabaquera—a tobacco farmer who'd picked me up like a stray at the edge of el Río Humacao after the San Ciriaco hurricane. Any trace of my blood relations had gotten knocked out of my head, swept away in the swollen river. After all that, the idea I could walk through the side door of the Albemarle right into a new family was nuttier than the rugelach I just ate.

But I'd been a janitor aboard the *USS Carolina.* I'd worked in tobacco fields, then foundries. I learned to speak English, only to realize in frustration that I'd also have to *read* it, then I did that too. I'd lost track of all the times I had melted myself down just to recast myself as someone with a slightly better shot at *belonging* someplace, and here I was being offered the brass ring, no new skills required.

I looked around at the liquor-warm faces anticipating the end of my sentence. Even Emmett looked halfway resigned to putting up with me.

"But when would I get a turn in the kitchen?" I finished to everyone's apparent satisfaction.

Bueno. Almost everyone.

Emmett stuck his finger at my face. "When you give back my damn socks."

I lent Lulu my arm to lean on as she led us slowly up the creaking staircase to a narrow hallway of living quarters on the third floor. "The company sleeps up here, but Timmy and I are downstairs so as not to disturb anyone's peace," she said with a smirk to indicate peace might just be subjective where her nene was concerned. At the end of the hall, she unlocked the cherrywood door and pushed it open, standing aside to let me through. "You get Saul's old room."

Remnants of the Human Skeleton's spartan existence still lay about—an ivory comb and pomade on the dresser, a silk top hat hanging off the standing mirror in the corner, and a writing desk by the window where a few framed photographs were arranged, including one of him and Lulu together onstage smiling wide in monochrome to an invisible audience. I picked it up.

Saul looked like un hambriento, the way his skin draped across his skull like soaked linen, the knobs of bone and cartilage poking sharply through his three-piece suit.

Lulu walked me through the keys on the key ring. "This goes to the side door, this one to the main door, this one to enter the park, and this one"—she singled out a tarnished brass key—"opens our dear old Menagerie."

I took it and ran a finger over the heart-shaped knot in the middle of the bow. "Mr. Morgan won't mind me having one of these?"

"What belonged to Saul belongs to me now. And I'm giving it to you."

Tití Luz would have warned me not to take the room of a guy so recently departed. But if Saul's ghost was still hanging around, I didn't mind if it meant having a real bed and a cotton quilt that smelled like starch and labdanum aftershave instead of charred coal.

But as lamps went out across the Albemarle that night, not even the comfy bed could keep the merman's steely glare from haunting me. Not that I wasn't used to being glared at; between the brethren of Irish ironworkers and the gentry of Nueva York, it was the daily reality of living where my existence was offensive.

Despite all that, the merman's judgment felt different. I kept wondering why I was its target instead of Morgan who'd been the architect of his circumstances. But if I had to guess, the merman wasn't leering at me because I'd killed the mermaid or helped kidnap him. In the same way I resented everyone who'd ever stood by while Farty Walsh tortured me at the furnaces, el tritón leered at me because I'd watched.

And I'd done nothing to stop it.

SEVEN

The first face to greet me the next morning belonged to Matthias, who strolled out of the kitchen with a plate of tosineta in a too-small apron, his sleeves rolled up to expose a tangle of tattoos. "Hope Porto Ricans like bacon."

I shot him a look and decided it was safe to drop the American act where my island's name was concerned. "*Puerto* Ricans invented bacon."

"Jesus," he said, shaking his head. "Been here, what, two minutes, and you already picking fights?"

But a fight was already happening above us.

"Vera Campbell, you loon! They looked perfect on you!" echoed Sonia's voice from above as Vera stomped down the stairs, her hair spilling out of a messy braid.

"Keep your manky ribbons!" snapped the fire-breather. "I amn't a bleedin' birthday parcel! Ah. Morning, Benny."

"Morning, Vera."

Harassments continued over breakfast, more to Lulu's dismay than anyone else's. She seemed to take it upon herself to parent everyone in the house, not just her son, breaking up an argument between the Rhodes brothers over Emmett's need for a new prosthetic ("You ain't spendin' a leg just to get me a new one!"), scolding Timmy for nicking sugar cubes from the pantry, and calming Navya's temper when Igor purposely tried to step on her foot. The madam had accidentally stepped on his first, at which point, I learned that Igor and other superstitious Russians believe trading one stomped foot for another avoids future conflicts. And bueno . . . there went *that* theory.

By the meal's end, I was weighed down with enough bacon and eggs to send me back to bed, but I was too eager to put Saul's key to use. I ventured briskly back to the Menagerie, saluting Oscar as I let myself into the playground that had, by some trick of fate, become my new workplace. The stuffed monstruos in the museum didn't faze me this time, but a shout from inside the theater did.

"Hellfire and damnation!"

I poked my head in. The curtains were open, the tank so big in my field of vision I almost missed Sam Morgan in his green vestido, perched on the ladder beside it like a cranky iguaca. His hand clung to a rig suspended from the ceiling, the other knotted in a long cloth banner that spilled to the floor.

"Sir?"

"Benny, be a gentleman"—he jutted his chin toward the ground—"and lift up the other end, would you?"

I scooped the cloth off the floor. Through the creases, "THE PRINCE OF ATLANTIS" read in sea-blue letters against a lemony background.

"Painted it yesterday," he grunted, maneuvering the cloth for a better grip. "How do you like it?"

"It's nice. Very . . ." I needed a kinder version of "chillón."

"Bright!"

"The better to see from the ground!"

I peeked involuntarily toward the tank. El tritón was right where we'd left him, curled against the glass in the same corner where the sunlight didn't touch, sleeping.

"There another ladder?"

"A single ladder is all this blasted production is fit to own at present," he grumbled, looping a swath of fabric around his forearm. "Get on top of the cage. I'm sure you can reach from there."

I carried the other end of the banner to the rungs I'd built into the tank and hauled it up. Halfway to the top, I noticed something downstage: A double-boiler engine sat attached to a long rubber hose that ran up the tank side through the grill to dangle in the water. A second hose lay idle on the ground next to it.

"What's that?" I asked.

Morgan shook out his arm and rested it against the ladder's top cap. "A retired steam pump from the fire brigade. I was hoping that prodigious brain of yours might help me come up with a way to convert it into a circulation system for the water—sooner rather than later if you don't mind. We wouldn't want a swampy tank on our hands!"

I was about to say I didn't mind, but then my foot came down on the tank's roof, making the metal—and my knees—vibrate. The last time I'd stood here, we had just hauled the merman's bleeding body up those rungs.

I willed my focus back to the topic at hand; there were logistics to work out if the pump was going to filter the water without clogging.

Except there was nothing in the water. It was completely clear.

"Does the merman . . . ?" *Bendito, how could I put this?* "Does he leave any . . . mess?"

"One assumes it metabolizes food like any other sea animal," Morgan said, delicately. "Not that I've seen it eat. So far, all it does is seethe and sleep in that corner like a defanged viper. I keep finding the salt cod I've been feeding it tossed back out of the tank, the slippery ingrate."

"Do mermen *like* salt cod?" Without proper soaking, that stuff could break teeth and make your eyes water.

Morgan huffed. "I hardly think that matters. I'm running a sideshow, not a Bavarian beer garden." He pointed above my head. "The hook's up there."

While the showman repositioned himself to hang his end of the banner, my jellied legs inched toward the edge of the roof. With some direction from me, Morgan managed to hang the eyelet from the metal hook on his side of the tank, after which I slipped my own into place.

"Splendid! Stay where you are; it might need adjusting."

He gingerly made his way back down the ladder. "Rather nice having someone with a work ethic around here. The exhibits are positively useless in the offseason," he said dryly. "Though I might have saved myself a mountain of effort had I just bought the silly patents from Harry, that Hungarian bastard."

I blinked. "As in *Houdini*?"

"You're right, he wouldn't have given them up," he grumbled. "Fame makes a man cagey, if you'll forgive the pun."

Morgan examined our handiwork from the audience, his pointer finger tapping an impatient rhythm on his bottom lip. "Lighting's a travesty," he concluded after a pause, "but an overhead spotlight might fix it. Add a bit of drama. I'm sure there's a spare in the ballroom they'd never miss." He turned on his heel to march back toward the curiosity museum. "I'll just pop over and get it."

"Should I—"

"No, stay there! I'll be back before the coffee's gone cold," he called back, then left me stranded on the tank roof like underwear hung out to dry. The height was making me dizzy. I backed away from the edge wondering if the air was thinner up here or if I'd just never known the unique displeasure of standing two dozen feet above the ground with a slumbering merman under my boots.

I could just as easily wait for Morgan on the stage floor, so I turned back to the ladder.

I made it only a step.

A splash like a cannonball blasting into a lake sent spray flying up at me from below.

Before I could react, something hard struck my ankle and I buckled, falling cheek-first onto metal.

A sea-stained hand—wet, webbed, and rougher than sand-paper—caught my wrist through the grill. I couldn't get to my knees before another closed around my neck and yanked me down, banging my face into the iron. Through watering eyes, I saw two limpid blue irises glittering with lethal intent.

My lungs shuttered.

"Have you no voice to scream, fiendish parasite?"

¡Manos a Dios! He speaks English!

"I will tear out your throat," he continued in a quiet voice as deep and fearsome as distant thunder. "I will dine on your flesh, you flea-bitten sack of terrene entrails."

I gagged and gasped against the bars. "L-let . . . go . . ."

"*No*," he snarled. "You will release me from this cage or, so help me Neptune, I will gouge out your eyes with my fingernails. I will take you apart with my *teeth* and season the water with your blood until my fins are stained red."

Saul's key ring was in my pocket. I wrenched my free hand behind my back and fumbled for it, praying for even an ounce of Sonia's flexibility.

"Can't . . . breathe . . ."

"*Die*, then! You shall have the same mercy you showed my mother!"

A hairsbreadth from blacking out, my finger hooked around the key ring. As hard as I could, I swung out and stabbed the

Menagerie key into the merman's hand. The blow only glanced off his wet skin but loosened his fingers enough for me to rip myself from his grip and roll onto my back, sending him falling tail-first into the tank. Water sprayed up, drenching my newly liberated ass up to my shoulders.

I clawed my way to the edge of the roof and half fell down the rungs. At the bottom, I collapsed onto my knees and stayed there. My vision was swimming, my breathing all wrong; if I made myself walk, I'd faint the second I stood upright.

But el tritón wasn't finished with me. I looked up in time to see him launch himself at the glass. The impact rang like a gong, but to his visible fury, the glass held. He flew into a fit, careening in a circle along the walls, hammering his tail against them as if he intended to burst them from the inside. How was his speed even possible underwater?

He was terrifying. A tornado in a tank.

His strikes at the glass eventually slowed until he stopped and clung to it, his hunched shoulders outlined in cold, filtered sunlight. When I hazarded to meet his eyes again, the fire had gone out of them. His despair hadn't.

Morgan was carrying a large round lamp in his arms when I staggered blindly into the daylight outside the theater.

"Benny?"

I sidestepped around him to hide my drenched backside, rationing my inhales to keep from coughing. "Air's a little . . . thin . . . over the tank," I croaked.

At first, he squinted suspiciously at me, but then his eyes widened.

He could hear it. The whistling.

"So it would seem." An uneasy frown inverted his mustache. "That doesn't bode very well for our aquatic circulation system—"

"I'll . . . come back," I panted. "Tonight. I'll be . . . better by then."

"I don't favor the idea of leaving you alone in the theater at night—"

"It's just this once."

I held Morgan's gaze until he relented and dug a key out of his pocket that wasn't on Saul's key ring.

"For the new padlock to the theater. I'll be in town tomorrow conducting business. Lock up after yourself, then return the key to me on Friday." He leaned in to add, "Guard it with your life."

With an enthusiastic nod, I took it. And before the coughs could explode out of me, I tore out of the park straight for the beach.

The chilly wind blew inland. I tried frantically to inhale it, gripping San Cristóbal until his haloed face was practically stamped permanently into my palm. Once I felt aerated enough not to swoon, I headed back to the Albemarle where I snuck in like a shadow. I sat on the corner of my new bed, cold, damp, and breathing easier by a margin too small to find relief in.

When I'd taken this room, I had accepted the risk I'd be haunted.

But not like this.

I didn't tell anyone about my confrontation with el tritón. I wrapped Matthias's wool scarf around my collar, earning me a few side glances from my housemates at dinner. I told them I thought I might have a cold.

"Probably caught it getting dunked the other night," Eli observed through a mouthful of biscuit, "'cause I ain't felt right since neither."

"You got your arse dragged by a sea lady. That ain't a cold, that's humiliation," Vera chided.

"Eli coulda died," Emmett murmured, instantly quashing Vera's wisecracking.

"Hey." Smiling, Eli put a hand on Emmett's arm and squeezed. "I'm still here, Em."

"'Tis natural to fall ill when one's life path has shifted," Navya said sagely. "The former self must be purged that the new self may emerge."

"*Or* Benny just has the sniffles," Lulu said.

"Well, we'll fix you right up, won't we?" Sonia said, shifting in her seat to reach for my scarf.

"No!" I yelped. Her hand froze in midair. "I mean, no thanks. I just gotta lie down or something."

"Do what you gotta do," Matthias said, then stuffed half the steak into his mouth.

"Right. Uh, buen provecho."

I abandoned my dinner and avoided their puzzled gazes as I left for my room. When I reached the mouth of the stairs, a hushed voice from the dining table stopped me in my paces.

"Are we sure about this Benny guy?"

It was Emmett.

"Here we go," groaned Matthias. "You afraid he's gonna murder us in our beds with his shrimpy guitar?"

"Something's off about him, and it ain't a cold."

"Oh, give it a rest, Em," said Sonia.

"Didn't you see how he flinched just now? He's a flincher, and flinchers always got something on their conscience! You don't really believe that thumper he told us last night, do you? All that tripe about stowin' away on a—"

"Emmett, do the damn world a favor and shut the hell up," Matthias whisper-shouted. "You act like you and Eli got the monopoly on running away. Like nobody else done had it rough as you. Of course I believe him, 'cause I know a survivor when I see one. And if I was you, I'd take a long look at my pale-ass face in the mirror and think about how that Caribbean kid crossed an ocean for a slice of freedom America ain't never gonna give him."

I waited. Then I padded up the stairs.

Seemed no one had anything to say after that.

 The Merman

I had the human in my grip. The last thing you touched. Had he
not struck my hand, he would have been slain by it.

Is this what captivity has wrought in my heart? Have I bowed at
last to the savagery our harmony has condemned in humans
since their relentless voyages across the Salted Deep began?
Never have I so misplaced myself to violence that I had
loosed my voice to the air, hissing into the face of a
creature no larger than a bluefin!

Merciful Neptune. What would you think of me, Mother?

"They have souls," you had told me once the smoke had cleared
from the estuary. "You saw how they grieve."

The other man, vested like an eel with eyes like a
trench-dweller—whose thunderous blast took you away; I am
loath to believe he has *ever* grieved.

But the one I harmed today does not have such eyes. When you died, he looked at me, and in his gaze was my own horror reflected.

Perhaps that is why I leapt for his throat.

EIGHT

Parasite, he'd called me. Even mermen thought I was a leech. All evening, I lingered at the mirror to check my bruises, the ghost of long, wet fingers still squeezing my neck. My duffel was sticking out of Saul's open armoire, still packed for the possibility of jobs where the occupational hazards didn't include getting my head bashed in by a sea creature.

No one was forcing me to stay. I could leave right now. Just kiss the cozy mattress and suspiciously high wages goodbye, and let fate pick some other cabrón to make nice with a mythical being smart and angry enough to list terrifyingly specific ways to kill a guy.

Except I couldn't.

Jesucristo, I wished I'd never heard the merman speak. Then I might never have known that the one who'd traded her last word for my healed hand had been his *mother*. El tritón hated my guts, but unlike the baseless loathing that used to follow me around the ironworks like a shadow, I'd absolutely earned it.

I'd built the cage that held him. Made it damn near indestructible. And ever since, the universe seemed pretty insistent that his welfare was my new head-smelter to solve.

Once five doors clicked shut and the hall lamps gave way to the dark, I slunk back downstairs, grabbed my coat, and nicked a can of sardines from the pantry.

I had an aquatic circulation system to build.

As creepy as the Menagerie Curiosity Museum was during the day, this place at night could give Gravesend Cemetery a run for its money. Before anything came to life in that graveyard of stuffed atrocidades, I grabbed the oil lamp from behind the ticket counter and hustled out of there—only to find out the theater was an even blacker hole than the museum.

Morgan had been busy after I left. The benches were now stacked along the wall, leaving a wide, empty space for my footsteps to echo, the plaster gods' kerosene-lit eyes following me as I walked. With the sardine can thunking against my thigh, I jogged up the stage stairs toward the rim of blue light and paused.

It'd take a cannon to break that glass, I reminded myself, then pulled back the red velvet, and stepped behind it.

I was back in the lagoon. Rippling moonlight danced on everything, from the curtains to the walls to my clothes and skin. There in his corner, wide awake and staring at me like my bones would make a decorative addition to the bottom of his tank, was el tritón.

I steeled my jaw and approached with the lamp.

"Hey. I, uh . . . I think we got off on the wrong foot." *Dios purísimo.* "Not foot. 'Cause you don't got foot—I mean, feet. What I mean is . . . I figured we might start over."

I couldn't be sure, but his glower seemed to get more glower-y. I set the lamp down.

"You should know, I don't usually help steal merpeople from the river, in case you thought I wanted you to get stuck here. 'Cause that was an accident. Mostly. I didn't know that they would—you know. Like, no one ever told me you were even . . . *Cristo.*" I bit my useless tongue and tried again. "I ain't gonna hurt you, all right?"

He didn't so much as nod. Or sneer. Or do anything to prove my words weren't just ricocheting off the glass. I was out here pouring iron without a cast, and he knew it.

"I get it. Most times, I don't trust me either."

Caramba, he was unnerving to look at. There was no reconciling the human and the sea creature in him, because he was both and neither, with eyes that stayed blue even in orange lamplight and a perfectly symmetrical scowl that made the faces in the Grecian friezes look jolly. And yet, somehow, his glare wasn't as scalding as it had been before. I thought he might just be tired, but then I noticed his arms wrapped tightly around his waist.

I used to do that. On the hungry days. Press in on my stomach so I couldn't feel how empty it was.

El tritón was starving.

"Morgan said you haven't eaten. I figured, maybe salt cod ain't your favorite, so I brought you these." I pulled out the can. "Says here, these are American sardines. From . . ."—I squinted at the label—"Maine."

Crossing myself (*En el nombre del Padre, el Hijo, y el Espíritu Santo, amén*), I made the climb back up to the tank roof. We could have been eyeing each other through cellophane the water was so still, nothing moving so much as an inch except the direction of his leering gaze. I crouched on the grill, peeled back the can lid, and, without ceremony, let a fish drop through the lattice. It hit the water with a humiliating *doink.*

He side-eyed it all the way down until it reached the floor, where it stayed.

"Bueno, you don't have to eat it *now*."

I left the can on the bars and got my ass off the roof in case his craving for human flesh had lingered from this morning. "I'll just do a bit of work while you get your appetite back. I ain't much of a talker anyway." I hesitated on a rung. "Then again, I'm the idiot hanging around here talking to myself."

Just then, I saw it: He rolled his eyes! I'd take it; at least he could translate the flood of tonterías pouring out of my mouth into something to sneer at.

I meandered over to the steam pump and started looking for valves and couplings to connect the other hose. "The other folks in the company are a lot more interesting to listen to than I am. They think you're gonna put them out of a job, but that's only 'cause they know the public's gonna go batty soon as they meet you. I mean look at you, you're . . ."

A backwards glance at the silky glimmer of his fins in the lamplight nearly derailed my train of thought.

"Gosh, you're gonna make them forget Dreamland ever existed."

His eyes flashed over pursed lips. With a flourish of his tail, he turned his back to me, a violent tremor running through the sharp fronds along his spine.

"Miércoles." I winced. "Sorry. We'll talk about something else. You speak English. Do you speak Spanish too? La sirena me habló en español—"

He sat up straight as a mast the moment I'd said the mermaid had spoken to me in Spanish. If he didn't speak it himself, then he surely understood it, because when he slowly turned back to me, the acid was missing from his expression, replaced by a blend of shock and grief so raw and open—and *human*—that my stomach clenched at the sight of it.

"The thing is," I murmured, "I'd probably try to kill me too if I was you. Doesn't much matter that I didn't know better. I helped them cage you, I built this tank, so you're allowed to hate my guts. But your mother"—and for the briefest moment, the merman's iron stare wavered—"she told me to save you. Shouted it right into my mind. I ain't stopped thinking about it."

Looking at his stricken face was like staring into a blast furnace, so I looked at my feet instead.

"Believe me, I don't get it, either. I can hardly help myself; I don't understand why she thought I had any power to help you. But she wanted you to survive, and this," I said, pointing to the sardine at the bottom of the tank, "is the only way I know how to do what she asked. So, uh . . . please? You've gotta eat."

I made myself look up at him. El tritón held my gaze for a long, silent moment with shoulders tensed until, reaching some kind of decision, they loosened.

My heart began to thud in my throat as I watched him rise slowly out of his corner, bite his pewter lip, then float gracefully toward the abandoned sardine, his tail sweeping out behind him in a streak of blue and silver. Just when I thought my words had run out, one came to mind that I didn't dare say out loud.

Hermoso.

He picked up the fish with lithe webbed fingers, inspected it, then shot a withering look in my direction.

"Sorry. I'll just get back to work."

I'd won a second victory. Suppressing a grin, I turned around to attach the hose to the couplings and hoped the sound of shifting water at my back meant he'd begun to eat. In a moment, there was a soft burble and the metal scrape of the tin when I knew he'd decided to finish the rest of his dinner.

Some of the tension ran out of my body too, as I tinkered away amidst the milky reflections swirling around me. This wasn't the same as sitting on the pier after work—hanging out next to a tank in an amusement park in the dead of night—but there was some of the same lonely serenity here as there was looking out on the Gowanus after dark.

Solitude had become a fixture of my life, but something told me the life of a merman wasn't lonely. Not if his mother could show up like lightning in his hour of need. I pulled San Cristóbal out of my shirt and wrapped a finger around the chain.

"It might not help to hear this, but . . . I lost someone too," I said. "A lot of someones, if you count my real parents, but Tití Luz was the one I remember. She wasn't really my aunt. Just sort of adopted me after my family disappeared in the hurricane. I was a kid when she found me. Pulled me right out of the river."

Just like you, I stopped myself from saying.

"But she wasn't murdered or anything. She was one of the revolutionaries who wanted independence for Puerto Rico, and I guess, after el Grito de Lares was a bust, waiting for a real revolution was too much for her, especially once the change from pesos to dollars bankrupted her farm."

I let out a short laugh. "I remember, she used to hate the word 'pronto.' Means 'soon.' *Soon* there would be crops. *Soon* there would be work. *Soon* there would be food. Freedom, money, peace—pronto, pronto, pronto. In the end, she got so tired of waiting, it wasn't hard for la tisis to finish the job. ¿Quién sabe? Maybe that's just a different kind of murder."

I squeezed San Cristóbal, forcing back that old, smoldering anger before it could burn its way into my eyes. The breath left my lungs in a hiss.

"Forget it. I didn't come here to say all these dumb things," I whispered. "I just thought maybe it might help, hearing you're not the only one who lost someone who tried to save you."

The room had gone very quiet. Turning back toward the tank, I found el tritón suddenly right next to me, hovering off the floor and sizing me up with those eyes, blue as sapphires and sharper than arrowheads. I shivered.

⌒III⌒

My whole life, no one had ever looked at me this way. Like they could see past the layers of shirt and skin and rib cage and find the X that marked the spot where I'd buried myself.

Slowly, I rose to my feet. In case one quick movement might disturb this fragile thing forming in the silence between us. He watched, still as a stone, as I laid my fingers lightly against the glass.

What I said next came out in Spanish. Because all my truest thoughts were in Spanish and because I knew he understood it.

"It is no wonder you cried out," I breathed. "I cannot imagine losing your liberty and your mother in the same breath. I am so very sorry."

El tritón tilted his head wonderingly at me like I was the most confusing creature he'd ever dined with. If he rejected my apology, I decided I wouldn't take it personally. But then, to my surprise, he raised his silvery hand.

And he placed it on the glass against mine.

A long moment passed before I pulled my hand away, then rushed past my revolú and back up the iron rungs. This time, I sat cross-legged on the lattice, hoping he'd accept the unspoken invitation.

His face broke the surface first, then his shoulders. Below him, a rippling outline of tail wafted gently to and fro, keeping him aloft. My brain idled at the sight of him, which accounts for the idiot thing I said next.

"How was the fish?"

He swallowed. Averted his eyes as if he were weighing something carefully in his mind. Finally, in a voice deep and far smoother than the one he'd used to threaten me, he spoke.

"Adequate."

I was fascinated. Just as he'd done when listing all the gruesome ways he planned to dismember me, he spoke aloud—instead of directly into my head. I also realized I couldn't locate his accent on a map; his words had notes of British and even the Mediterranean but couldn't be pinned to any single country.

Before I could think of a better conversation starter, he asked, "What *are* you?"

My mouth opened, then closed. "I'm a guy. I mean, a—a man."

"Is that all?"

"And a . . . blacksmith?"

He studied me like I was the head-smelter here. "You said my mother spoke to your mind. But you are"—he looked me over with bored disdain—"a blacksmith."

"What about you?" Remembering Madam Navya's mutterings about imprisoning deities, I asked, "You're not like a—a god, are you?"

His expression went frigid. "A god who could not save himself or his kin from death and captivity?"

"Right. Sorry." I cleared my throat. "You should probably eat the bacalao Morgan's been giving you, you know."

"Morgan," he repeated, like the name tasted bitter on his tongue. "Is that the trench-dwelling shark who circles this cage all day?"

If I weren't a heartbeat away from shaking out of my skin, I might have laughed. "Yeah, that's him."

His jaw tightened. "My kind are not beholden to humanity."

"Be that as it may," I said, aiming for diplomacy, "if we want to keep this up"—I drew a line in the air between us—"you're gonna have to eat what he gives you too."

He didn't roll his eyes so much as held back a glower. "I will eat it, but not because the shark wishes it." With a shudder, he added, "It tastes of the Dead Sea."

"That's just 'cause it's cured. I'll get him to soak it in water. It's so much better that way. Not so salty, or chewy . . . or, um . . ." My audience was looking at me like I could use a good soaking myself. "I'm Benny, by the way. That's short for Benigno."

"Benigno," he repeated. "Your name means 'kind.'"

I grinned. "Yeah. Yeah, that's right."

An eyebrow—the one with the gash carved into it—arched at me. "We shall see."

"What's yours then?"

The corners of his eyes pinched. "Humans cannot say it."

I held in a scoff. If Igor's voice could come out of my mouth, this merman's name couldn't be so hard. "Try me," I said.

"No."

"I should call you 'merman' then?"

"No."

"I mean, you don't want me to pick a name for you." We blinked at each other. "Wait, you *want* me to pick a name for you?"

He closed his eyes like I was riding the farthest edge of his patience. "If you must call me by a name, then you will choose it," he said. "To give you my name is to give you the last of myself, and humanity has taken enough from me. My name is my own. *You may not have it.*"

I found I couldn't argue. The name I'd given everyone I had met in America wasn't my real name either, but rather a loaned-out version that matched everything they thought I was: simple and easy to wrap their sharp tongues around. The only place I existed as Benigno was in my memories.

"Well, I don't want to give you one that doesn't fit. Couldn't you tell me something about yourself?"

His eyebrows lowered.

"All right, all right, forget I asked. Lemme think."

I sat up on the lattice and let myself look at him, reining in my urge to ogle. I'd never seen features like his—like he had evolved to blend perfectly into Atlantic waters, with variegated blue-green skin and hair that fell in waves around his athletic shoulders like copper-colored tributaries.

Tributaries made me think of the river we pulled him from, then that made me think of el Río Humacao. I wasn't sure about the path that connected the merman to the swollen, rushing current that stole my memories during the hurricane, but it produced a name nonetheless.

"How 'bout 'Río'?"

"Río." He mimicked my rolled *R* like a native boricua. "Why that name?"

A river can be both devastating and beautiful. I shrugged. "It suits you."

He tipped his head to the side, seeming to carefully assess my selection. "All right, Boy Named Kind," he murmured. "You may call me Río." And without taking a breath, he dipped back under the water, his tail cresting the surface before slipping noiselessly away.

After he summarily ended our chat—and ignored my farewell—I went back to work on the pump. It wasn't long at all before I'd made use of all the parts Morgan had on hand, but I'd need to spend tomorrow gathering materials and preparing to cast the rest: another valve for the boilers, some spindles, and other odds and ends.

In the meantime, I had the theater to myself and some exploring to do.

The wing of the stage that sat opposite from the exit to Morgan's tent branched off into two locked rooms. I tested Saul's keys until one opened into a narrow room with a long vanity running the length of the wall. My housemates had probably dressed in this room for performances before Morgan went and packed it full of sea salt, rows of cured codfish, and the six wheels he'd stripped off the tank.

I threw a few of the rock-hard filets into my pockets for the meal I had volunteered to cook for my housemates. I'd have to save my pennies for something better than sardines if I was going to keep up Río's health.

When I cut back through the stage to leave, Río lay sleeping—truly this time—his body forming a long S across the floor and his fins draped over him like a blanket. His chest rose and fell in slow intervals spread out over minutes as if his lungs didn't need to pull in much air—or water—to keep his heart beating. I shook off my jealousy and added the observation to my expanding list.

Before leaving, I put my hand on the glass again and closed my eyes in silent petition for the second time in a week—for both of us. If I was going to make friends with the prince of Atlantis without getting caught, fired, or sent upriver to Blackwell's Island penitentiary, then I needed a miracle.

And in the meantime, it was a damn good thing I was just a blacksmith instead of whatever Río expected me to say. On my way out, I wrenched the brass claws off the stuffed dragon and pocketed them.

This padlock key wouldn't copy itself.

When I see the sea again, part of me knows I'm dreaming.

She calls my name from the horizon with a voice like a chorus, my feet leaving ripples instead of footprints as I run across the water toward her. I still can't get closer.

"No te alcanzo," I shout, but the sound is absorbed by the wind.

I can feel it in my stomach, the moon's command over a new fleet of waves that rise up and choke the sky. I'm the one they devour this time, in water like blood. As the light vanishes over my head, I wonder if I can find them—mi familia—here in the depths.

NINE

My cooking day had arrived. Thankfully, there was enough in our pantry to make a large vat of cinnamon-spiced maicena—the cheap, easy way to warm up a creaky boricua in winter.

Everyone ate and went about their morning discussions like I'd been in the rotation all along, sweeping in and out of the kitchen for plates and saltshakers, me holding the stool while Madam Navya climbed up to reach the cupboards. Even Emmett forgot to leave a nasty editorial on my cooking before heading out with Eli to "chase seagulls on the beach," whatever that meant.

Maybe that's what Morgan took for being "useless on the off-season," because Lulu sent them off with an overflowing picnic basket like they wouldn't come back until April.

I was washing dishes when Igor ducked into the kitchen to start a fresh pot of café. As la cafetera began to heat, he folded his long torso over the counter to inspect the pot I'd set out.

"Mr. Benny, this fish in water—is on purpose?"

"Hm? Oh, yeah, it's gotta soak to get soft."

"Why not get fish fresh? More trouble, this seems . . ."

"Guisado needs salt cod, actually," I explained. "Don't worry, it flavors the sauce."

"*Sauce*," Igor hummed. "Very fond of sauces, I am. My wife make most beautiful borscht, you know."

My washcloth paused over the plate. "Wife?"

"Ekaterina. Moy tyul'pan. My tulip."

A woman eight feet tall—with skirts that began at my shoulders the way Igor's trousers did—thundered into my imagination. "Where is she?"

The way the giant's eyes bore into that pot of soaking fish told me we'd stumbled onto a subject he didn't often discuss. He cleared his throat and refocused his gaze slightly closer to my face. "Is gone."

Caramba. My mouth was getting too careless in these new surroundings. "I'm real sorry."

"No, no. Is my fault," he sighed somberly. "I leave Moscow during Great Famine, you know. I make promise to go to America, and I say to her, when I have house and job for us, she will follow."

He pulled out a stool and dropped down onto it. It looked like a matchbox under him.

"On foot, I walk to Sankt-Petersburg, and I sail to America. I find apartment, get job in shoe factory—but it take so much time, you know?" he said, as if to himself. "It take almost three years before I can send letter for Ekaterina to come." As he spoke, he dug a folded-up paper out of his vest pocket, torn at the edges, and browned from handling. He held it out to me.

Inside was a crinkled photograph of Igor standing larger than life beside a woman who stood level, not with his shoulders, but with his waist, her light hair braided under una corona of flowers. I squinted at the handwritten letter wrapped around it. "I can't read Russian."

"Ekaterina die of cholera, it say."

My ears tensed around that word. It sounded the same in every language, and it wasn't until I came to Nueva York and heard it repeated in the multilingual mutterings of other immigrants on the waterfront that I realized why. A deadly contagion that raged across the globe like fire didn't have time to change its name.

"That don't sound like your fault, Igor," I said quietly.

I gave him back his mementos, and he returned them to his pocket. "Maybe. Madam Navya tell me is no help to look back with regret," he admitted with a shrug. "But I miss Ekaterina. Before I join Menagerie, she was only person in the world who look at me and see Igor Rybakov."

How could anyone *not* see Igor Rybakov? You could pick him out of a crowd from the top of the MetLife Tower. "I don't think I know what you mean."

He lurched to his feet, took la cafetera off the stove, and lumbered back toward the hallway, pausing to smile wistfully at me before ducking under the rise.

"To Ekaterina, I was devoted husband," he said. "Not giant."

Now that the merman and I had made Timmy-sized steps towards civility, I was looking forward to peeking behind the Menagerie curtain, but a note from Morgan stopped me at the ticket podium. It listed all the renovation supplies he wanted me to purchase, along with his written permission to pay for any materials I'd need for the pump as long as I could account for everything I'd bought. An envelope of cash was waiting at the gate with Oscar Barnes for my use.

Checking on Río would have to wait until dark.

Morgan's directions led me to the stables behind the theater where a pushcart sat next to a wooden basin and steel cask on wheels, no doubt abandoned there whenever he'd topped off the tank. I rolled the pushcart through the rear auxiliary exit of Luna Park toward Eighth and Surf where a friendly voice called out, "Benny!"

Matthias was striding toward me, an easy smile raising his round cheeks high enough to lift the glasses right off his nose. He had a pencil tucked behind his ear, and his large hand all but eclipsed the small notebook in his grip.

"You following me?" I called back.

His laughter pulled his coat seams taut. "For your information, I am *absorbing* the setting of my memoir and taking notes. Just so happens you're part of the scenery." He snatched Morgan's shopping list out of the pushcart and examined it. "Looks like I showed up right on time too. Ain't no way you gonna tow all them buckets of paint without snapping your arms off at the elbow."

"I ain't weak," I said defensively. "I hammer iron."

"*Hammered* iron. Past tense. And like hell you ain't. I've lifted potato sacks heavier than you."

I snatched back the list. "Just tell me where a smithy can buy a furnace around here, will ya?"

We headed east toward the residential part of town where Matthias promised we'd find a general store to suit my needs. He played tour guide while we walked the main drag, and I swear, every block that wasn't already cluttered with carnival rides played host to a hotel or inn, sometimes both. A person could probably come to Coney Island every day for a year and sleep in a different bed each night.

And suddenly, there it was. Not that anyone with eyes could miss it. Its shadow ate up the whole street.

Dreamland Park.

Por Dios, the gang was right to be nervous about this place. An archway bigger, grander, and whiter than Luna Park's sloped over our heads, held aloft by a giant plaster angel that stood like

a winged effigy to Venus between a pair of knock-off Italian frescoes.

Over the angel's head, white light bulbs spelled out the word "CREATION."

"She's . . . naked."

"Yeah?" Matthias sniffed. "I hadn't noticed."

"But, how's that . . . *allowed*?"

His glasses magnified the tired contempt in his eyes. "Reynolds is smart, that's how. He sold the *Creation* ride as a scenic railway attraction about the Book of Genesis. And just like that, all the Roman Catholics on the oversight commission were fine with a two-story-tall tomato with her bare breasts hanging out on Surf Avenue like fishing tack— Oh, hey, how's it goin', Georgie?"

A young guy with an upturned nose and boxy shoulders hunched up to his ears was rolling up to Dreamland's gates with his own pushcart, this one loaded with barrels of tar. "Hiya, Matty," he said in an oily voice. "Business goin' so bad across the street, you had to come snoop on our doorstep?"

"Not remotely," said Matthias with a relaxed grin. "I was just introducing our new hire here to Luna Park's illegitimate offspring."

All the smug dripped off Georgie's mug. "We'll see who's legitimate at the end of the summer season," he sneered and gave the pushcart a shove. "Give my regards to that sweet li'l contortionist o' yours, will ya?"

"Aw, I would, but Sonia told me to tell you she's fresh outta room for regards. See ya, Georgie." Then, Matthias leaned down, muttered "Dreamland's slimy gatekeeper" into my ear, and led me out of the angel's long shadow.

I glanced back over my shoulder at *Creation*. As unseasoned as I was in the art of luring pleasure-seekers, I didn't think a gaudy plaster monument invited any profound ruminations on God. And I'd read the Book of Genesis a dozen times. Aloud.

Río, on the other hand. The sight of him ripped up everything I thought I understood about creation. One look at him and you had to wonder if the Bible had been selling God short this whole time.

"Is that all the merman's supposed to compete with?" I asked.

"Nope. *Creation*'s a tiny slice of a much bigger cake. In Morgan's mind, it's his merman exhibit versus the whole of Dreamland." Matthias rolled his shoulders, quickened his step, and muttered, "and hopefully, he ain't bettin' our necks to win."

I rushed with the pushcart to keep up. "What's that mean?"

"Nothin'."

"You're the one who brought up our necks. I'm kind of attached to mine."

His gaze shifted around, scoping for nearby eyes and ears. "Here's the thing," he said in a lower voice. "Since '04, Luna's been fighting a losing war to keep up with Dreamland, right? Ain't no way the Menagerie would've lasted this long unless some charitable donations of the criminal variety were in the mix."

I gawped. "*Criminal?*"

"Jesus, keep your voice down," he hissed. "Yes, criminal. Take you, for instance. Luna's dying a slow death, yet somehow Morgan found the clams to pay for a tank, theater renovations, and *your labor?*" he said, ticking the items off his fingers. "'Patrons,' he calls them, but it don't take a genius to figure out he and Sonia been spending the offseason cutting deals with folks too shady to show their faces in Manhattan Beach."

"What's Sonia got to do with it?"

He raised an eyebrow. "The man don't go anywhere without her. I got my suspicions why—and none of 'em look good."

It didn't take a second to run those calculations; Sonia's flimsy handshake masked a hidden strength for maneuvering folks any way she wished. She probably could have convinced half the

Ironworks to show up with their own paintbrushes and pitch at Fulton Ferry station if she'd wanted.

"You think Morgan's in trouble then?"

Matthias sighed like he'd already run that question into the ground. "I dunno. That man's brain train only runs in one direction. Don't leave much room for considering consequences once he's fixed himself on something he wants."

I frowned. "Consequences like . . . the mermaid?"

He scoffed in my face. "You think killing a mermaid keeps Sam up at night? Anyone tell you what got him so bent on hunting mermaids in the first place?"

I shook my head.

"The way Saul told it, Sam *Dixon* was just a kid when his rich pop took him out on the ocean for a ride on the family sailboat. While they're out there, a storm sweeps in and, *BAP*"—Matthias clapped his hands—"he gets knocked overboard. As he's sinking, he notices he ain't the only thing in the water trying not to make like a stone. When his pop pulls him out, he gets a better look. There and gone in the flip of a fin is a real live mermaid. And well, you can guess what happened after that."

"No, what?"

He lowered his voice further like the plaster angel might be a spy for Reynolds. "He lost his goldang mind, that's what. Gabbin' to anybody with ears about fish ladies out to kill us or, at the very least, watch us drown. When no one believed him, he started wasting his father's dough on pricy voyages to see if he could catch one—until his folks cut off his inheritance and tossed him out."

"Caramba."

"Yep," Matthias said. "That's when Jack-the-original-Morgan found him. Brought Sam into the fold as an outside talker, seeing as Sam's tongue was nice and polished from sucking on that silver spoon so long."

The cart rolled over a stone that nearly tripped me up as much as Matthias's English. "What's an 'outside talker'?"

"Oh, you know. The straight-lacer who sells the show on the promenade and gets the crowds through the front door. Sam's probably the best one there is," he explained matter-of-factly. "Problem was, he never really got in with the rest of us odd types. Lulu thinks he was holding onto his old family too hard to take up with a new one. *I* think he thinks he's too good for a crew like ours.

"Either way, he kept himself outside our world just like his work stayed outside the tents—until Jack choked on a chicken bone, and Sam inherited the operation along with the Morgan name. That was the very moment Sam's crusade to redeem his trashed reputation turned into Coney Island's most successful sideshow."

"You say that like it's a bad thing," I remarked.

"It ain't bad. But lemme teach you a thing about showbiz, Benny."

He laid a thick hand on my shoulder. "Inside every showman is two people—the one on the poster and the one you leave offstage. Poster Sam can charm the pants off the governor. But Offstage Sam is ruthless. Chases what he wants like a hound on the hunt.

"Now, you can rely on an ambitious man to do ambitious things. But an ambitious man with a grudge has got a powder keg in his pocket," he went on sagely. "Sam's been stewing over the mermaid that made a fool of him since he was a kid, and something about this war with Dreamland picks at that old scab—makes him believe he's got something to prove all over again. And now that he's got the honest-to-God mythological beast locked up in his theater, I've got a hunch we're gonna see a lot more of Offstage Sam."

My uneasiness must have been plastered across my face because Matthias stopped walking to look at me.

"Listen," he said. "The pay's good. The company is even better. And for all his flaws, Sam's the reason the Menagerie is still the best sideshow in Coney Island. Just keep your eyeballs open and stay out of Sam's business, same as I do, and you won't get kicked back to the curb all because you accidentally lit the powder keg."

"All right. I will," I said as we started walking again. "But can I ask you something?"

"Shoot."

"How'd he know that mermaid was gonna drown him?" Specifically, I thought of Río, pulling Sonia's boat to shore instead of dragging her down to join the victims of the *General Slocum* disaster.

Matthias puffed a short laugh. "Great question. Now, I'll ask you one. You ever heard of a person who can see underwater?"

"Uh . . . no?"

"Exactly," he said. "My guess? Sam just *assumed* it was out to get him. Which oughta tell you something about how that man sees the world."

TEN

That evening, I dragged myself into the theater with my pushcart in tow. I'd just spent two hours under the boardwalk casting spindles for the boiler using nothing but beach sand, an apple crate, and a cheap blacksmithing kit from the general store. While I was at it, I melted down the dragon claws I'd purloined from the museum which earned me a copy of Morgan's padlock key—and a chest full of concrete.

I thought about dropping off the pushcart and going home, until a soft splash coaxed me the rest of the way up the apron ramp.

Río was hovering off the floor looking like he was seriously reconsidering our arrangement. He drifted along next to me with the weightless grace of a silk scarf on a breeze while I trudged around the tank's long viewing pane to leave the cart by the pump, climb the iron rungs, and slump down on my backside to wait.

He met me at the top, wavy lines of wet copper hair drawn over his cheeks. "You are here again."

I cleared my throat enough to speak. "You'd prefer I wasn't?"

He crossed his arms over his chest. "I did not think you would come given your professed aversion to conversation."

"Good thing I ain't here"—I sipped in a breath—"for conversation."

Earlier, I had cooked un bacalao guisado to convert the culinary religions of everyone at the Albemarle, and had made sure to set some apart for Río in a jar. I pulled it out of my pocket and nearly fumbled it into the tank at the eyeful I got of his wet skin and swirling hair.

"I think I mentioned . . . salt cod's better when you soak it," I wheezed.

He leveled a mistrustful eye at the jar. "You mentioned."

"This is the same stuff, just . . . soaked and cooked. Thought you might . . . like this better."

I unscrewed the lid, then paused. I hadn't thought through the business of sharing food so it wouldn't dirty the water. Manners be damned, I took a piece of the cod in my fingers, got down on my stomach, and fit my arm through the lattice to offer it to him.

Río's face was all damp suspicion. He plucked it away without touching my fingers, and though the piece was small enough to swallow whole, he nibbled off a corner and rolled it around his mouth like he'd bitten off a hunk of day-old queso blanco.

I licked the sauce off my fingers. "Well?"

He swallowed the microscopic bite and grimaced. "Merfolk do not adulterate our fish by cooking it."

Bueno. I didn't know what "adulterate" meant when it came to food, but it couldn't be good.

"You did improve it, though," he conceded, catching my disappointment.

"You don't have to say—"

My voice snagged in my throat. Suddenly, and with no concern for dignity, a coughing fit muscled its way out of me. Below, Río watched with wide, startled eyes as I clambered back to sitting, and my useless lungs hawked air out instead of in.

"What in Neptune's name is wrong with you, Benigno?"

I tossed my arm over my mouth to smother it. "It'll pass. Just . . . dame un momento."

Río observed me sideways while I barked into my elbow, then ducked underwater. He began swimming in a wide, slow circle, and as I tried to catch my breath, he went around again, then a third time, until I got the powerful impression he was *pacing*.

Less than a minute later, he resurfaced. "Are you recovered now?"

I scowled. "Of course not."

"I suppose the noxious air over your city has done this to you."

"This ain't my city," I snorted, which spawned another fit. "*Carajo.* I . . . I was probably just born this way."

"*Born* with traitorous lungs?" The concept shocked the snooty right out of his voice. "How can that be?"

"I dunno, it just *is*."

"Have you been poisoned? How does it feel?"

"How does it *feel*?" I gawped at him. "Ave María, why would you ask me that?"

Río peered up at me with the tired impatience of a royal forced to mingle with commoners. "It interests me."

This guy was a riot. No one had ever asked me what it was like to have asthma, and it especially defied description when I considered my audience. If Río couldn't imagine being born this way, then he definitely couldn't imagine the iron clamp around my ribs, the sense I'd inhaled something black and sticky that crowded out everything else in my chest, nor the bone-deep terror that somewhere a clock was marking the minutes before my lungs gave up breathing altogether and killed me instead.

How do you describe asthma to someone who can't drown?

"It's like thirst," I rasped, finally. "Except instead of starving for water . . . it's air."

He shook his head, disturbed, which was an improvement over pitying me. "That sounds grave."

I hacked. "It . . . it's n-no picnic, that's for damn sure."

"What is a 'nic' that it must be picked?"

"No. I just mean"—I grasped at more air—"I don't much enjoy it."

Río laid back on the water, the liquid parting around his muscled chest. "Humans are such vulnerable creatures," he mused, frowning. "I cannot understand how your fragile kind persists in blighting the globe with such rigor."

"Well, we ain't all perfect like you," I sniped. "Most humans have good intentions . . . when we're not stepping on each other's heads just to stay alive." My tetchiness hedged at the subtle change on Río's face. "What?"

"You think I am perfect?"

"That's not what . . . I mean . . ." I jabbed a warning finger at him. "Hey, stop mixing me up."

A shadow crossed his face, then vanished. "Well, you should swim more," he continued with the authority of a doctor. "That would help."

"Can't swim," I muttered. "And anyhow, what makes you the expert?"

"I am mer," he said, like that explained everything. "My lungs have four chambers compared to your two, half of which breathe water."

"*Four* chambers?" I gawped. "But how does your body just . . . know what to do?"

Río's detached expression took on a mischievous hue. "I would invite you in for a demonstration," he said smoothly, "but I fear you would not enjoy drowning."

My scowl came back. I hadn't cared when Río was just a blood-thirsty sea creature with haunting eyes and sandpaper palms, but now that he'd proven himself a busybody *and* a snob, wheezing in front of him felt no better than wheezing in front of Farty Walsh.

"You know what?" The words blew out of me with a whistle. "It's time I got back to work."

He sat up in the water, eyes scrunched in bafflement as they watched me hastily screw the lid back onto the jar and nearly drop it into the tank.

"You are embarrassed."

"I'm tired."

"You need not feel shame," he said. "Who is to say what would happen to my lungs if I was out of water and had nothing but soiled air to breathe? This ailment is a part of you that you did not choose and cannot help."

I got to my feet and teetered on the bars. "Easy for you to say, Mr. World's-Best-Pair-of-Pulmones." I headed for the ladder.

"It is the simple truth of every creature with a soul. You are not your body, Benigno."

I froze in my step. When I turned back to snap at him, the look on Río's face made me pause.

He was chewing his bottom lip, staring off like he was weigh-ing the stakes of a gamble. A moment later, he looked up. "I can help you. If you will allow it."

"Help *me*? ¿Por qué?"

"Because you need it."

Cristo. Between his liquid voice and the always-blue-ness of his eyes, he had a very inconvenient knack for making my ears burn. I stepped away from the ladder, not because of my ears, but because the biggest insult of having asthma was being desperate enough to do anything if it meant breathing properly. I sat back down.

"Sit taller," he said like he was schooling me in table etiquette.

I tried.

"Good. Place one hand over your heart and another over your belly, but do not press in."

Overlooking the fact that I didn't generally touch people, myself included, I set my right hand on my chest, the other on my stomach. "All right," I wheezed, "now what?"

"Listen closely. Make your throat thin, just a little, and breathe through your nose so it makes this sound . . ."

Río breathed deeply, his eyes fastened on mine as his chest expanded, except it was surprisingly loud, like drawing air through a vent. He took several breaths this way, his shoulders rising and rolling back in slow arcs, and as I listened, I realized I'd heard this sound before.

"That sounds just like the ocean," I said.

He clicked his tongue impatiently. "Obviously. Now you try."

I straightened up a bit more and drew a ragged breath in through my nose. It immediately caught in my throat. "I don't—think—"

"You waste air by talking. Be quiet and try again."

There are few things I hate more than being a novice, which might be why I didn't clock out on Río's challenge despite a lifetime of never getting my lungs to do a single thing I wanted them to do. It took several tries to make it work without coughing or closing up—but then, to my surprise, I started hearing it. A *shish* sound, like rolling tides.

"Well done." His voice went suddenly low and calm. "Take in more. Enough to make both your hands rise up."

I licked my lips, then drew the air in. My ribs resisted around it, hardening like sealant left to dry—

"*Relax*, Benigno."

"*I'm trying.*"

"You called it thirst. Air surrounds you, yes?"

A cough escaped. "Y-yeah?"

"Then drink it in like water. Close your eyes."

I closed them.

"See it in your mind. Touching every corner of your chest. The way a flame is doused in a rising tide," he hummed. "It is cool . . . and calm . . ."

The eye of a hurricane is calm. Tití Luz was talking about surviving a war when she'd said it, but the metaphor felt apt as I wrestled for control of organs that resisted me like the Armada resisted McKinley. In my mind, I saw the storm, a rotating mass under my palm. I pulled in all the air I could . . .

There. A break in the clouds.

"You are doing well. Keep going."

There had to be something to the siren lore after all. Río's voice was deep. Musical. He kept reciting encouragement. I kept doing what he said.

Eventually, my mind started wandering. To Red Hook pier, stagnant, stinking, the color of café con leche. My next inhale swept the Gowanus clean as the jewel-toned waters of la Playa del Condado took its place. I imagined the surf rolling up to my ankles, erasing my footprints in the sand.

I felt a little dizzy. Also, my eyes were prickling, which didn't make sense, because I'd long forgotten how to cry. It was as if all this breathing was thinning out the mesh of dirty gauze inside me, a moldy knot that had never touched air. I was breathing into it now. Felt it loosening, unwinding. Which roused a sensation I didn't expect.

Fear.

That gnarled net was all that held my mutilated heart together. If it came undone—

"Open your eyes, Benigno."

I opened them. I was swaying in my seat, my head so light, I nearly forgot where I was or what I was doing before I took a breath—the normal kind—and felt my eyes go wide.

The whistle was gone.

Río's tail was treading the water so evenly he could have been standing with legs on solid ground. "Better?"

I inhaled again just to make sure. "Yeah," I said in a gust of air. "What'd you do?"

He shrugged. "Nothing. You did that yourself, and you should do it more often if you do not want your lungs to betray you as much."

My hand still lay over my heart. For a long moment, I rifled through my bilingual vocabulary for a word to describe the odd feeling under my fingers, but there wasn't a precedent for it.

Río cleared his throat. "We should not speak any longer tonight. Your lungs need rest."

"Right," I whispered. "I'll, uh, just finish up the pump then. Thanks for the breathing lesson."

"Thank you as well. For el guisado."

I puffed a short laugh. "You didn't like it."

"But it was kind of you," he said, not laughing. "And kindness is its own food."

His blue eyes, rimmed with golden lamplight, sent a current of warmth up my neck.

"De nada."

Silently, I took my jar of bacalao back down the iron rungs and returned to my work.

Several hours and one completed circulation pump later, I gathered myself to go home and ventured a last look into the water where I expected to see Río sleeping. Instead, he was reclined against the wall, arms folded, silent and watching.

I waved goodbye. He didn't. But there was something in the tilt of his head, in the thoughtful set of his mouth I hadn't seen before. Whether he liked my company or just didn't want to be alone again, he seemed a little sorry to see me go.

I probably imagined it.

RÍO

I have abandoned trying to break apart my prison. The walls will not yield, and if they did, my effort would only strand me in the shadows to parch until such time as the Shark discovered me and found some cruel new use for my body. Harvest my teeth. Cut off my fins. Expose my carcass to the gulls just like the whales humans ravage then leave to rot on the beach.

And yet, the other one returned tonight. Benigno.

With food.

I strive to discern what rarity in this human made you choose him for my protector, Mother. His attention allows me to observe him more closely. He stands as tall as the Shark, but leaner, with a formidable strength in his webless hands that defended him from my violent rage before they began toiling over the instruments beside my cell. Still—he is not without frailty.

The sounds his lungs produced. I could find no amusement in his condition. What blight lives inside Benigno's chest that makes him drown above water?

As he labored for breath, he called me perfect—an ignorant assumption, for there is nothing perfect in the choices I made under the moon's light. But perhaps the word's meaning differs for a creature who dwells in shame of his body's strange deficiencies.

I should not have helped him. Our elders would have surely condemned it.

But I felt you closer to me when I did.

ELEVEN

I returned Morgan's key the next morning and found his mood a little hard to peg. He was pleased I'd been so quick to deliver his circulation system but frustrated that I hadn't also riddled out how to sneak in bulk quantities of coal under Oscar's runny nose to test it. He decided I should start on cosmetic repairs in the curiosity museum, which was how I wound up standing next to the yeti while Morgan paced around like the room had committed some personal offense.

"Christ." Morgan lifted a decrepit wing off the dragon and a flurry of red paint flakes drifted to the floor. "For a place where first impressions are made, the tone in here is 'mausoleum meets sculpture garden for the criminally insane.'"

It's fine for white guys of a certain means to insult what's theirs, but que Dios te perdone if you tell them they're right. I kept my mouth shut.

"These ancient relics from Jack Morgan's old traveling show all need new bones, so I expect you'll have to sculpt from scratch. Ah, but what am I saying," Morgan said with a patronizing smile.

"A craftsman like you will figure it out. Should you need me," he sighed scornfully, "I'll be domesticating our new tenant."

Claro. That explained his finicky temperament. As he strode toward the theater, I mustered my courage and stopped him at the threshold. "Mr. Morgan?"

"Hm?"

"I was just wondering how the merman was taking to the food." To justify my inquiry, I quickly added, "I made some cod for the company yesterday."

"In the meal rotation already," he mused. "The exhibits have taken a shining to you, eh?"

The way he called the company "exhibits" wasn't exactly endearing. With his expression falling just shy of pleased, I tried to make myself look as benign as my given name suggested I was and shoved my hands in my pockets. "They don't hate me, I guess."

"Well. As long as you're asking, I thought the creature would be hungry enough by now to eat its own tail, but it remains insufferably"—his nose twitched—"*resistant.*"

Aquí voy. "I'm no expert, but I grew up on salt cod. If you don't mind my saying, it might be easier for the merman to swallow it if you soak it overnight."

Morgan blinked. I didn't know if he was the sort of yanqui who put insults and consultation from brown day laborers in the same box. When his grin came back, it reached no further than his mouth.

Same box, then.

"I will take that into consideration," he said. "After all, *I* grew up on red meat."

Then he left me to fix his gallery of atrocidades. Good thing the pantry wasn't out of sardines yet.

I decided to start on the dragon with a mind to salvage whatever didn't outright disintegrate into my palms. My spackle knife was positioned to lift off some of the chipped paint when a sudden, shrill noise made my hand flinch, sending dragon scales scattering.

It was a whistle. Not the kind my lungs made, but a high-pitched, tooth-grinding *FWEEEEET.*

Was Morgan trying to *train* Río? I stilled and waited for the *gong* of Río's tail defiantly colliding with the tank side—but there wasn't so much as a splash.

The whistle introduced a pattern of activity in the theater while I worked, beginning with Morgan stomping around the stage, barking commands like "Look *here*, I say!" and "Swim, dammit!" and "Get off your blasted tail!" which he'd keep up for about twenty minutes before storming off to his tent because Río wouldn't react to any of it.

During one of those silent gaps, I found termites in the baseboards under the dragon display. On my way to give Morgan the news, I looked in on the tank as discreetly as I could and found Río facing away, tucked in his shadowy corner except for the shaft of light shining across his brilliant tail. Though the blue was so vibrant it dulled every other color in the room, something else had caught my attention.

Río's hands were covering his ears.

"Everywhere I look, another blasted expense," Morgan groaned at the ceiling when he heard his museum was infested. "Just find Lulu and tell her we need to borrow the Albemarle's exterminator. You two may as well work out upholstery estimates while you're there—and tell the rest of those lazy nincompoops I expect them to help dismantle the museum tomorrow so they can kill the little bastards!"

"Will do, boss." I touched the rim of my cap and turned to leave.

"Before you go, Benny . . ."

I paused at the tent flap. "Yeah?"

He plucked the pipe from his teeth. "Fetch a bowl from the storage room. Fill it with water. And," he growled through his nose, "soak the damn fish."

That night, before heading out on a "walk" as I put it to my house-mates, Sonia let it slip that Morgan always left early on Fridays to "unwind with his Victrola after a long week." It gave me an idea.

"Is that a lyre?" Río asked as I scaled the tank ladder.

"It's my cuatro."

"I see ten strings, not four. The name is misleading."

"Noted. I'll inform the mayor."

I toed my way to the middle of the bars and sat, balancing the sardines on the grill and trying not to crack wise at Río's face when I positioned the instrument on my lap. I was beginning to learn his expressions, and this particular one was his default—nar-row eyes, furrowed brows, and pinched lips that all seemed to ask what earthly continent was responsible for breeding a human as confusing as me.

"You are a musician, then?" he asked.

I strummed the open strings and grimaced; it sounded just like my eviction from Red Hook had felt. "My tití thought so. Boleros were her favorite."

"Boleros," he murmured, exploring the word with his mouth as he drifted closer. "The ocean has not carried such a word to my ears."

"It'd have to go a long distance." I gently twisted the peg until the sound rang true and I could move on to the next string. "So you know what music is. What sort of music do you get in the ocean, anyway?"

When he didn't answer, my fingers paused over the strings. I peered over my lap.

"The ocean is my native song," he said. His voice was usually so melodic, I hadn't thought him capable of sounding so toneless.

"'Native song.' ¿Qué significa eso?"

"It means the ocean's music is my language. The way yours is Spanish. The way the Shark's is British." Rolling his eyes, he added, "Though he tries very hard to seem otherwise."

A guffaw fell out of my mouth. "Mr. Morgan, *British*? Are you kidding?"

"I always hear that word, 'kidding.' There is not a juvenile goat for miles. What does that even mean?"

"Nothing, forget it. So, you're saying your language is *music*?"

"All language is music, all music is language. But the song of the sea is a dialect unlike any other." His eyes took in my cuatro and dimmed. "I was a voice in a once vast choir."

I wanted to ask why he spoke of his kind in the past tense, but the dark turn of his expression told me that would be a mistake. I'd come to cheer him up, not depress him.

"I keep meaning to ask how you know Spanish," I said, moving on to the next pair of strings. "Or English, for that matter. I didn't think merfolk would bother with human words."

Río splashed some water over his head to rewet his hair. "We excel at absorbing the utterings of land dwellers. Especially those who navigate the water," he said simply. "When you live as long as we do, there is time enough to swim in as many seas and learn as many human tongues as you desire."

"Ave María. And here I thought *I* was pretty good at picking up voices."

Just then, a circuit connected in my brain.

"Río, how old *are* you?"

He lifted an arm idly out of the water, watching the beads roll over his tinted skin. "Quite young by our standards. Quite old by yours," he said thoughtfully. "How old do you think I am?"

"Qué sé yo." I scratched my neck. "You look my age."

"And how old is that?"

I didn't have an immediate answer. After the hurricane, when finding any documentation of my birth had proved impossible, Tití Luz declared my birthday the first of January, and decided I was probably about as old as the other muchachito who hung around the revolutionary sect, Ramón. He would turn twenty-two in July.

"I'm twenty-two."

After brief consideration, he gave a satisfied nod. "Then I am twenty-two as well. Now did you plan to play something, or will your cuatro play itself?"

"Sure," I said, testing a chord. "I'll play something soft."

"Is that customary?"

"Well, I can't imagine wanting to hear anything loud after Morgan practically busted the windows blowing that maldito whistle."

There was a pause. "You heard it?"

"How could I not? They probably heard it in Queens—"

"Yet you did not stop him."

His voice put an end to my tuning. I looked down to find Río staring, his blue eyes relit in anger like a pair of kerosene flames. "Were you amused? Entertained?" he demanded.

"Claro que no. It was awful to hear—"

"But not enough to intervene in my torture?"

Torture. The word bore down on my heart like a brick. "I couldn't," I insisted. "He got peeved when all I did was suggest he soak the cod!"

I didn't realize how pathetic my excuse was until it came out of my mouth. Obviously, Río thought so too, because the next moment, he was gone in a rippling swirl of marine blue and burnished hair.

"I just gotta be careful," I half shouted at the water. "I can't free you if he tosses me out. Río? Río!"

Carajo, I was earning a reputation here as Brooklyn's worst bystander. Calling down again got me nothing but a dose of the defiance Río had been showing Morgan all day, and if the whistle had taught me anything about the merman, it was that his will was made of stronger metal than mine. I looked around helplessly for a way to coax him back to the surface—but a couple of measly sardine cans were a weak offering in exchange for his forgiveness.

So I started to play. *"Palomita blanca del piquito azul, llévame en tus alas a ver a Jesús . . ."*

My fingers were a little stiff from taking apart monsters all morning. But I never wheezed when I sang, and the notes I strummed were as sturdy as the iron I cast, taught to me by tabaqueros who knew just how to make a song speak truth where words failed. It felt like I was praying for the third time in a week.

Ola, ola, ola,
Ola de la mar
Qué bonita ola para navegar . . .

It wasn't hard to steep every chord in remorse for letting him suffer. I played until I ran out of refrains. Until it seemed like God had finally reached His threshold for doling me second chances. The theater was quiet again, leaving me alone to figure out another way to repair what I'd broken, but then Río's form began growing larger in the water.

When he finally broke the surface, he didn't emerge past his chin. "You sing," he whispered.

Gracias a Dios. I nodded.

"You would truly free me?" he asked, an edge of disbelief in his voice. "If you could?"

"Sure I would."

He closed his eyes and rose further until the water was level with his shoulders once more. It felt like he might be weighing my integrity again; I didn't want to speak in case it tipped his opinion back in the wrong direction.

When he opened his eyes, he said, "Your voice is . . . surprising."

"In a bad way?"

A subdued smile pulled at his lips. "No."

Relief unclenched my muscles. I laid my instrument aside to lower my face to the lattice.

"Forgive me," I whispered in Spanish, to make doubly sure I meant what I said. "You are right. I should have done something. If I were braver—if I had known better—I might have found a way to stop him. It won't happen again."

He studied my face—for honesty or contrition or both—while sweat dampened the rim of my cap. After a long moment, he spoke Spanish back to me. "I think you are right to be afraid of the Shark. I have seen enough to believe him capable of doing great harm. But not to me."

"¿Cómo?"

Río's tail crested and flicked, propelling him to the cage side where he reached over the rim of the glass to touch the bars with a webbed finger. "It appears I am valuable to him. He would make my ears bleed a thousand times before my resistance would persuade him to kill me." Turning his serious face back to me, he added, "Your life, I think, he would not spare."

Diablo, I'd been worried about getting fired, not killed. Río didn't know that, compared to him and his mother, I was safe by virtue of my species, or so I figured. Even so, his assumption had a cold logic to it that made my neck prickle.

He wrapped his palm around the iron. "I do not understand humans, but I think I am beginning to understand you."

"You are?"

"You heard the whistle, and so you came to soothe my ears with music."

I cleared my throat and pulled my cap lower over my eyes. "So?"

He tilted his head thoughtfully and, in English, said, "So, your name suits you too, Boy Named Kind."

And like a crank on a phonograph, something in his words whirred my heart into motion the way it hadn't since I last sat under a warm Caribbean sun next to Ramón. I didn't think I'd earned it.

"I forgive you," he announced, reclining on the water. "Sing another bolsillo, if you know one."

"Bolero."

"Yes. That."

I stayed for another song. And another after that. And as I sang, Río floated in a lazy circle, his eyes fastened on the little window near the ceiling where moonlight lined the glass. I refused to play him a third until he polished off both the sardine cans I'd brought him, then promised him fresh fish next time. When two more hours had passed without another offense on my part, I collected my cuatro, dropped down the ladder, and touched my hand against the glass in farewell.

I didn't head for the promenade. Instead, I took the path to Morgan's empty tent where I hunted around until, tucked in a nest of paintbrushes, I found his whistle.

Tin. Malleable.

Good.

I set it against the edge of the table and took off my necklace. With the medallion, I pushed a dent into the reed, so small you'd miss it altogether if you weren't looking closely.

Satisfied with the pettiness of my crime, the whistle went back into the brushes, San Cristóbal went back around my neck, and I walked home like an innocent man.

Río

Could you hear him sing from where you are, Mother? The
whales would welcome him to their choir, so mystical a sound
does Benigno's voice make. And given so freely! Does he
not comprehend its value?

If this prison is punishment for my entanglement with humans,
I cannot fathom the meaning of this man's attentions—nor that
he sings about the sea whilst under the waves our elders' songs
are abundant with human barbarism. Their refrains interrogate
the Deep: What of the endless Age of Warships? Of men who,
battling from nearly every shore, murder without mercy nor
necessity nor care for the poisons their ear-rupturing weapons
spray into our waters? What of the ocean kindred we cannot save
from their harpoons? Of the brutality humans committed on
their trading vessels—*to their own kind*?

"I have heard their strange music and found peace in its noise,"
you once told me. "Many humans are lost. But not all."

My cell is haunted by a man who would destroy me by my ears—
and guarded by another who would relieve me by them. Our
elders were not wrong. But you were also *right.*

A new ache dwells in my spirit tonight I dare not examine,
and yet, what else can I do in this cage with so costly a gift as
Benigno's song except place it in my heart beside the moon?

Would that he had sung for me until the dawn.

TWELVE

When the waves return for me in my dreams, I capsize like a ship.

And though the sea is crushing and the color of blood, moonlight hews the darkness overhead with its luminous bands to show me I'm not alone.

Copper hair. Sea-colored skin. Eyes blue, bottomless, vast as a horizon.

Are you my captor or my savior? I ask.

His answer is a musical refrain my mind plays over and over again until I wake.

Benigno, you and I are both.

Morgan was a fuming inversion of the Steeplechase Funny Face when he strode into the curiosity museum on Monday morning to ask, "Any of you witless wonders know how to fix a dead whistle?"

Matthias pushed up his glasses in mock interest. "Have you tried blowing harder?"

Per the showman's grumpy insistence, the whole company of human curiosities had come to help take apart the make-believe ones. By the way Morgan wound up and pitched the whistle at the promenade like a Yankees outfielder, it seemed he was profoundly regretting his decision.

He turned back but hadn't made it past the vestibule before something outside the glass pane caught his eye and his spine went rigid. Sonia glanced up from her bundle of velvet ropes. "Sam?"

"If you'll excuse me." Morgan licked his palm, ran it over his unrumpled hair to no apparent effect, then strode outside.

Madam Navya clung nervously to a feather duster next to the hydra's wireframe remains. "So it begins."

"What is beginning?" said Igor.

She started dusting more furiously.

"Don't you know, Igor?" Vera stood up in the men's trousers she'd borrowed from Eli and pulled a cigarillo out of the pocket. "When a shite whistle's banjaxed, means something spooky's afoot!"

Navya jabbed her duster at Vera like a sword from the top of her stool. "Today it's a whistle. But karma takes time to unfold. A horse does not stop the moment you pull on the rain."

"You mean 'reins,'" sighed Lulu.

"Do not scrutinize my words and forget to listen," the madam snapped. "Who is to say we have not stolen the next incarnation of Vishnu from the river? Has anyone even spoken to the creature?"

I choked on a cloud of dust.

Beside me, Eli hoisted up the rear end of the mummified basilisk. "Karma? Ain't Fares selling that stuff on the pier for a jitney?"

"That is *shawarma*. Karma is the earned outcome of our *deeds*." Navya smeared an exasperated hand over her face. "Goodness knows what I did in this life or the last to win myself the company of an ignoramus like you, Mr. Eli."

"Hey, who's the guy gabbing with Morgan?" said Emmett from the window.

Eli left the basilisk tail to join his brother. Following suit, Matthias and Vera sidestepped Timmy Porter, who was quiet for once now that he was busy fashioning medieval weaponry out of leftover museum scraps. Igor only had to bend at the waist to get a good view over their heads. "It seem they know each other," mused the giant, to which Vera added, "But they ain't bloody mates, that's for sure."

"Get a load of the ring on that guy's meat hook," Eli murmured.

Sonia dumped the velvet ropes onto the ticket counter. "Clear outta here, ya nosy parkers," she scolded, squeezing herself in front of Emmett. "He's a patron, and their business ain't none of ours!"

Emmett swaggered back to his spot at the front end of the basilisk. "If I didn't know better, Fraülein, I'd say *their* business and *your* business were the *same* business."

Lulu clapped dust off her work skirt. "Aw, put a lid on it, Em, and finish polishing your damn snake."

At this, Emmett and Eli shot each other a silent plea for help, but it was no good. Their snorts turned into wheezes of laughter, and the rest of us tumbled headfirst into the gutter after them— save for Navya, who shook her feather duster into the trash with something like contempt.

I coughed out my residual chuckles and swept a path over to her with the broom. At the sight of me, she pulled back her shoulders and doubled her dusting efforts. I wasn't insulted; when no one takes you seriously, you learn to doubt it when someone does.

"Say, Madam," I began. "I was just thinking that stool you use all the time must be a pain in the neck to drag around. What if you kept that thing here, and I built you something at the hotel that made it so's you didn't have to use it?"

Without looking up, she whacked the feather duster hard against the bin. "I haven't the money for such an undertaking."

"I wouldn't take it from you if you did," I said. "It's bad enough livin' in a world that don't fit. I just figure you should have a home that does."

She lifted a leery eyebrow. "Trying to change your karma, are you, Mr. Benny?"

I laughed. "Nah. I've ticked off too many gods already. Although," I added in a lower voice, "I wouldn't mind hearing what makes you think that merman's something special."

Her feather duster paused mid-whack. "Why are you interested?

"Maybe I don't want my karma getting any worse."

Madam Navya's defensiveness thawed before my eyes. From her stool, she seated herself elegantly on the little platform where the dragon once stood, produced the world's smallest set of eyeglasses from her pocket, and smoothed her tunic over her lap. "Do you know where I am from, Mr. Benny?"

A trick question no matter who asked it. "I figured probably . . . India?"

"India is bigger than New York with borders well buggered by British colonial rule. One must be more specific," she said instructively. "I am from Punjab, so named for the five rivers that flow into the Indus from the Himalayas. Our civilization has been tied to the sacred convergence of those life-giving veins for thousands of years."

She reached into the handbag behind her, feeling around for something that, after a moment, it became apparent she couldn't find.

"TIMOTHY PORTER!"

Timmy's dusty curls poked out from behind the ticket booth.

Madam Navya thrust her open palm at him. "Give me back that picture," she whisper-hissed, "or I will tell your mother who's been sneaking sugar cubes out of the pantry again!"

Terror blanched his rosy cheeks before he shuffled over with the picture in his grubby hands like he was heading to the baby gallows. Navya snatched it back, and Timmy bounced off to resume building his armaments.

"This"—she held out the picture to me—"is Matsya, the first avatar of Vishnu."

Goose bumps crawled up my neck. By the illustration, Matsya was a beautiful four-limbed man from the waist up, crowned with gold and draped in red and white garlands, his skin tinted a rich blue. Below his waist, an apron draped over a long fish tail.

Cristo. If I'd grown up worshipping this Matsya instead of a man on the cross, you could've convinced me easily enough that Morgan had made us drag a god out of the East River.

"In the *Mahabharata*, Matsya appears to King Manu as a small fish," she explained. "He asks for protection, and so the king cares for it. It thrives and grows until, with the king's help, Matsya is returned to the river. As reward for Manu's care and devotion, Matsya instructs him to build a ship. 'Tie the ship to my horn and you will survive the flood,' he says. And so, Matsya carries Manu through the storm—up the river, to the Himalayas—and there reveals his true self: Lord Vishnu, the savior of creation."

"Then you think the merman is this Matsya?"

She shook her head. "Vishnu's avatars do not repeat. But I sense a nobility in this creature that makes me quake with unease. From the moment I saw it, I felt a foreboding. As though we had lit a fuse on a stick of dynamite."

I gulped dust. "What do *you* think our deeds earned us?"

"My imagination can produce too many fitting consequences for imprisoning an exalted being." She wrapped her arms around herself and shivered. "Perhaps a flood comes for us too, and we have doomed ourselves to drowning."

I almost said something then. To confess that, where that maldito whistle was concerned, the hand of fate was my own, and Río was far more interested in going home than visiting his wrath on anyone—except maybe Morgan.

But then the Menagerie door flew back open and the man himself tramped through it looking more pressed than a cork in a soda bottle. Everyone stopped to sniff him for clues about his mysterious visitors only to be disappointed when he stuck his casual grin back on his face and started moving at a trot toward the theater.

On the way, he pointed at me. "Benny, come along. We have some things to discuss."

Madam Navya's wary gaze met mine in the split second before she went back to dusting. I followed Morgan to the stage exit.

"Looks like I'll be in Manhattan for a number of days," he said, walking too fast for me to steal a glance at Río. "I've been tasked with promoting our little production there."

Chilly air exploded into our faces as we strode outside. "What's that mean?" I asked over the wind-whipped canvas and crunching gravel.

He forgot to hold open the tent flap for me, and it nearly hit me in the face. "A lot of botherations, that's what. It's easier to sell a bar of soap than a sideshow nowadays, what with those barking psychologists trying to make us all ashamed of ourselves."

The wind that came in with us disturbed some papers on his table, so I threw a hand down to catch them. Glancing at what I'd caught, I paused and looked closer. "'The Prince of Atlantis: Eighth Wonder of the World'?" I read aloud.

"Designed the flyer myself. Stunning likeness, wouldn't you agree?"

Under the ornate lettering was a gaudy illustration of a man with the lower half of a mackerel, complete with crown, trident, and waves of fluffy curls. It looked like King Ferdinand II. With a tail.

"It's stunning, all right."

I sidled into the same chair I'd sat in the day he hired me, while Morgan disappeared behind the partition wall. A second later, he stumbled out with a small suitcase, dropped it heavily onto the table, and clicked it open.

"Now then. I have a very critical task to add to your duties. While I'm gone, I'll need someone to look after the properties." He pulled his green suit coat off his chair and commenced slapping dust off the sleeves. "That includes our occupant on the stage."

The refrain to this tune was always *Sure thing, boss*, but I faltered. "You want *me* to look after the merman?"

He stalled in his slapping. "Are you resistant to the idea?"

"No! I just thought you'd ask one of the others, seein' as they've been here longer and all."

He pivoted to his desk and rummaged around for a moment before finding a roll of twine. "Out of the question. All those little whispers they think I can't hear—I can tell they're a bit threatened by our new exhibit. But you don't seem to have that problem, do you?"

More rummaging. From the center drawer, Morgan drew out his derringer.

"No, sir—uh, Sam."

"Besides"—he waved the gun around in a casual flourish—"the tank is just as much yours as it is mine, isn't it?"

"Right," I said with gaunt enthusiasm.

"Capital!" The roscoe went into the suitcase. "You can let the others know when your shift is over."

"*I'm* telling them?" I choked. "But what do I say?"

Morgan paused from tying twine around the flyers to twist his mustache between his fingers in thought. "Tell them you're our new . . . production assistant in training! That has a lovely ring to it, doesn't it? Oh, don't look so terrified, it'll be fine. There's salt to treat the water in the crates behind the tent and plenty of dried cod in the dressing room. Open the hatch and drop it in thrice a day—and yes, soak it if you must. Though, I'll advise you not to get too close," he added with a frown. "I haven't broken the beast in yet, which leaves it somewhat unpredictable. Wish I'd had the forethought to chain it up, but alas, we can't all be fortune tellers, can we?"

I wanted to point out that Morgan's impression of el tritón as a vicious animal was as far from the real thing as the flyers he painted. But I just stood up and nodded. "Salt for the water, cod for meals."

In a torrent of words my brain stumbled to keep up with, Morgan rattled off instructions on maintaining everything from the motorcar to the horse stalls, concluding with proper use for the heavy wad of banknotes he slapped into my palm in case anything broke. I'd never held so much money.

"Oh! And for pity's sake, get our pump running, would you? Sneak in coal in the middle of the night if you must. There's a good fellow." He clapped a hand on my arm. "Been less than a week and I already can't remember how we ever survived without you!"

I had no idea what to do with his gushy praise other than accept it with a vague sense not to trust it. So much in Coney Island was embellished, it made me wonder if I could believe anything I saw, much less heard a ruffled Sam Morgan say.

Río was the exception. In a counterfeit world, he alone was the real deal.

Morgan practically shoved me out the tent. For the rest of my shift, and all the way back to the Albemarle, my gut churned. On one hand, this was the kind of promotion I'd always hoped I would get at the Ironworks, even if I couldn't really understand how I'd earned it. On the other, as much as I was relieved to have Río in my keeping, I hated the idea of keeping him in the first place.

And if I was being honest, something in Navya's warnings felt prescient. That somehow, we'd all pay a price for Morgan's star exhibit. And if Río didn't visit his wrath upon us, then maybe something else would.

"A production *what*?"

Nine faces stared blankly at me over bowls of Eli's spaghetti and meatballs.

I coughed into my napkin and repeated myself. "Assistant in training."

"Yeah, I heard that part." Emmett put down his fork and spoon, the better to leer at me openly. "What I can't wrap my noggin around is what the hell he's thinking putting a greener-than-grass *blacksmith* in charge of a sideshow!"

"I wouldn't be in charge of you," I replied, the air in the room suddenly thinning. "There's the renovations to look after and the tank and, you know . . ." I caught Matthias's wide eyes and quickly looked back at my bowl. "The merman."

Emmett yanked his napkin out of his collar and tossed it on the table. "I knew it. Eli, didn't I just say it this morning? Morgan's already fixing to replace us with that *thing*!"

"No one's replacing anyone," Lulu interjected calmly. "Ain't no reason to jump to conclusions."

"No reason?" Emmett squawked. "This kid's been here, what, a week? And Morgan puts *him* in charge while he runs off to put ads in the croakers?"

"Why you gotta be so damn paranoid?" Matthias asked.

"Yeah, Emmett," said Vera with the calm of a priest, twirling more spaghetti onto her spoon. "That's Navya's job."

Navya scowled at the fire-breather and aggressively speared a meatball with her fork.

"You're drunk on scandal soup, Em," Sonia remarked. "It only makes sense to put Benny in charge of the merman if he's around it all day and built the stupid cage."

Emmett swiped a finger at her. "You don't get a say, Sonia. Yours is the only job that's *safe*, and everyone knows you been sweet on Benny ever since you shared a backseat in the coach!"

Sweet on me? I glanced at Sonia, at the open-mouthed silence that only seemed to confirm Emmett's accusation, and promptly lost whatever was left of my appetite.

"Morgan is not fool," boomed Igor sagely. "Luna Park need extra help to survive next season, and Mr. Benny is extra help. Merman? Is extra help. We keep park open; we keep jobs. What for you need to suspect Benny?"

"He ain't one of us," Emmett said without missing a beat. "You're all so eager to trust this wisenheimer just 'cause he speaks English like a Brookie. How do you know he ain't gonna sell us down the river when money pours in and Morgan finds out how much more of it he can keep with only a merman and a Porto Rican scab to pay for?"

"Emmett!" Eli gasped.

Suddenly, every face turned to look up at me. I'd risen to my feet without telling my body to do it. My head felt so hot, I thought smoke might start leaking from my eyeballs.

"I ain't a scab," I snarled, "or a dope you can talk about like I ain't in the room! I'd *never* sell out anybody here." I glowered at Emmett. "Not even a two-bit, peeled-potato, grousing come-mierda like *you*!"

Timmy giggled "Peeled potato!" into his milk, which made me feel only marginally better about calling Emmett a shit-eater in front of a kid.

I turned to Lulu, whose face had gone completely pink. "'With it, for it, never against it,' huh? You said everyone in this house was family, and I believed it. Jesus, maybe I *am* a dope."

Sonia reached out a hand but didn't touch me. "Benny—"

"I'm going for a walk."

I left my dinner in the dining room and took the stairs two at a time up to my room.

No. *Saul's* room.

As I stood in front of the mirror, trying to fit my cap back on my boiling cabeza, Sonia appeared in the doorway. "You sure like to go on walks at night, huh?"

I whipped Matthias's scarf off the chair and wrapped it around my neck. "Habit."

"Well, you just missed a great show," she said with a giddy lilt. "Lulu gave Emmett a talking-to like she ain't never gave Timmy. I thought she might take away his dessert and send him to bed for good measure."

"Bet that did the trick."

She took the hint and dropped the artificial levity. "He didn't mean it, you know. It was a poor choice of words."

"Oh, come on." Overheated, I ripped the scarf back off. "You think he's the first white guy to throw a poor choice of words in my face?"

"If you knew him better—"

"No thanks." I yanked my coat off the hook. "I know all I need to know about that paranoid pendejo."

Sonia watched me hunt around for my keys in silence, opting not to strong-arm me for once. Meanwhile, guilt prickled on the borders of my anger for snapping at her. If Emmett was right, and she really was sweet on me, then as much as I *really* didn't want to think about it, she'd had her vulnerabilities poked at too.

Was that why she was still standing here?

Suddenly, she blurted out, "Sam's taking me with him."

"What?" I stopped buttoning my coat. "Why?"

"Well, I'm his—gosh, how'd he put it—sideshow ambassador!" she exclaimed with flat enthusiasm. "Says it attracts new patrons to have someone with some sparkle hanging off his arm."

"Huh. I didn't take you for an ornament."

The forced smile on Sonia's face wilted away.

"I'm sorry," I moaned. "I didn't mean that. It just don't seem like you're that excited."

She pulled back her shoulders. "Why wouldn't I be? Manhattan's hep, and going means I get to learn the ropes. I mean"—she let out a nervous chuckle—"*someone's* gotta take over the show when these goops get too old to run it."

"Morgan tell you that?"

"Not everything's up to Sam," she said pointedly. "Anyway, this will all blow over as soon as we're outta the way, you'll see. You'll still be here when I get back, won't you?"

I sighed. "Yeah. I'll be here."

Like I had anywhere else to go.

THIRTEEN

Per the usual routine, I stepped behind the curtain that night ready to coax Río out of his corner. Instead, I found him propped on the glass rim and peering down at me like I hadn't held up my end of a business agreement.

"I expected you earlier."

Climbing up the tank side to resume my seat was a little trickier with a lamp in hand and a newspaper bundle under my arm. "I didn't think you were the waitin' type."

"There is naught else to do in this cursed cage but wait," he grumbled, flicking away an offending bubble.

"Hopefully, you won't mind so much when you find out what kept me."

Río's eyes livened as I unwrapped the newspaper and held its contents up to the lamplight. "Snapper," he gasped. "Where did you catch it?"

I fit it through the lattice and let it fall into his open hands. "At the Clarendon. If by 'catch' you mean 'bribed el camarero.' Buen provecho."

He melted like I'd just dropped a bouquet of roses through the grill, then tore into it with startling gusto. As much as watching Río finally enjoy a meal was a balm on a shitty evening, I thought he deserved better than snapper to soften the news I was about to give him. I didn't think he'd be too pleased about my sudden promotion—even if the extra cash it put in my pocket had paid for his meal.

"Morgan's leaving for a while, so he's put me in charge," I began. "Says I'm supposed to look after you."

Río regarded me askance. "Have you not been doing this already?" he asked through a bite of fish. "A barnacle could not look after me with as much tenacity."

Abashed, I took off my cap. "Means I've got the key to your tank."

My turn to wait for him. When he finally spoke, it was barely above a whisper.

"You cannot free me, can you?"

Don't ask me how he was still floating. If it were me finding out the key to freedom wasn't enough to liberate me, I'd have sunk like a stone.

"Not on my own," I murmured. "And after what happened tonight, I'm not sure I could get anyone here to help me if I tried."

"What happened?"

I chewed my lip and tried not to bite through it. "They don't know what to do with us. On one hand, they'd celebrate if you left, they're so sure Morgan's trying to replace them. On the other: the park's in trouble and they think you can save it for 'em. As for me? Soy un extranjero." I balled up the newspaper and flung it as hard as I could over the side of the tank. "Even around a bunch of foreigners, I'm too foreign."

Río's expression went gray. "Perhaps you should seek a better harmony."

I had a hunch he wasn't talking about music. "What's a 'harmony'?"

"To you? A bunch of foreigners," he said dully. "'Harmony' is how we refer to our family groups."

No one who'd ever heard a merperson speak could deny it was the perfect phrase. "A harmony of merfolk," I said, amused. "That's got a much better ring to it than 'a school of fish' or 'a murder of crows.'"

"'A *murder* of crows'?" Río made a disgusted noise. "Drag me on a reef, but humans are vulgar!"

"What about yours, then? Where's your harmony?"

There was a pause when it seemed Río wouldn't answer, which I quickly realized was his only sensible option. Río would never risk his kin by telling a human where to find them, whether or not the human was me. I was about to take the question back until, surprisingly, he spoke.

"With my mother returned to Neptune's robes, I am all that is left of it."

My heart foundered at the stoic restraint with which he spoke such awful words. "Perdóname. I shouldn't have—"

"It was inevitable," he said in an empty voice. "Our race only persists, it seems, out of sheer stubbornness. We have been dying off for centuries."

"Dying? But you seem so . . ." I took in his strong, sculpted frame, and felt my cheeks burn. "Sturdy."

"Ocean water is life-giving and ages us far more slowly than our earthbound cousins," he explained, rubbing absently at the scar over his eye. "But changing seas have made us vulnerable. Most harmonies have fled to the deep or taken refuge in other waters. The kind without large fishing nets or steam-powered ships turning the tides to acid."

"The East River seems like the worst place in the world to dodge a net," I said. "What were you even doing there?"

"The East River is not a river at all, but a saltwater estuary."

"You didn't answer my question."

Río exhaled, caught out. He laid back on the water and gazed past my face at the metal rigging above us. "I struggle for words, Benigno," he said softly. "I have followed the Currents all my life. Of late, I have wondered whether they have failed me, or I have failed them."

"'Followed the currents'? To where?"

"Not where." He touched his mouth as if it could summon the right words. "The Currents are the wisdom and intuition of the living tides. Guidance for all water-bound souls."

"Wait, you believe the water is . . . alive?"

Río's fingers swept delicate figure eights through the ripples. "Your skepticism is human. Your kind worships your individuality, injuring yourselves in the delusion of being separate from each other and the world," he explained without his usual snobbishness. "The children of Neptune live as waves on the water—unique and separate only in appearance, for we are united in spirit by the vastest element on earth. Thus, when the Currents call, we obey."

Waves on the water. The way his sharp eyes softened as he spoke those words wrought an ache in my chest that didn't feel like asthma.

"Except I misinterpreted them, I think," he continued. "I might never have approached the woman in the boat otherwise."

"You mean to say you towed Sonia back to shore because the Currents *told* you to?"

At this, Río's eyes closed like he was forcing himself to think through a bad headache. "You ask why I was in the East River. Perhaps you know of the tragedy that occurred there."

"A tragedy," I said, then instantly knew what he was referring to. "You mean the *General Slocum*?"

When his eyes opened, they stared out at nothing. "My harmony was larger then," he said. "A dozen of us saw the ship succumb. Watched as the humans aboard it—women and children, mostly—cast themselves to the water wearing garments too heavy to float, hoping to spare themselves from burning alive. We felt the calamity at hand before we had even broken the surface, but the Currents' ache was so great, we knew not what to do.

"Our elders had taken it as confirmation that humanity would be frightened into violence if we interfered, having long decided that to save humans from themselves was to advance the destruction of our race and our home. After all, choirs of harmonies had already heeded the instinct to swim deeper, to migrate to the farthest reaches of the Atlantic lest we find all merkind obliterated on the tip of a harpoon.

"But the horrors would not leave me. Human screams rang in my ears like whistles long after the vessel surrendered to the estuary. When I could not withstand my guilt at letting them drown, my mother alone sympathized. A mermaid from the Tailfin Sea—what your kind call the Caribbean—she believed in human virtue and perceived a different warning in the Currents' ache: that we

too would find ourselves lost—extinct, even—if we abandoned humankind."

I sat on the lattice, dumb with shock. Not only because he'd witnessed the worst maritime catastrophe in New York history, nor because Río's kind had stood by and let it happen—but because, by the looks of it, his elders' fears were justified. He and his mother had believed humans deserved saving, and humanity had punished them cruelly for it.

"The harmonies fled the estuary that day. But I chose to stay, and so," he concluded, "my mother stayed as well."

As he finished his story, my mind assembled another. Of a merman who finally found someone to rescue on a cold moonlit night, and the mermaid who wouldn't let him do it alone.

"Río, you don't blame yourself for her murder . . . do you?"

His eyes went red-rimmed and wet. He draped a webbed hand over them. "Out of seawater, I cannot learn what purpose has killed her and driven me to this prison, except that my foolishness is to blame."

It dawned on me, perched on the metal bars with a clear view of Río's crisis of faith, that we were going through the very same thing.

"Oye," I said, "your mother died because Morgan killed her. As for the rest, I don't know the Currents, but I know what it's like to get pulled somewhere by something you can only know by how strong it tugs. Sounds to me like, when the Currents got muddy, you followed your heart, and that's gotta be the same thing. It's what got me from Puerto Rico to Nueva York."

He sat up in the water. "What did the Currents say that made you abandon your homeland for a shore so far away?"

The truth found its way to my mouth—in Spanish—for the first time in four years.

Río

"I was a lost boy," he begins in his native song. "Different from other young Puerto Rican men following the path of their fathers and uncles who scheme about liberation, marry young, and, in hardship, drink too much."

Benigno's garment twists in his restless hands, speaking for an agitation I realize I recognize within myself—as tremors that bristle my scales and drag like weights off my fins in the Shark's presence.

"Tití Luz foresaw me on an island of loneliness and pain without her," he continues, "so before she died, she made me promise to follow a different path to liberation in New York. My courage had faltered at the thought of leaving, but once she was gone, the person I was disappeared with her. I guess I came here to find him."

I listen, rapt. His words issue forth swiftly, but meticulously arranged. Indeed, his clipped Spanish sounds as though it were spoken by a different person entirely.

"And did you find yourself?" I ask in his tongue.

He answers with an acrid laugh. "I am even more of a stranger to myself here. This country has no better idea of what to do with me than it does of what to do with my island. They won the Spanish-American War and inherited an angry, wounded youth in the Caribbean. I often wonder if the people of Borínquen will always be caught between the master who conquers us and the master we wish we could be for ourselves."

"It sounds like your Currents have failed you too," I say.

He shrugs and resumes his saw-toothed version of English. "It hasn't been all bad. If I hadn't come to Luna Park, I'd still be breathing poison air at the ironworks. At least here, the sourpusses are made of plaster."

In vain, I try not to smile. There is genius in the way Benigno softens bleakness with humor.

"Maybe, if it weren't for my Currents," he says, "I wouldn't have this job, and I wouldn't be here to . . ."

I say what he cannot. "Save me."

Unexpected warmth rolls through my fins when he leans over the bars to observe me more closely.

"I won't give up if you won't," he says. "At least Morgan'll leave you alone for a while. Not that I'm a more welcome sight . . ."

From my view below him, Benigno's face is partitioned, the bars crossed over his sultry skin and midnight eyes like a netting of iron. Still, his presence is a warm glow over my lightless captivity, and only now do I realize it—how thankful I am at once again being able to gaze skyward and know I am not alone.

"You are a welcome sight, Benigno. I never expected to find an ally in this dreadful place." I reach for humor as well and add, "You are a rather pleasant sort of barnacle."

"Thanks. I'm getting used to the hours."

His smile is shy, and though his lungs are quiet tonight, I worry for the rest he does not give them conversing with me while the world outside sleeps. "I regret my mother did not charge you with a simpler burden."

"You might regret it." Benigno scratches a fingernail over the bars. "But I don't."

His words, reservedly spoken, make me feel buoyant in the water. "Then be assured. I will not give up."

FOURTEEN

Once Río had filled my head with the Currents, I couldn't drain them back out. Morgan stayed gone for another few days, leaving me free to ruminate on Río's strange convictions without getting any closer to understanding why he held them. His mother was slaughtered, himself imprisoned, yet he still believed something greater than himself had a plan or at least a *reason* if only he could make it back to the water to hear it.

What the hell did *I* believe?

I was about four years removed from the day my fate became chiefly dependent on whoever handed me a paycheck. But whenever I looked at the tank and remembered all the weird synchronicities that followed its creation, I wondered if the Currents ever bothered to work their strange magic on land.

While I wrestled with the matter in private, I decided to ask Río if there was anything he thought might cure his boredom whenever my workload kept me away.

"Seashells," he said. He lifted the end of one of his braids where a few small cowrie shells were threaded into his hair like beads. "My mother enjoyed carving them. Perhaps I would as well."

"Seashells, it is."

Being ahead of schedule with my renovations, I took myself on a treasure hunt for Río down Stratton's Walk toward the sand. As my shoes sank into powder, the commercial amusements world gave way to the shoreline like vellum peeling off a painting. Now that the March breeze had lost its bite, it was easier to imagine this place in summer, warm, noisy, and packed so tight with bathers you couldn't move without stepping on one.

I sifted a few nice unchipped shells out of the pebbles and cigar butts, then looked eastward where the craggy silhouettes of fishing boats lined the horizon.

It'd be fun to rent un barquito out here. To sail so far out that Dreamland's tower, the Ferris wheels, and the Iron Pier would fit comodito in my palm.

Then a shock of blond hair at the corner of my eye interrupted my fantasizing.

"I can resist anything but temptation!"

A dozen yards away, Emmett and Eli were watching the waves roll in, propped up on elbows with their three-and-a-half legs outstretched. Emmett's yell drew a dramatic gasp out of Eli who retaliated by shoving his brother sideways into the sand. Surely Emmett was the sort to hit back, but to my surprise, he started *laughing*—a cheerful, mischievous cackle. He grabbed one of Eli's suspenders and yanked him down with him, the pair of them a sandy heap of giggling malcriados.

Was this what they meant by "chasing seagulls"?

As if he could sense they weren't alone anymore, Eli looked past Emmett's shoulder and saw me. His boyish smile converted to a curious stare.

I nabbed a last scallop shell and shuffled out of the sand. Emmett was still laughing, and I didn't think I ought to ruin a moment that produced such a rare and pleasant sound.

"What in Neptune's name is that noisy contraption doing?"

The circulation system was, after a bit of elbow grease—and more Ave Marías than I could count—finally up and running. I was clearing away extra parts while Río watched the effervescent bubbles fluttering up from the hose with barely controlled outrage.

A finger at a time, I wiped my grease-blackened hands off on a rag. "It's aerating the water."

"I can see that. I just do not understand *why*."

At this point, I didn't entirely understand myself. The water looked clearer than a spring, even after I'd convinced Río to end his hunger strike.

"You know. To keep the water . . . clean," I said uncomfortably.

"Why do *you* need to keep the water clean if *I* am already cleaning it?"

I snapped the rag over my shoulder. "Whaddaya mean *you're* cleaning it?"

Río's eyes rolled to the ceiling and back. "Merfolk are purifying to water. It is the defining trait of my kind." I gawked at him for several moments before Río folded his arms across his chest and said, "Is that so hard to believe?"

"Of course it is! You eat fish!"

"So?"

As far as Río and I had come as polite conversationalists, grilling a merman about his bodily functions felt like a Brooklyn Bridge too far. "So, do you never . . . I mean, you don't need to . . ."

He was eyeing me like I'd gone bobo. "Defecate?" he supplied helpfully.

"Aw, *jeez*, Río—"

"Sky and sea, must every function of your human bodies humiliate you?" he huffed, somehow more offended at my prudishness than that *mierda* had become our latest discussion topic. "The water gives me life. As a Keeper of the Sea, I give it back. A forest does the same for the air. What could be easier to understand?"

"But that ain't easy, that's—" *Milagroso*, I thought, but rather than call him a miracle to his face, I said, "Magic."

He cocked an indignant eyebrow. "Merfolk do not lie."

"Oh yeah? How about all that stuff you said about tearing me apart with your teeth?"

"That was not a falsehood. I simply altered my intentions."

"Ave María—"

"If you cannot believe me, then pass that cloth through the bars."

I glanced down at the grease-smeared rag hanging over my shoulder and, grimacing, picked up a fold of it between two fingers. "What, this?"

"Yes. Bring it to me."

That seemed like a terrible idea. I knew what happened to fish that wandered into the Gowanus by accident, and as tough as Río seemed, I wasn't keen to poison his water by casually dropping industrial lubricant into it.

But Río was resolute, and I was curious. I hauled myself up the rungs and dangled the greasy rag through the grill.

He glared at it so judgmentally, I thought the grease might melt off it from shame. But he snatched it away, and to my disbelief, smoothed it all over his agile hands as if it were a washcloth. When he flung it back at the bars, I caught it on the hook of my fingers—then almost dropped it again once I saw what had become of it.

"¿Cómo . . . ?"

It was perfectly clean. A bright linen white. I turned it over and over for even a hint of the grime I'd left on it, but apart from being soaked through with salt water, it looked the same as it had the day I'd bought it.

I stared at him with bulging eyes. "Can you do this . . . to anything? Could you, say, clear up the Gowanus Canal?"

"There are limits to our capacity to heal water," he said soberly. "The canals are beyond anyone's salvation unless human cretins can stop polluting them."

"Still, that's . . . increíble."

"Not incredible," he contested. "I am mer."

He gave no further explanations. But after what I'd just seen, I decided I didn't need them.

"All right," I said, recovering. "And now I'll tell you why we should keep the pump running anyway."

Visibly disappointed that his demonstration hadn't earned him a silent tank, he asked, "Why?"

I answered in Spanish. "Because it will keep your gifts a secret. If the Shark ever finds out what you just showed me, he will find a way to exploit it."

Río's face darkened in understanding. "I see."

"Almost forgot . . ." I dug out a handful of seashells from my pocket and lowered them through the grill, balancing them in my open palm. "I tried to find good ones, but you know how lousy that beach gets with litter."

His expression pivoted from surprise to anticipation. With a slow, graceful roll of his tail, Río rose high enough out of the water to examine the collection, somehow avoiding touching me as he plucked out the shells one at a time.

"You'll need this too," I said, handing down my small carbon steel graver. "It's for engraving metal, but with a soft hand, I bet it'd do the trick on shells too."

He lifted his face to smile at me. It made me sit up a little straighter. "Thank you, Benigno."

"No problem."

Río had started examining his gifts more closely, but before I could descend the rungs, he stopped me. "The noise shall keep us a secret as well, I expect?"

"'Us'?"

He held up a pearly-white coquina shell. "Our friendship."

My cheeks warmed. For a guy who usually made enemies just walking into a room, making a friend like Río felt like a big deal. "Yeah. If you can tolerate it—the noise, I mean, not the friend. Ship."

"You should know, Benigno," he said with sudden seriousness, "that violence is not in our nature. I regret the threats I made."

I stared dumbly at Río's contrition, not daring to mention how small his regret should be compared to mine.

"Thanks. But save it for the day I get you out."

On the second to last Friday in March, Morgan and Sonia returned from Manhattan. The showman congratulated me on getting his circulation system running but was otherwise wound up tighter than a wristwatch for reasons he wouldn't share with anyone. Lulu waited past Timmy's bedtime to tell me she was sure Morgan had resumed "embalming his liver," which I guess explained the acetic tang in the pipe smoke aroma coming off his green suit.

As for Sonia, she withdrew to her bedroom for the day, claiming that traveling in corsets had left her spine "stiffer than a lousy plank" and she needed to unwind.

Once Morgan had returned to the theater, there was no way to keep him away from Río's tank whenever he felt the inclination to "train" him. But in the showman's absence, I had prepared an arsenal of distractions to pull out whenever Río's refusal to so much as look at the guy made him ready to combust, from weathered upholstery to rusted electrical fixtures to rats in the walls.

It was a goddamned miracle I got anything done when the Avocado Man was around.

Gracias a Dios, I'd had extra hands in the museum earlier that week. Vera had helped me rip up the old carpeting on the nutty condition that I let her try on my old guayabera. It cheered her up so much, she forgot to snipe back when Sonia yelled about finding crushed cigarillos in her silk hatbox. Once the carpets were gone, Matthias had volunteered to be my right hand at restoring the wire skeletons of the museum's monstruos—me using a pair of needle-nose pliers, Matthias just using his fingers. (We'd decided it might be time to retire the Chimera after we found its crumbling head hidden under Timmy's bed behind his shoes.)

Even Igor had lent his massive height toward fixing some faulty bulbs, albeit he'd seemed far more interested in playing rummy with Madam Navya while she complained about the Trolley Dodgers' disappointing starting lineup. I had my suspicions about why he let her go on like that when Igor himself was a Yankees fan.

Then there was Emmett. Despite Sonia's mostly accurate prediction that things would go back to normal after the dinner table incident, he still gave me a wide berth and barely said a word to me if he didn't have to. Meanwhile, Eli campaigned for a seat as Emmett's only human credential.

So it happened that, on the rainy day Morgan left work early, Eli came to visit me in the theater while I was repairing the friezes. "Need an extra set of hands?"

I glanced nervously back at the stage where Río slept behind the curtain.

"Sure," I said. "Just, you know . . . keep it down."

He cut his eyes to the stage. "Sounds like you've got a motorcar running back there, I should still keep it down?"

My eyebrows went up. "How bad do you want a merman listening in on your conversations?"

Eli shuddered. "I'll keep it down. Jesus, I dunno how you get anything done with Moby Dick over there. Gives me the heebie-jeebies." He rolled up his sleeves as he walked toward the spot where I was sanding down sculpted walls to prime them.

I tore another sheet of sandpaper from my pile and made room for him to stand next to me. "Don't rub too hard."

He chuckled and started scrubbing the paper gently over the peeling surface of a trident protruding from the frieze. "I gotta tell Emmett he's missing out."

"On what? A chance to polish Poseidon's prick?"

"Ha! You got a funny bone, you know that?" he remarked as flecks of faded gold cascaded to the floor. "He woulda come, ya know, but he wasn't up to walking today."

"If you came to make excuses for Emmett," I said tightly, "I ain't the right audience."

Eli dropped his head and sighed. "He's just . . . protective."

"Right. 'Cause I'm such a threat."

This wasn't like me. When folks made a stink about where I came from, I never fussed. But despite everything, I wanted that pasty-faced gringo to like me, and I hated how helpless I felt that he didn't.

"It ain't about you," Eli said. "Not really, anyway. He's just got a hard time trusting people thanks to some no-good louses we grew up with."

"But you don't have that problem," I remarked, "and you're his brother."

The look on Eli's face, like he'd bitten into salt expecting something sweet, paused my hand.

"What?" I asked.

He glanced over my shoulder at the theater doors to make sure they were closed. "Benny," he said in quiet disbelief. "He ain't my brother."

My eyes squinted over my O-shaped mouth. "What do you mean he ain't—"

And then, as if Poseidon's trident had fallen out of the wall to thump me over the head, I understood him perfectly.

Their constant closeness. The playful way they touched each other. Emmett's ferocious protectiveness of Eli, and Eli's infinite patience.

Chasing seagulls.

"He's . . ."

The sandpaper fell out of my grasp. Fumbling to catch it, I backed into the ladder, and it tipped. I had to leap to catch it before it crashed to the ground. Eli folded his arms over his chest. "You oughta be in the ballet."

"Sorry—"

"Does it bother you?"

"No!" I said quickly. "It don't bother me at all. I just . . . I ain't never met a man who— Who—"

"Loves another man?"

I nodded.

Eli pulled a bench away from the wall where Morgan had stacked them and sat, leaning forward on his elbows. "Let's be honest, most people would be bothered."

My cap felt too hot, so I took it off and sat down next to him, sticking the mask of casual interest back on my face.

"I ain't the judging type," I said.

He snorted. "Everyone *thinks* they ain't the judging type, but they can't all be telling the truth, right?"

"What's there to judge? I ain't never been in love."

"What?" He balked dramatically. "Handsome guy like you? Somebody chain you to that Red Hook furnace so's you'd never meet a girl?"

I shrugged. "There was no one to meet."

It wasn't a lie, exactly. Hardly anyone ever tempted me; I'd left the one person who did behind in Caguas when I was thirteen.

Since then, I'd been too distracted with surviving to ask myself if I still knew how to want someone that way, and in the meantime, my heart became like iron left too long in the flames: charred and brittle beyond salvaging.

"Matthias mentioned you and Emmett ran away," I said.

Eli cast me a bittersweet grin. "We was acolytes together at Saint Joe's Episcopal outside Jersey City when we figured out our enthusiasm for Sunday service had nothing to do with sneaking the communion wine. You wouldn't have recognized us back then—not just 'cause I was Rudy, he was Lenny, and neither of us was blond, but because that kid I grew up with was so different. Lenny was a handsome, freckle-faced dope who ate too many taffies and loved his horses—almost as much as he loved me." Eli bumped his shoulder into mine and added, "Well. I guess he's still a handsome dope."

I looped my finger around San Cristóbal. "What changed him?"

"Some nosy rat in the neighborhood told the priest she saw us foolin' around. When my pops heard I was kissin' the altar boy behind the hay bales, he laid into me like buckshot with that leather belt of his. I thought nothing could ever feel as bad as I did gettin' whipped by my pops. But then, when he was done with me, he shouted, 'I'm gonna give that fairy a leveler he'll never forget.' And that felt even worse."

There was a word in there I'd never heard before. I wasn't sure I wanted it defined for me, but I asked anyway. "What's a leveler?"

Eli looked down into his lap and scraped his thumbnail across the sandpaper. "He beat him, Benny. Left both his eyes in mourning, busted some ribs, and snapped his leg so bad it nearly killed him."

"Then that's why his leg is . . ." My fingers went numb. "Cristo."

I could see it on Eli's face, the ghost of a devastated kid named Rudy, his lips pulled into a line only Emmett ever got to cross. "Yeah, well. Once the leg was gone, he healed up so fast I thought he'd done it on purpose to spite my pops. 'Cause as soon as he could walk again, Em got me out of that house and away from my father," he murmured. "He saved my life, kid. And I've been his extra leg ever since."

For a full minute, my jaw hung open. I'd never known a love like that—the kind that paved a road through Hell and motored you to freedom. How many chumps had come to see the Conjoined Twins on stage, and never *seen* what they were looking at?

"And the company?"

"Oh, they know," he said, relaxing into an easier topic. "They only call us the Twins 'cause that's our gaff."

"Ave María." I scrubbed my cap over my sweaty neck. "You two ever think you'd find yourselves attached at the hip in a sideshow?"

Eli chuckled. "Nah, but I ain't got no regrets. The show keeps us together and safe from folks who don't understand. And that's a damn sight better than bein' alone and dead."

"Yeah . . ."

Eli swiveled on his seat to look me in the eye. "Emmett's not a bad guy, Benny. He's just been broken in more places than his leg, and sometimes it's hard for him to understand that the whole world ain't tryin' to take what's his. Especially if he thinks you're . . . hiding something."

I swallowed, but nothing went down. Eli's gaze had nailed me to the bench.

"See, he's got this crazy idea," he said carefully, "that maybe we three got something in common."

I tried to laugh, but it came out thin. "What gave him that idea?"

"Could be the way you look at Miss Kutzler. Or don't look, I should say."

My lungs wasted no time with their tontería, squeezing around the air in my chest while the rest of me sat stiff as a beam. I'd been here before, my bare palm sizzling against a glowing bar. "Emmett's the one who said she's sweet on me. I'm just trying to be careful around her."

"Then you gotta be the most careful guy I've ever seen." Eli's face softened. "Listen. I'm the last person on earth who's gonna judge you. I just know what it's like to live in a skin that ain't mine. Onstage, that's the act, but offstage, I get to have Emmett and a family who loves us like there ain't nothing wrong with us. Because there *ain't*."

He placed a hand on my shoulder, and everything around it tensed.

"Ain't nothing wrong with you either, Benny—"

"I'm no *invert*."

My voice came out blunted. Like a bat. It was a reflex, the way a cornered perrito bites in fear without meaning to. Eli let go of my shoulder like he'd touched a hot stove, and my regret filled in the outline of his missing hand.

"I'm sorry," I breathed. "I wasn't trying to—"

"It's all right," Eli said through a weak smile. "My fault for prying."

Without another word, he went back to work on Poseidon's trident until the sky went dark behind the curtains. Before he left, we moved the ladder and drop cloths to continue my work the next day.

But I already knew, when the next day came, he wouldn't be back to help.

Río

In my dreams, I burn alive.

There is little to see beyond the blinding conflagration that surrounds me and licks at my face. The heat curls my scales, blackens my fins, and boils my blood right from my wounds. I feel as though my body has run ashore on the smoldering surface of a red-tide sun, the Currents' call reduced to a whisper on the arid wind.

With waning strength, I try to raise my fluke to shield myself, but my tail is restrained. I realize then that I am moving. Through parched eyes, I force myself to look.

Human feet?

My eyes fly open. Heavy footsteps beyond the curtained room have stirred me from my fitful sleep. I flee to the furthest edge of my cage, grip the walls, and wait.

The Shark has come back to circle.

"Sovereign of the Seas," he says, his voice sluggish and low. "Heard me coming, did you?"

He places the lantern at his feet. A shiny vessel—swishing with a dark liquid I do not recognize as water—swings from his fist as he approaches. I sink farther into shadow.

"You look a good deal larger than that mermaid that tried to capsize us when I was young. With that mineral tint in your skin, you'd have the aspect of a prehistoric porpoise if you weren't so *sssymmetrical*," he slurs. "If my father could only see you for himself; the simpleton was so sure your species was just a myth."

Lifting a finger into the air, the Shark's posture contorts in mockery. "'You're a nuisance and a maniac, Samuel T. Dixon! You'll not squander another dime of my money on this ludicrous fairy tale, now get out of my sight!' If that pompous bastard weren't already six feet under the ground, he'd drop dead at the sight of you."

Every scale on my body raises with the serrated sound of his bitterness, but I dare not react. His whistle is gone—Benigno disabled it himself—but the Shark knows that, in the absence of metal armaments, his voice is his deadliest weapon. Alone with him in this moonless room, his sweat-sheened face fills me with a wild fear I cannot let him see lest he use it to unravel me.

Instead, I bore my loathing into his glistening forehead with my eyes.

He sees it and frowns. "Sitting there, staring daggers at me all day long . . . Isn't it tiring, pretending you can't hear or understand a word I say when I know you have better ears than every cur on the Eastern Seaboard?"

Lifting the vessel to his lips, he drinks, then wipes his mouth upon his hand. "That's right, I know everything about you. I've collected lore from every region on Earth that has something to say about the infestation of sea creatures whose humanlike appearance exists solely to lure us toward our undoing. Years of study and travel tend to make one an expert on the subject."

He leans his forearm against the pane and stares at me from beneath it.

"Although it seems I'm still learning a thing or two about your kind," he says softly. "For instance, did *you* know dead mermaids leave no bodies behind after you fire a bullet through their hearts? I didn't. Turned out to be quite the convenient trait," he mumbles. "Beast didn't even scream."

The scorching blaze from my nightmares erupts in my heart. I fly at the glass with strength insufficient to break it, but the human stumbles backward and falls on his seat, washing his sleeve in the dark drink he has been soaking his tongue in since before he set foot behind the curtain.

The Shark laughs—a sound so unlike the bright, glittering noise I have heard Benigno make when something I have said amuses him. His cheerful laughter is as warm and light and colorful as the Tropics.

The sound of the Shark's mirth sends a glacial chill
through my fins.

"Well, what do you know," he exclaims. "It understands
me after all!"

Cursing at his stained garments, he staggers to his feet and leaves
me, though not in peace. A tremor—sudden and sinister—
vibrates beneath my scales, and though I quiet my thoughts
enough to invite the water to heal it, it seems to take an age.
This water is not Ocean, and the Shark's leering face, twisted in
cruelty, pushes into my mind against my volition.

Relief comes only when I force my thoughts away from his
ugliness and toward something else . . .

A shy, lamplit smile. Kind night-sky eyes. Webless fingers that
dance upon lyre's strings as his mossy singing voice sets the
water rippling around me.

I cling to Benigno's seashells until the tremors cease,
and sleep carries me to oblivion.

FIFTEEN

That Sunday, Igor went out for shoe polish and brought home *The Brooklyn Daily Eagle* instead. It had a headline to cast a pall over the entire Albemarle, if not the entire city:

OVER 150 PERSONS, MOST OF THEM GIRLS, DIE AS FIRE TRAPS HAPLESS FACTORY WORKERS IN MANHATTAN SKYSCRAPER

The disaster—this one out of water—had everyone in the parlor that afternoon heartsick and stuck for words to explain how a three-story fire in a ten-story building could eat up that many souls in less than half an hour. If the article had its facts straight about what happened at the Triangle Shirtwaist Factory, then most of those girls were immigrants from Brooklyn younger than Sonia.

Lulu and Igor took it especially hard, having both spent their pre-Menagerie years working in Garment District factories, Lulu sewing skirts she couldn't fit into herself, and Igor cobbling work shoes. "You couldn't hardly breathe in those rooms," Lulu said, wiping tears and holding tightly onto Timmy, who sat surprisingly still against his mother's side. "I can't stand the thought of those innocent kids having to choose between jumping out a window or burning alive."

"Is proprietor's crime," said Igor quietly as Navya brought him a fresh cup of café. She sat down next to him and put her small hand on his enormous one. "When laborers is sick, when they working too long hours, when people is crowded in unsafe building . . . they do *nothing*."

Matthias pushed up his glasses and sighed. "Greedy is as greedy does. What do they care so long as the cash flows into the bank?"

"I dunno, but I amn't smokin' indoors no more," whispered Vera.

There was little I could add when I'd just escaped factory life by the skin of my scalded hand only ten days ago. I didn't miss my old workplace, but when I thought about Farty, Dan, and the others still sweating at the furnaces in Red Hook, I was surprised to find sympathy for them lurking under all my resentment.

The mood was too glum for evening drinks, so the Albemarle's lamps were all turned off by nine o'clock, making it easy to slip out to the theater unnoticed. When I arrived, Río looked as if someone had turned down his lamp too, until I showed him what was wrapped in the *Eagle*'s ad page.

"Salmon," he sighed happily. "Neptune bless you."

"De nada."

I handed it to him through the grill and pulled out a canteen of Igor's café while he ate, noting a slight dip in his usual energy. I wondered if the pump had interfered with his sleep, and tried not to think about how Río was trapped in his tank the way those girls were trapped in that factory.

"Tell me that story again, Benigno," he said through a mouthful of fish. "The amusing one from the other night."

"Wasn't much of a story," I said. "The pig got loose, and we found it eating the communion wafers in San Juan Bautista's bell tower."

His giggle sparkled like water. "An earthbound creature in a tower. Absurd," he mused between bites. "Everything is so much heavier on land, climbing seems impossibly difficult."

"That's exactly how swimming seems to me," I said.

Río licked his lips and dabbed the corner of his mouth. "Swimming is easy. Even a tailless creature like yourself can do it."

"Ballsy assumption from a guy with a tail."

"It is a fact," he insisted. "Mankind has bathed in Neptune's robes for generations. How did *you* never learn to swim?"

"Bum lungs," I admitted. "The hurricane too. Tití Luz believed in her own kind of Currents, and she figured if the water had spat me out, then I was never meant to swim in it."

"Odd. She was right to believe in the Currents," said Río, thoughtfully, "even if her interpretation of them was wrong."

"Says you."

"Indeed. And I will prove it when I teach you to swim."

"When pigs stop climbing and start flying, you mean." I choked down a lukewarm sip of the café and grimaced at the bitterness. "Have you done anything yet with those shells I gave you?"

"Yes, though much practice lies ahead of me before my hand is steady enough for the task," he said with a grimace of his own. "I have chipped a good many."

"I can always bring more," I said. *And some sand too,* I thought. It would give him something more comfortable than a steel floor to sleep on.

He glided closer. "Where did you find the carved shell that hangs from your neck?"

"This?" I held up the medallion. "This ain't a shell. It's San Cristóbal, the patron saint of travelers. Tití gave it to me for protection on the way to Nueva York."

"So that you could find a new harmony?"

I didn't usually like poking around the old, abandoned corridors of my past. But Río was a natural at getting my malas mañas out of the way. Tactless though he was, when I turned over my memories to him, he handled them carefully.

"Feels like I've been hunting for a harmony my whole life," I said. "I'm beginning to think there's nowhere on earth where someone like me can even find one."

"Someone like you? A Puerto Rican boy, you mean?"

Since Río first spoke to me almost two weeks ago, he'd called me a parasite, a coward, and a barnacle. But he never lied, and he never cracked wise about the parts of me I couldn't help. He'd told me his darkest secret when he spilled his guts about the *General Slocum*; maybe it wouldn't kill me to spill some of mine.

"Brace yourself for a stupid story," I muttered, so he laid back on the water, settling in to be entertained.

This particular memory would be easier to share in Spanish.

"Tití Luz had found me in Humacao where she had business, but then she brought me home to her tobacco farm in Caguas, where I met Ramón—the son of an insurrectionist who lived in the sugar plantation nearby. He was the sort of rascal everybody liked: cheerful and fearless and more handsome than a jíbaro had any right to be. He was tall, even though he ate like a juí bird, with coffee eyes and a smile as bright as a coquí's chirp whenever there was some mischief he wanted to include me in. Ramón was my best friend. And I had no words for what I felt whenever I looked at him.

"After long days working in the sun, the dirt would be all over our skin and clothes—Ramón smelling like sugarcane, me smelling like pigs and tobacco—so we often went to the shallow stream to bathe. One afternoon, we sat on the bank waiting for our clothes to dry and the feeling came over me again. Like warm honey."

I opened my palm, recollection rising to the surface of my skin. "I took his hand. Just to feel it against mine. But as soon as I did it, he yanked it back with a glare like I'd attacked him. 'What is wrong with you?' he said, disgusted. And he grabbed his wet clothes and ran back down the yellow path away from me."

"Benigno," Río breathed, but I couldn't look at him. If I did, I'd lose the nerve to tell him the rest.

"When I called on Ramón the next day, he puffed himself up and blocked the door frame as if I was an invader. He had obviously told his father what I had done, because he wasted no time telling me there was no place in an independent Puerto Rico"—I ventured a look at Río—"for a nameless queer like me."

The fronds of his tail fin came up behind him and draped over his shoulders. He shrank into them. "What did you do?"

I cleared my throat of the rock that had lodged itself there and fell back into English. "I bloodied his lip."

Río nodded soberly. "While generally I disapprove of violence, he appears to have earned it."

"Yeah, well"—I shrugged—"I learned all I needed to know about what the world thinks of 'someone like me,' by which I mean . . . Manos a Dios, I don't know how to say this . . ." I drew a deep breath. "A Puerto Rican boy who falls in love with other boys."

If I hadn't had it already, I had Río's complete attention now. I thought my whole body might dissolve through the grill from shame.

"What ridiculous savagery," he breathed in English, "would make humans spurn a person for something so . . . so . . . *ordinary*?"

I squinted at him. "You mean merpeople don't care?"

"Benigno, why in the Seven Seas should it *matter* who we love?"

Instead of an answer, a different question slipped out before I could catch it. "Have *you* ever been in love?"

"Young as I am, and sparse as we are, the souls that have drawn my affection have been few indeed, but if my heart sought the love of another merman, we would not be hindered by senseless rules meant to separate us for being the same sex. A host of sea creatures would cease to *exist* under such constraints." He folded his arms across his chest. "Honestly, Benigno, I despair for your race!"

"Obviously, not *all* humans have this hang-up," I said, compelled to defend humanity from an outraged merman's judgment. "Turns out Eli and Emmett, the two men who pretend to be twins, aren't brothers at all."

Río looked like his brain was about to combust from all the human nonsense it was trying to interpret at once. "They are lovers?"

"Yeah. And I guess they figured it out. About me," I muttered.

"You've a trait in common. This is good, is it not?" he said when my sullen expression didn't go anywhere.

"I denied it."

His tail slipped off his shoulders. "*Denied* it? But why?"

I groaned into my hands. "I didn't know how to admit it. Because, not counting this conversation, I've *never* admitted it. I should've been happy—finally, people who understand, who might show me how inverted folks survive in America without burying themselves alive," I said, my voice climbing to a hysterical pitch. "And it's because, after everything, I still wish it wasn't true. Everything else in my life is so damn hard already, couldn't God give me one less complication?"

I chanced a glance at Río and instantly regretted it. He looked stunned.

"See?" I muttered. "Estupido."

For a moment, it looked like he might agree with me.

He dove under the water instead.

"Uh . . . Río?"

His blobby shape swam a slow oval path several times before he reappeared at the surface looking refreshed and resolute. "I have given it some thought, and what I think is this: Guarding your heart because it has been broken is not una estupidez."

I pursed my lips. "Really."

"Yes. Revealing your truth is like swimming, Benigno. It may not come naturally or easily. But in still waters, it can be learned," he said firmly, his hair painting a rusty halo around his shoulders. "Though you feel regret about what happened, I am glad you have found others like you. Perhaps one day you shall feel safe enough to tell them what you have told me."

"Safe," I repeated, looking down at his conviction with envy. "In my whole dumb life, I've never felt as safe anywhere as I feel sitting on a metal grate twenty feet above the ground with you."

As soon as I said it, I wished I had the good sense to stop spilling my guts into that tank. The habit would be hard enough to break later. But Río just raised an eyebrow and said, "Spoken like a true barnacle."

We both cracked up. It left behind a sensation I didn't expect. Half ache, half ease, I didn't know what to call it.

"¿Río?"

"¿Qué?"

"Won't you give me your name?"

His smile faded slowly. "No."

"Why?" I whispered.

"For the same reason you could not confirm aloud what Eli and Emmett already knew about you."

Sure, I was disappointed. But I couldn't blame him. I looked down at my hands—the ones that had built his prison—and knew whatever safety I felt around him would always be one-sided.

"Lo siento," he said quietly.

"Don't apologize. You're right to hold on to it."

"I am grateful you told me your story, though," he said, "and sad indeed to learn you are not free to love who you wish. Perhaps you were right. Perhaps the Currents brought us here because they knew we would meet."

My face flushed. "Why do you say that?"

He looked pityingly up at me through the iron bars.

"Because we are both caged."

RÍO

We all know the Songs of Sorrow. The chronicles of unimaginable cruelty from the humans who bound their own kind in chains and filled the hulls of their creaking vessels to bursting with fledglings and the grown. When in desperation these prisoners would cast themselves to the sea, our kind laid their bodies to rest in Neptune's robes, horror-struck and confused. What terrors would tempt men to abandon their lives to a sea that could not heal them?

I had once asked you, Mother, what had marked them for such treachery. "They were not light-skinned," you said.

Benigno's skin, though lustrous, is dark. Thus, when he spoke with distant eyes of seeking a harmony that would accept him, I assumed his appearance was the only reason such fear lived inside him. Imagine my dismay at learning humans would also condemn him for the tender leanings of his heart! His willingness to sing for my comfort surprises me less having now heard how generously he gave his affection to a companion who understood not the exquisite pearl Benigno had cultivated for his keeping.

"Estupido," he called himself for being afraid when he shares his meals with *me*, who had exploited my first moments alone with him to strangle him. Can he not see how valiant an act his protection is?

Benigno is braver than I. With every seashell he gives me, I long to meet his courage with a shell of my own. And yet, though the desire to give him more of myself rises each day like a tide, when Benigno asked for my name, I could not share it.

I told him revealing his truth can be learned like swimming. What I did not say was that I am learning as well—to tread the waters of a truth more frightening than anything I have learned about humanity.

Something in his nature calls to mine with music both familiar and strange. Despite the wisdom of my harmony, despite everything I believed possible, my heart is cultivating a pearl. For a *human*.

And the more I learn about Benigno, the more he teaches me to swim.

SIXTEEN

For the rest of March through early April, Morgan took Sonia on an exhaustive tour of the five boroughs, returning in quick daylong spurts where Morgan blustered through the theater like a gale force wind, nitpicked my progress, then hid in his tent with his pipe before it was back on the road with them both. I got the feeling that Sonia's resilience as Sam Morgan's compañera was wearing thin because we hardly ever saw her anymore.

It was nice having the theater to myself, though. While the primer on the friezes dried, I towed the wire skeletons of museum monstruos into the orchestra seating and took down the curtain—for scrubbing, but also to leave the stage exposed so Río and I could carry on a conversation over the lip of his tank to cure our mutual boredom while I worked.

Generally speaking, Río was a snob who found everything about the world of men barbaric and extreme, but it didn't stop him from indulging my questions or enjoying the impressions I did of Oscar Barnes, Farty and Dan, or my old foreman in Puerto

Rico, whose missing teeth lent a squeak to all his consonants that had him avoiding *v*'s and *f*'s altogether.

I got the feeling Río liked the attention.

Little by little, my merfolk education deepened in ways I was certain Morgan's research never had. Apart from the babel of languages he spoke—and his attachment to calling me "Barnacle"—Río knew things about the ocean I'd always wondered about, like whether Atlantis exists (it used to) or if the Devil's Triangle is as dangerous as they say ("Claro que no."). Among the more fascinating things I learned was that merfolk were not born ni macho ni hembra—that becoming male or female in body happened only once one's soul had chosen "its truest form."

"Some are neither maid nor man. A good many are both, though Spanish and English have yet to accommodate such realities," he remarked dryly. "For all your words, your language is rather primitive."

"*Primitive*, eh? There a word for 'comemierda' in your language?"

He smirked. "If I stare at you long enough, I am sure I can come up with one."

"Ah, shaddup."

Now that all my lunch breaks took place over Río's tank, I started leaving the house earlier to pick up fresh fish from the Iron Pier markets, necessary for charming Río into answering ruder inquiries like the one I was about to ask.

"What's with the sharp spines on your fins? Do they make you especially hard for predators to kill?"

Río laid back on his watery hamaca, scratching shapes into a seashell. He pointed the graver at my shirt. "I see you have stripes on that garment, Barnacle. Does that make you an especially dim-witted bass?"

"Vete de aquí," I muttered, reining in my laugh. Then, after a beat, "What's a bass?"

He sighed wistfully. "Delicious."

"All right, well, if you're not dangerous and you're not magical, did marineros make up *everything*? What about wrecking ships and luring sailors down to the depths?"

Río rolled his eyes mightily. "Sky and sea, they were bound to conjure some idiotic fantasy to explain their limited encounters with our kind and skirt blame for their shipwrecks." His tail flicked in irritation. "When water claims a human life, fault the sailor, not the sea."

I took a bite of my hot dog, mopping up the juice before it could run off my chin and into his water. "You sound just like Tití Luz. '¡*Todo lo prieto no e' morcilla, Benigno!*'" I said in her lilting mountain accent.

Río's eyes drifted to the center of my chest where San Cristóbal hung. "You loved your tía very much."

"Couldn't be helped," I admitted. "When your family and ten years of memories get swept away in a hurricane, it's easy to love the one who thought you were worth saving."

"You do not remember your family?"

My last swallow of lunch went down dry. "Tití tried to find them after the storm. She put out the word that she'd rescued a banged-up muchachito from the river, but when nobody came to claim me, everyone figured my family got washed out in the rapids with the hundreds of other boricuas who disappeared."

Río held himself like he was bracing against a chill. "You speak as though it does not pain you."

"I ain't gonna cry about it," I said, tucking San Cristóbal back into my shirt. "You can't change what happened. Better to just accept it and move on."

"Benigno." He brought himself upright again. "Do you mean to say you do not cry?"

I crumpled the wrapping. "What does that matter?"

"It *matters*," he insisted. "Salt water has healing properties. That is why our tears are made of it. Why should you hold them in?"

I wasn't sure how to answer him. As awful as I often felt—not just about the San Ciriaco hurricane, but about *everything*—my brain had figured out that, if I dwelled on the injustices of my life, the hurricane would rage in me long after the clouds had dissipated and wash me out as well.

"Do you want to know what I think?" he asked.

"No, but I bet you're gonna tell me."

"I think you have not yet grieved."

"Of course I've *grieved*—"

"If that were true, then your eyes would not have forgotten how to perform their most basic function," he said with more concern than judgment. "Like the armored sea cradle, you are protecting yourself."

"From what? ¿El cuco?"

"From a pain that has followed you here and demands to be felt."

That hot dog was souring in my stomach. "You don't have to make me sound so heartless."

"To the contrary. The softest hearts wear the thickest armor. I have seen enough of your heart to know it exists."

Santa María. Every time he dug out bits of me to redeem, I worried the dirt it kicked up wouldn't rinse off later. "Well, it's how I am. Not even God can fix me, all right?" I let out a hollow laugh. "I oughta know, I've prayed enough times."

"Perhaps that depends on what you call a god," he said solemnly. "And what you are praying for."

"I stopped praying after Tití Luz went. Although . . . bueno, I guess that's a lie."

"Is it?"

"That night. You know the one. I prayed for comfort," I said, heat creeping into my ears. "For you."

I ventured an embarrassed glance in his direction only to find him staring up at me like the point between my eyes was a horizon he was trying to reach.

"Then your petition was heard," he said. "You became that which you prayed for. Perhaps *you* are a god, Benigno."

There it was again. A twinge, like the sides of an open wound being painfully drawn back together with thread. I rubbed my chest uncomfortably. "We've already established that I'm a sea cradle. What about you?" I pivoted. "What kind of occupation is a 'keeper of the seas'?"

He clicked his tongue at me. "Humans are obsessed with occupations."

"All right then, what do you do in the ocean all day?"

"Merfolk do not *do* anything. We flow," he explained, reclining in the water again and resuming his shell carving. "We commune with the deep, rescue the occasional marooned creature, protect our harmonies, explore. But we age too slowly to behave like time is a thing you can outswim if you fill it up with enough *doing*."

I would've laughed if I wasn't so jealous. Whether I was picking worms off tobacco leaves or sweating before a furnace, not a *maldito* day in my life had passed when I wasn't working. "Is that what you miss the most about the ocean?" I asked. "All the, uh, flowing?"

"No."

His tail flicked again, and it spun him at an angle where he could look at the windowpane. He held the little white shell out in front of his face. "What I miss most is the moon."

Río rarely gave me an answer that didn't lead to more questions. "What's the moon got to do with the ocean?"

I expected another eye roll, but instead, he turned a wistful gaze on me that washed my neck in tingles.

"The moon and the ocean are lovers. Companions in the night," he murmured. "When the moon is full and the sea is calm, it hangs so large and luminous in the sky; I would go to the surface just to bathe in the silver glow and feel the tides rise to greet it."

His voice seemed to carve a path through the noise directly into my heart as he added, "Would that the moon could know the depth of my gratitude for its comforting light."

We stared at each other, and Dios purísimo, that's when I realized how poorly I'd hidden myself from him. I nearly asked him if he knew. If, when he fixed his blue irises on mine, he could see into my dreams and find himself there.

I cleared my throat. "You'll have the moon again one day," I said. "Te lo prometo."

He smiled at me, then closed his eyes to the rumble of the pump. I laid down above him, and we stayed that way until drowsiness pulled me off the lattice to go back home.

Before I left, I put my hand against the glass. A promise to return.

He came and placed an argentine palm on the glass against mine. A promise to wait.

Asthma woke me up ahead of the dawn the next day. I creaked up to sitting—but before I could lapse into panic, I put a clammy hand over my chest and the other on my belly the way Río had told me to. I closed my eyes.

"You are just thirsty," I whispered in Spanish to the empty room. "The air is water . . ."

Río's techniques were calming my breathing a bit, so I figured a bath might settle the rest. Moving my wheezing lungs to the Albemarle's porcelain tub, I sank into liquid warmth, inhaling VapoRub-scented steam through my nose. My hand went back over my heart, fingers tangling in my necklace and the sparse hair on my chest, the other hand on my stomach.

My skin felt different in the tub. Awake in ways the rest of me wasn't.

As I relaxed into the water's silk touch, without meaning to, my thoughts floated back to Río. To pewter lips and copper hair. To the glittery luster of warm lamplight on his skin and scales. How his blue eyes came alive when he talked about the moon and looked at me with an almost aggressive compassion for the ways I fell short of the man I pretended to be.

I could almost ignore it before. Río was objectively beautiful; it was easy enough to write off my fascination as the probable outcome of daily exposure to a mystery of nature. But the more time I spent with him, the less monster waves invaded my nightmares, and the more I dreamt of Río and me, the open sea, and his deep, musical voice delivering me to the sunrise.

I breathed in, closed my eyes . . . and let my fingers venture down . . .

Just past my navel, I stopped them.

I dragged my body out of the bath, toweled off, and dressed without looking in the mirror in case something had washed off in the water that I didn't want to lose. Before I left, I braced myself at the sink, listening to water drip off San Cristóbal like a ticking clock.

Santa María, ayúdame, I prayed. *I think I am the fish, and he is the net.*

RÍO

Benigno's cart overwhelms him today. His jaw tight and a sheen
of perspiration across his bare forearms, he pushes the heavy load
up the path to my cage. A hazard of large sacks is
balanced before him, the contents of which I cannot
make out from where I float.

He tells me he has come to "decorate the tank" and hopes
I will assist him in the endeavor.

While there is still daylight, he carries each sack to the grate
and sets loose more sand and gravel from the beach than I have
touched in an age, a trove of small seashells embedded in the
grains like treasures meant for my discovery. I shape it in gentle
slopes across the floor with my tail. I want to burrow
in its familiar comfort.

When the last of his burdens is carried up to my roof—a thick
branch of driftwood for a seat—he pauses to rest himself.

Deft fingers sweep stray curls of his black hair aside, clearing a
path for the cloth he drags along his cheek into the supple
cleft of his throat. When was his last sip of water?
His lips look far too arid.

A kiss would restore their shine . . .

I catch myself again, watching Benigno with my heart
alight and heat in my eyes.

What would he do if he knew that, when he is near me,
I hunger for more than my freedom?

SEVENTEEN

The cuatro was out, and I was celebrating my first full month working at the Menagerie. With Morgan and Sonia still running around the city, I took the liberty of improving Río's living conditions on the pretense of dressing it up like a real aquaterrarium. Río was so pleased, I forgot to care what Morgan might think of what I'd done.

"Mm, I like that melody," he said, popping a last bit of flounder into his mouth. "I would like it even better without a steam engine in my ears."

I grimaced apologetically. "You know I can't turn it off."

"Then I shall keep complaining," he muttered. "Are there words to that song?"

"Some, but I could use some help with the rest." I picked up the pace:

> *Llévame, río, hasta el mar,*
> *Sobre olas azules de agua cristal.*
> *Porque soy un muchacho al que le gusta cantar . . .*

I hummed through the rest of the verse. "And that's it. I'm stuck."

Río's fluke appeared in front of his chest, folding over flat like a table so he could prop his elbows on it. "Why, Barnacle, have you made up a song about me?"

I busied myself with adjusting strings. "Oye, 'río' means 'river.' It's not always about you, your highness."

"What a shame I lack legs," he said, his fins slipping elegantly back under the surface. "I rather like your boleros, and dancing seems a perfectly civilized way to enjoy them."

"Who says the way you swim isn't dancing?"

He pulled his shoulders back and swept a thick wave of hair off his face. "In that case, when I teach you to swim, you will learn to dance as I do." Brightening, he added, "And that shall be your next lyric! 'Con tritones y sirenas, me gustaría bailar.'"

"Y'know, that ain't half bad." I tweaked a string back into tune and sang through the completed verse:

> *Carry me, river, out to the sea,*
> *Over the blue waves of crystal water.*
> *For I'm a young fellow who likes to sing.*
> *With mermen and mermaids, I would like to dance.*

"That'd be something, huh?" I said once I'd finished. "A human dancing with merfolk."

Río cupped his hands in the water and lifted them, visibly enjoying the sensation as it dribbled over his wrists. "It reminds me of a merfolk legend from the Tailfin Sea. About a woman—a human chieftain who mated with one of our kind."

"Can that sort of thing happen?"

He shrugged. "Any waters that might authenticate the tale are far away."

I strummed him a regal introduction. "Let's hear it then."

"As the song goes, she had revived a merman wounded and washed ashore during a great cyclone," he began with slightly histrionic flair. "Not realizing merfolk heal in seawater, she wrapped him in wet garments and ministered to his injuries until he was strong enough to call the sea to his aid, but by then, his attachment to her was so strong, he grieved the notion of a life without her. Hence, after he returned home, his visits to her shore continued as they each became the other's heartsong—an immutable bond. Perceiving the sea in her spirit, the Ocean gave her safe passage to join her lover in Neptune's robes, uniting her tribe to his harmony. It is said their descendants persist today, and that their song can be heard when one journeys to the shore where she saved his life."

Of all the mer-culture novelties Río had shared with me so far, this story surpassed them all as my favorite. "I thought you were gonna say she served him up for dinner or something, the way merfolk think humans are out to ruin the world," I quipped. "Where'd you hear that legend?"

"My mother told it to me."

I smiled. "I liked the bit about the heartsong."

He cocked his head thoughtfully at me. "From where are you descended?"

"That's anyone's guess. My tití saw all kinds of blood in me. African, obviously. Some taíno, some Dutch. Bit o' this, bit o' that."

Río went quiet again and let his eyes rest on my face, the way he often did when the night deepened, and sleepiness thinned out our banter. Except now, his gaze held something more, a curious intensity I'd been noticing more often as spring grew warmer.

"Why're you lookin' at me like that?" I ventured through half a smile. "What? I got something stuck to my face?"

"It brings me pleasure to look at you."

My hands tightened around my cuatro.

"Though," he added, surveying my surprise, "you seem strangely unaware of your beauty."

"*Beauty?*"

His voice lacked the sarcastic punch I'd grown accustomed to whenever he was kidding around. But he was still wrong. People didn't cross the street to get away from beautiful people. Beautiful people didn't invite ridicule or hate just for breathing the same air, for taking up space—

"Merfolk do not lie," he declared, as if he could hear the mean thoughts stomping around in my head. "But as it seems you do not believe me, let us make an agreement."

No. No agreements. "Río—"

"One day, I shall tell you how beautiful you are and why it is so. And on that day, you must believe it."

"Aw, just cut it out, will you?" I snapped.

Confusion washed the remnant ease from his expression. "Cut what out?"

I rifled for words without sharp edges. "You can't . . . just *say* stuff like that. Not to me."

"Why not?"

"'Cause it ain't right! Mírate, you're so"—I gestured furiously at his entire mythical self—"and I'm just—I'm not . . ." With no command of my mouth, I got to my feet and grabbed my cuatro. "I gotta go."

"Benigno?"

"It's nothing, I'm tired. See you tomorrow."

Río sank down to his chin and nodded. "Tomorrow."

I left. Chased out of the building by my own shadow.

How could I explain it to him? How *cruel* his kindness felt sometimes? Brown, Puerto Rican, and inverted, I was a walking composite of undesirable traits, and every time he said I was something more, I wanted to shake him, make him understand that I couldn't survive in this stupid town if I believed I was better than the petty allowance of scraps I lived on. More treacherous than hoping for a seat in Ornamental was believing in a world where Río wanted me.

I strode back to the Albemarle missing Tití Luz so much my insides felt bruised. There was no one to hear me confess what a rompecabezas my life had become. No one to place a cool hand on the back of my burning neck and say, "Give your problems to your guardian angels, nene. Y todo será curado."

But there's no adage or saying for a man who falls in love with another man, let alone un *tritón*. A story like that only ends with a broken heart and God's judgment.

"Bit early for work, isn't it?" came a voice from behind me.

Vera stood in a thin violet dressing gown at the bottom of the stairs, her cigarillo propped in the V of her fingers, thin streams of smoke pouring from each nostril. A smirk canted her lips as she took another drag.

"Vera! What are you doing out here?"

"Keepin' me promise. No smokin' indoors. Also"—she gestured to a large potted flowering plant at the door that hadn't existed when I left—"Igor let it slip that Madam Navya never got to celebrate Ram Navami, so I went out and got some marigolds. Put 'em out late so she wouldn't know it was me."

"Wow." My eyebrows lifted in surprise. "That's real considerate of you, Vera."

"Aye, well, if karma's real, mine could use some help." Glancing past me at the screen door to check for unwelcome ears, she leaned in. "So, which is it? Henderson's? Conner's? Go on, you can tell ol' Vera."

I wasn't nearly clearheaded enough for midnight interrogations. "What are you talking about?"

"Come *on*, Benny." She waved her cigarillo at my cuatro impatiently. "Which music hall are you playin' at?"

Chilly air collected in my eye sockets. "*Music hall?*"

"Tuck your jaw in. You ain't the first lad in Coney Island to ever hold down two gigs," she scoffed, dropping the butt and grinding it into the ground with her heel.

How should I temper a lie I hadn't even come up with? "Oh. I thought about it, you know, but I got my hands full with the theater and . . . decided I'd better not."

She reclined against the banister like I wasn't fooling anyone. "That does it," she announced. "Sit down, ya great sod. We're havin' a chat."

I looked helplessly over my shoulder at the screen door, then sat on the bottom step beside her. Seemed to me that saying no to a fire-breather came with more risks than benefits.

"I'm the only member o' this company what chose the carnival life, you know. Everyone else were run out of options or scouted but me." She looked sideways at me. "And now, you."

"You don't think I was scouted?" I snorted. "Morgan practically sold me a dog to get me to come to Coney Island."

"You had a trade. You made a choice," she said, "and that's 'cause you was lookin' for something when you walked off that steamer from San Hoo-ann. It's why every time I walk into that theater, I catch you staring at the walls wishing they'd paint themselves. I stared at me own walls that way when I were a proper housewife."

My teeth bit down so my jaw wouldn't fall open again.

"Don't look so surprised. It were the only way to stop bein' a burden on my da. Or so I figured," she murmured.

"There were always a little piece of me what knew I were never meant to play house. A spark—in here," she said, tapping her chest. "It made me an odd duck as a scrap, sneaking my brother's trousers, playing' rough with him and his mates when the other lasses was learning to tempt a lad. But then one day, fate got me a ticket to see Lord George the Imperial Sanger: The Leading Show of the World!"

Her eyes grew soft with nostalgia. "It were the first time I ever saw someone breathe fire. I thought to meself, 'Feck, if only I could make the deadliest element on earth obey my command . . . I'd burn the world to the ground and come back to life as a phoenix 'stead of a lady.'"

I let out a laugh. "That's a hell of a wish."

"Yeah, well, eventually the wishing turned to needing." She propped her elbows on her knees. "My man started drowning hisself at the pub at night only to come back wanting what I weren't willing to give him. One night, he comes into the kitchen after goin' for a swall at the pub, blathering on about when we was gonna have children and be a proper family. And I says, 'When you stop pissin' away every goddamned farthing we have on ale, ya great caffler!' So he raises his hand to slap me, but damn if he missed and got the boiling kettle instead!"

My hand clapped over my mouth, to which Vera tipped her head back and hawed with laughter against the banister. "Seamus were so drunk, he passed out right there on the rug! So, I just wrapped up his daddle, packed me things, took the rest of his drinking money, and dropped me surname," she said between giggles. "And well. Seamus couldn't find his own prick, much less a woman who left his house dressed up like his brother."

"How old were you?"

"Nineteen. I woulda been no performer yet, but the thirst for a crowd put me on the train all the way to Sandringham to catch up with that two-mile-long caravan. I marched right up to Lord George himself and told him I wanted to learn something no proper lady'd ever done before. So he brings me by the hand to the Fakir. 'This one's got a blaze in her heart,' he told him. 'Teach her how to wield it.'"

I shook my head. "Vera, either that's the biggest thumper I've ever heard, or you're the battiest lady—er, person—I've ever met."

She nudged my knee with hers. "You'll see the truth with your own eyes soon enough."

"So . . . do you really wish you were a man, then?"

Vera shrugged. "Would be nice to be the next Ella Wesner, but I don't feel much one way or the other. Some days the dress fits just right. Other days . . . it's a skin I'd like to peel off. Either way . . ." Vera pulled back her shoulders and smirked mysteriously, her hair half pinned, half falling in tawny curls around her shoulders. "On stage, I'm the Phoenix."

Ave María. Who would've guessed I'd wind up sharing a house with living proof humans could be just like merfolk who were neither man nor maid?

"That, I believe," I murmured.

"You and me, we're the lucky ones, Benny," she said, grabbing my hand and holding it firmly. "Life ain't taken away our choices, even when we been tricked into thinking it has. Way I see it, you can spend the rest of your dreary days hammering metal or painting walls 'cause that's what the world's told you you're good for. Or you can ask yourself what you really want."

I remembered the last thing Innis said to me. About living instead of surviving. What was happening in the theater each night made me feel more alive than I'd felt since the hurricane had struck through my memory. Until now, I'd held off admitting how much I wanted it—maybe even needed it.

"What if I'm not allowed to have what I want?" I asked.

"Not allowed? Or too afeart to go after it?" she said, sizing me up. "You and I know fire, Benny. Don't waste your damn life trying to smother a spark what wants to be a blaze."

Back in my room, I satisfied the momentary winding-down-for-the-night requirement by draping my bones over the duvet fully dressed. All the lamps in the Albemarle were out but mine, so I shut it off then turned my head on the pillow to stare at the April rain pelting at the window.

Eli and Emmett shared the room across from mine. I wondered distantly if they held each other at night. The only thing occupying the space beside me was my shadow, except tonight, the sight of it brought a loneliness that settled over my chest like the smoke from one of Vera's rompepechos. Before it could gather in my lungs, I closed my eyes and laid my hands over my heart and my stomach.

I breathed in. Made it sound like the sea.

As air filled my chest, my imagination filled Saul's room with water. The bed and armoire lifted off the floor, and I floated above

the sheets with them, the old props and costumes coasting over my head like manta rays. Instead of rain at my window, my mind supplied a full moon casting cool beams and ripples across my legs—until a silhouette eclipsed the silver light.

In a whiplash of sparkling scales, I imagined Río gliding through my window. Reached my hand out to meet the ghost of his sandpaper palm and pull him close. I could almost see his long copper hair swirling around our faces like paint and stilled under the covers trying to conjure his pewter smile, not four feet below a metal grill, but close enough to kiss.

How would it feel to wake up to the ocean of his eyes? To measure his perfect dimensions against my imperfect ones, breathe in the turquoise sea off his skin, and feel like home had come to find me instead of the other way around?

Don't waste your damn life trying to smother a spark what wants to be a blaze.

I got out of bed.

RÍO

I always hear Benigno before I see him, Mother. He treads so
differently upon the earth than the Shark.

Wordlessly, he climbs the steps to my cage where we observe each
other for a long moment in the din of chugging and bubbles.
He looks tired and wet from rain and, by the pinch of his
brows, almost lost. It is a meager improvement to the wounded
expression he made at hearing me call him beautiful.

He finally sets down his lamp, slips past me, and disappears into
shadow, returning with a heavy cloth coated with paint and a
long wooden seat, which he pushes flush against the open pane.
With relief as much as curiosity, I watch him lie down on it and
drape the cloth over himself for warmth, his hat tucked under
his dripping head and body curled toward the glass. Shivering,
he presses his palm against it in a wordless bid—for what?
Forgiveness? Consolation? My very heart?

He can have them all. Beautiful Benigno, who works so dutifully to bring comfort to my circumstances, then sacrifices his own by sleeping on a cold ledge. I would tell him that remembrances of his kind loveliness are all that calm my tremors of late, if only he could bear to hear me say it.

Despite the engine's relentless noise, I feel it—the quiver of his pulse through the water, swift as a sailfish—and dare to wonder if his heart beats this way for me.

I traverse the sand on fingertips toward him, my fins drifting back into place across my shoulders as I lie beside him and press my hand to his against the glass. I thought I had grown accustomed to his night-sky eyes, but they look at me differently tonight, holding my gaze like a question.

So I answer.

My other hand reaches for him, and meeting the pane instead of his cheek, traces the gentle outline of his face on the surface. Benigno's eyes close—as if he can feel me. As if, indeed, he has never felt a tender caress in his life before I tried to convey one through the glass.

Would that I could touch him again, in affection instead of rage.

When at last he sleeps, I open an eye to appreciate the softness of his body at rest, his hard edges smoothed, serene as a lake.

He looks like he is floating.

EIGHTEEN

I was in trouble. For all of Holy Week, I slept on a bench next to Río's tank, which, despite the minor discomfort of trading Saul's quilt and pillow for a drop cloth and a burlap sack, meant opening my eyes each day to fanned eyelashes, parted lips, and waves of rust-red chestnut hair drifting across the slope of Río's fins. As if I needed another reason to watch him sleep, the sun through the hopper window set his iridescent scales ablaze every morning, and *Jesucristo*, it was enough to make me give up on air altogether and try my luck breathing water instead.

None of this was exactly motivating where freeing him was concerned.

Given my updated sleeping arrangements, the extra trips between the Albemarle and the theater gave me time to wrestle with the obstacles to Río's freedom—ones that didn't involve my growing attachment to him. Between Luna Park and the ocean was Surf Avenue and that behemoth Dreamland, not to mention a public beach crawling with fishermen, vendors, and hustlers. I considered reattaching the tank wheels, but it would still take every set of arms in the Menagerie to push it through the theater's barn doors where the mares could be hitched.

One obstacle that loomed even larger than Dreamland was asking the company to betray Luna Park, to which they were nearly as loyal as they were to each other.

Not that I wasn't earning goodwill with my housemates. With leftover museum materials, I set aside time in the afternoons to install some retractable platforms in the kitchen that Madam Navya could use to access the countertops more easily. While I was at it, I got permission from Lulu to replace the back of her settee with something that wouldn't require her to prop her aching back against a bunch of flimsy pillows. On Easter Sunday, we raised our glasses to the Resurrection at a table overflowing with Igor's lamb roast, kulich, and pashka with a side of my escabeche.

But whenever riddling out Río's freedom brought me to another dead end, and it always did, I'd consider what might happen if he just stayed in Luna Park—before guilt and shame dead-ended that thought too.

Guilt because I'd considered breaking my promise.

Shame because I didn't want him to go.

On the afternoon of the first warm day since I'd arrived, the Albemarle's door opened to Sonia and Morgan, returned from the city. The showman hollered for everyone to meet him in the parlor, where we found him completely refinished in a new suit even greener than the last, single-breasted with cuffed sleeves, white piping, and engraved buttons down the front. As we took our seats, he leaned against the mantle with an impatient eye on his pocket watch, visibly uncomfortable in a room he obviously never visited.

Looked like he'd taken Sonia shopping too. She practically had to duck when she entered the foyer, so generous was the plumage on her new hat.

Madam Navya looked the Fraülein up and down. "You look like a condor landed on your head."

"I am ignoring you," Sonia declared, directing a curtsey at Igor instead who clapped his enormous hands and bellowed, "Krasivaya!"

"Whaddaya think, Benny?" She lowered herself gracefully onto the settee beside me. "Ain't I a proper lady now?"

"You were always a proper lady," I answered, then regretted it the instant she blushed.

"Well, I'm a *Manhattan* one now! What fun to roam around Fifth and Broadway in a motorcar!" She touched my arm with her gloved hand and giggled. "I can finally say I've seen Central Park, and you wouldn't believe how different it smells over there without all the horseshit in the—"

"Miss Kutzler," said Morgan sternly.

I hated the way he scolded her. Sonia's name in his mouth was sufficient to make all her cheerful energy retract like a parasol. It might be easy to confuse as fatherly if it wasn't laced with the same cruelty he used whenever he spoke to Río.

"Well now!" Morgan exclaimed brightly once everyone had seated themselves. "Aren't we a lively bunch!" A glance around the room revealed a row of drowsy stares, save for Timmy, who was under the end table taking apart the mantle clock with a stick.

"As you know, Miss Kutzler and I made good on my promise to promote, promote, promote the coming season. Within the next few weeks, you shall start seeing your faces in the *Times*, *The Sun*, and the *World*. Our investors have expressed quite a bit of eagerness for a summer season that will well outperform the one before. Which is why I've guaranteed them that this summer's earnings will not only top last summer's but outearn the sideshows of Dreamland and Steeplechase combined!"

A low din of groans filled the parlor before Lulu said what everyone was thinking: "Why'd you go and tell 'em that? The merman's a wild thing. We got no idea how it'll take to a crowd."

"Picture this . . ." Morgan strode into the center of the room as if taking the stage. "A brand-new backdrop—painted by yours truly—of ocean waves on a moonlit night. Stars and a moon hang above a mystical atmosphere of danger and intrigue! As both our outside *and* inside talker," continued Morgan with a flourish of his hat, "I simply regale them with the story of how the merman rescued Sonia from certain death, steering her safely back to shore before being fallen upon by ruffians!"

"Beggin' your pardon, but ain't *we* the ruffians?" asked Vera, gesturing around the room with her unlit cigarillo.

"Heavens, no. Let me finish." He opened his arms to the room. "The curtain parts and, behold, here dwells the water-bound hero I saved from dismemberment! No one will even know we've passed a glorified tadpole for a prince."

I stared at Morgan's act with burning eyes and sharp twinges in my palms where my fingernails had dug into them.

Across from me, Matthias reclined in his armchair, large arms folded under an expression like extreme fatigue. "So, what happens to the rest of the show with this ball o' yarn stuck in the middle of it?" he asked.

Morgan straightened his cuffs and smiled. "Not to worry, Matthias. You will all have your time to shine in a separate show of your own. Now, now," he added when Emmett started growling, "no need to fret. Morgan's Menagerie of Curiosities will remain our flagship production, and all of you, our leading players. But to whet the appetites of amusement-goers, we will prepare an exclusive two-for-one show that will open a day ahead of the season as a preview."

"A day ahead?" Eli sat up. "Who made *that* call?"

"Why, Mr. Thompson and Mr. Dundy, of course. At my recommendation."

Igor's disapproving hum rumbled through the floorboards. "No one will come on workday," he argued. "We play to empty house."

"Oh, it won't be empty." Morgan reached into his pocket, withdrew a folded-up sheet of paper, and stepped across the rug to hand it to Igor. It was the same flyer I'd seen in Morgan's tent less than a month ago, with a small change.

"'Prince of Atlantis, Preview Exhibition'?" Igor read aloud.

"That advertisement is already on every wall in Manhattan, Staten Island, Brooklyn, Queens," Morgan said. "New Yorkers can't even piss in an alley without seeing our name."

Eli snatched the flyer out of Igor's hand for a look. "That's a lot of alleys."

"And a lot of piss," mumbled Sonia.

"Consider what we are up against," Morgan exclaimed. "Steeplechase is well in our shadow, but Dreamland? The only way to beat them is to get a head start. One day will be more than enough for the Prince of Atlantis to reach renown across the city without giving Dreamland the chance to catch up!"

"But what happens when the crowds only want to see the fish-man?" Emmett demanded. "When a million cash-paying chumps realize we're a buncha gaffers compared to what's in the tank?"

Morgan's eyes narrowed. "I realize most of you began here under Jack Morgan's proprietorship, God rest his soul, but as far as I have brought this establishment since taking the helm, I don't think I need to remind you what alternatives await should your popularity . . . falter."

Shock deadened the room at the threat Morgan had made between his genteel teeth. You didn't have to live in Coney Island to know that prisons and asylums were full of curiosities without a show to perform in.

It was enough to revive Matthias, who leaned forward with a warning glare on his face. "Ain't no one here in need of your reminders, Sam."

"A little motivation hurts no one," he said with a chilly smile. "I'm counting on all of you to *plumb* the depths of your imagination—so that all who see your enchanting faces in three weeks will be reminded why the Luna Park sideshow is here to stay! What say you all?"

Gray-faced, Madam Navya threw up her hands. "We are mired in catastrophe anyway. I shall meet you all again in the next life to undo this mess."

"That's the spirit!" Morgan popped his top hat back on his head. "I'll confer with you all within the week to help you revise your performances. In the meantime, secrecy is paramount from now until opening night," he said, his eyebrows knitted in warning. "You never know who might be watching. Understood?"

A round of muttering to the affirmative brought the pleasantry back to Morgan's eyes. "Capital," he said. "You can all get back to lazing about or whatever waggery you were up to before I got here."

And with that, everyone got to their feet and scuffled anxiously out of the parlor, Igor ducking under the archway in front and me bringing up the rear.

"Benny," Morgan said. "You stay."

A quick glance over my shoulder treated me to Matthias's concerned stare before he exited the room.

Morgan leaned in close enough for me to smell the smoke already hanging off his new clothes. "I am most eager to hear you explain," he said, "what you've done to my tank."

"Oh. I figured you'd want to dress it up a little—for the show," I answered with as much indifference as I could fake. "It didn't cost a penny."

"And the merman let you do it?"

I nodded.

He sucked on his teeth. "Interesting," he said. "Has it perchance . . . said anything?"

Río withheld his voice just like he withheld his name. I felt duty-bound to protect it.

"No, but he's not looking at me like I'm a snack anymore," I said.

"It *looks* at you," he repeated. "As in, not glaring? Not sneering?"

I'd have to thread this needle just right. If Morgan thought Río actually *liked* me, he might feel justified taking back the responsibilities that had warmed the merman toward me in the first place. "He tolerates me, I guess. I know his routines now. Figured out what he likes to eat. I could keep taking care of him—if you think it's a good idea, I mean."

He took a step back and looked me up and down. "Paint me impressed," he declared. "Good thinking, making the tank an aquaterrarium. As for the rest, steady on if you believe your efforts have made an improvement on its vile temper. I'll expect you to show me just how tame it is in your presence soon enough."

Miércoles. How the hell was I supposed to show him that? "Will do," I said in a thin voice.

"You know, Benny, you remind me of myself at your age," he mused, buttoning his overcoat to leave. "Focused. Hardworking. Unperturbed by a challenge. I daresay, with some grooming, you might be a decent showrunner yourself one day. Land of opportunity and all."

Ave María, if I had a jitney for every condescending compliment a white man gave me whenever I did something too hard for them to do themselves. "That's awful nice of you to say, Mr. Morgan."

I watched him leave with my hands sweating in my pockets. Why did every solution have to spawn a new problem?

Janitor. Blacksmith. Hired hand. Of all the hats I'd collected since leaving my island, there was one I had yet to declare, and I bet it would wind up on my headstone.

Here lies Benny Caldera, Puerto Rican Fraud.

It was small consolation having dinner preparation to occupy me after Morgan's announcement. The mood at the Albemarle had curdled with the announcement of an early opening and two separate shows, leaving the company pricklier than a pincushion over what it would mean for them. I was so distracted, I burned the canned onions like I was Vera.

What would Río say once he learned I'd set up Morgan to watch us? Río's trust was a fragile thing more valuable to me than anything I owned. For all I knew, he'd retreat to his corner and never look at me again.

Igor said grace in Russian, which no one asked him to translate, and we dug in.

"I swear to Christ, Benny," murmured Eli, his eyes rolling back. "How does someone do this to a can of beans without fairy dust?"

"Don't like beans," Timmy grumbled, flicking the habichuelas off the rice with his spoon until Lulu spanked his wrist.

I grinned. "Well, I'm glad *you* like it, Eli."

"I love it," Matthias remarked. "When I performed with Buffalo Bill, the cooks there didn't have no education on making beans taste better than salty mud. That said . . ." He leaned back and wiped sauce from his mouth with his thumb. "Bill Cody ran a tighter ship than this cracked-up circus. Sam-the-Ham-Morgan telling us we gotta come up with new acts after six years keeping this damn park afloat"—he wedged a whole potato in his mouth—"all so he can play Shakespeare with his pet merman."

"You'll all be jake," muttered Lulu. "What about me? There ain't nothing special about a fat lady without a human skeleton standing next to her. Without Saul, I need a whole new gimmick. I'm gonna wind up begging Benny to teach me to play his guitar."

I wasn't sure why Lulu was so worried about her act if she and her nene enjoyed the financial security of the Albemarle Hotel. Then again, the way she mothered everyone in the company, maybe she felt responsible for more welfares than Timmy's.

"Bet Sonia don't need to come up with nothing," said Vera with a sharpness that made Sonia's cheeks redden. "Mighty fine dress you got there, princess."

"Put a cork in it," Sonia muttered. "I'll have to spruce up my act, just like everybody else."

"Ah, but you're part of the bleedin' *Prince of Atlantis* show," singsonged Vera. "Reckon all you need to do to keep your job is touch your toes."

"Like you weren't already looking for an excuse to—to start swallowing *swords* or something!" Sonia dragged her napkin roughly across her mouth, smearing her lip rouge off. "I didn't get a say in this business any more than you did. This was all about making his stupid patrons happy!"

"Now, now, settle down, you two," Lulu commanded.

"I will say," ventured Eli, "the way Morgan's been dropping dough on the renovations and motorcars, you'd think he was getting cozy with the Carnegies."

"Don't kid yourself," Matthias said. "They ain't no Carnegies. Ain't that right, Sonia?"

Her eyes were glued to her plate. "How would I know? I don't say more than two words to them."

"Why bother taking you, then?" I asked.

Sonia turned from her plate with a look to slaughter me where I sat.

"Yeah," Vera pressed. "Why did you go?"

"Don't ask me," Sonia snapped. "Sam's got this silly idea that I'm good for publicity or something."

Madam Navya shook her head. "That man is a wolf. It's a wonder he did not barter your life to those patrons if it meant an extra donation to the show."

"*Can it!*" Sonia was on her feet. "You think I don't know what all this bellyaching's really about? Reading me the riot act just 'cause I get to go downtown while you stay here twiddling your thumbs next to an empty promenade! You're all jealous!"

"Sonia," Lulu said gently, "we're only saying that something about all this smells bad. No one would ever accuse you of throwin' us under a trolley."

Vera cleared her throat and reached for her glass. "Exceptin' me. I'm definitely accusin' her."

"Oh, go jump off a bridge, Vera," Sonia spat. "You want answers, take it up with Sam. I ain't hungry no more." She untangled her skirts from the table and stormed off.

Igor folded his hands, making his plate disappear underneath them. "Vera, you are too harsh with Sonia," he boomed. "She is barely woman."

"Nineteen's old enough to stop being bloody naive about Sam Morgan," she said. "You think that posh dress and hat has anything to do with publicity? That she's the star of the Prince of Atlantis show because she's Helen Gardner? I know bribery when I sees it!"

"She wouldn't betray you," I said, then quickly added, "I mean, us."

"Rice and beans with a side of opinions nobody asked for," Emmett sniped with an eye roll.

I ignored him. "You shoulda heard her talk when she first met me. She loves the company and the show more than anything."

Matthias pushed up his glasses. "Brother's right. She's protecting us in her backward Sonia way."

Navya tutted in concern rather than her standard disapproval. "Miss Sonia needs more protection than all of us."

Vera forked the last bite of rice into her mouth and washed it down with the rest of her cider. "You lot can have your fun—how'd Sam put it?—'plumbing the depths of your imagination'? Well, if anyone cares to join me, I'm gonna go plumb the depths of the rum bottle in the parlor."

Eventually, everyone took Vera's invitation, leaving me to tidy up. I didn't have the heart to throw out Sonia's half-eaten dinner after the way she left the table, accused of things she had so little say in. I knew that feeling too well.

I took the plate to her door and knocked. Sonia answered with her hair down around her shoulders, rougeless lips, and pink eyes. She looked . . . her age.

"Thought you might still be hungry," I said.

She took the plate from me and sniffed. "I'm glad you don't think I'm a scab."

My finger threaded nervously around San Cristóbal. "You heard that, huh?"

"You should know . . . I ain't a perfect person, but I'd never do anything to hurt the company. Sam always says"—she dropped her voice low and mimicked his high-class, no-accent accent—"'What's good for the show is what's good for us all.' And, I dunno. I just think he's right."

I couldn't tell whether she was trying to convince me or herself that this was true. "That's one interpretation of 'with it, for it, never against it,' I guess."

She smiled down at the plate in her hands.

"I was wondering," she said softly. "Monday's Light the Night, and I thought maybe you'd want to go with me."

"What's Light the Night?"

Her eyes livened a bit. "The maintenance crews come back to Luna Park on Monday. Light the Night is when they turn everything on for the first time since the last season ended—the lights, the music, the rides—and that way they get to see where stuff needs fixin'. It's a helluva sight, and the only night of the year you get the whole park to yourself. I never miss it."

"You mean, you get to ride the rides?"

She slid closer and winked at me. "Sounds fun, don't it?"

It did, but her manner of persuading me was having the opposite effect. "Well, uh, I dunno. Won't we get in the way?"

"Not a bit. They'll be keen to see a couple o' kiddos like us having fun on the roller coasters. *C'monnn*, Benny," she whined. "It's a Coney rite of passage!"

I looked into her large, tear-stained eyes and rocked uncertainly on my feet. The very thought of visiting Luna on a night when the park was lit up was so enticing, I could almost feel the electric arcs of all those lightbulbs along my neck. I'd heard that entering the park at night was such a jolt to the senses that first-timers think they're hallucinating.

Going with Sonia didn't have to mean anything. It *wouldn't* mean anything. She and I would be just a *couple o' kiddos* having a romp at America's Playground. And anyway, by the injured way she lashed out at the table, I didn't think she deserved another rejection.

"All right. If it's a rite of passage."

Sonia bounced on the balls of her feet like she hadn't just been crying alone in her bedroom for an hour. "Oh, it's gonna *abso-tively* make you scream, just you wait! We'll walk over together after dinner tomorrow!"

Then, balancing her plate on one hand, she reached up on tiptoe to kiss my cheek, stepped back into her room, and shut the door, at which point one thing became abruptly clear.

I was *abso-tively* gonna regret this.

I wasn't yet halfway down the aisle in the theater when Río shouted, "I have a new verse for your song!"

A grin pulled at my lips despite my nerves. "The pump's louder than a Model T Torpedo. How do you always know when it's me?"

Lamplight lit my steps onto the stage until Río's face smirking over the glass came into view, his tail undulating in its usual hypnotic rhythm. "I can always tell," he said. "Your legs have a . . . manner about them."

"I thought I was being quiet."

He let out a genuine Brooklyn *pfft*. "Quiet, yes. As a bob of seals."

I stepped across the grill until I'd made it halfway, folded my legs under me, and sat. "I want to hear your verse, but first . . . I've got some news you're not gonna like."

Río listened stone-faced as I recounted the details of the announcement Morgan delivered in his bright new vestido—his plan to open the park ahead of schedule, the Prince of Atlantis exhibition, and how it had thrown everyone in the company into chaos as soon as they realized they'd have to compete with a second show starring none other than Río himself and the woman who'd helped snare him.

By the time I was done, he was carving a slow circle below me, scowling like I'd just polluted his water.

"The Shark has an obscene talent for aggravating me even when he is not here to do it himself," he spat. "However did you manage to convince him to make you my permanent caretaker?"

Aquí vamos. "I might've told him you were warming up to me."

He stopped pacing. "You *what*?"

"But that was it," I added quickly. "I didn't let him think you've done anything more than just look at me so he wouldn't think that . . . you know."

"That you have heard my voice." Río stared fretfully into the water. "We must be especially careful not to speak if he is near."

My ears warmed at realizing I was the only human who'd ever earned Río's conversation, but the thought of further limiting our talks was an injustice I couldn't tolerate.

"Your mother talked right into my head," I offered. "Is there a reason why you can't?"

He resumed pacing. "I can only speak to your mind if we are touching."

"There goes that idea," I muttered. "Well, we won't need to talk. Just, acknowledge my presence a little when he's watching, and that way, he'll keep me around and you won't have el Tiburón circling your tank."

Río had stopped listening. "'Prince of Atlantis,'" he hissed, thrashing his tail to send water fanning out at the bars. "That merfolk would *ever* put a crown on their own heads for—for Neptune knows what purpose! And this Sonia. Am I to be terrorized by her as well?"

I shook my head. "At this point, she's a bigger danger to me than you."

"To you? Why?"

"Apparently"—I rubbed the back of my neck—"she's sweet on me."

Río wasn't in the right temperament for interpreting yanqui slang. "What does this mean, 'sweet on you'?"

I stammered trying to come up with a way to explain it that wasn't just another colloquialism he couldn't make sense of. "It means, she *likes* me. Romantically."

He cut me an incredulous look. "Does she not know that you feel no passion toward women?"

"Río, *no one* knows that but you."

At this, he raked an exasperated hand through his hair that nearly unraveled his braid. "Drag me on a reef, Benigno, how can you expect to get me out of here if you persist in keeping yourself a secret from anyone who might help?"

"I can't just come out and say it! I know, it's human *tontería*, but I swear I'm working up to it!"

He halted in the water, splashed some over his face, and rubbed it into his eyes as if it could put out his temper like a fire. "I am sorry," he sighed, "for suggesting you endanger yourself more than you have already. I am going mad in here, Benigno."

More absurd to me than the state of human preoccupations with love was the idea that Río had anything to be sorry for. I was about to tell him so when I remembered what I'd nicked from the pantry for just this occasion. Hopefully, Timmy wouldn't be blamed for it.

"I brought you something to soften the news, but I probably waited too long." I laid myself flat on my stomach over the lattice and held out my closed fist. "Not the moon, I'm sorry to say." Then, I opened my palm to him.

He took the sugar cube between his wet fingers, turning it slowly to inspect it. "It is a white stone," he said flatly.

"Just put it in your mouth. Quick. Before it melts into the water."

Tentatively he placed the sugar in his mouth. As soon as his lips closed over it his eyes widened. "Oh," he breathed. "Oh, it is *wonderful*. What is it?"

I rested my chin on my hands, pleased at having managed to bring Río something to eat from the world of men he didn't find completely repellant. "*Azúcar*. It's cheaper to get here than it was in Puerto Rico, but I know what sweetness really costs even if these *yanquis* don't."

He surveyed me with tired eyes and managed to smile. "You always surprise me, Barnacle," he said. "Thank you for the sweetness."

"De nada. And I'll tell Sonia the truth about me tomorrow night," I said. "They're turning on the park and I promised I'd go with her. It's this big thing."

"I see . . ." Swallowing the last of the sugar, he laid back on the water below me, giving us the effect of standing face-to-face. "I hope for your sake that she will be accepting."

"Me too."

"With the Shark returned," he went on, "you will go back to your bed at night?"

I'd purposely put off thinking about that. Thinking about it now felt like getting evicted all over again, if everything I cared about had stayed locked inside the apartment.

"Guess so," I said without looking at him. "I still need to hear your verse, you know."

"All right. Sing yours first. Then I shall add mine."

I sat back up on the lattice and cleared the trace emotions from my throat.

> *Llévame, río, hasta el mar,*
> *Sobre olas azules de agua cristal.*
> *Porque soy un muchacho al que le gusta cantar.*
> *Con tritones y sirenas, me gustaría bailar.*

"Now you."

"'*Acércate más, amante del mar,*' dijo las olas de agua cristal," he sang—in a voice so rich and resonant it stopped my breath. "*El ritmo que sientes, la tentación fluvial, el latido de mi corazón es tu cantal.*"

Río's verse took on the perspective of the water, connecting the rhythm of the waves to a heartbeat that lured the human singer to the sea like a lover. Incredibly, my eyes were prickling. "Río," I breathed. "You brought the waves to life."

"They *are* alive. I thought they deserved a say. Do you not approve?"

I might have told him everything right then and there. That his words were more precious to me than I had words to express. That I'd never slept so easily as I did beside him and wanted to give him so much more than the bit of sweetness I could fit in my palm. Part of me—the part he'd woken from a decades-long sleep—was desperate to say he'd leveled the fortress around my heart the moment I first locked eyes with him in the East River.

But freedom and I were mutually exclusive. And Río could only want one.

"Es perfecto," I whispered. "Absolutely perfect."

Río

When the Shark returns in the morning, his footsteps
do not drag.

"Miss me?" he asks with a smile tipped like a sinking schooner.

From his pocket, he produces a small bowl with a long black
stem that he places in his mouth. His other hand flicks open
a little case, and a small flame sparks to life, which throws my
heart back into my nightmares like tinder. I make fists of my
hands to stay my fins as he ignites the kindling within, and
smoke begins to rise.

"I see your accommodations have greatly improved since I've
been away. You've a proper aquaterrarium now, not that you've
earned it," he says, puffing dirty vapor into the air. "Benny says
the improvements to your tank were a product of his
own initiative."

Though tremors threaten, I smother them at the mention of Benigno's name lest losing command of myself invite the Shark onto new prey.

"In the wake of so many improvements to your accommodations, one can't help but wonder where his motivation is coming from."

He begins walking his usual path around my cage. "The selkies of Scotland. The ningyo of Japan. The Iara of Brazil. La sirène and Mami Wata. So many varied accounts of sea-dwelling mimics and shapeshifters, and yet they all share a particularly powerful feature in common: a voice so mystical in its properties it can induce insanity. Infatuation. Even death," he murmurs. "Personally, I no longer have any delusions of dying from the sound of your voice, but it is a downright mystery to me that I've never heard you use it again since the night we collected you."

He turns and heads back the other way. "Benny claims you haven't said a word to him. But I've deceived enough people in my life to know a second-rate liar when I see one."

The Shark pauses by the shadow where I sit, but I do not meet his eye. "So, try me. You have no problem seething at me, so why not shout? Howl watery profanities? Punish me with a shriek to burst my ear drums? I know you can do it," he hisses softly.

I remain silent as a trench.

"No? Well. There's still time." He draws another breath of smoke from the pipe. "It doesn't matter what delusions you tell yourself; your voice, along with the rest of you, belongs to me."

He leaves, and my jaw aches with restraining myself from doing exactly as he asks. Far from punishment, what he truly wants from my voice is command over it—a power I would sooner die than give him.

The Shark must never know Benigno has heard me sing. The revelation would surely bring an end to Benigno's life.

And if anything were to happen to him, neither pride nor dignity nor the condemnation of my ancestors could prevent me from using my voice to beg for death.

Nineteen

onia didn't dress in anything as extravagant for our
Monday night jaunt as she had the day she returned
with Morgan. Rather, she swept in with a burgundy
skirt and matching box coat, which she complained was out
of fashion by several years. I told her I didn't know jack about
fashion beyond making sure my union suit went under my
shirt and pants.

"Men don't worry about clothes unless they're Sam Morgan,"
she remarked. "He thinks he's a walking billboard for the show."

"Is that why you can see his suit from Midtown?"

"Benny!" She slapped my arm in mock surprise. "Who knew
you had some bite in that mouth of yours!"

Since March when I'd first arrived in Coney Island, the
Surf Avenue strip had gradually drawn more tourists; mostly
night-trippers looking for an excuse to get out of the city for
lower-key amusements. As we meandered down the avenue, a
small crowd of gentry smoked in front of Buschmann's Music Hall
waiting for the evening's entertainment to begin.

Sonia took my arm on Twelfth Street and squeezed it. "I finally get to join you on a nighttime walk," she said blithely. "What do you get up to out here anyway? Offseason wages ain't enough to buy you more than a cheap thrill unless . . ." She wilted under the brim of her lacy hat. "You're not hitting up those peep shows on the Bowery, are you?"

"No!" I laughed. "I just like the water. The view's nice at night."

It was almost the truth. Seeing Río and visiting the shore weren't too different. In either case, my proximity to drowning felt dangerously close.

We arrived at the front gates of Luna Park only minutes before seven. As we approached, I gently pulled my arm out of her grip to dig out Saul's keys before a Brooklyn accent thicker than Sonia's interrupted me.

"Eyyyyy, Fraülein!"

We followed the sound to the little booth where Oscar Barnes stood in a new pair of coveralls. A pipe poked out of his mustache.

"Why, Mr. Barnes," declared Sonia as the portly man sauntered toward us. "I do believe you're wearing a new coat of paint yourself!"

As she tucked into my side, Oscar's bright eyes shifted onto me. "Benny!" He snapped his fingers and pointed one back in my face. "Calzone, right?"

"Caldera."

"That's what I said!" He turned back to Sonia. "This must be your third Light the Night, ain't it? I'd've thought this was old hat for you by now."

"I wouldn't miss it!" Tugging on my arm, she added, "This is Benny's first."

Walking backward to his post, Oscar pointed his finger at me again and grinned fiendishly. "Hold on to your britches, kid." Then, he disappeared into the booth.

Sonia's breath brushed my ear. "Look up."

I followed her gaze skyward to the red corazón that held the words "THE HEART OF CONEY ISLAND."

There was a loud, echoing *chock* sound followed by another—then another. The hum of unleashed electricity crackled in my ears, and the next thing I knew, a light so bright it doused the stars exploded into my vision, sending me stumbling backward. Sonia, being stronger than the average lady, caught me easily by the arm before I could fall, though she was laughing so hard, she almost tumbled down with me.

The entire park lit up with thousands—maybe *millions* of lights. Lights on the spires. Lights lining the columns and adornments. Lights in every letter of "LUNA PARK" blinking on and off to their own musical meter. I had to shield my eyes with my hand, it was so bright.

"Dios misericordioso," I breathed.

"Come on, ya big goop." Sonia tugged me into the main promenade, empty and dark whenever I snuck in to see Río—now brilliant with artificial light.

I was Odiseo arriving in Ogigia, every tower and turret awash in a magical dreamlike glamour, even in the presence of maintenance men, electricians, and other carnival staff who came to delight in the promise of a summer season more prosperous than the last. We walked toward the towers that stood in the center of the main promenade, now surrounded by a lake of bright blueish-green water.

Sonia walked us right up to the edge. "Now don't get spooked when—"

A geyser erupted from a spile in the lake and I nearly jumped into Sonia's arms.

"—the fountains turn on," she finished.

I clutched San Cristóbal through my shirt. "Jeez, is this how the whole night's gonna go?"

"I sure hope so," she proclaimed. "If the fountain can get your heart racing, just wait 'til I get you on a ride!"

She dragged me by the wrist down the bare concrete walkway toward the Circle Swing, which had bloomed overnight into a massive steeple with long metal arms from which a set of candy-colored boats hung. At the base of it, a man tinkered away at a little metal cabinet with several keys sticking out of a flat panel on top.

"Oh, Errrnieee," Sonia sang, and he hit his face on the cabinet door.

Ernie was a youngish fellow, with pink skin and sandy hair that poked out of the bottom of his worker's cap. He rubbed his smarting cheek. "Dammit, Sonia, you can't just sneak up on a guy!"

"I don't sneak, you're just unobservant," she countered. "Anyway, Benny's the newest member of the Menagerie, and you have the distinct honor of hosting our very first ride of the evening!"

I stuck out my hand. "Nice to meetcha, Ernie."

He eyed the point on my arm where Sonia had wrapped her fingers and grunted. I drew back my hand, wondering just how many guys among the maintenance crew were as sweet on the red-haired contortionist as Ernie obviously was.

My pondering was short-lived. The moment he strode around us to open the metal gate that led to the ride, my head emptied of all thoughts except, *Me voy a morir.*

"So, we're, uh, sure it's safe?" I asked, following behind Ernie as he meandered to one of at least half a dozen miniature multi-colored boats. "I mean, you're testing these to see if they still work 'cause you don't actually know, right?"

Ernie scowled. "I'd never let Sonia step foot on a clunker. I ain't no barbarian."

"Then be a good non-barbarian and hold this," said Sonia, removing the hat from her head and handing it to Ernie, who practically bowed as he took it carefully in his calloused hands.

Gesturing to my cap, she added, "You're gonna want to tuck yours somewhere safe."

He undid the chain of a bright apple-red barquito and helped Sonia inside. Left to fend for myself, I put a foot in and felt the boat glide in the air away from me, making me hop after it until Sonia reached out her gloved hand and tugged me aboard.

The seats were slippery—varnished wood—and as Ernie redid the chain, my mind ran through about a dozen scenarios in which a solitary aluminum-link chain would do nothing to save my life in the event the boat detached from the metal rig that held it.

"You are abso-tively gonna love this," she squeaked.

"Can't wait," I said in a strangled voice. Another loud noise made me flinch, and my hands flew to the metal bar in front of us. Ernie had returned to his post beside the cabinet, his sunburned arms folded across his chest as the tower slowly began rotating, and with it, the boat.

We were picking up speed. The barquito started lifting away from the ground.

"Jesucristo . . ." I held on.

The faster it spun, the higher we rose. In seconds, I could see over the top of the front gate—a sight that whipped away as quickly as it had appeared. My eyes clouded over with tears from the chilly wind that lashed at our faces, my belly hollowed out like I'd left my stomach on the concrete.

Sonia was squealing.

Picking up yet more speed, the large metal arm that held us began to splay outward, tipping us sideways until I could look over my shoulder and see the ground parallel to us.

At which point, I lost my grip on my seat. But instead of careening to my death, I slid in the other direction and crashed right into Sonia's hip.

"¡*Coño!*" I yelled over the noise. "I'm so sorry!"

"That's supposed to happen!" she yelled back. "Now put your hands up! Like this!"

Sonia took her hands off the metal bar and lifted them over her head. She had obviously gone insane.

"Whooooooo!" she howled jubilantly. "Come on, before it's over!"

I swallowed hard. One at a time, I lifted my hands off the metal bar.

I did not die.

Qué locura. We were *flying*.

The Circle Swing was churning now, dipping in the air only to crest the next moment into the wind. I worried that the force of my body against Sonia's hip was crushing her, but by the manic joy on her face, I realized she couldn't feel it. She was laughing and laughing—at me, at the sky, at the ground below us—and feeling half-hysterical myself, I started laughing too.

Emancipated from gravity, we cut a path into the wind. My face was numb, but I didn't mind.

It felt like I had no body at all.

Sonia escorted me all over Luna Park. With every ride, I learned to think less and less about the indignity Sonia might be suffering every time a sharp turn or dip forced her into my lap, because there was no getting around it, and it didn't seem to occupy her thoughts at all. Like everyone else who had ever entered Luna Park, Sonia and I had checked social propriety at the front gate.

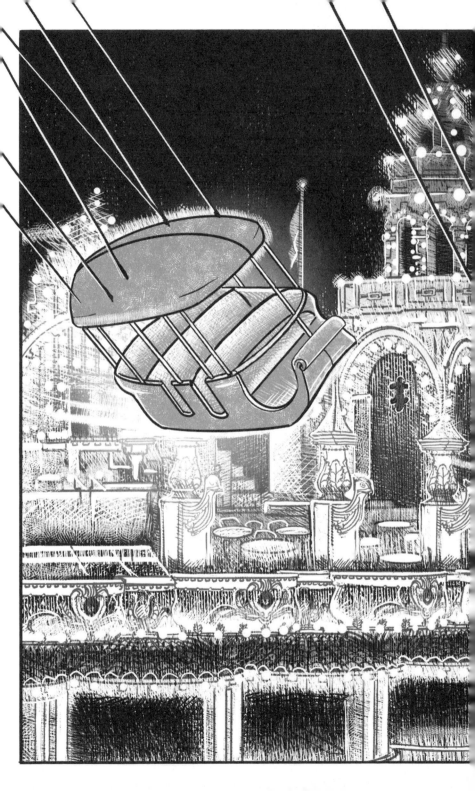

At some point, Sonia walked us past a chained gate, behind which stretched a shaded avenue of straw huts in disrepair. She explained it was the now-abandoned Igorot Village, an attraction not unlike the Menagerie in that humans were the paid exhibit. When I asked why Luna Park had decided to host a commune of Filipino natives, Sonia explained that it was meant to teach Americans about "our new conquest in the Pacific"—before the proprietor got himself thrown in the clink for fraud. I wondered uncomfortably whether Puerto Rico would ever find itself represented in an American amusement park somewhere, or if annexation had spared it from such a crude display.

Then I thought of Río, who wouldn't be paid and had no commune of his own. If only Morgan's intent to erase Río's culture and replace it with a fake one was the sort of fraud he could get locked up for.

We meandered around for hours, boarding as many rides as we could until my throat was raw from yelling and my hair looked like I'd lost a brawl with a barber. It was nearly nine thirty when we finally got to the rear enclosure where the Menagerie Theater stood across from the ballroom, the waning moon bright overhead, as if to remind us no electric light bulb could compete with the real thing.

"I saved the best for last," said Sonia, tugging me toward the enormous, brightly lit open-air dance floor.

The ballroom facade was bordered with archways for onlookers and dancers alike to come and go as they pleased, with chandeliers and shining wood-paneled floors. On a wide platform in the corner sat a red wagon calliope with golden pipes glistening behind the gilded window. An older, sloped-backed man pushed a large industrial broom around the dance floor, kicking up little clouds of dust as he did so.

"Mr. Davis! Do your girl Sonia a favor and fire up that calliope!"

The man aborted his sweeping and squinted at us. "Henh?"

"Cal-li-oh-pee . . ." She pantomimed a cranking motion with her arm. "Turn it onnn!"

"Oh, you wants old Orpheus to play sumthin', do ya?" Mr. Davis adjusted his hat and waddled over to the red wagon.

Meanwhile, Sonia walked around to face me. "You know how to waltz, don't you?"

My hand searched for San Cristóbal. If I was going to tell her my secret, now was the time. "You know, I don't really dance—"

"Lucky I'm a good teacher." She stepped toward me and took one of my hands in hers. The other, she removed from my chest and placed on her waist. Across the floor, bright, airy music filled the air, poor Davis leaning into every crank of the machine. I wondered if Río could hear it.

"Now then. One, two, three, one, two, three . . ." Sonia lifted our hands and steered me in an arch around her. "Hey, you're a fibbing fibber, Benny Caldera! You're a better waltzer than me!"

Sweat had started gathering across my forehead. "We had la danza back in Puerto Rico. My aunt taught me."

Sonia studied my face in a way that made it impossible to meet her eyes. "There's a lot we don't know about you, huh."

"Nothing special."

"You don't gotta be special," she said, as we turned on the floor. "You just gotta be real."

Tell her now, I thought. "You're right. Sonia, there's something—"

"Take me for instance," she went on distantly. "I'm not real."

My eyes snapped back to hers. "What?"

"I'm a figment of Sam's imagination." Suddenly, her smile looked stilted. "Every person in Coney Island looks at me and sees a walking poster of the Flexible Fraülein—they don't know there's a heartbeat under all the paint. I ever tell you my real name?"

I shook my head.

"It's Mary. Mary Schneider, after my grandmother. Sonia Kutzler's just the stage name Sam gave me. Said it sounds more exotic. Imagine that."

Still wearing that forced smile, she looked over her shoulder at the calliope, then up at the ceiling, willing away the tears that had suddenly gathered in the corners of her eyes.

"It don't matter," she said quietly. "It's gonna be mine one day, ya see. I'm the youngest one in the company and the only one who knows the business side of sideshow business. When the rest of the Menagerie retires, I'll be the next Morgan, and with a young guy like you in the company now, we could even manage it together! It'll all be worth it . . . as long as the show *keeps running*."

My stomach twisted as I realized she was trying to say something without saying it. I leaned close so I wouldn't be overheard.

"Sonia, what really goes on in Manhattan?"

Her eyes met mine, and the confident coquette was gone. Then she glanced about nervously, as if Morgan might be hanging around the corner with his derringer cocked at us.

"Sam's been borrowing money from some dicey folks in the Lower East Side," she answered tightly. "It's how he's been paying for everything—the tank, the improvements, the clothes, the whole nine yards. But these folks . . . they don't do nothin' gratis."

"'They'?" My heart was beginning to pound. "Who's 'they'?"

"Frankie Agostinelli and his goons used to run the Coney numbers racket back in the day. Well, Sam hunted 'em down. Told them they'd get back their run of Surf Avenue if they helped him compete with Reynolds. Every time we go back, Sam asks for more dough, and now they're antsy for proof that Sam's gonna make good on the deal."

She rattled in a breath the very same way I did in an asthma fit.

"He thought I might soften them up."

I spun her around. My turn to look for eavesdroppers, but there was only Mr. Davis perusing yesterday's *Sun* with one hand as he cranked Orpheus with the other. "Sonia, did they do something to you?"

Her face blanched beneath her rouge. "Frankie took a shining to me. Said he wanted to see m-more of me," she stammered, her voice suddenly frail.

I stopped dancing.

"Dios mío. That bastard *sold* you to them," I said breathlessly. "Didn't he?"

Sonia looked anywhere but my face, like she was searching for a hole in the ground to jump into. "With a couple drinks in me, it's . . . it's not so bad. W-what else was he supposed to do?"

"What else was he—*Sonia*." I was losing it. My English too. I backed away from her so my profanity wouldn't hit her on its way out of my mouth. "¡Me cago en ná!"

"I know, I know, but once the debt's settled, I'm free, you know? One more reason why, in the horse race between Luna Park and Dreamland," she said through quivering lips, "Luna's just *got* to win!"

The Heart of Coney Island twisted before my eyes. A fantasy land running on electric light bulbs and corruption.

"Benny, *please*, you can't tell no one—"

"Sonia, the company's gonna lose their minds when they find out Morgan's done this to you! Matthias'll crush him *and* Frankie What's-His-Face to a powder!"

"That's exactly why it's gotta stay a secret!" she insisted. "Don't you get it? Frankie owns half the cops; if anyone else finds out, he won't just go after Sam, the whole company will be in danger! Promise me, Benny. *Don't. Tell.*"

"Coño, carajo . . . Fine! If it's really life or death, I won't," I growled under my breath. "But Sam Morgan's a dirty louse and a liar and I *hate* him for what he's done to you!"

"You don't have to say that—"

"I do have to say it! The way he treats you. The way he treats"—I caught myself before I said Río's name—"*everyone*! Like you're not people, just *things* he can just pawn off on a stage for fifteen cents a head. You deserve better!"

"Oh, Benny," she murmured. Her eyes were big, green, and leaking tears onto her grateful smile. "You really mean that?"

"Of course I—"

I didn't see it coming. Sonia dug her fists into my vest and crushed her mouth against mine so eagerly, her teeth nearly sliced open my lip. I took her wrists with both hands—I tried to push her off—but her grip was so strong, I didn't know what kind of force I could use without hurting her or implicating myself in something a whole hell of a lot worse in front of Mr. Davis. There was nothing to do but pray she'd end it soon so I wouldn't pass out from holding my breath.

She did. It only took an extra second for her to notice I'd gone stiff as a statue.

Ashen, she stepped back. "Oh my God," she whispered. "Oh *God*, I'm an idiot . . ."

I was panting. "Listen, Sonia. There's something you gotta know about me. Something I should've told you a while ago—"

"How did I not see it," she moaned.

"It's my fault for not—"

"There's another girl, ain't there?"

The sentence died on my tongue. "*What?*"

"All the late-night walks and, oh God . . ." She covered her mouth and started retreating farther away from me. "I'm such a *fool*."

I lunged forward and held onto her shoulders. "You're not a fool or an idiot! You've got it all wrong— Aw, Sonia, please don't cry!"

The ballroom went suddenly silent. "Miss Kutzler!" Mr. Davis pointed at me. "This man upsetting you?"

"No, no, he's all right," she called back, backing out of my hands. "I gotta go."

And she gathered her skirt and hightailed it, stranding me under the chandelier with Mr. Davis who, by his puckered brow, had already decided who was responsible for the sudden change in her disposition.

If I ran after her, he'd think I was pursuing her. So, I ran in the other direction.

To the Menagerie.

TWENTY

The electric daylight penetrating the theater was scant, so I lit the lamp and rushed toward the only person I didn't have to lie to.

"It sounds like a maelstrom out there," Río shouted as I jogged through the empty house. "What in the Seven Seas is happening?"

"The whole park's turned on, remember?"

He frowned, following me around the tank side as he stuffed his fingers in his ears. "Hardly a worthy excuse to pollute the air with such barullo!"

"Yeah, well, air pollution's a permanent fixture in this town." I tore off my coat and dropped it absently on the ground. "It's right up there with hot dogs and subway rats."

Whether all the flashing lights and blaring sounds had lit my nerves on fire, or I was suffering some kind of kiss-induced sensory collapse, for once, I felt just as antagonistic toward that stupid, noisy pump as Río felt all the time. In two strides, I went over and turned off esa maldita cosa.

Río dropped his hands slowly, watching me and my lamp come up the rungs and slump down onto the lattice.

"Benigno, are you well?"

I reached for San Cristóbal and tried to settle my breathing. I wasn't sure what I was searching for in Río's company. I wanted to banter in the easy way we always did together, but my thoughts were caught in a loop like I'd left my brain on the carousel.

Sonia's colorless face when I didn't kiss her back. The wounded way she ran off. The horrifying secrets I had no choice but to keep unless I wanted to endanger the livelihoods—and lives—of my housemates. What would happen once the rest of the company saw her in that state? How hard would they have to pry for her to tell them how I'd—

"*Benigno.*"

"Yeah?"

"Your mind is far away."

I wanted to be far away. But I also didn't want to be alone with my panic. It felt like my ribs were caving in . . .

"Tell me what is wr—"

"Sonia kissed me."

Río's tail went still. "Kissed you. But . . . she is a woman."

"I know what she is, Santa María." I scrubbed a hand over my clammy face.

"Benigno, did she . . ." His voice faltered. "Force it?"

My words were gone. I had none, in any language, to describe what had happened.

"*Benigno*—"

"I wish I could say no." My voice was barely there. "I wish I could say *I* kissed *her* and it made us both happy because, carajo, wouldn't it just be so much *easier*? Every guy wants a kiss from Sonia Kutzler, but she had to go and fall for the only idiot in Coney Island who can't kiss her back. You shoulda seen the way she looked at me."

"Just because she looks at you does not mean she sees you," Río said with all the steadiness I couldn't muster myself. "Otherwise, she would not have taken what you did not offer."

"Doesn't matter," I muttered, my breaths coming shorter and faster. "'Cause I know what's next. Soon the rest of the company will figure out what happened. Matthias'll cut me down for being careless. Eli will know I lied to him. And Morgan? God knows what he's letting his patrons do to Sonia for money. If he finds out what she told me, he'll fire me, and that's if he decides I'm not worth plugging with a bullet and dropping in the Hudson. I'll have to run, go back to the beginning, make it alone all over again in this stinking, *godforsaken* city with nothing but smoke to breathe every day of my life—"

"Benigno," Río said with alarm, "you are punishing yourself most cruelly for something you did not cause. I insist you stop."

"I cause things just by existing!" I covered my face with my hands. "Madre de Dios, why'd I even come here? What was the point of crossing the ocean just to find a different hell everywhere I go?"

"Do not say that," he said gently. "What would become of me without you? Where would I be without my Barnacle?"

"Where would you *be*?" I raked an exasperated hand through my wind-whipped hair. "*I* built this tank, Río! You wouldn't be trapped in this maldita cage, you'd still be in the East River—"

"Saltwater estuary—"

"You know what I mean!" I half shouted. "You'd be free! You'd still have a harmony!"

"You could not influence the Shark's actions any more than I could," he argued, his voice finally rising. "Merciful Neptune, have you no compassion for yourself?"

The answer, we both knew, was no, though the word never found its way past my clenched teeth. I wanted to run without stopping, bury myself in the ground. Anything to stop feeling like a wounded animal being hunted by a ruthless god.

"Si te digo la verdad . . ." My eyes squeezed shut as the darkest secret I carried rose up my throat like an oil slick in water. "Sometimes I think the hurricane hadn't meant to leave me behind. That everything I am is an accident because I should've been swept out to sea."

"Enough!"

I looked down. Río looked stricken.

"Enough of this," he said again. "Come into the water."

"¿Qué dijiste?"

"I wish to comfort you. I cannot do it with bars between us."

My stomach dove into my heels at the suggestion. "Comfort *me*? But—"

"Do humans not console each other when they are in pain?"

"They do—*we* do, but . . ."

"But what?"

Staring unblinkingly at him—at the scar Morgan had carved into his skin—I said the words in Spanish so I didn't have to bear the sting of them in English. "No lo merezco."

His blue eyes flashed stubbornly. "You do not know what you deserve. You think yourself unworthy for your hand in my captivity when I have already forgiven you! Why do you refuse to forgive yourself?"

"After everything I let happen—"

"Of everyone who dragged me from the water that night, *you* are the only one who has sought to right the wrong," he said emphatically. "What have I needed that you have not tried to give me? Food, music, protection—hope! *You* have been my comfort and my friend. If I have any chance of surviving this place, it is because of *you*."

His hand rose out of the water, silvery palm upturned.

"I cannot take your burdens," he went on. "But if you let me, I can bear them with you for a while."

I stared at him with his arm lifted over his head like Lady Liberty, his open hand offering promises I was afraid to believe in. With his eyebrows bunched up and low over his wide eyes, he looked nearly as grieved as I felt.

"I can't swim," I whispered.

"I can carry you."

"My lungs—"

"Benigno, I will not let you drown."

Something about Río's expression touched a long-neglected corner of my mind like an echo from a forgotten dream. I stood up on the metal grate and slid off my shoes, placing them neatly out of the way along with my socks. He watched patiently as I rolled up my trouser legs, undid the buttons of my shirt, then shrugged out of it. The hatch groaned as I lifted it, and I made a mental note to grease the hinges later.

Crouching at the lattice's edge, I reached down, and for the first time in the weeks since el tritón had called me "friend," our palms touched without glass between them. Warm, wet fingers curled around mine, the sandpaper roughness I'd felt on them the day he attacked me, gone.

"Come to me." Río lifted his other arm. "I will catch you."

Not since my days with Ramón had I known what it was like to stand at a bluff ready to jump, but the three feet down to the water might as well have been a drop off the roof of my old tenement. I swung my legs over the iron ledge, made a silent petition to el Arcángel Miguel, and with a *sploosh*—

"¡Coño!" I yelped as lukewarm water met all mis pedacitos. Río caught me under my arms, keeping my chest level with the surface while the rest of me tightened like a cooling ingot. He tried drawing me closer, but my fingers clamped around his biceps and held him back, as if a few extra inches could short the electricity crackling through me from every point of contact between us.

This felt like hallucinating, albeit differently from my first view of Luna Park lit up. From this distance, I could make out the glint of water clinging to Río's thick eyelashes, the exact texture the lamplight painted on his skin, the tiny glyphs carved into the small seashells braided into his hair. I looked over my shoulder into the blackness below us just for the distraction and immediately regretted it. We seemed to float over an abyss.

Río cleared his throat. "It would be easier if you held onto my shoulders. Like this."

As if trying not to startle me, he slowly guided my hands up his arms one at a time, leaving them on his shoulders so he could take my waist. Long fingers stretched across my back, pulling me toward him. A warm breeze brushed against my legs. His tail.

"Boy Named Kind," he said softly, "when was the last time someone showed you kindness?"

My agitated brain stuttered in search of an answer. Kindness was Tití Luz. The steward on the *USS Carolina* who didn't toss me overboard and gave me a job. Even the Menagerie, despite everything, had offered me a life away from fire and smoke. "I wouldn't be alive without it," I said.

"¿Y ternura?" A hand left my waist to move a curl out of my eyes. "What of tenderness?"

I swallowed. "Sonia kissed me."

"That was not tenderness."

He firmed his grip until our stomachs were pressed together, the fronds of his fins curling protectively around my ankles. As one arm locked around my waist, another hand tipped my head gently onto his shoulder where his hair brushed wet against my cheek. With every part of himself, Río held me, and as my arms stretched unsteadily to hold him back, I realized with a leaden pang that he'd grown thinner since the time I'd carried him, knocked out and bleeding onto my coat . . .

"Eres inocente, Benigno." His voice carried only as far as my ears—so I'd be forced to listen.

"Don't—"

"Escúchame bien. You are innocent."

I wanted to argue, but I had been breathing in sips since the moment Sonia ran away from me. Finally, out of air, I inhaled.

Bendito. Río *smelled* like the ocean.

Like a sunlit morning on a pier in San Juan. Like the world San Ciriaco, President McKinley, and la consumición had stolen from me.

My eyes burned. My shoulders shook. Grief welled up so black and thick in my chest that I clung to Río harder out of an irrational fear we might both sink like stones under its weight. Before I could stop them, tears were scorching a path out of my eyes and into the rivulets on his shoulder.

When my sniffles turned to strangled gasps, he whispered, "Release it."

As if his voice had cut the tie, it all came out—years of painful isolation in an audible gush from the shunned recesses of my heart. I could hardly stand the sound it made, broken and desperate and raw as iron-scalded flesh. I *sobbed*.

If Río was put off by the messy spectacle of human grief, he didn't show it. Instead, his arms tightened around me until I was crushed against him. Until I couldn't tell whose heart was drumming against my sternum. He molded himself to my body as if it would somehow keep me from splintering apart, and it was a relief to let him so I didn't have to.

I don't know how long we stayed like that. Time lost its rhythm in the tank. Just when I thought it might overflow with my tears, the convulsions that wrung out my lungs began to ebb, and my fingers softened their clawlike grip on Río's shoulders.

"Respira," he whispered. "Like I showed you."

I tried. Deeply in. Deeply out.

"Good. Again."

In.

Out.

As my breath calmed, I felt strangely lifted. Dizzy. I was back on the Circle Swing, my entire world spinning around the axis of Río's embrace.

In a thunderclap of clarity, I remembered where I was. I, who couldn't swim and never cried, had just emptied my tears onto a merman in forty tons of water. With nothing between us. No glass. No bars. Just Río's wet shoulder against my cheek, his arms around me like shields, and the rest of me tangled in green and blue. I didn't know how to leave him, to maroon myself where his careful hands couldn't reach me; not without telling him the one truth that mattered more than anything else I'd ever confessed to him.

"I dream of you."

I waited for him to drop me. He didn't.

"What do you dream, Benigno?"

My arms tightened around him to curb the shaking in my limbs. "That I'm with you. Under the water. Holding you just like this," I whispered into his shoulder. "They're the happiest dreams I've ever had."

His breath disturbed the last strands of dry hair on my neck as he spoke. "Then why do you sound so sad?"

I was wrong. The real leap off the tenement roof was about to come out of my mouth.

"'Cause the prettiest girl in Brooklyn wants me, but my heart wants someone else. Someone who knows me better than any human alive—including me. And I don't even know his name." Tears were forcing their way into my eyes again. "All I know is that he misses the moon. If I could, I'd ride a roller coaster to the sky just to steal it for him."

He pulled back to look at me with wide, startled eyes.

"Es una locura, I know. I'm human, and you're . . ." I let that thought dead-end on my tongue before it could make a bigger fool of me. "Dios misericordioso, I'm more broken than I thought—"

"*No.*"

With an arm still wound tight around my waist, he slid his other hand against my cheek like a warm compress over an ache. "Your emotions are not madness. Nor are you broken. Everyone else—the cowards who taught you that keeping your heart safe meant caging it—*they* are broken."

A look of hope and expectation took shape on his face, and not even steeping in water up to my shoulders could put out the blaze that flared to life in my chest once I realized what it meant.

"What if nobody taught me how to keep my heart safe"—my eyes drifted to the dark ribbon of his mouth—"from you?"

"Your heart in my keeping," he whispered, "would always be safe."

No one leaned in first. Our lips met and in one bright, moonlit moment, the whole cruel, confusing world dissolved in brine. There was only Río—fin and flesh, salt water and sugarcane—and I gave in to his touch like flotsam washing ashore after an age adrift.

It was nothing at all like Sonia's eager, bruising kiss. Río's mouth was careful, unhurried, and glided over mine with a gentleness I wasn't sure I deserved. I'd gotten so used to being treated like I couldn't feel pain; I was a machine meant to labor until the gears failed and I became just another punchline to a white man's joke. But I was one of Río's seashells in his hands—treasured, precious, apt to shatter if pressed too hard.

His tenderness wrought in me a needy enthusiasm I didn't know I was capable of. In a complete reversal of my earlier strategy to keep him away, I managed to relinquish one of my hands so I could thread my fingers into the damp waves of his copper hair and guide him closer, melting against him like the surf into sand. A sound I'd never heard myself make disappeared into the warmth of his open mouth.

Suddenly, he pulled back. "We should stop."

"What's wrong?" *Miércoles.* I understood too little about the romantic inclinations of merfolk to know if I'd crossed some unspoken line.

"Your breathing has become quite"—he gulped—"loud."

A laugh bubbled out of me at the worry on his face. "I'm fine. Better than fine. Just means I like kissing you." Heat filled my cheeks. "*A lot.*"

He smiled, relieved, and rested his gaze on San Cristóbal, floating in the water between us. "I did not know my heart could bend toward a human's touch," he said quietly. "Until you."

Still clinging to his shoulder, I ventured to lay my free palm upon his cheek. "Does that scare you?"

"Less than perhaps it should," he said soberly. "Are *you* frightened?"

I was terrified. But it was the exhilarating kind. Dreamland's thrills couldn't rival the thrill I felt kissing Río. "Only 'cause I'll be begging you to teach me to swim after this."

He touched his nose to mine and tightened the circle of his arms. "Then kiss me again, and it will make us brave."

So I did. Then again, on his cheek. On the scar across his brow. A kiss for every night I'd left him alone. And as I did, I wondered if, like the greasy rag that had gone clean in Río's hands, I'd been purified.

Because no dream, no fantasy or myth, had prepared me for this—for happiness that ran in all directions and watered every love-parched corner inside me until I felt as free and weightless as I had soaring above the earth in the red barquito.

"Río," I whispered, out of breath, and not from wheezing. "You make me feel like I'm kissing the tides."

"Benigno," he whispered back. "You make me feel like I am holding the moon."

TWENTY-ONE

Morning arrived at the Albemarle without anyone having gotten so much as a whiff of Light the Night's miserable finale. Meanwhile, I was still settling my pulse from everything that came after it. If not for my wet clothes hanging off the footboard of my bed, I would've had a hard time convincing myself I had kissed Río and managed not to die from happiness, much less that Sonia had kissed me and managed to keep it a secret from the Menagerie gossip brigade.

When I found her in the kitchen, pulling ingredients for breakfast croquettes with the harried focus of un tabaquero wrapping cigars, she ducked all my attempts to clear the air. It took me withholding the eggs for her to even look my way, and when she did, her eyes telegrammed the warning that she'd rather take a walk off the Brooklyn Bridge than talk about what happened last night.

I put down the eggs and backed away.

The workday might have passed like any other if not for the riot of feelings that soldered my attention to the velvet curtain.

Cleaned and mended, I'd hung it back up, leaving the pump turned off as well so Río could rest in quiet privacy after staying up all night with me. He'd held us for hours at the surface with only his strength, kissing away all the evidence that I'd been in shambles.

Santa María. I never knew a kiss could feel so good. I'd never sought one out before, though I was pretty sure it wouldn't have felt like this if I had, like touching my mouth to a circuit that lit up my body like a ballroom chandelier. A guy can hardly focus on stripping varnish once they've seen salt water roll off the curve of Río's bottom lip; I was out there sanding benches with the energy of a dozen men just to cope.

Back at the Albemarle, my housemates had their noses to the grindstone as well. When Morgan had made his announcement, I'd assumed the company couldn't exceed their current standards of oddity, but like every other assumption I'd made since taking up with them, I was wrong.

I was hammering nails on Lulu's new settee when the madam towed Igor into the parlor by the leg, donning a more lavish tunic than she usually wore, with ornate embroidery wrapped around the hem at her knees, bracelets jangling from both wrists, and a bright red shawl draped across her collar. Igor seemed to stand even taller dressed in his homeland's fashion—an oversized shirt lined with patterned ribbons cinched at the waist by a thick striped scarf.

"How is looking?" the dapper giant asked.

I gave the hammer a break and smiled. "Real spiffy. Both o' you."

"If the audience is going to gawk at our size, they shall learn a thing or two about the Eastern world while they do it," Navya said proudly. "At least it will be an improvement over sitting on a stool and smiling while Morgan asks impertinent questions about our shoe sizes and how many steps it takes for legs like ours to walk to the front gate."

"I suggest madam ride on my shoulders for good stunt, but," Igor laughed, "she call me 'beans for brains.'"

"If I wanted to sit in the sky, I would have asked Mr. Benny to build me a tower," she snorted, then walked around his legs back out of the parlor.

In the dining room, Eli and Emmet were having their own disagreements.

"Aw, c'mon, Em," Eli whined. "Vaudeville's hep right now! We could make a whole new name for ourselves!" He held up his hands to frame the billboard he saw in his mind. "Eli and Emmett: the captivating, comedic, *and* conjoined!"

"I ain't learnin' to juggle with your leg in my pants, end of story." Emmett sealed the argument with a pound on the table—then immediately relented after Eli unleashed a pout so pitiful it made Timmy's look dignified.

Not everyone was thinking in pairs. Donned in breeches and one of my work shirts, a cigarillo hanging from her lips (unlit per her recent pledge against smoking indoors), Vera contemplated the aesthetic virtues of tattoos while studying pictures of the New York Botanical Gardens in the *Saturday Evening Post*.

"Forget it, fire breath," Matthias said, passing her on the way to the kitchen. "There's room for only one tattooed freak in this show, and that's me."

"Go get 'killjoy' tattooed across your bloody face." She threw down the magazine. "What're *you* doing to save the show?"

He emerged with a fresh cafecito. "Nothin'. Morgan's a fool if he thinks I'm about to mess up the reputation I spent a decade building just to buy stage time from Moby Dick. Trust me, y'all are better off if I just stick to expanding the circumference of my biceps."

A small gasp of profanity from Lulu's corner of the parlor interrupted my eavesdropping. Looking up from the hammer, I found her eyes holding in a sheen of tears as she sucked her finger and shook it out.

Timmy abandoned an anthill of shredded magazine paper to climb up her dress. "Mama?"

"You all right, Lulu?" I asked.

Quickly, she stuffed whatever she'd been working on into her sewing bag and molded her face into a placid smile. "Just pricked a finger, sweetie," she said to Timmy, then to me: "Everything's jake. I think I just need some air."

Timmy dutifully gave his mother her cane, and she rocked onto her feet with her sewing bag under her arm, making for the door without a glance in anyone's direction.

Must've been one hell of a finger prick. I put down the screwdriver and tried to make myself inconspicuous as I wandered after her.

Soft sniffles lured me onto the porch. Lulu didn't look up from her seat on the top step when the door clicked shut behind me; instead, her focus stayed on her lap where something resembling the museum's Chimera pelt was bundled in her sewing bag.

"Want some company?" I asked.

"Aw, Benny. You don't need to be out here right now."

"Sure I do, it's a nice evening."

I pocketed my hands and waited against the banister. If I'd learned anything in the last day about consoling someone, it was that talking was overrated.

Predictably, the silence wore her down. "I envy you, kid."

"Envy *me*? Why?"

"Look at all the lives you've lived. A blacksmith. A seaman. Now that you've taken up with us freaks, you're a regular butcher, baker, *and* candlestick maker," she rambled, waving her hankie emphatically at me before blowing her nose into it. "You're young. Changeable. Which is exactly what I'm not. Not anymore."

"I don't think that's true."

"Oh, but I *do*. Sam came back asking this old dog to learn a new trick when the fact is, I can't change no more. This body's all I've got to help this family stay afloat, and I was already stretching the truth with that whole 'takes seven men to hug her' claptrap. Without Saul, I've got no gimmick, and you gotta have a gimmick, Benny."

"Is that what you're making?" I gestured at her sewing bag. "A gimmick?"

Lulu's eyes welled up again. She raised her hands so I could get a better look at what they were holding.

It was a beard.

The moment she caught my startled expression, hers crumpled. "I'm g-gonna b-be so *ugly* . . ."

Quickly, I dropped down next to her and wrapped an arm around the soft slope of her shoulder. "That's not possible, Lulu. You're so pretty, there's nothing a beard could do to change it."

I meant it. She had better style than Sonia, curves she didn't need whalebone to achieve, a permanent rougeless blush on her cheeks, and a cherub mouth she'd passed onto her lucky nene.

Lulu dabbed at her nose with her hankie. "You sound just like my Charlie."

"Must've been a smart guy. You know," I said, rubbing her arm, "I knew a lady with a beard in Porto Rico. She put ribbons in it. Said it kept the mosquitos off her neck. And she was married and had seven kids, so I guess it didn't matter what anyone thought if the person she made all them kids with thought she was a doll."

At this, her sobs mixed with laughter—the kind that disappears into silence before coming back in an infectious blast. "You're fulla shit, Benny," she said through a soggy smile. "I know you didn't bet on living in a house full of lunatics when you left Red Hook, but I sure am glad you're here."

"Me too, Lulu."

She tipped into my open arms so I could hug her. It didn't take seven of me to do it either.

After dinner, I rushed back to the theater with pockets full of haddock and sandwich, powered by an eagerness that all but made me sprint across the manmade lake just for the shortcut.

Río was waiting for me at the glass. This time, he followed me up the ladder, his expectant smile greeting me between each rung, the lamplight turning his copper hair russet. He met me at the lattice where I knelt above him, my blood singing in my ears.

"Buenas noches, Río."

"Buenas noches, Benigno."

I passed the haddock down to him through the grate, unwrapped my sandwich, and an awkward moment passed when all you could hear was quiet chewing and the gentle burble of water as Río's tail did its dance to keep him afloat. I hadn't noticed how quickly he'd gulped down his dinner before I caught him staring at me like he was still hungry.

"Are you waiting for an invitation?" he said softly.

I choked down an unchewed bite. "Am I invited?"

His fins skimmed the surface as he backed away from the hatch, making room to catch me. "Come awn in, the wua-tah's fine," he drawled in perfect Brooklynese.

"Your impressions are almost as good as mine." I ditched the sandwich. "Almost."

I skipped right past yesterday's nervous impulse to fold my clothes if it meant delaying another taste of Río's salted lips. They landed on the ground, and wearing only San Cristóbal and my union suit, I gathered my courage and lowered myself into the water with slightly more grace than I'd done last night, giving in immediately to a grip so solid, it could have been made of cast iron itself.

How had I held out this long? My gaze followed the rivulets of water down his forehead and off the steep end of his straight nose. His eyes gazed back, two blue stars on a horizon of dark, wet lashes.

I'd waited all day for this—

"You know," he whispered, interrupting my trajectory to his mouth. "I seem to remember you telling me you were going to beg."

I remembered no such thing. "Beg?"

"For me to teach you to swim."

"What, you mean . . . *now*?"

"I have a theory, you see," he murmured, lifting my arm off his shoulder to kiss a water droplet off my wrist, "on the elasticity of human lungs."

Another kiss, this time to my fingertips, and all the muscles above my neck immediately stopped working. "W-which is w-what?"

His fingers found their way to my chest, tracing the silver chain down my sternum. "That holding your breath for extended periods underwater may increase your capacity for air."

The floor of my stomach dropped out, and I didn't know whether to blame his maddeningly gentle touch or my complete terror of what he was suggesting. "How 'bout you just tell me how to do it, and I could, like, try it in the bathtub or something?"

His quiet laugh sent a breeze of warmth across my face. "As much as I relish holding you for hours at a time, you are a rather heavy barnacle. And I am not as strong as I once was."

"Not as strong? What do you m—"

"The first thing you will learn is how to float."

I glanced warily down below us. Now that we were entertaining ideas of my independence in the water, it looked like we were a hundred feet in the air.

"No te preocupes. I have your arms," he reassured me. "You will now lean forward, with your chest in the water, extend your legs behind you, and just . . . keep your eyes on me."

That part was easy. "Jesucristo, ayúdame," I muttered, which wasn't begging, but close enough. Slowly, I leaned forward, then lifted my legs up one at a time so my stomach rested flat in the water. "Like this?"

"Perfect. Let us take a turn together."

His tail unfurled elegantly beneath me, blue and silver and made of myths. As we started to move, I noticed the sandpapery feeling was back on his palms, confirming my theory that the texture helped him grip things in the water.

Río propelled us around the tank. Eventually, as I gave in to the motion, my panic and the day's labor washed off in the brine. It felt *good*. My body had always been this clunky, wheezing thing I tolerated against my will, but the water seemed to bring out a gracefulness I didn't know I had.

Getting an eyeful of Río's upper half didn't hurt either.

"I believe you are ready to dip your face in the water," he observed. "Shall we?"

"We don't gotta be hasty—"

"It is easy. Breathe in deep and hold it while you are under. Here, would you like an incentive?"

Taking my waist, he leaned backward until his head disappeared into bubbles. As he went under, he pulled my hips over his, so we were both horizontal in the water—me looking down from above the surface, Río grinning impishly at me through a halo of copper hair and ripples. I was gonna kiss that comemierda smile off his face.

I mumbled the world's fastest prayer to Santa María, gulped air, squeezed my eyes shut, and dunked my face in. The world went silent, and just like that, I was weightless.

One at a time, Río's hands released my waist, and like a miracle, I didn't sink. I felt soft kisses on my eyelids—the right, then the left.

When I opened them, there he was. Beaming at me.

I took his face in my hands and reached for his mouth. He backed away, a teasing glint in his eye, so I kicked my legs out—clumsily, the way cabras kick trying to get a foothold on a craggy cliffside. It got me closer.

This time he let me catch him. Or maybe he caught me. We floated into a kiss that could've boiled water, his hands on my neck and mine skating over the folded ridge of fin that lined his lower back. When I couldn't hold my breath anymore, I let it out in a stream of bubbles between our faces.

Río tipped us back above the surface and the world splashed into bright, noisy focus. I was puffing like I'd run a race, my curls dripping into my eyes. I shook them out—

"Stop, you insidious urchin!" Río cried, nearly dropping me to shield himself from the spray.

"¡Oye! Did you see that?" I gasped.

"Of course I did. I was there," he said, recovering. A proud smile took shape on his lips. "I daresay you will be swimming circles around me before long."

I pulled him closer. "I can't believe I get to be with you like this," I whispered, sweeping his hair back over his shoulder. "I think you're even more beautiful underwater than you are in my dreams."

Halfway to his mouth, I saw Río's eyes widen, and I paused.

"Benigno," he whispered, "can you *see* underwater?"

"Huh?"

But before he could answer, the ease drained from his face. He snapped his head toward the proscenium, and in a terrified whisper, said, "Someone comes."

I jerked my head to look. "*What?*"

"Hush," he hissed. "You must go!"

He spun me around and hoisted me up by the waist toward the ledge. I grabbed onto it and pulled, Río pushing up my legs.

Caramba, *why* hadn't I turned the pump back on? In case there was still time to thwart discovery, I put out the lamp then padded blindly down the rungs, gathered my clothes, and tiptoed to the edge of the curtain, where I waited.

All was silence, and then: The scuff of a shoe. The groan of a bench skidding across the stripped flooring.

An intruder was inside the theater.

I flattened myself against the proscenium wall and gave my lungs a stern command to shut up. The trespasser's steps were hurrying away; once they had faded enough to suggest a safe distance between us, I stuck my head out and raced on bare feet all the way to the entrance of the Menagerie in hopes of catching a glimpse of whatever Dreamland interloper had come to spy on Río in the middle of the night.

By the time I reached the door, they were gone.

I squinted across the darkened promenade. When my eyes failed to show me anything, I tuned my ears.

The silence had never been so loud.

RÍO

I wish at moments like this that Benigno would stay away from me. Though the footfalls we heard tonight did not belong to the Shark, I dwell in terror of the day they do. What wrath would he visit upon Benigno for standing guard over my sanity in this place of nightmares?

Selfishly, I also never want Benigno to go. I have not kissed nor held any mer, maid, man, or otherwise, in an age, but my yearning is not founded on loneliness. He tastes of *sky*, this tender man who sings of the sea and named me river before he had ever heard of the Currents. And when I hold him, every anxious thought subsides with the pleasurable novelty of his human heart fluttering against mine like a gentle tern.

Though I may deceive myself in dreaming we might see each other again after I leave this place, I am teaching him to swim. He falls into my arms with the crustaceous agility I expect from one whose contact with the sea has never surpassed gazing at it from a pier. His body was a configuration of sharp corners, so unyielding had the fear of drowning made his limbs. Foolish hopes are still hope. The progress he made tonight gives me faith where there is little to be found.

The tremors have returned. They reappear each time my captivity presents some new threat to my peace. Any healing this water may bestow has run out, and without Benigno here, I can find no distraction sufficient to quell the burning in my fins.

He left me to search for villains in the dark, though my ears tell me they have gone. Otherwise, with eyes as evolved as his, I feel certain he would find them, Mother.

Benigno sees in water.

TWENTY-TWO

My spare drop cloth made a decent towel in a pinch, though I was hot enough around the collar to air dry. The front entrance's only lock was undone, and apart from an empty promenade, all I could see was red. Anyone with half a brain might've expected snoops and intruders after Morgan had wallpapered Manhattan in those maldito flyers!

To thwart entry from the outside, I hooked leftover wire from the creature displays around every door handle but the stage door exit to Morgan's tent so I could leave. Installing new deadbolts would be my morning priority; I'd have to sell it to Morgan as a precaution, since there was no way I could tell him about trespassers without owning up to being one myself.

After securing the theater, I took the longest route possible to Luna Park's front gates, hoping I'd trip over one of Reynolds's goons. I wasn't sure what I'd do if I found one, but the only punch I'd ever thrown in my life had drawn blood, and that seemed promising.

"Stop right there," came a voice from behind me. I spun around, and my bravado promptly withered away.

It was a policeman.

"What's your business wandering out of Luna Park at four in the morning?"

I eyed the club dangling at his hip and tried to look harmless. "I work at Luna Park."

He stepped closer. "And loitering's part of the job description, eh?"

I raised my hands to show I wasn't armed. "Honest. I'm just looking after an exhibit."

"What's the exhibit, then?"

Morgan would have my head on a spike if I told anyone the Prince of Atlantis already resided at Luna Park. "I . . . can't tell you."

"Now, *that* I believe."

He reached for my arm, but as I dodged the cop's fingers, his remaining patience seemed to slip through his hands too.

"Please, sir," I said without any amusement at the irony of having to beg twice in one night. "There actually *was* someone else here—someone who broke into the—"

I wasn't fast enough this time; he grabbed my swim-sore arm and twisted it behind my back. "You better rethink your next words, or I'll bust you so hard you're gonna forget how to lie!"

"There a problem here, Joey?"

We both looked over the cop's shoulder. Matthias was strolling over with his hands in his pockets, doing his most leisurely impersonation of a brick wall. Out of the corner of my eye, I saw the policeman's spine go straight as a tentpole.

"What brings you out here, Matty?" he said in a squeak ill-suited to a guy with a badge.

"Ain't I told you I'm writing my autobiography?" he said, smiling. "*The Heaviest Weight: A Mighty Memoir* is gonna be in every souvenir shop on Surf Avenue, if I can ever finish the dang thing. And wouldn't you know, the only cure for writer's block is a good walk around the corner, so here I am. Anything I can help with?"

"Just a loiterer making like he works at Luna Park," Joey spat.

"That's because he does," Matthias said coolly. "Meet Benny Caldera, our new day laborer."

Officer Joey's grip loosened, then let go. Even in the twilight, I could see his face flush. "All right. Then what's a day laborer doing here when it ain't day yet?"

"Matthias, I tried to tell him—"

"Stop your damn mouth, Benny," Matthias hissed before turning a placating face back to Joey. "You're gonna have to forgive lunkhead here. Fact is, Sam's got him looking after a very important, very *expensive* attraction and Mr. Caldera here don't know how to manage his time is all."

"Very expensive and important, huh?" The officer squinted in my direction, baffled. "And they left *him* in charge of it?"

I opened my mouth to protest, but Matthias clapped me on the back and sent all the air out of my chest. "Crazy, right? Turns out Benny's the only one with the right credentials. Now"—he walked up to Joey and clasped his hands amiably—"he ain't hurting no one, is he? Just look at him. Harmless as a seagull with half as much meat on his bones. He ain't even fit to hawk shoes."

I scowled.

"And I guarantee, sir, that brother here is gonna do a better job managing his workload from now on. *During the daytime*," he added through his teeth.

The value of my silence dawned on me as Joey's posture visibly loosened under Matthias's influence. I nodded emphatically.

Joey took the baton off his belt and stuck it in my face. "Don't let me catch you out here off hours again."

"You won't," I croaked.

"Thank you for your service to our humble neck o' Brooklyn, officer." Matthias took me by the shoulder and tipped his cap. "You have a good night."

"Night, Matty."

We turned back toward the Albemarle, the strongman's grip about to chip off a piece of my shoulder. For several blocks we walked like men fleeing death, my insides roiling, but when we finally reached the hotel's back door, Matthias took a giant step ahead of me and blocked my path up the stoop.

"For a goddamned genius, you sure are *stupid*," he snapped. "I ain't never seen anyone so desperate to have his brown ass scraped across pavement!"

"I'm sorry—"

"What in the fool shenanigans has got you dancing a jig on the tightrope between arrested and *dead* at four in the morning?"

"I'm just looking after the merman! Someone broke into the theater tonight—"

"Yeah, *you* did!" He turned in a furious circle. "To think I been defending your behind every time Emmett spouts off about not trusting you—"

"C'mon, Matthias, I'm no traitor!"

"Then tell me the truth!"

"It's not— You don't—"

He leaned against the rail. "Go on. I just had me a nap and Igor's coffee, I got all damn night."

I was a lousy liar. It was always miles easier to just shut up and let everyone else come to their own conclusions about me, which they were usually bound to do whether I had anything to say about it. But now that mine wasn't the only neck at risk, all the angst I'd felt after Sonia kissed me came right back like I'd escaped Officer Joey's billy club only to back into quicksand.

I'd gone quiet when Matthias finally threw his hands up. "Fine. You don't wanna tell me? That's just fi—"

"*I love him.*"

Matthias couldn't have looked more stunned if I'd told him I was President McKinley's illegitimate Puerto Rican son. "Come again?"

I slumped onto the bottom step. "Madre de Dios, don't make me say it twice," I whispered into my hands.

"You mean to say, Sam put you in charge of the fish-man," he said in the most high-pitched voice I'd ever heard him use, "and you went and fell in *love* with it?"

"*Río*," I corrected angrily. "Dammit, he's not a *thing*!"

He yanked his cap off his head and paced across the walk. "But . . . I thought . . . you went with Sonia to Light the Night—"

"Yeah, God knows I regret it. I been trying to tell her I'm not the guy for her."

"'Cause of Sam?"

"'Cause I ain't *made* that way."

Matthias's face went slack. "I don't believe it," he murmured. "This whole time, I been thinking you was Mr. Shy Guy when really, you're just like Humpty and Dumpty!"

"Who?"

"Eli and Emmett. You don't want Sonia 'cause you don't want ladies, full stop. I get that right?"

I stared down at the ground. "You gonna put that in your memoir?"

He teetered away from me, his hand over his mouth, then spun back. "Brother, I am far more concerned about what Sam'll say when he finds out the merman who's been giving him the cold shoulder since day one is playing Romeo and *Julio* with the hired hand."

Dread snapped me back upright. "Shit, you're not gonna tell him, are you?"

He blew a sharp breath through his nose. "Hell no! I value my peace too much to be the bearer of *that* news."

We slipped into a tense silence. I figured Matthias probably needed a moment to let all this sink in, so a moment is what I gave him before nerves made me ask, "Does me being . . . you know . . . bother you?"

He shook his head. "Nah, brother. I been in the sideshow business for ten years, six of them with the twins. Men sweet on other men, ladies sweet on ladies, folks sweet on nobody at all—who cares so long as everyone's living happy and hurtin' no one?"

My relief mingled with gratitude and an entirely new appreciation for Matthias's mightiness.

He dropped onto the empty space next to me on the step. "All right, so. You love him. He love you?"

I almost said no, but then I thought of the proud look on Río's face after my first strokes in the water—of kisses against my eyelids and lines drawn over my heart with wet fingertips—and said, "Maybe."

"And like"—he cleared his throat uncomfortably—"the tail and the fins and whatnot. That don't bother you?"

"Aw, *jeez*, Matthias—"

"What! It's an honest question!"

"Well, I dunno, on him they're nice," I admitted, my ears on fire. "When Río swims, Ave María, it's like the most beautiful thing I ever seen."

"Well butter my ass and call me toast," he snorted. "I seen a ton o' shit in sideshow work, but this takes more than the cake. This takes the whole goldang bakery!" Glancing sideways at me, he bumped my shoulder. "So, then, the two of you been . . ."

His eyebrows actually waggled at me.

"What? No! He never even kissed me before yesterday."

"What's with the wet hair, then?"

I shifted in my seat. "He's teaching me to swim."

Matthias laughed so loud I had to shush him. "I forgot your Caribbean ass can't even swim! Holy shit, Benny, what does this merman even *see* in you?"

In spite of myself, I cracked a smile. "Who knows. Something. It don't matter to him that I'm colored and speak Spanish, or that my whole family's gone, or that he'll outlive me by like a thousand years or something. It's like what Igor said about his wife," I murmured. "He just sees me, Matthias."

"He sees you."

Matthias leaned back on an elbow and cast me a bittersweet grin. "Benny, I'm happy you're happy. I am. But how do you think this ends?" he asked quietly. "You think he's still gonna feel tender for you when the crowds pour in to stare and laugh at him—as they *inevitably* will—meanwhile you're standing around in the wings like the Porto Rican Statue o' Liberty? What, is he gonna stay in that tank for the rest of eternity or however long fish people live?"

I looked back at the ground. I hadn't considered that.

"Brother, you ain't thought this through," he said, echoing my thoughts. "Not by a long shot."

"What if I don't want to think it through?" I demanded. "Every day of my life, I'm thinking. About the next Officer Joey waiting around the corner. About how to keep my head down, how to perfect my impersonation of someone who's lived here his whole life so no one figures out I'm not supposed to be here, how to *work* my way to liberty the way Americans are supposed to do." I tore off my cap. "¡Qué idiota!"

Matthias let his head hang. "Just because this country sold you the same thumper they sell everyone don't make you an idiot."

"Yeah, well, Río makes me *feel* free," I said. "Like I don't gotta prove anything—because he thinks I'm enough as I am. When I'm with Río, I feel like maybe all my dumb decisions weren't so dumb if they brought me to him."

"Damn, man." Matthias propped his chin on his knuckles. "They could see the stars in your eyes from Staten Island. Look, I get it. You're in love. But there ain't no being free on the outside if you ain't free on the inside, and that starts with accepting reality. What you have in that tank ain't just a merman. He ain't even your sweetheart. As soon as Sam sells his first ticket to the Prince of Atlantis show, you and I know *exactly* what he'll be."

My gut clenched around a sudden wave of nausea.

"So, the question is," Matthias continued, "are you gonna free him?"

I gulped, and nothing but dry air went down. I had promised Río I'd return him to the sea.

But that was before he kissed me. Before he called me innocent and said holding me felt like holding the moon. Before Lulu told me she was glad I was one of the gang and Eli told me about Rudy and Lenny. Before Sonia told me what would happen to everyone if Morgan's plans failed.

"It ain't so simple," I answered.

Matthias chewed on that for a second before getting to his feet and wedging his fists back into his pockets.

"Sure, it ain't. But it's what you're gonna do. If not now, then eventually."

I looked up at him. "How do you know?"

He shrugged. "You're the one who said you loved him."

TWENTY-THREE

Following my twilight encounter with the mystery intruder, I gave up on convincing Matthias or anyone else it had happened. Río's peace of mind was already suffering without inviting Morgan's paranoid attention to the tank or, failing that, more cops.

Río demanded I stop visiting him at night for my welfare, which was ridículo. I told him he was in no position to decide whose welfare was at risk; with the city wallpapered in Prince of Atlantis flyers, who knew how many goons would risk the end of Joey's baton for a shot at stealing a live merman? If keeping watch meant having to sleepwalk through my daytime duties, then so be it.

And sleepwalk I did, until Río brought me back to life in the tank.

He was a patient swimming teacher when he wasn't scolding me for being so distracted; though, in my defense, Río's lithe backstroke would wreck the focus of a monk. He'd often hang off to the side to observe or let me propel him around, and by early

May, I'd learned to tread water and hold my breath for as long as it took to recite the Pledge of Allegiance in my head twice. I could even dive down and pluck his carved shells from the sand, which came as a shock to us both the first time I did it.

I hadn't had an asthma fit in days.

Río said I had natural talent, though if you asked me, learning to swim is easy when catching a merman in your arms is the reward at the end of a lap. The thrill I felt just being allowed to touch him. To be the person who, in the peaceful moments between telling stories and teaching me not to drown, he reached for and kissed.

I'd never *wanted* someone like this. Like a drought was inside me that a kiss alone couldn't quench. Along with the possibility of ever breathing freely, I'd accepted that physical intimacy wasn't in the realm of things I could do. With anyone. After Ramón, my body had become a greater mystery to me than any of the human curiosities I lived with now, so skilled was I at suffocating everything I was into oblivion—my language, my island, even my name. My stunted heart had become another foreigner in a sea of extranjeros, but when I was with Río, it seemed to come back home.

What would become of it if Río left?

The thought got interrupted on the way to Río's tank when I noticed a lamp was already lit behind the curtain. Someone had turned off the pump. I froze.

"I did not sink a chunk of brass into this joint to have you tell me two weeks ahead of opening day that you caught a sea monster who don't do nothin' but look at us like we're on the menu at Lombardi's," came a gravelly voice I didn't recognize.

Morgan's nervous laughter followed. "Now, now, Little Frankie—"

"It's *Mr. Agostinelli* to you," the man snarled. "I will carve it into your face the next time you call me 'little,' pezzo di merda!"

Miércoles.

Crouching close to the ground, I crept toward the gap between the curtain and the proscenium to get a better look. Morgan stood in the space between Río's tank and a set of three dark-suited men, the shortest of which stood in the center, flanked by his taller, slightly dim-looking cohorts.

Sonia stood stiffly to the side, her face paper white despite a generous daub of rouge on both cheeks.

"My deepest apologies, Mr. A-Agostinelli," Morgan stammered. "I'm simply articulating the modifications we've had to make for our star performer. The merman came to us wild, practically untamable. This actually represents a marked improvement in its ability to communicate. To think it was unwilling to even look in our direction when we first pulled it from the river!"

Saltwater estuary, I thought darkly.

"I'm hearing an awful lot of excuses and no solutions," said Little Frankie. He turned to the man on his right. "Qual è la tua opinione?"

"No solutions," Righty repeated.

"Ah, but we do have a solution!" Morgan insisted. "We will plan the entertainment around the creature until such time as it is properly trained to engage with the human world. And we do have reason to believe it will eventually engage, don't we Miss Kutzler?"

Sonia's face blanched further. She'd be a ghost before the night was over. "Yes," she squeaked. "We got a new member of the company who's taking care of the merman. He's been spending loads of time with it. I've even heard him talk to it."

My mouth fell open. That night. The mystery intruder hadn't been a goon. Or a thief.

It had been *Sonia*.

"I think," she added, taking her cue from Morgan to keep talking, "the merman could even be a willing performer."

Little Frankie shifted his feet into a wide stance. "*Could* be? Or *will* be?"

"Will be," Morgan answered confidently. "I'll make it my personal priority."

"That you will, Sammy." Glancing first at Righty, then Lefty, Mr. Agostinelli turned his sneer on Morgan and started walking toward Sonia. "Because we got a business partnership, you and me. And so far"—he lifted Sonia's hand and ran his fingers over her knuckles—"I been holding up my end of it while you let us play with your pretty puttana like that's gonna pay back the five grand I loaned you outta the goodness of my heart."

"Goodness of his heart," parroted Lefty.

Frankie dropped Sonia's hand. She let out a visible breath and resumed staring at the floor. "It's already May. I came to see some return on my investment. But you've disappointed me." Then, tipping his head gently to the right, he added, "Vincenzo, show Sammy what happens when I'm disappointed."

In three long strides, Lefty reached Morgan, but before the showman could move in his defense, the goon sank his square fist into Morgan's gut—then backhanded him across the face.

Sonia shrieked as Morgan crumpled, a thin strand of pink spit dangling from his bleeding lip. Vincenzo straightened his tie back out and reclaimed his spot next to Frankie, abandoning Morgan in a writhing heap on the floor.

Río backed straight into his corner, horrified.

"What'd you do that for?" gasped Sonia.

"Aw, don't worry, principessa. That was a little love tap." Frankie grinned, baring a set of tiny teeth. "An incentive to earn back my good opinion. 'Cause me and my brothers here are gonna be back on preview day to see if Mr. Morgan's made good on our arrangement, or else Vincenzo will have something of a more permanent nature to exchange for my disappointment. Understand me, Sammy?"

He was on his hands and knees, looking up at them through watery eyes like a kicked dog. "C-completely," he choked.

"Next time, don't stutter when you say my name." Then, turning to his brethren, he said, "Andiamo. We got a ferry to catch."

They filed down the stage steps and out of the building like they'd just been let out of Catholic Mass. As their footsteps faded into silence, Sonia's strangled terror gave way to tears.

"Oh my God, Sam, are you all right?" She knelt beside him, but Morgan was already fencing off her ministrations.

"Stop," he croaked. "I'm fine."

She tugged at the arm he held against his belly. "*Fine?* You need a doctor—"

"I don't need a damn doctor."

"Just let me see it—"

"Oh, for Christ's sake, get out of my sight, you useless whore!"

Sonia's tears seemed to retract back into her eyes. While Morgan scowled at the ground, she took an unsteady step away from him, then dashed noiselessly out of the theater.

It was just the showman, the merman, and me now. Haltingly, a red welt rising on his cheekbone, Morgan rose off the ground and faced the tank.

"Bet you enjoyed that," he mumbled, his words slightly slurred. "We're all about the fucking *thrills* here at Luna Park."

Río watched wide-eyed from his shadowy corner. Morgan straightened as much as his injured gut would allow and scoffed at him.

"Look at you. Sitting in that exquisite enclosure bought and paid for by some of the most powerful people in New York City, looking down your nose at me like you're some kind of J. D. Rockefeller instead of the misshapen mackerel you really are," he hissed.

"I oughta tell the world the truth about you. Heartless, soulless devils who think nothing of watching children drown," he continued, his voice rising. "If you had half a brain in that briny head, you'd thank me for rescuing you from the river, you ungrateful brute! While the rest of your race goes the way of the dodo bird, you'll be preserved and glorified by the masses because of *me*, but you won't even cooperate! Do you think people will come from miles around to see the Eighth Wonder of the World if all it does is glower at them from the bottom of a tank? Well? Say *something*, goddamn you!"

Morgan waited for an answer Río would never give him. As the seconds ticked, Morgan's bitter scowl degraded into something noxious and terrifying.

"But of course, you'd rather converse with the hired help," he sneered. "I'd ask what's so special about that greasy dock rat, but I suppose one bottom-dweller recognizes another."

Every muscle in my body wrapped itself around my rage like a tourniquet, and not because he'd insulted me.

That yanqui pendejo had called Río heartless.

Morgan stabbed a finger at the tank. "I've eliminated bigger obstacles than you. Just see what happens when you outlive your usefulness. I've an entire museum full of things that were once pretty and profitable, and a bit of stuffing can turn anything into a curiosity people will pay a nickel to—"

Suddenly, Río was out of his corner. In a streak of blue and green, he rushed at the glass wall where Morgan stood and, at the last second, swerved his long tail to send a massive tidal wave of water over the tank side—and directly on top of Morgan's head.

The sound of Morgan's roar was so completely removed from his manicured speaking voice, not even *I* could impersonate it.

"So help me, God, I will tame your savage spleen if it's the last thing I do!"

Uneven footsteps came alarmingly close, then faded as Morgan stomped away from Río's tank, soaked in water down to his skin, clutching his stomach and snarling cusses furiously to himself. I thought back to that conversation with Matthias in the shadow of Dreamland's plaster angel, because there he was.

Offstage Sam.

TWENTY-FOUR

waited for the sound of the padlock before I slipped onto the stage. I was afraid to light the lamp, but the moon was waxing through the small window above, and once my eyes adjusted, I could see Río leaning against the glass with his forehead in his hand.

I gave a gentle tap to the tank before climbing up the rungs. With a worried glance at the curtain's edge, he rose to the surface to meet me.

"You should leave," he whispered, a deep crease between his brows. "He might return."

"Not while he's banged up and dripping como un perro ahoga'o," I said, undoing my shirt buttons. "Besides, the tank's probably the safest place to hide from a guy with a gun. My old foreman said it'd take a cannon to break this glass."

Río watched anxiously as I stripped down to my undergarments and slid quietly into the water. As soon as I was afloat, I opened my arms, and he swam into them.

"For all the years I have watched your kind, I still cannot understand humanity," he whispered into my neck, gripping me with his sandpaper palms. "Such violence and cruelty. I can hardly believe you are one of them."

"I'm no saint," I admitted, rubbing his back while I did my part to tread the water below us. "I could've started a riot when I heard him yelling at you like that."

"A riot sounds like a terribly unwise course of action. I am glad you resisted."

I chuckled and wondered if Río knew he was being funny, but when I pulled away to look at him, what I saw made me pause.

He looked drawn. A trick of the light, maybe.

"Are you all right?"

He nodded and lowered his head against my shoulder. "His presence often leaves me . . . shaken."

"Come on, then." Taking him by the waist, I swam us toward the wall where I could hold the rim of the glass and tuck my legs in. I steered him onto my lap where he leaned into me wearily, folding in the sharp spines on his back.

"Benigno?"

I kissed his salty shoulder. "Hm?"

"What does 'return on my investment' mean?"

"Means trouble," I muttered. "Those guys who beat up Morgan paid for this nightmare, and now they got Morgan stuck under an anvil of debt."

"They want a dog, not a merman. A noisy, obedient thing that does tricks. Why can these walruses never understand merfolk have no masters?"

His voice sounded so heavy. I turned his chin to search his face, and it lanced me through the chest to find fear in it.

"Oye," I whispered. "I've been around plenty of cabrones like him, and they mouth off 'cause making dogs of everyone around them makes them feel better. Morgan might look at you, but he sure don't see you."

Río touched two fingers to the medallion hanging from my neck. "What do you see, Benigno?"

I didn't have to guess why he asked. Morgan had unearthed Río's weakness without even trying when he'd called him soulless and willing to watch children drown. Without a language that could do Río justice, my "native song" would have to do.

"I see someone brave and beautiful and too noble for a world as unjust as mine," I said in Spanish. "With a heart as wide as the ocean if it was willing to bring a lonely, broken thing like me into it. You saw a man starved for air and tenderness and gave him both. You are so much more than a fool like Morgan could ever comprehend."

I covered his hand with mine and traced my thumb over his knuckles. "From the moment I first saw you, I knew you were a miracle."

He gazed down with wide, glittering eyes and took my cheek in his palm, guiding my path to his mouth. I kissed Río the way he breathed: Slowly. Deeply. Until the cords in his muscles dropped their traumatized grip.

The cage blended into the shadows, but even in the dark, his loveliness shone over me like a star. Through a veil of wet hair, he smiled and raised his tail to the surface, draping it loosely over my shoulder so I could skate light fingers across it. I pressed another kiss to the pearly gems that decorated him, warming at the low hum that vibrated in his throat at being touched the way he liked.

"*Llévame, río, hasta el mar,*" I sang in a quiet voice.

"*Sobre las olas de agua cristal,*" he sang softly back.

"I have a secret to tell you."

"What is it?"

"That song?" I nuzzled my cheek against his tail. "It's about you."

"Barnacle." He smirked at me. "That is not a secret."

"Yeah, well, it's your fault I can't keep anything from you. This tank's got more confessions than a Catholic sacerdote."

He sighed. "If only confessions had greater uses."

"Bueno. That depends on the confession."

My heart had gotten ahead of my brain, palpitating before I even realized what I was about to say. Without the pump to drown out the sound, I was sure he could hear it, because his stare deepened, and he whispered, "Will you tell me another?"

There was only one secret left to tell him, something that made me feel weightless all the time, whether or not I was suspended in ten feet of water. After all the monstrous lies Morgan flung at him, I could have shouted it to the night.

"Te quiero, Río."

I reached into the water, found his hand, and lifted it to my chest.

"You call me the moon, but it's you. You're the beacon. Dios mío, I've loved you since the moment you touched my hand through the glass." When Río's eyes went suddenly wide and unreadable, I hastily added, "You don't have to say you feel the same if you don't. Doesn't change anything. I just wanted you to—"

Río stopped my mouth with his fingertip.

"Benigno, surely you know," he breathed. "*You* are my heartsong."

In one fluid motion, he slid off my lap and kissed me against the glass—arms and tail winding around my body like he was el Leviatán about to swallow me whole. I met his eagerness with something like desperation, drinking him in like I walked the earth by day with a Río-shaped hole in my chest.

He loved me.

And I thought: What if passion—the sort that melts down all your raw, untempered pieces in another's heart—needed something more? A different ingredient. A higher temperature. What if intimacy had always been out of reach because I'd never loved anyone like I loved Río? I was deep in the crucible now. Molten. Glowing. Here in the water, kissing with my eyes half-open for the miraculous vantage of seeing his affection up close, all I could think about was how badly I needed to show him what I felt.

Panting, I pulled my lips away. "Do your kind make love?"

I'd shocked the hell out of myself with that question, while Río didn't so much as flinch.

"Even dolphins breach the surface to taste the heavens," he replied in his silkiest voice.

"So, that's a 'yes'?"

He laughed softly. "It is quite different from the ways of humans. But yes. Of course, we do."

"Different how? Or—" I blinked. "You mean. You don't. That there's not—"

"I have the requisite anatomy for reproducing, Benigno. I am just not as"—his eyes drifted downward at my obvious arousal—"exposed as you are."

I was one more embarrassing sentence away from disintegrating in ten thousand gallons of water.

"Your shame has no place here, Benigno. There is no part of your body that does not tempt me," he murmured. "But what you are asking about has little bearing on the furtherance of our race. It means more than my fervent pleasure in touching you or being touched, however much that may feature in the undertaking. Making love, for merfolk, is a consummation of a different sort."

"What sort?"

He brushed my hair from my eyes and let his fingertips trail the curve of my face. "Two rivers converged," he whispered. "Two breaths made one." His caresses traveled farther down. "A union most sacred."

Río had taught me how to breathe. Though he hadn't meant to, he'd taught me how to cry, and later, to swim. As he touched me with the same sureness I saw in his eyes, I realized I had something important left to master.

"Teach me how to love you, Río."

He didn't blush since blushing, I'd learned, wasn't something merfolk could do. But he bit his lip and looked at me as though for once in his long life, modesty had overtaken him. "A human might find it overwhelming."

"And if I wanted to be overwhelmed?"

I ran my thumb across the seam of Río's mouth. His eyes fluttered closed. "Then your soul would bind to mine. And mine"—he firmed his iron grip around my waist—"to yours."

The idea took my breath away. I imagined us, bronze and pewter, melting together until we glowed with the same light. I smoothed his hair back over his shoulder, the better to taste the salt along his neck. "My soul is yours. If you want it."

His swallow sent a ripple across my lips. "Neptune knows how deeply I want you. But . . ."

"But?"

"Benigno," he said quietly, "you still don't know my name."

The words fell like stones on my heart. I was about to apologize for my atrevimiento when Río laid a palm against my chest to stop me.

"But perhaps it is time you knew it."

I searched his face for shadows in the dark. I couldn't tell if he felt pressured. "You don't have to—"

"Hush." He brought his mouth to my ear. "I give it freely."

Río's arm traveled the familiar path under my shoulder blades, pulling me closer. His other hand skimmed over my thigh to hoist my leg gently over his hip while, below the waterline, his tail curved around my other ankle. I wasn't undressed, my union suit still clung to me like a second skin, but we were so completely entwined I couldn't tell where he ended and I began.

"You feel certain?" he whispered.

Whatever was about to happen, I wanted it more than anything I'd ever wanted in my life. I nodded. "¿Y tú?"

Río took one last lingering look in my eyes before they closed. "Sí."

This kiss.

It spilled.

Spread across my chest and down my back. Warm. Like rain running thick down plantain leaves in a thunderstorm. I let go of the glass, and we stayed afloat, his body cooling against me like my blood had mixed with seawater. When I shivered, he hesitated.

"No pares," I gasped.

One-handed, Río undid the buttons over my heart, then slipped his fingers between them with a lightness that sent tremors through me like lightning had struck the water. His lips rolled in waves along my jaw and down into the hollow of my throat before I started hearing something unexpected. Something impossible.

Two heartbeats pulsed in my ears. I knew mine only by the way it slowed to match his. With each beat, ordinary noises seemed to resound, to turn to music. The wet of our lips. The water colliding gently against our shoulders. His sighs played like a symphony in my ears, and Dios misericordioso, was this how all merfolk heard the world?

Returning to my mouth, he hovered there and sent his voice into my mind just as his mother had done.

Respira.

I inhaled. As I did, he blew a breath into my open lips that came alive inside me, pure as a spring and familiar as a song.

It was Río—the raw, unbounded essence of him—and in the space of a heartbeat, a hundred of my questions about him were all answered. He was young; uncertain and innocent, an elemental spirit pulsing with bravery being tested for the first time. Río's yearning for the sea now throbbed like a subterranean ache inside *me*, as if an invisible cord had reached through the metal and glass to pull me powerfully by the chest.

My next exhale, Río breathed in, and I watched the bond take him too, his breaths coming faster, his expression opening with bliss and wonder at whatever truth he sensed in me. I held him through it while my blood resisted the human urge to race and calmed in my veins instead.

And not just my blood—*everything* was slowing down. Water rippled in protracted motion. My breathing had gone almost still. I sank into blue until the margins of my body blurred, then disappeared.

If Río's soul was an ocean, then I'd found the sea floor. Here, I saw his mother's face—not pained and desperate, like it had been at Lawrence Point, but glowing with the same compassion and kindness I saw in her son.

That's when, like a blow to the chest, I remembered. I'd seen a face like hers before.

In the rapids. In the hurricane. That face had been *mer*. I felt it confirmed down to my fingertips alongside the sudden certainty that this moment with Río was no accident. The part of me climbing to the surface ever since we'd met had been searching my whole life for exactly this—for a love that didn't burn, but *flooded,* until all I could see behind my eyelids was the sea spread out in all directions, as boundless and blue as Río's eyes.

My next breath stayed held. I didn't need air.

Llévame, Río, I said in his mind.

He pulled us under.

Río sang to me in his language. The rarest, most beautiful sound I'd ever heard.

Without opening my eyes, I saw moonlight reflected on water, glittering like stars on the ocean's skin. Turns out merfolk have a word for that.

Río's true name.

Laying together among the sand and seashells, he named me just like I'd named him. A melody sung prayerfully into my mind where only I could hear it.

I'll never tell it to another soul.

TWENTY-FIVE

I slept beside Río's tank like I'd left half my heart in the water. Once his hand had returned to its place across the glass from mine, sleep came instantly to him; meanwhile, I watched over his rest for as long as my tired eyes would let me, imagining I could still see through the scales and skin and feel the incomprehensible warmth of his spirit. I felt awed and grateful and too alive with the echoes of his music inside me to dwell on the chilly injustice of lying under a drop cloth where I couldn't rest my head on his chest and hear his unhurried pulse.

Qué milagro. I understood what heartsong meant now.

When the blue tint of dawn filtered through the hopper window, I took myself home on boneless legs, detouring once to buy Río's meal at the market so I'd at least have an alibi if Vera was out for a smoke again and happened to see me on my way in.

Only it wasn't Vera waiting outside this time.

"Matthias?"

My voice stopped him mid-pace and he rushed at me, grabbing my shoulders so roughly he nearly shook the bundle out of my arms. "Get your ass back to the theater, and I mean *now*."

My stomach dropped. "What's happened?"

"Sam was just here looking for you," he said in a loud whisper. "Practically kicked your door in, and as soon as he couldn't find you, he grabbed Sonia and walked her out in her nightgown like a creampuff convict!"

I was too terrified to ask whether all my secrets—worst among them, my romantic affair with Morgan's prized exhibit—had been spilled like blood before the entire company. "Breathe, kid," Matthias said, reading my mind. "No one knows about *that*. Not yet, anyway."

He spun me around but never got the chance to shove me back toward Surf Avenue.

I was already running.

The red curtain was wide open when I stumbled into the theater wheezing and coated in sweat.

Río was, of course, wide awake—and taut with fear. I jogged up the aisle and bypassed the tank toward Morgan's tent, hiding my panic behind what I hoped was an encouraging smile in Río's direction.

I passed through the tent flap directly into pipe smoke. In the middle of it sat Sam Morgan at his desk, dry but glowering, his lip scabbed and a shiner on his cheek courtesy of Lefty. The hand without a pipe in it held a liquor flask, which accounted for the Van Brunt saloon–like stink in there. Across from him, Sonia sat with her leg twitching like one of Timmy's windup toys. She glanced up at me, then quickly resumed drilling her eyes into the floor.

Morgan set down the pipe. "Tell me, Benny," he said, picking at a stick of drawing charcoal, "what exactly does a production assistant in training have to accomplish away from home at this hour of the morning?"

"Sorry you couldn't find me. It's just that"—I held up the small bundle of newspaper in my hand—"the market has the best cuts of fish if you go early."

His bloodshot eyes raked across my features, and he leaned back in his chair. "Fish," he intoned. "For the merman."

"Yeah."

"I'll get right to the point," he said in a low voice. "You spend an awful lot of time and resources on a beast that's done little but stare daggers at us and prove itself—and, by extension, *you*—a worthless investment. What say you to that?"

I lifted my chin. Right into the smoke. "I've done everything you've asked me to do."

"Miss Kutzler claims you've spoken to it. Is that true?"

Here it was—the head-smelter I'd put off solving because I didn't want to solve it. I'd had *weeks* to figure out what to say when Morgan inevitably came looking for reasons to throw me out, and sure enough, the moment had arrived and found me unprepared.

"Yes," I said.

"*And?*" he snarled.

"And . . . he won't take orders from you."

Morgan's curled lip dented the straight line of his mustache. "Now, you listen to me. This production has less than two weeks left before we open the gates to the public. The very future of Luna Park hangs on our success. I am out of time and out of money to spend on a *tenement rat* who caters to a merman's whims and has nothing to show for it!"

Fire erupted behind my eyes, but I held it in check. Morgan got to his feet and leaned over the table, sending the sour whiff of booze up my nose.

"You're done! Finished," he barked. "Pack your things and get out of our establishment."

Sonia sat up. "But Sam—"

"What I meant to say"—I matched his steely gaze with my own—"is that the merman only takes orders from *me*."

The showman's eyes bulged. He *thwack*ed down his pipe against the table. "Don't toy with me."

"I wouldn't."

I glanced at Sonia, still ashen and holding herself around the middle, then back at Morgan.

"The merman is stubborn," I said, trying to sound like I knew what I was talking about. "But I've earned his trust. He'll listen to me."

Morgan stared through two slits under his manicured eyebrows. "Show me."

I led the way back to the stage, slightly nauseous now that my heart was trying to make a run for it out the backside of my rib cage. When I finished walking, I found myself in the same spot Morgan had stood in only last night—before Vincenzo had leveled him.

Río sat in his shadowy corner, arms folded, tail tucked, and face concealed behind a curtain of dark hair. With the pump off, he had to have heard every word we'd said.

"Go on," Morgan said. "Make a believer out of me."

I walked a bit farther so I could reach between the bars and put my hand against the glass.

"Merman," I said, loud enough for everyone in the room to hear, "would you come closer? So they can see you? Please?"

Río stared at me, unmoving. I could feel his alarm and confusion through the glass. God only knows what he was thinking after all that garbage I told Morgan.

"No one's come to hurt you," I tried again.

Still, Río didn't budge. Behind me, Morgan growled. "The beast is laughing at us."

"He's not, he's just . . ." My eyes lingered on the shadows of his face. They had deepened since the last time I'd seen him in the daylight.

"Tired," I finished.

I leaned in close to the glass and whispered in Spanish so he alone could understand me. "Please. Give him something. Anything. Do not give him a reason to hurt you. I could not bear it."

Río's eyes lowered. The muscles in his jaw twitched. Slowly, he rose off the bottom of the tank and drifted toward me.

"Jiminy Cricket," Sonia whispered.

When Río finally reached me, I smiled at him in a way I hoped hid how I truly felt, which was somewhere between wanting to empty the contents of my stomach and wanting to make like Lefty and backhand Morgan in the face. Río didn't even look at me. It was a long moment before he lifted his hand and gently placed it on the glass against mine.

"Incredible," breathed Morgan. "Go on, what else can it do?"

"Well, uh . . ."

An idea came. It was wild and ridiculous and a shot in the dark, but if it worked, it wouldn't just exorcize Morgan's rage—it would seal Río's place in history as the most valuable curiosity in Coney Island, if not the world.

Once more I looked up pleadingly into Río's silvery face and relied on my Spanish. "Do exactly as I say, my love," I breathed. "Just until he has seen enough. Trust me."

I looked back at Sonia and Morgan. Like I was taking over for Tití Luz again as lector of the tabaquería, I announced, "The Prince of Atlantis reigned over the East River when he *followed* the cry of a damsel in distress."

Maintaining my fingers against the glass, I walked around the tank side to the ladder. Río followed uncertainly beside me.

"Her boat," I continued, pointing to the roof of the tank, "drifted on the *rough waters*."

Río's lips pursed. I gave him my best I'll-make-it-up-to-you grimace. Whether or not he bought it, he soared to the surface and swam in a wide circle around the top of the tank until the water became a swirling, churning rapid.

Meanwhile, I climbed up the rungs, stepped onto the lattice, and unwrapped the fish.

"Before it could capsize, the prince appeared . . ." Río's face broke the surface, dripping and expressionless. I threaded my hand through the iron grill, the fish filet in my palm. He examined it through narrow eyes.

"The lady reached out to him. She begged for help." Whispering, I added, "Por favor."

With an almost imperceptible eye roll, he took it, then obediently replaced it with his fingertips.

"My word," came Morgan's voice from below, thick with emotion. "When you said it would listen to you, I never thought—but never mind what I thought! This! This is miraculous!"

I gently pulled my fingers away from Río and looked down over the edge at our audience. Morgan's hands were fastened on his hair, his mouth stretched in a crazed smile like the Funny Face on the wall at Steeplechase Park. Sonia's expression was stranger: she bit her lip like a disobedient thought was caught between her teeth.

"Do you understand what you've done here?" he said, beginning to pace around the foot of the tank. "No one in the history of mankind has ever tamed a merman, but look—he's practically a poodle! My God, the crowds will go positively fanatical at the sight of him!"

"Then Benny should be in the show."

We both gaped at Sonia. "¿Perdóname?" I choked as Morgan simultaneously said, "Beg your pardon?"

"The merman won't do any of that for you or me, Sam," she said. "It's Benny it listens to, so Benny's gotta be onstage. We'll build him right into the act!"

Morgan's glee shriveled. "Benny is completely unseasoned—"

"He can do impressions! He can sound like anyone you've ever met, I've heard it!" she insisted. "And he plays the guitar!"

The way she was talking me up, I felt like one of those all-in-one fire extinguishers at Sears, Roebuck, and Co., priced up just for the illusion of being useful. "Sonia, stop—"

"Can he?" Morgan gawped.

"No. I can't," I said, louder.

"Just think of it, Sam . . ." Sonia put a hand on Morgan's shoulder. He glanced down at it with restrained derision. "You could narrate while me 'n' Benny did all the work. I'll train him up myself. He don't need nothin' but some polish."

Morgan sized me up with the same veiled skepticism he'd had the day he discovered the skinny, asthmatic Puerto Rican had designed his custom tank. He reached a wary decision.

"You and you," he said, jabbing a finger at each of us. "Seven days to sort out your performance. I'll redraft the script tonight."

I'd thought my heart couldn't sink any lower, but at that moment it buried itself in the sand under the Luna Park firmament. I clung to the iron lattice like a pigeon on a wire, wondering what new hell I'd just created for myself. I looked down for Río's impression of all this, but he'd become a blob of blue-green and silver under the water.

"Yes, sir," I wheezed.

"It's Sam to you!" Morgan glanced cheerfully at his pocket watch. "Go home and alert the others that Benny has been added to our cast. Then it's back here, Benny, to finish the floors. I'll be returning to my studio for the next few days, seeing as Mr.

Caldera needs a poster." He produced a comb from his pocket, spit on it, and ran it through his rumpled hair. "And Sonia, *try* for pity's sake. You look ridiculous in that frock."

Sonia scowled at the back of his head as he left, while I climbed down the rungs. At the bottom, I crumpled the newspaper from Río's fish, at which point she remembered I was there and turned to meet my dismay.

"What the hell was that?" I demanded.

She shrank away from me for only a second before glazing her face in another winning sonrisa. "You can thank me later."

"*Thank* you? Christ, you don't know what you've done!"

"What *you've* done, you mean! Jeez, Benny, you did so great," she crooned, her voice gooey with excitement. "Morgan was happy as a clam in high tide—"

"Sonia, I ain't a performer! Neither is the merman!"

Her grin twisted skeptically. "Sure could've fooled me."

"That was just for Morgan!" I paced in a small circle, bashing the newspaper into a tighter ball. "It was hard enough making him do that act for two people. He's never been in front of a crowd—"

"Oh, honestly." Sonia's arms flopped down at her sides like I was nuts for missing the crackling potential of this whole sham. "The Albemarle is busting with folks who never thought they'd ever wind up in front of a crowd. Your pal in there is gonna be a star! The tourists will wrap around Surf Avenue just to see it!"

"*Him.*"

"Him, flim, whatever he is, he's gonna save the park! Aw, come *on*, Benny . . ." She hooked her arm on mine and steered me down the stairs into the audience. "You remember how scared you was the first time you rode the Circle Swing? You trusted me not to walk you off a cliff and look what a great time you had. Can't you trust me now?"

I peered over my shoulder at Río. He was facing the wall, but his ear was trained on us, visible just beneath his billowing hair.

I gently removed her hand from my arm. "What about Light the Night?"

A shadow passed over her face and disappeared. "What about it?"

"Sonia. You *kissed me*."

Her pale face reddened. "It was a mistake, all right? We were dancing and I was spilling my guts and you were being so damn *nice* . . ." She shook off the thought like she was shaking off a fly and sat down on a bench. "Benny, is it so hard to believe I'm just trying to help out a friend? You are my friend, right?"

"I am," I said, and I meant it. "I just didn't think friends spied on each other."

Sonia's eyes darted to the ceiling and back. "I just wanted to see where you kept disappearing to every night. I regretted it as soon as I walked in and heard you . . . *splashing* around in there."

My stomach lurched. "What else did you hear?"

"Enough to know you're more of a conversationalist with that thing than you are with the rest of us," Sonia pouted. "You might've let somebody know it spoke English."

"If you heard us talk, then you know he's not a thing," I said quietly.

"Fine. And since he's not a thing, he oughta thank me too. Everything's jake now!" She leapt to her feet. "Little Frankie and his goons'll be over the moon! With all the money the show rakes in, we could get out of Lulu's hotel and get our own homes—in *Sheepshead*! Leave Coney Island to the out-of-towners, and come in on the train for work like all them highfalutin Long Islanders do. And *Benny*," she gasped, holding out a palm at a blindingly bright something in the distance, "you're gonna be *famous*."

"Aw, lay off the absinthe, Sonia—"

"I'm serious! Once your name's up on that wall, kiddo, everything changes. The hotter the summer gets, the louder they cheer.

Ain't no feeling like it. You're a god among men, you can live forever!"

I once cast fences for houses like the one Sonia dreamed of. Wondered what it was like on the other end of the custom order—to be the sort of yanqui whose happiness got bought in cash. But what was the point of a big Long Island house without someone to share it with?

As for being a god among men, Río made me feel that way every time he touched me.

"What about the merman?" I murmured.

"I dunno, he gets all the fish he wants?" She laughed. "With the money he rakes in, he can have his own lake with the pretty coral decorations like them fancy aquaterrariums in Castle Garden if it'll make him happy."

That wasn't likely. Río was fond of coral reefs. Real ones.

At my lack of enthusiasm, Sonia's sparkle waned. "I dunno what else to tell you. If you care about your friend in there, you'll convince him to put on a show," she said with pleading eyes. "If he won't, it ain't just his life on the line. It's everyone's."

I looked past her at the theater—a box of wood and plaster I'd spent nearly two months painting, restoring, and polishing until the pantheon on the walls looked alive. Like every other job I'd ever done with my two hands, it was precise and perfect, because I'd never accepted anything less from myself, nor had anyone else.

Río was right. Between his tank and this theater, we were both caged. And my hands had crafted our prisons.

"Let's go home." Sonia tugged my arm. "You'll feel better after breakfast."

I nodded numbly. "I'll meet you at the gate. Gotta turn the pump back on."

With Sonia off my arm and headed toward the entrance, I climbed the steps to look in on Río a last time before I'd have to ruin the quiet with steam-powered chugging. I was going batty wondering what he thought of all this, but when I arrived at the glass, Río was sleeping, his back toward me.

In the center of the tank lay the fish I'd bought him, untouched.

Río

I did not know how binding my soul to Benigno's would feel. I expected to meet him in the ether between our hearts—that our natures would touch but resist each other. Instead, my spirit joined his readily and with powerful need, winding around his passion like an anemone. A tide courses through Benigno unlike anything I have ever felt, older and deeper than a seabed, and it consumed me as a storm swallows vessels upon the waves. The elders of our harmony could not fault me my transgression, for I felt the whole of the Atlantic sing in his heart for me. His love is so sublime I thought it might turn me to foam.

How is it possible to soar in ecstasy and the next instant, be plunged into icy despair?

Benigno is betrayed by the woman who stole his kiss. That he might save himself—and me—he engaged me in a falsehood I fear shall bring about my end. He delivered my compliance to the

Shark as if it were a gift, and though I trust Benigno not to harm me with intention, the harm is nonetheless done.

The burning tremors that wrack my fins have not ceased since the Shark's return, Mother. Desperate for relief, I reach for the joyful memory of Benigno's love in hopes it will quiet the wrath in my skin, but when it is not enough, I try to smooth the sensation away with my palms.

My scales come off in my hands.

Merciful Neptune, without the Currents' call, I pray for guidance some other way. For if Benigno cannot free me from this cage with haste, I will be foam in earnest soon enough.

TWENTY-SIX

Jesus Christ on a cracker, lemme get this straight . . ."

Emmett had the floor. Matthias's breakfast offering sat undisturbed in front of nearly everyone but Timmy, whose grits had migrated into his curls. Sonia was the only person at the dining table who didn't look like someone had spit in their café.

"You mean to tell me Caldera not only got the sea monster to do tricks, but he's gonna be in the show now too? Like, on stage? In a costume? With his own goddamned *poster*?" Emmett demanded in a voice that rose in pitch with every question mark.

"Is not terrible idea," rumbled Igor. "If Mr. Benny has trust of sea creature, why should he not also be on stage?"

"Better than Sam trying to tame it," muttered Eli, who stared at his bowl to avoid Emmett's glare. "I'm just sayin'. The way he bumped off that mermaid, if *I* was a merman, I probably wouldn't do a damn thing Sam said." He shivered and shoved his hands in his armpits. "I get nightmares just thinking about it."

"*You* get nightmares from the Galveston Flood show," Vera commented, plucking a crumb off her cornbread and licking it off her fingers with disdain.

Not to be sidetracked, Igor raised his fork. "In Russia, merman is 'vodyanoy.'" His chuckle made the bowls rattle. "Is much more older and more ugly creature than merman we capture, but anyway—vodyanoy is master of water, eh?"

He gestured at me.

"Mr. Benny is master of fire. Is make sense for blacksmith and merman to be paired. Is complement. Like Navya and me."

In a rare moment of outward affection, Navya grinned at the giant. Despite a stomach full of knots, so did I.

"He's *green*," Emmett fired back. "I don't see why Benny doesn't just share what he knows and let the professionals handle it."

"By professionals, surely you don't mean you and Eli," Navya scoffed. "The two of you have been a comedy act for longer than Timmy has been alive and have yet to be funny."

Eli sat up. "Hey!"

"You're all missing the point here," Sonia snapped. "The fact is, Thompson and Dundy are barely holding Luna Park together, Morgan's in debt to *gangsters*, and if they go down, guess who goes down with 'em?"

The Fräulein's hand clapped over her mouth too late, and an excruciating pause fell over the table. I buried my face in my hands.

"I *knew it*. That son of a bitch," Matthias hissed. "I swear, no one knows how to dig a hole straight to hell like Samuel Morgan!"

"But we're saved!" Sonia declared, as if it could rescue the conversation from its doomed trajectory. "Thanks to Benny, folks are gonna choose us over whatever copycat act Dreamland cooks up. And we needed someone to replace Saul, didn't we?"

"*No one* can replace Saul," said Lulu quietly, prompting nods of agreement around the table. "No offense, Benny."

I grunted into my palms. "None taken."

"I personally don't give two figs what any o' you boneheads think," said Matthias. He jerked his square chin in my direction. "I want to know what *he* has to say about it."

The company swiveled to look at me.

"It don't matter what I have to say," I murmured. "I ain't got a choice."

Another long silence threatened to harden the cornbread when I thought maybe telling them about Río would solve this whole stupid thing. If the idea of sharing the stage with me was so awful, maybe they wouldn't mind helping me get Río back home and out of the competition. Bring back some of the normalcy they'd had before Morgan decided to upturn their lives by courting mobsters and kidnapping mermen.

But where would that leave me?

"Aye, glad that's resolved, then," said Vera, butting in on my ruminations. "We got work to do if Benny's gonna get up on that stage for previews without makin' a right bags of it."

I stared at her. "'We'?"

Vera pulled out a long cigarillo and tucked it behind her ear. "You don't think we'd feed one of our own to the matinee dogs, do you?"

One of our own.

Eight faces eyeballed me like I was dumber than I looked if it had taken me this long to figure out that "with it, for it, never against it" included me too. Even Emmett shoveled a forkful of cold eggs into his mouth in a gesture of forbearance.

"All righty then," said Lulu, picking up her fork. "Finish your breakfast, Benny, then meet me in the parlor."

"What for?"

"To fit you for a costume."

For a half hour, Lulu tried and gave up squeezing me into a shiny thing that once belonged to Saul the Skeleton. "No worries, kiddo," she said. "I'll just let out a few seams and it'll fit you like a glove."

By "a few seams," I had to assume she meant all of them.

After that, it was off to Sonia's room to hear her ideas for dramatizing everything Río and I had improvised that morning. She had real intuition when it came to coordinating gags and tricks by the reaction they'd get from the crowd. If I were capable of paying any attention, I might've mentioned how little difference my input would make if I died of stage fright before the curtain even went up.

Moreover, that botched kiss still hung over our heads like the smoke from Morgan's pipe. I got the feeling Sonia's efforts to make me a sideshow headliner had something to do with it, a misguided olive branch that only made me desperate to finish what I'd started telling her in the ballroom. But when she asked my opinion about foregoing high wires and hoops in favor of staging her acrobatics around the tank's metalwork, my head emptied.

"Wait, so we'd be making like the merman kidnapped *you*?" I asked, catching up.

"It's so simple. A little backbend behind the tank, and voilà! I've been whisked away to the bottom of the ocean," she said brightly. "Oh! Then you can say, 'He made her his Queen of Atlantis!'"

"Like Persephone?"

She squinted at me. "That some kind of gramophone?"

"No, the goddess of spring. There's Hades, who rules the underworld, and he steals Persephone to be his wife. There's a frieze of them in the theater. You never noticed?"

"When in my illustrious career of standing on my head would I have noticed the friezes?"

"Never mind," I said. "I just don't think kidnapping's very romantic."

"I don't usually hear you talk about romance." I looked up to find Sonia pink-faced and staring intensely at her stage diagram.

Now. Now was the time.

"Sonia, I should tell you. What you saw this morning with the merman," I ventured, "wasn't real. I'm—I'm not his tamer."

She leveled a skeptical grin at me. "Huh. What was all that razzmatazz about then?"

"He did it for me," I said. "I begged him to."

Her grin faded. In its place a bewildered frown took shape. "What, is he an actual prince of the ocean that you'd be begging him for favors?"

"Of course not," I said quickly. "He's something else altogether. Especially to me."

Comprehension flickered behind her squinted eyes like a crank engine struggling to start. I couldn't rely on her to say it. Maybe the idea of two men together was no big deal to the surrogate sister of a pair like Eli and Emmett, but the idea of a man and a merman romantically attached had to be too great a stretch, even for a Coney Island contortionist.

I took her hands.

"Sonia, I'm his . . ."

My big confession fizzled halfway out of my mouth as I suddenly *got it*. Why Morgan had balanced the success of his criminal scheming on her shoulders—and why I wasn't just some guy she was sweet on.

I'll be the next Morgan, and with a young guy like you in the company now, we could even manage it together!

While Morgan sold her off as a side dish to thugs and the faceless bureaucrats of Luna Park, she was safeguarding the Menagerie's future from a Galveston Flood–sized disaster *alone*.

Enter me: Someone who could pick up her hankie and inherit the whole rapidly aging establishment with her.

"His . . . what?" she asked, her voice just above a whisper.

A shriek outside the door grew louder until Timmy burst into the room. He jumped onto my lap with a tiny blue statue in his pudgy fist.

"Demon child! Give that back!" Navya shouted from her bedroom.

"I just *wooking* at it! Benny, help," he whined against my chest, huddling over the statue like a little curly-haired camarón. "I not gonna bweak it!"

Bueno, that was a lie. Nearly everything Timmy touched shattered or came apart almost instantly, as if by some sinister brujería de chiquitín. "You gotta stop nabbing things without permission, nene." I cast a glance in Sonia's direction; she had shifted in her seat away from me, busily gathering up notes.

Navya stomped into the room, a flush across her brown cheeks. "Mr. Benny, please escort this thieving pest back to my room to return Krishna to his proper place," she commanded.

"Yes, ma'am."

Timmy grumbled unhappy noises into my shirt all the way to Navya's room—by far the most lavishly decorated room in the house, with a small shrine and expensive furniture perfectly sized to her stature except for a ceiling-high bookshelf that was crammed to bowing with books, framed portraits of bearded holy men, and statuettes of many-limbed deities I didn't know. When I first saw it, I wondered how on earth she scaled it before I noticed the ladder and felt like a nincompoop.

My eyes lingered over Matsya's picture as the kid placed the statue back on the shelf with less-than-gentle hands.

When I returned to Sonia and Vera's room, it was empty.

That night, I found the fish I'd brought Río earlier still uneaten in the center of the tank floor. Río himself was lying with his head against the driftwood, facing the wall.

Huh. In the dark, I couldn't be sure, but the water looked a little cloudy. Maybe two months was enough time for even a merman's powers of purification to prove no match against Brooklyn tap, steam-powered circulation pump be damned.

"Amor," I whispered from the lattice. "Are you awake?"

Río's shadow slowly grew in the water. When his face broke the surface, his eyes were pink-rimmed and set in dark circles, as if all our late nights had finally caught up to him. I immediately set about pulling off my suspenders so I could join him before his low voice derailed me.

"You should not come in tonight."

My hand stalled over my shirt buttons. "Why not?"

He looked dimly into the water. "I am unwell."

"I had a feeling. You left the fish." Worried, I laid down on the grill. "Last night, you didn't feel right either. When we . . . Was it too much?"

"No, querido. I do not regret anything we did last night," he reassured me with a half smile like his lips were torn between happiness and sorrow. "Your love has been a shield and sustenance to me. You revived me."

I blushed at him through the bars. "Me too."

"Would that you were mer," he said in a voice I strained to hear. "You would like the ocean, I think. Can you imagine it? A liquid universe, infinite in its mysteries, and still it holds you as though you are its most precious star. A place where, no matter which sea realm surrounds you, you are always home."

My neck prickled. "Río, what's got you talking like this?"

He looked up at me, his lip quivering. I reached my hand toward him. He backed away from it.

"Let me in," I said in Spanish. "You can rest on me and—"

"If you come in, you will not be able to get back out."

There was a three-foot distance between the grill and the water. Río would lift me up so I could leave each night. It could only mean . . .

"You're too weak."

Río drifted to the wall and touched his forehead to the glass. "I resisted. I swore my captivity would never conquer my dignity. But my body can go no further, Benigno. I feel it."

"Your dignity?" The anxiety that had been filtering into my chest like poison gas all day was thickening with every word Río wasn't saying. "If this is about this morning, I'm so sorry. I didn't plan it; I just thought it'd get Morgan off our backs so he wouldn't send me away from you. You and me, we're just trying to survive."

"At what cost?" he asked, a new hoarseness in his musical voice. "Perhaps *you* are in the habit of pretending to be what you are not, denying yourself happiness, working to exhaustion for the good of everyone but yourself—of making yourself agreeable to a *murderer*—and for what? To exist without freedom! To wake each day with only half your humanity intact! Merciful Neptune, how can you bear it?"

I hadn't seen him so indignant since the day he'd grabbed me by the throat. "I don't have a choice," I tried to explain. "In this town, choices are for white men with money, and the rest of us do what we can to get by. When the options are getting sick or shot or thrown in jail, what choices do any of us really have?"

"Do not speak to me of choices when *you* have not been locked in an iron box," he said icily. "You have choices, but you are too frightened to make them!"

Too frightened to free him was what he meant. He was right. But I couldn't bring myself to say it—that falling in love with Río had changed everything for me, and I'd assumed it had changed everything for him too. At some point, I'd convinced myself he wouldn't be in such a hurry to leave if he felt like I did. If he knew that staying in the Menagerie meant we could stay together.

Maybe he knew no such thing.

"I'm choosing *us*. I'm just trying to be smart about this," I said. "If we play our cards right, you won't have to—"

"By the time you finish being smart, I will be dead."

The words dealt un golpetazo to my chest before I fully understood their meaning. "What?"

"Benigno, *look at me*."

I did. And, for the first time, I *saw*. It had happened so gradually I'd completely failed to notice it. His skin, lustrous as a pearl the first time I spied it in the light, was now as dim as the curtains I'd spent days scrubbing. His tail, once vibrant with shimmering blues and greens, now matched nearly everything else in New York City—coated in a thin gray sheen. Even the webbing between his fingers looked brittle and thin.

I rifled through memories of our nights together: Río hanging off to the side during our nighttime swims. How he'd taken to letting me carry him around.

In an instant, all the air in the room seemed to escape. "No."

"Until today, I remained uncertain," he murmured. "No one mer has ever been taken away from the Currents, so how could I have known? I had convinced myself it would pass. That somehow, I could will myself to overcome it, but my fins burn without ceasing."

"No. *No*. You're so *young*," I protested, "and strong! I felt it last night!"

He smiled grimly. "The condition of my spirit does not match the body that houses it any more than yours does."

"*My* body wasn't made to last for hundreds of years!"

"Benigno, would I lie to you?"

He wouldn't. I knew that.

But he was also *wrong*. Because if he wasn't, then that'd be it for me. I'd finally fold. Neither starvation, illness, violence, nor occupation had done me in yet, and as much as I'd abandoned notions of God, I wanted to believe that whatever omnipotent being lorded mercilessly over my life would look at everything I'd done, at how hard I'd tried, and not find cause to punish me by taking away the people I loved over and over and over again. Losing Tití Luz was bad enough, but losing Río . . .

I was clinging to tree roots in the middle of a hurricane again.

"You can't be dying," I said. "You've lost some luster, but that's my fault, keeping you awake so late. I'll take better care of you. Hell, I'll dig you a lake just like Sonia said—"

"A prison the size of a lake is still a prison," he snapped in frustration. "I need the *ocean*."

My voice felt suddenly fragile under the weight of my growing panic. "You don't know what you're asking of me."

"I do know. Do you think I want to part myself from you?" He paused. "But something else prevents you from setting me free. Something the woman Sonia said to you. What makes you hesitate?"

Of course he'd heard everything. "I— I dunno what you want me to say," I stammered. "It's not about just me anymore. The whole company relies on this place to survive."

Río's eyes narrowed to slits. "Since when has the fate of this hellish place been your concern?"

"They're decent people," I said, sweat forming at my temples. "Their lives are staked into this show."

"Then I should die to earn them a living?" he demanded.

"Of course not! Because you're not going to die!"

He scrubbed a hand over his face and gripped the glass. "You needed allies, you said. You told me you would not give up on freeing me. You *promised*."

"I haven't given up!" I insisted. "Just give us the summer. Morgan could pay off Frankie and after that, who knows? There might be enough money to pay for a way to keep us together."

Río punched the water with his tail. "Or you could release me *now* and damn Morgan and his Menagerie to the depths!"

"*Escúchame*." Desperation was already crowding out the remnant air in my chest while tears gathered along my eyelids. "Anyone who believes the flyers knows merfolk exist now. If you stayed, I could protect you, keep you safe from all the Morgans and Reynolds and Frankies, otherwise it's off to the Atlantic with you until the next human drags you back out."

"Protect me. Keep me." Bitterness curled his pewter lips. "You sound like the Shark."

His words could have leveled me all by themselves. "How can you say that?"

Río didn't answer. Just stared at the water with the same hopeless disappointment that had squatted in my heart before Río's affection had chased it out.

"My whole life, I've never loved anyone like I love you," I whispered. "How can you expect me to cast you back to the water when I've only just found you?"

He sighed and looked despairingly up at me through the bars. "So says every man who has ever hooked a fish."

"Río—"

"I tire of talking, Benny," he said, and I flinched at the sound of my American name. "I wish to rest."

And without looking back, he dove away from me.

I called after him. When he didn't come, I climbed back down and placed my hand against the glass—a gesture, once intimate, that I'd put on display before his captor just this morning. I curled my fingers around San Cristóbal and stared into the shadows, where Río stayed until I got the message he'd rather be alone.

That night, the heat in Saul's room stuck to my lungs like coal tar. Crying only made it worse; once the hacking started, I sat up, lit my lamp, and gave up trying to breathe the way Río showed me because nothing about the air felt remotely breathable.

What makes you hesitate? he had demanded. Three months ago, I would've told him nothing. Surviving was easiest when you had no one else to save but yourself.

I didn't plan to get pulled into the center of Morgan's criminal tempest, but maybe a tempest is where the Currents needed me to be. I could help my friends *and* Río, and if it meant shipwrecking whatever was left of my heart on the Menagerie stage, then so be it.

TWENTY-SEVEN

The hours until dawn were a drowsy stretch of tears, asthma, and nightmares of Playa del Condado after the hurricane. In them, my nose clogged with the unbreathable stench of corpses floating facedown around my legs until their bloated hands took me by the ankles and dragged me under. I woke up with Saul's sheets in my mouth and, with the added insult of a pounding headache, decided I'd slept enough.

That same day, an unseasonable heat descended on the city. It was only the second week of May, but seemingly overnight, the temperatures had climbed high enough to draw a fair number of city folk away from the unventilated tenements and fetid sun-baked streets out to Manhattan Beach. They came seeking the sea breeze, but there didn't seem to be any breeze at all.

On my way into work, loudmouths in stained coveralls trudged around Luna Park with ladders, toolboxes, and carts full of bricks, lightbulbs, and steaming vats of pitch. Familiar as I was with tropical heat, I worked up a sweat just looking at them and tried to ignore the itch as my wool pants stuck to me like wallpaper.

I'd just reached the ballroom when a shrill sound from inside the Menagerie made my heart nearly give out on the promenade.

A whistle.

I exploded into the theater. "Hey . . . HEY!"

Morgan stood next to Río's tank with a brand-new metal pipette between his lips hooked from a chain around his neck. He spit it out. "Benny, do you *mind*?"

"You can't use that thing!" I shouted.

Sonia, observing from the center aisle, wasted no time getting right in my way. "Benny, Benny, everything's jake, all right?" she coaxed softly, pushing me backward. "Why don't we let them have a moment?"

"What? *No!*" I shoved past her. "His ears can't take the sound, Sam! It hurts him!"

Morgan slanted an incredulous look at me. "A few weeks of soaking codfish, and suddenly you're the expert," he scoffed. "As I recall, *I* taught *you* about their sensitive ears."

Then he didn't care. "But what's he done? Why are you punishing him?"

"Escort Benny to the museum, Sonia. I'll be along when I'm through with our session here."

Sonia recommenced yanking my arm, but I was staring at Río. He braced himself against the wall with a hand on his ear. The reams of daylight across his back gave him a sickly, matte pallor as if his iridescence had gotten washed out with dirty laundry water. His skin had paled overnight like leaves left too long in the dark.

"Come on," said Sonia, yanking harder. "We'll talk outside. I can clear things up."

I didn't want to talk. I wanted to rush the stage. One swift tackle, and I'd force-feed Morgan that *maldito* whistle until his inhales sounded as reedy mine. Instead, I snapped my arm out of Sonia's grip and strode past her into the hallway, watching Río over my shoulder until he disappeared behind the swinging doors.

As soon as her feet crossed the museum threshold, I got right in her face. "What the hell is going on?" I demanded. "*I'm* the one who looks after Río, not Morgan!"

"What's a 'río'?"

"The merman!" I started pacing as an alternative to kicking walls. "Madre de Dios, I should've gotten him out when I had the goddamn chance!"

Sonia gaped at me like I was concussed. "It's just a *whistle*, you maniac!"

I whipped around, and she shrank back.

"You've never seen me be a maniac. But just *wait* until I hear that sound again."

The thud of the partition doors announced Morgan's arrival. I turned to find him staring at me with an irritated dent in his mustache, his new torture device swinging loosely from his neck.

"For a green performer, you've certainly learned how to make an entrance," he intoned.

I had to cool my head. Without a grip on my rage, I'd lose something a lot more precious to me than my job. "I'm just a little . . . confused," I said haltingly. "See, I thought *I* was the merman's keeper. Wasn't that why you wanted me in the show?"

He turned a scolding eye on Sonia. "Miss Kutzler hasn't told you?"

My eyes jerked in her direction to find her standing behind the reupholstered dragon.

"She telephoned last night," Morgan continued. "Helped me realize it might look a bit odd for our newest member to debut as a merman tamer. Thought it might send something of a mixed message to see the creature obedient to an unknown when it's my surname on the awning. Isn't that right, Sonia?"

Morgan's words seemed to wrap around my windpipe and squeeze. "But he won't obey you."

"You think not?" he said in mock consideration. "Because it's certainly been *very* responsive to this little gem I picked up downtown." He held up the whistle, and a fresh wave of revulsion spider-crawled down my neck.

"Now, I understand the natural desire to be *important*," Morgan went on with icy detachment. "You've broken the beast in, well done for that. But I'll advise you not to let your head get too big lest you lose it next time you question my methods."

"I'm sorry," I said without defining what I was sorry for, or to whom. "But if it's all the same, I'd still like to be in the show."

"And do what? Put on a tail and make yourself a member of the prince's royal court?"

"I'm a musician. I've got my cuatro. The act might benefit from some Caribbean"—I broke off in search of the right English word—"atmosphere?"

He shot me a cynical smirk. "'Caribbean atmosphere.' By that you mean humid and oppressively hot?"

"With all due respect, New York City's already humid and oppressively hot."

"I think it's a good idea," Sonia chimed in suddenly, her mouth already plastered in her trademark sonrisa. "We could set the scene in the tropics, couldn't we?" She turned to me. "What can you play?"

"Boleros, mostly," I said warily. "Music from my homeland."

"Don't sell me a dog, Sonia," huffed Morgan. "What on earth would Coney Island tourists know about . . . whatever he's talking about?"

"Nothing, of course!" Sonia was reviving a bit now that she was solving problems again. "And all the better. Anything they're dancing to down in Cuba—"

"Porto Rico," I inserted.

"—is exotic! And exciting!" she continued. "I'm imagining palm trees, an ocean backdrop. We'll build a sandy beach right on the stage . . ."

Incredibly, Morgan looked poised to take the bait. "A nighttime scene, perhaps . . ."

"With a moon! And this way, Benny gets to stay in the show without having to worry about"—she glanced at me—"anything else."

What the hell is her angle?

Morgan's frigid gaze passed between Sonia and me as though he was seriously questioning whatever wisdom had compelled him to employ us in the first place. Finally, he blew out a sigh reeking of pipe smoke and brandy. "You're both lucky I'm in a good mood," he muttered. "We'll try it. Goodness knows we could use the extra flair when our special patrons decide to visit."

I faked a tight smile. "I'll just go back for my cuatro—"

"No," he said tersely. "We need the second greenroom cleared to house those exotic set pieces before we can start building. Move the food and salt to the stables. And keep away from the tank lest the merman forget who its master is. Understood?"

Carajo. I might have seen that coming. "Understood. But . . ." Whatever I said next had to tread that thin line between persuasive and pushy. "Couldn't you try something less painful than a whistle?"

"Mr. Caldera." His mustache twitched. "The pain is the point."

He straightened his waistcoat and strode back through the doors and down the hall, away from us.

Sonia relaxed next to me. Or a girl who looked a lot like her, anyway. After that *maldito* dance in the ballroom, someone had hollowed her out and installed a scab in her place.

"You don't know what you've done," I whispered.

"I was only thinking of you—"

"No, you were only thinking of *you*. You must think I'm an idiot. I could see it on your face before Timmy busted in on us like a pint-sized tornado. You know *exactly* what Río means to me!"

"Benny," she whispered with forced patience, "he's not human. No matter what you think you feel, it ain't real."

"What do you know about what's real?" I hissed. "You spend six months out of the year pretending to be someone else in a plaster fantasy land! Your name's not even Sonia!"

Her frown hardened, adding years to her face. "That's rich coming from you! Getting steamrolled every day by a buncha sooty ruffians in a Red Hook factory—was that where *you* felt more real?" she snapped, tears brimming. "You think you can stick someone like me in a kitchen somewhere with eight kids hangin' off my apron strings while my old man digs ditches? That life's the bigger lie, Benny! Look around you. Luna Park might be a fantasy land, but this show is where I *live*, and it don't work if you're sweet on the headliner!"

"Santa María, there won't *be* a show if Río dies!"

For once, Sonia didn't have a smart retort. "What're you saying?"

"I'm saying to hell with this goddamn Menagerie." My broken voice grated against my own ears. "And to hell with me too."

Sonia stood there with wide, wet eyes. I pushed past her into the hallway, past the empty rectangle where my stupid poster would be hung, while the tinny screech of Morgan's whistle echoed off the Grecian friezes right into the marrow of my bones.

But between my ears, I was louder. Screaming inside my own head, as Río swam in an obedient circle at the top of the tank. On the next turn, he spied me through the bars—from across a universe, it seemed—then looked quickly away before Morgan could catch him.

I didn't have to wonder what had changed. In a body that was turning against him, Río's last recourse for survival was to do what I'd become an expert at doing my whole life.

Comply.

There was no anger in his face. I wished there was. Rage meant he still had fight in him, and God knows I deserved it. I locked the door behind me in the windowless greenroom and gripped the sides of the nearest crate as my stomach convulsed. The burn of vomit followed, surging up my throat like phosphoric acid on rusted steel.

And, like every urge to let out what I felt, I choked it back down.

TWENTY-EIGHT

I wound up obeying orders just like Río. Manual labor was all I had to distract me from feeling I could punch a hole in the tank with my bare hands, like Matthias probably should have done the first day we met. Every crate I moved wrought a burning hatred that coalesced in my stomach like liquid metal.

I hated Morgan. I hated Sonia. The whole Empire State could go to hell.

But I hated myself most of all. I was about to lose a genuine article in a sea of impersonators, the only person left who truly knew me, and I understood with bone-crushing certainty that part of my soul would go with him, never to revive. I thought of what Igor said about Río and me, water and fire. Whether or not humanity deserved it, Río was the sort to pour himself out in compassion for humans.

Me? I wanted to burn down the world.

The rattle of the handle jolted me out of my violent thoughts. Suddenly, the door swung wide to reveal a sweaty, self-satisfied Sam Morgan, who did a quick examination of the room while I stood in the back corner balancing an overfull crate of costumes in my arms.

"I'm retiring for the evening," he said. "Clear out of here."

He waited for me to join him at the door, then walked me past Río's tank—no doubt to make sure I didn't linger there. I kept my head down, so it wouldn't be too obvious when I peered hungrily through the iron bars. Río lay in his corner, his arms wrapped tightly around himself.

Is he sleeping? Injured?

"The Menagerie was once a traveling exhibition, you know."

Morgan's gravelly voice wrenched my attention away from the tank. "You mentioned," I mumbled.

"A small caravan of curiosities," he said with a strange lilt, as if he rarely shared this information with anyone, much less his troublesome hired hand. "The creatures that stand in the museum today were once on display in towns from Burlington to New Orleans, drawing hordes from their sleepy villages like a pied piper on the promise of seeing a stuffed being or beast lured from the edges of the earth."

Morgan sucked his teeth breezily. "Of course, mummified relics could never compete with a living curiosity. Whenever the everyman confronts the abnormal, the deformed, and the deviant, he apprehends the oddity within himself. From there, he grows an appreciation for the perfect, the divine, and the noble. And then"—he pointed toward the sky—"he *aspires* to it."

A shadow had settled over Sam Morgan since the night he tangled with Frankie Agostinelli's goons. Even in stagnant heat, it sent a chill down my backbone.

"Nowadays, the freak is no longer evidence of God's judgment, but an object of . . . scientific *contemplation*," he grumbled sourly. "Scholars explain away the riddles of the natural world with their lengthy papers and Latin names, and the public imagination shrivels. It then falls to other men to restore their sense of wonder."

"Men like you, you mean?"

He glanced sideways at me and grinned, baring his bright teeth. *Especially* men like me. Old Jack Morgan didn't have the requisite language, business sense, or ambition to draw in larger, more sophisticated crowds. Luckily, I did. And unlike my predecessor, I don't tend to tolerate obstacles. Had he not bequeathed his establishment to me, Luna Park might never have become the Heart of Coney Island."

"Must've been hard to do all that by yourself."

Morgan's eyes darkened over his smile.

"I can see why the exhibits like you. How nice you've all taken to each other so quickly," he said, though he didn't sound like he thought it was particularly nice at all. "They disagree with my approach, I know. They have their silly little motto that they never stop saying."

"'With it, for it, never against it'?" I offered.

Morgan snorted to the affirmative. "A quaint philosophy for those whose aspirations don't exceed eating tinned food thrice a day and escaping the asylums. That attitude does little more than fool them into believing they can protect each other from the derision of the outside world," he said, biting each consonant on its way out of his mouth. "But not even a person's flesh and blood can protect them from that."

A sneer twisted his lips. "A mermaid I saw in my youth damn near ruined my life," he murmured. "No one believed me. My family rejected me. But I knew that, were I to capture one, I'd do better than unshackle myself from the assumptions everyone had made about me. I would awaken in the masses a new understanding of the natural world and our place in it."

Jesucristo, nothing makes a lowlife feel high like stomping on folks more spurned by society than they are. I bit back the urge to ask him what his lime-green suit purchase did to advance his "aspirations."

"Why are you telling me this?" I asked instead.

"So you can understand my intentions. That creature will send a message—one which will resonate throughout the populace—that gods still dwell among us, and my Menagerie is the sole establishment on earth fit to keep one. For this reason, it is imperative that you trust me enough to stay *out* of my way," he said coldly. "Do you?"

We'd finally reached the front gate of Luna Park. The sun no longer blazed overhead, but there wasn't so much as a draft to cut the malevolent haze rising off the pavement. I was burning too—with a desire to grab his silver chain by the whistle and strangle him with it.

"Yes, sir."

"Capital," he said with a smile. "I knew I could rely on you."

The Albemarle and the Culver Depot were in the same direction, but he guarded the gate until I was far enough in the distance that there was no chance I could turn around and sneak back in without him catching me. He knew I was lying when I said I trusted him, just as I knew he was lying when he said he could rely on me.

He hadn't asked me to call him Sam.

I never made it to the Albemarle. Once Morgan's watchful eye was on its way back to Queens, I took the path between Feltman's and Dreamland toward the beach.

It gave me a closer look at the park that had made so much trouble for my friends, with its gold-leaf-encrusted carousel, towers, and roller coasters, the maintenance workers hanging off them like paint-spattered Christmas ornaments. Dreamland would open the day after Luna Park's previews.

For the evening, the moderate crowds had dwindled, and there was only the scuffle of my shoes against pavement and the rolling drone of ocean waves growing louder as I approached the beach.

Concrete gave way to boardwalk, powder gave way to wet sand. I didn't bother taking off my shoes. Just staggered right into the water.

The unceasing breakers surged and crashed, spread, and retreated. Though I dug my heels in to steady myself, the tide still pulled the silt right out from under them, leaving me wavering on my feet. In a battle for supremacy, I was no match for the Currents.

"Why?"

My whisper disappeared in the din of waves.

"*Tell me why, ¡carajo!*"

I plunged both my hands into the water, scooped up dripping wads of sand, and flung them as hard as I could at the sea.

"You left him," I hollered, "¿Y pa' qué? So he could die alone in a cage after that yanqui diablo maims him with a five-penny whistle? What kind of shitty deity are you?!" I grabbed another fistful of wet sand. "How could you just *strand him here?*"

I flung the wad of sand as hard as I could and took it as an accusation when it slapped lamely into a slow wave near my feet.

You were the one the mermaid had begged to save his life, it seemed to say.

"Yeah well, I got news for you," I spat. "Río's mother picked the wrong guy. I can't save anyone. Not Tití Luz, not my parents, not the Menagerie." I kicked the water as hard as I could. "Not even my own"—*kick*—"sorry"—*kick*—"ass!"

I lost my footing in the undertow and fell onto my knees. The water ran frigid over my thighs and forearms, ice against the fire on my skin, and I just stayed there, shivering on the warmest spring day New York had seen in decades, waiting for a reason to stop believing I was completely, infuriatingly alone.

"Which god do I gotta pray to?" I gasped through tears. "No me importa. I don't care who's out there, just don't let him die. Please, I'll do anything. *Anything.* Just tell me what to do . . ."

A flock of noisy seagulls soared over my head. As the waves retreated, they landed around me, dozens of them, to peck at horseshoe crabs that had climbed up in pairs along the shore.

"The hell—"

Without warning, a stealthy wave slammed into my side and knocked me flat on my back, soaking me through. It chased the seagulls away.

Suddenly, I knew exactly who I needed to talk to.

"If you're knocking to see Eli, he's—*ergh*—in the kitchen so I don't gotta—*goddammit*—poison nobody!"

I'd never given much thought to the limitations Emmett's missing leg placed on him because it frankly never seemed to slow him down, but as I stood outside his and Eli's bedroom, I suddenly wondered if he'd had an accident.

"Do you need help?" I called through the door.

"Not in the mood, kid," he grunted, and I heard a loud thud as something large thumped against the floor.

"What was that?"

"A warning shot! Go away!"

I tried the knob. It was unlocked. "I'm coming in," I said and pushed my way into the room.

Garments were scattered around Emmett like rainbow-colored seaweed, and he, the hapless seagull perched in the middle of it. From the waist down, he wore something too wide for his hips but too small for his leg, red and satiny with a tear in the inseam where his gray union suit poked out.

His peg leg lay across the room where he'd apparently thrown it.

"Nice . . . pants?"

"Aw, shut up," he grumbled. "The costumes are always a little tight before the season starts. Lulu will fix 'em." Sitting at the vanity, he rummaged on the ground for something else shiny and bright. "You here to stink up my evening?"

"I need your help."

"Go milk a bull. I got a whole other person to fit in these pants, so if you don't mind—"

"*Please.*"

Emmett lifted his head to shoot me his most hostile glare, but as soon as his eyes landed on my face they popped in surprise.

"Jesus, Benny. You look like shit."

I glanced down at myself. I might as well have been run over by a streetcar in a rainstorm. I didn't care.

"Let's get something straight," I began in a low voice. "I know you don't like me. You make that plain enough every time I gotta suffer through your grousing at the dinner table. I also know you only hate me 'cause you're spooked by a certain kind of foreigner, just like every pale-faced pendejo in New York who thinks I don't deserve to be here."

Emmett made an indignant noise, but I plowed on. "You're just another back-seat bully who can't stand bein' so goddamn scared all the time, so you made up a version of me you could blame for all the bullshit you can't fix. That's why, when it comes to me, you're wrong about everything––except one thing."

I turned and slammed the door closed behind me. "And I know you know what it is."

For the first time ever, Emmett looked at me like I was a real person instead of the villain in his paranoid delusions. He shrank in his seat.

"It's true then. That you're . . . ?"

"Yeah. I am."

He glanced down at the crumpled mound in his hands and rubbed uncomfortably at the red silk stretched over his thigh. "All right. So, what's that got to do with me?"

"Tell me how you did it." My voice came out ragged, a sound like mortar scraped across bricks. "Eli told me what you did for your freedom. When everyone and everything was trying to end Rudy and Lenny—when you had to be scared outta your mind and it'd be easier to just go back to whatever life was like before the neighbors caught you—how'd you get him out? How'd you find a way when there wasn't a way?"

He let out a sardonic *pfft*. "Why? You fixin' to lose a leg?"

"If that's what it takes."

Emmett stilled, frowning at me. But before I could make a second attempt at convincing him, he made a fist in the shiny red fabric and, with a loud *rriiiippp*, yanked it off, letting the shredded pants fall to the floor.

He leaned his forearms on his thighs and sighed.

"The way you tell it, you make it sound like I had some kind of secret. I didn't have no trick for getting Eli and me outta there. Hell. I don't even remember that night."

My face fell. Everything fell. "Oh. I see."

"But what I do remember," he continued quietly, "was thinking I was gonna die getting Eli out, or I was gonna die without him, you get what I'm saying?"

I swallowed back the hard knot in my throat and nodded.

"I ain't a smart guy like you, Benny." A bittersweet grin crossed his lips. "But if there's anything I've learned just being human in this lousy, jacked-up world, it's that love and hate—they got something in common. They put blinders on you, so's you can't see nothing but whatever it tells you to see. When our folks saw we was a couple of inverts, they did what hate makes people do. But me . . ."

Emmett's rugged features melted into an almost unrecognizable softness. He spoke just above a whisper.

"All I could see was the boy I loved."

I stepped closer to him. "You ever regret it?"

He chuckled and shook his head. "Nah. I got everything I need and better—'cept maybe a goddamned costume that fits. What I want to know is why you and your sweetheart are stuck. This is Coney Island, not Connecticut. The Brooklyn waterfront's got more fairies than Neverland."

He could've knocked me over with a feather. "*What?*"

"And anyway, it ain't like the company cares about that kind of thing. Do I even know the guy?"

Suddenly, everything from my hair to my toenails seemed to weigh a thousand pounds.

"Sort of."

Emmett sat up. "Who?"

Ignoring the unhappy fact that confessing my affair with Río to the guy who'd pegged me as a threat would basically confirm everything Emmett had ever suspected about me, I let the whole history out, from the mermaid's dying wish to the intimacy that bloomed between Río and me—all while Río's health wilted right under my nose. I couldn't believe how easy it was to spill my guts when Emmett and I had nothing in common without the shared experience of loving someone we weren't allowed to love.

It seemed to be enough.

"Now Morgan's back to torturing him," I concluded, starting to shake. "He won't even let me near the tank anymore. I gotta get Río out of there. And I know the show will be done for and I'll lose him forever, but Emmett, I just can't l-let him—"

A sob smothered the word I couldn't bear to say. Without Río to keep me afloat, I backed toward the wall, sank to the floor, and wept into my grainy sleeve. Somehow, even weeping in Emmett's humiliating presence felt better than preserving myself like one of Morgan's museum pieces behind a wall of numb indifference.

A succession of thumps halted just ahead of where I'd crumpled. I looked up, and Emmett was standing over me with his hand out.

I took it. Balanced solidly on his one leg, he helped me to my feet.

"I'm real sorry, kid," he whispered, gripping my hand harder than I could grip back. It wasn't the lengthy amends you expected from somebody who looked as contrite as he did, but even I knew how much those words cost a guy like Emmett.

"How much do you love him?" he asked.

My voice still sounded like steel wool. "I can't breathe without him."

He nodded. "Then there's only one thing left to do."

"Rob a bank?" I sniffled.

"What? No!" And he slapped me upside the head like I was Eli. "Abduct the merman, ya knucklehead!"

My eyes bulged at the suggestion—and at the man who'd been so protective of the Menagerie but was now offering to demolish it. "What about the company?" I asked. "The show will probably close, not to mention Morgan'll go batty on everyone the second he finds out his star performer is gone."

"Oh, I know." Emmett hopped to my side and put his arm around my shoulder. "*That's* why we're gonna frame Dreamland for it."

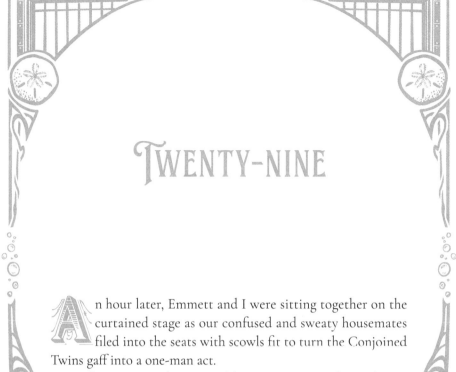

TWENTY-NINE

An hour later, Emmett and I were sitting together on the curtained stage as our confused and sweaty housemates filed into the seats with scowls fit to turn the Conjoined Twins gaff into a one-man act.

"Tell me again why we couldn't just meet in the parlor," I whispered.

He rolled his eyes. "We're selling a jailbreak, kid. It won't work if they don't know the inmate."

After I had finished spilling my guts to Emmett, he took it upon himself to summon everyone to the Menagerie ("Emergency meeting at the theater, ya numbnuts!"), then walked ahead with me to sneak me back into the park in case Sam had tipped Oscar off about keeping me away. It meant finally getting to see Río after this morning's torturous training session.

As soon as I'd tucked myself behind the curtain, I'd had to hold in a gasp at the sight of him huddled and clinging to his tail. Río's skin now had some sort of film on it that floated around him in a smoky haze, and a quick glance at his lower half showed patches of matte, colorless flesh where scales used to be.

They were scattered across the sand like pennies in a fountain.

"Confía en mí," I had whispered, then quickly summarized Emmett's plan through the glass. I didn't want Río to panic in the sudden company of everyone he'd seen at Lawrence Point, plus some new strangers.

"Goddamn, Em, I got another half hour of lifting before I'm available for the airing of idiot grievances," sniped Matthias, whose muscles weren't remotely in need of more weight lifting. He threw himself onto a bench between Navya—whose breakfast debate with Igor on the World Series starting lineup was still going—and Vera, who slumped down looking more like Eli's sibling than Emmett did in an outfit made up entirely of my spare clothes.

Sonia was last through the partition doors, overheated and pushing Lulu in the wheelchair with Timmy drowsing in his mother's lap. Lulu had apparently been in the middle of making Sonia's costume adjustments when Emmett whisked everyone out the door.

"This better be good, Em," huffed Sonia. "Twelve pins is all that's holding this onesie together. Twelve!"

Emmett got up and shuffled toward the proscenium where the curtain tucked into the wing. "You'll get your petticoats back on as soon as we're done here."

She sniffed at his own state of semi-dress, Emmett having only bothered to throw on pants and suspenders. "Speak for yourself."

"Actually, I ain't here to chat." Emmett pointed a thumb at me. "Benny is."

Everyone's mutterings ceased, leaving only the chugging of the circulation pump for me to talk over. I slid off my cap, got to my feet, and wondered briefly where my anxiety had gone now that the truth was one speech away. A moment later, with a loud hiss of metal rings dragging against the steel track, Emmett parted the curtain to reveal the tank.

The lit chandeliers had left Río without a shadow to hide in. He backed away from the glass and shielded his bloodshot eyes.

"*Matsya!*" Timmy's squeal made both Río and me jolt. The brazen little manganzón made a dash up the stage steps. Madam Navya looked like she might faint dead away from shock.

Lulu grabbed Sonia's arm in a move to leave her wheelchair behind. "Timothy Porter, you get back here!" But the kid had already smushed his face against the glass, bouncing on his toes like his underpants hid a set of hydraulic pistons. "He wooks just like the madam's picture, Mama!"

"Benny," Lulu implored.

I already had my hands on the kid's shoulders to steer him away, but when I caught the lonely ache in Río's eyes, I got a different idea.

"Amor mío. This is Timmy." Behind me were rustles to intervene, but I held up a hand. "It's all right."

Río's uncertain gaze shifted between my face and Timmy's before he brought himself level with el chiquitín, who was comically flattened against the viewing pane. He reached out a webbed finger and gently tapped Timmy's nose through the glass. Not to be outdone, Timmy blew a raspberry.

A mischievous grin took shape on Río's lips, and he stuck out his tongue.

"Oh my God," breathed Lulu.

I turned back to my housemates and gestured to the glass.

"Everyone? This is Río."

"This a joke?" asked Eli. "What's goin' on here, Em?"

"Emmett asked you here on my behalf," I answered. "So I could convince you to help me set Río free."

Everyone in the company sat up, except Sonia, who slouched like she was trying to shrink out of existence.

"I know you don't think he's one of us. Maybe, now that I've said this, you won't think I am either. But you can see it, can't you? That he's not a *thing* you ditch behind a curtain! He ain't your competition either. And he sure as *hell* ain't Morgan's prize for being a bigger maniac than Reynolds." In Navya's direction, I added, "He's not even a god."

Pulling my cap off, I straightened my shoulders. "But he is a philosopher. A storyteller. A singer and an athlete and, yeah, a stubborn knucklehead when he wants to be. And it shouldn't take me having to vouch for his soul to justify his right to be free.

"My aunt used to say, 'Hay una infección sobre la humanidad.' That humanity had a disease. It took meeting Río to figure out what it was. It tricks folks into thinking the only way to survive a lifetime getting pissed on, is to piss on somebody else. It locks a person in jail or some other institution for being different unless they're willing to get on a stage and let folks pay three jitneys to call 'em 'freak' to their face."

I stared down at my cap where my tears were darkening the tweed. "Río's kind believes they're one. Like waves on the water. And *Cristo*"—I wiped my nose on my sleeve—"we dragged him away from it. Killed his mother. Cut him off from the one thing that keeps him alive. And maybe it's Morgan's fault, but I ain't innocent. I built his prison. This stupid, maldito tank!"

Vera's hand was over her mouth. "Benny—"

"Don't, Vera. It's my fault no one knows Río like I do. I was so afraid of losing everything that I lied to everyone, especially myself. I thought I could buy time just looking after him and keeping Morgan away, but the joke's on me, 'cause none of it matters now."

Here was the truth we were all accountable for, only it felt too heavy for my voice to carry it. My eyes found Matthias nodding encouragingly. It helped me push out the rest.

"Río's dying."

Timmy turned away from the glass to stare at me. This was Tití Luz's funeral all over again, the whole theater shrouded in the gloom of inevitable change.

"You all know what it's like to beg, so here I am, begging. I can't do this alone. I love him." I glanced back to make sure Río was listening. "*I love him*," I repeated. "And he loves me. And I don't care if that makes me the wrong kind of freak. I can live with losing the job and the warm bed and the only family I've ever had in America. But I *can't* live with myself if he dies, and neither should you. 'Cause this world ain't worth a damn if he's not in it."

Río hands were pressed to the glass. The small seed of hope in his blue eyes was enough to loosen the sorrow that had absorbed all the space inside my ribs. Everyone else had gone stock still and quiet until—

"FINALLY."

Matthias made the whole company jump. He bounded up the steps onto the stage to take me by the shoulders. "You did it, kid," he whispered. "Ain't no being free on the outside if you ain't free on the inside. Though I bet you'd've convinced us without making a goldang speech."

"Thanks, Matthias." I wiped a sleeve over my wet face. "But the speech wasn't for you."

He smiled. "I know."

"I need some bloody clarification," Vera declared. "You're meaning to tell us that you *wasn't* out tryin' for a gig at Henderson's? Why didn't you just say you was out chattin' up the merman?"

"Don't be stupid," Emmett said haughtily from the wing. "With you guys going on about the show like the world was gonna end, what else was he supposed to do?"

"You get amnesia, man?" Matthias said as every last person in the room leveled an incredulous look at Emmett, including me. "*You* were the one making a rear end of himself about Benny threatening the show!'"

"Well, I'm helping him now, ain't I?" Emmett squeaked. "Benny came to me 'cause I know a thing or two about getting someone you'd die for outta the ditch, all right? What, you think they amputated my *heart* below the knee?"

Lulu turned her stunned expression on me. "Is that true?"

I nodded.

At this, Eli stood up and gazed at Emmett the way I often gazed at Río, eyebrows drawn up in the middle over a melted smile. Without a word, he leapt onto the stage, slipped a hand behind Emmett's neck, and kissed him on the mouth. *Thoroughly.*

"Well, I for one support Mr. Benny's wish," said Madam Navya soberly, "though as I recall, *I* had said from the very beginning that we should make amends to the—"

"Yeah, yeah, your sainthood's secure," interrupted Vera. "What now, then? Is there a plan?"

Looking back at Río, his expression matched my own, a blend of hope and disbelief. "We bust him out," I said. "The night of the previews."

"That's in a week!" Vera gasped. "We'd be sneaking a merman out of Luna Park when Coney Island's crawling with half a million people—right under Sam's nose!"

"So we do it anyway," Lulu said, getting to her feet. "Río's one of us, ain't he? I'll be damned if he goes the way Saul did."

"Whoa, whoa, whoa . . ." Eli swatted the air like reality had suddenly descended upon him like a swarm of bees. "I know I'm the village idiot here, but what about our *jobs*?"

I swayed uneasily on my feet. "Emmett was thinking we could maybe pin it on Dreamland."

All eyes fell on Emmett's pink face. "What?" he snapped. "It ain't un-residented!"

Navya trudged up the ramp to join us, rubbing her temple. "You mean 'unprecedented'?"

"That too! I mean, what have we got that Reynolds and his gang didn't wind up stealing and taking the credit for later? I bet my other leg the bastards are over there planning to gaff their own Prince of Atlantis right now!"

"Oi, Emmett's two-fer-two on acts of intelligence now," Vera said as Eli helped her hop onto the stage. "Better check the sky for pigs."

Emmett threw Vera a scornful look.

"We can't do this."

It was Sonia. She stood up from her seat in the audience, her coat sliding off her tensed shoulders, leaving her looking as young as a schoolgirl in her frilly onesie.

"What do you mean we can't?" Lulu asked.

"I mean we can't! What about the Agostinellis?" she snapped. "What about not letting Luna Park sink like the *Slocum*? Don't you think Sam's smart enough to figure out a mutiny's going on?"

"With Río, we've got ten heads to his one," Matthias said pragmatically. "Sam's been beggin' for a mutiny if you ask me. And ain't nobody afraid of a couple o' two-bit gangsters."

"Well. I am," Eli admitted sheepishly. "But I'm still in."

"You don't understand," Sonia protested.

Emmett walked to the edge of the apron. "*What* don't we understand, Sonia?"

"Me, dammit! What about *me*? When do *I* get freed?" she shouted.

Sonia's frantic expression seemed to liquefy before our eyes. She slumped back into her seat and sobbed into her hands. I made to go to her, but Vera beat me to it. She jumped off the stage, sat beside Sonia, and pulled her into her arms.

"I c-can't keep this up no more. If Frankie doesn't kill me, S-Sam will," she wept into the fire-breather's shoulder.

"There, there, princess. None o' them feckers is gonna hurt you," Vera whispered, rocking Sonia gently. "They'd have to get through us. Go on, say it with me, lass."

"With it, for it, never against it," they murmured in unison, and tucked in the shelter of Vera's embrace, Sonia finally shared the sordid truth of her trips to Manhattan with Morgan, while the company listened in silent astonishment. Thankfully, Río thought to distract Timmy by showing off his carved seashell collection until she was done.

"That sniveling bastard," Emmett breathed as Eli growled, "Son of a bitch!"

"Aw, Sonia, I sure wish you'd told us," Matthias said without scolding. "It ain't your job to pay for Morgan's sins, same way it ain't Río's job to save the show."

"It's like Saul used to say," added Lulu, "'Sometimes a show's gotta sink'—"

"—'before it can be saved,'" finished Madam Navya.

Sonia smeared a tear off her cheek and nodded.

"It'll be all right, kid," Lulu continued. "No matter what happens after Río goes home, this company will stay afloat. Ain't that right, Igor?"

Igor, who until this point had had nothing to contribute, suddenly stood up. He put on his hat and lumbered back toward the museum exit.

Navya marched to the apron's edge. "Where do you think you are going, you great beenastok?"

"We plan escape for merman?" He raised a finger. "I get the vodka."

RÍO

I remember when I first beheld the little boat. Its silhouette had carved a path across the moonlit ripples above me, and though the Currents were silent, I could hear the woman's trembling through the wooden hull and knew she had drifted there in error. Thus, I took the tether in my hands and pulled it toward the bank where your life ended—and mine was forever changed.

Our harmony believed they knew all about humankind, Mother. Unpredictable, misguided devourers with inborn selfishness, humanity's dangers far outnumbered their virtues. Or so I had learned from all but you. When the Shark slaughtered you and took me prisoner, I felt sure the truth of their nature had been revealed.

I did not expect to find my views so challenged in captivity. Benigno's affections toward me have always seemed singular and strange, an anomaly for his species. When his human family gathered around him tonight, I felt little hope they would listen to his appeal for my salvation.

Instead, dear Mother, they called me one of their own. These beings who have never heard my voice will risk themselves to an uncertain future and even death to preserve me.

Humans. Complicated creatures of earth and light and shadow, just as merfolk are as varied as the waves. I am humbled to learn how mistaken about them I have been.

It also happens that the young woman in the boat was indeed imperiled. As I watched them embrace and vow to protect her, I began to think my choice to tow her boat to shore was not in error as I had despaired to believe before.

Perhaps that night in the estuary, the Currents had not been silent after all.

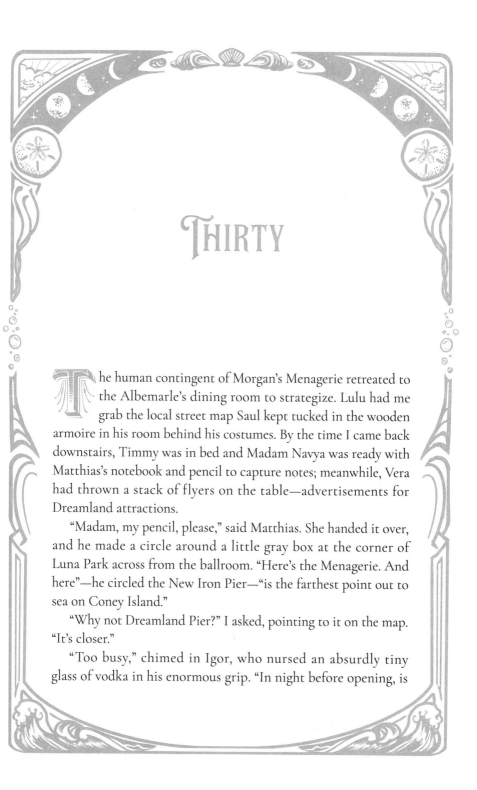

THIRTY

The human contingent of Morgan's Menagerie retreated to the Albemarle's dining room to strategize. Lulu had me grab the local street map Saul kept tucked in the wooden armoire in his room behind his costumes. By the time I came back downstairs, Timmy was in bed and Madam Navya was ready with Matthias's notebook and pencil to capture notes; meanwhile, Vera had thrown a stack of flyers on the table—advertisements for Dreamland attractions.

"Madam, my pencil, please," said Matthias. She handed it over, and he made a circle around a little gray box at the corner of Luna Park across from the ballroom. "Here's the Menagerie. And here"—he circled the New Iron Pier—"is the farthest point out to sea on Coney Island."

"Why not Dreamland Pier?" I asked, pointing to it on the map. "It's closer."

"Too busy," chimed in Igor, who nursed an absurdly tiny glass of vodka in his enormous grip. "In night before opening, is

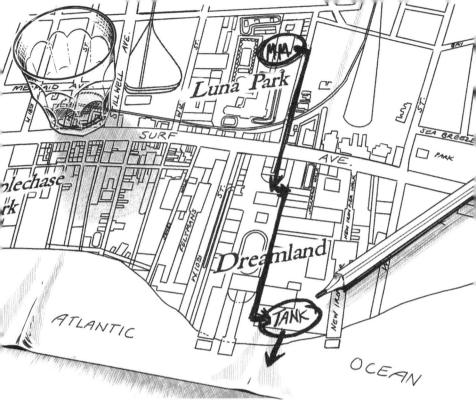

crowded with tourists for all the three parks. New Iron Pier is just fishermen and boats—"

"And prostitutes," Vera added helpfully. Sonia shot her a look. "What? It don't hurt to be prepared."

Lulu nudged Sonia. "How much time would we have?"

"The park's supposed to close at sundown on our previews day," Sonia replied. "We'll have from then until just before sunrise. After that, we won't be alone on the beach."

Eli was nervously tapping out a beat with his fingertips. "First things first. How the hell're we gonna get the merman off the stage?"

My area of expertise. "The tank's wheels are in the stables, we can put 'em back on," I said. "But we'll need to drain the tank to move it. Too much water and the swan springs could collapse—"

"And we go nowhere," finished Matthias grimly.

"I'll rig the pump to siphon Río's water out without circulating it back into the tank," I said. "The extra-long hose will route the water outside."

Navya resumed taking notes in the strongman's notebook. "Drain tank, reattach wheels," she recited.

Lifting an objecting finger, Igor threw back his vodka, then said, "There is problem. Is called Samuel Morgan."

"The Agostinellis too," added Sonia. "They're supposed to meet Sam *here* after previews close. To collect their dough away from witnesses."

"Aw, shit," groaned Eli, "those goons are coming to *the Albemarle*?"

"I guess if Morgan's meeting them at the hotel, that buys us time, but ain't he gonna come back?" I asked.

"I will handle that part," Navya volunteered. When all our eyebrows rose in surprise, she huffed, offended. "Am I not a show-woman? Igor and I will create a distraction to ensure the theater stays clear. Won't we, Igor?"

This was the most brazen thing she'd ever suggested in my presence that did not involve murdering Lulu's five-year-old nene. Igor poured another shot of vodka and rumbled a laugh. "Is true. I am very distracting."

Eli *tch*-ed in mock disapproval. "Framing Dreamland, and suddenly the madam's not concerned about karma."

"Not if *we* are Dreamland's karma," she retorted.

Vera clutched her breast. "Ohhhh, I *love* that!" She lifted her unlit stub in salute to Navya. "Morgan's Menagerie: Divine Instruments of the . . . Whatever-the-Bleedin'-Hell-Reynolds-Has-Got-Comin'-to-Him!"

"Well, seein' as I don't got any delusions about helping to move that iron monstrosity," Lulu remarked, "the least I can do is hide it under some fancy-looking tarps."

"That leaves"—Matthias's finger bobbed in the air to count our heads—"six of us to move the thing. We can take Luna's rear exit on West Eighth Street out to Surf Avenue—"

"And then we cut through Dreamland," Emmett finished.

"Yeah, about that part," I interjected. "How do we do it without getting caught?"

"Easy. We go right through the front gate."

Sonia's head thunked against the table.

"Well, what else you wanna do?" he snapped. "Roll it through Seaside Park and hope the philistines don't notice a fourteen-foot-tall iron box stuck in the sand?"

"I think Em's right. There'll be loads of cargo going through that front gate," Eli said.

"We can just wait for Gatekeeper Georgie to take a piss and ride the tank through on wheels," Emmett continued. "Anybody asks, we just tell them it's a new house for the Midget City."

Navya muttered a stream of angry Hindi at her paper with "Blast that Midget City!" thrown in for good measure.

Lulu put her hands on her hips. "I suppose I could whip up some fake mustaches," she said. "And we've got plenty of coveralls to go round."

Sonia looked aghast. "Are you suggesting I wear workman's clothes? As in working clothes? For a *man*?"

"I'll dress up Queen Mary here," said Vera, leaning over Sonia to slink an arm over her shoulder. "What fits me probably fits her."

"You're batty." She shoved off Vera's arm. "Georgie's sweet on me. If anyone's gonna get you past the front gate, it's me in a *dress*."

"What about you?" I asked Matthias.

Back in March, not even a winter coat was adequate to contain his persona.

He barked a laugh. "Those bums could look me dead in the face but ain't nobody gonna believe I would walk into our *rival park* hauling a live merman in a tank. Just you watch."

"Overalls, face fuzz, glad that's settled," Emmett summarized, grabbing the pencil from Navya. In the businesslike manner of a betting broker, he tapped the point against Dreamland's promenade, then drew a line right through it to a large rectangle adjacent to the shore. "We go in, we leave the tank in Balmer's Bathhouse, so everyone pegs Reynolds as the rat fink, then it's a straight shot to the water with Río and splitsville after that."

My worry may as well have been mounted on my forehead in incandescent lamps because Eli reached across Emmett to thump my arm encouragingly. "Nobody'll give us a second look. The night before Dreamland opens, it'll be like a beehive in there," he said. "It'll work."

Before I could reply, Igor put his enormous palm on my head and patted it, his wrist coming down over my eyes. "Molodoy chelovyek. You not need to fear for your love," he boomed. "All of us? Is survivor. Is strong. Morgan, Dreamland, patrons . . . we handle it. Mr. Benny's job?" He stuck a long finger into my chest. "Comfort sick merman. Yes?"

It seemed the sheen in Igor's eyes had nothing to do with booze. That Ekaterina had suffered through cholera without her husband at her side was a regret Igor kept folded in his vest pocket. He didn't want me to experience it for myself.

"I can do that."

I looked around the table at every ruddy face that reflected my reckless, hairbrained determination right back at me and couldn't believe the luck that had brought me to Coney Island. "Bueno. I, uh, thanks," I said thickly. "I'm just . . . Ave María, I don't know what to say."

"Tonight were the most words you've leaked in one shot since you got here," Vera snorted. "You was bound to run out."

"Actually"—I reached into Lulu's sewing bag and pulled out a remnant of leather from the dragon's reupholstered wing—"there is one more thing I need."

Sonia volunteered to sneak me back into the park, which left us walking down Surf Avenue together in awkward silence. When my eyes lifted from my feet to look at her, her gaze flitted in my direction, then quickly dropped back to the path ahead of us.

"You probably hate me," she said in a small voice.

"I don't hate you."

"I made a mess for you and Río. And I'm sorry."

I sighed, taking a moment to appreciate how much better embarrassment felt over secrecy and resentment. It seemed Sonia felt the same way: she'd changed out of her costume, choosing a white collared blouse and a work skirt the color of wet sand over one of her fancy vestidos, having left the burden of performing back at home. "I'm sorry too. I don't actually think you're selfish, you know," I added.

"*Pfft*. Like hell I'm not."

"Everything you did was for the company. And that ain't selfish."

She kicked a flattened wad of newspaper out of her path. "But I was *jealous* too," she groaned. "The signs were all there that girls weren't your cup o' tea. I just hoped . . . I dunno what I hoped."

"Mind reading's not your act," I pointed out. "I could've saved us both a lot of grief if I'd just said it."

"Well." Out of the corner of my eye, I saw her dab at her cheek. "He's a lucky man. Or mer. Man."

I shoved my hands deeper into my pockets. "I dunno about that."

"I do."

My heart ached for Sonia just then, this kid who'd borne the weight of the company's future on her shoulders in secret and simply wanted to be seen and loved. I was the last person on earth who could fault her for that. My arm came up, stopping just shy of wrapping around her shoulders, but she caught me in the act and leaned into the open invitation.

"Sonia"—I squeezed her arm—"you deserve a better man than me."

"Aw, Benny." She gave a watery chuckle and wiped her nose on her handkerchief. "Different man, yes, but not better. Ain't no better man than you."

"Querido," I whispered. "I'm here."

The electric glow through the hopper window backlit the shadowed lump of Río's resting body on the tank floor. At the sound of my voice, his head lifted to look for me, but before I could rush off, Sonia touched my shoulder.

"I'm gonna split," she said. Nerves or shame or both prevented her from meeting my eyes. "Tell him I'm sorry, would ya?"

I wrapped my palms around her wringing hands. "I don't have to. He heard you."

As Sonia's shadow disappeared down the hall, up the rungs I went to wait for Río. His ascent was so slow he seemed to waft more than swim, his skin bleached light gray by an illness with no name. Whatever was claiming his life before my eyes was working faster than I did, and it scared me stupid. I didn't breathe until his face broke through the water.

"Look at you," I whispered in Spanish, tears filling my eyes. "I was so afraid to believe you . . ."

"You overcome your fears quickly for a human," he murmured in a serrated version of his once silky voice. "You must be an evolved type."

"A selfish cabrón is what I am."

"Hush," he said, fighting his own welling emotion. "I am so glad to see you I cannot bring myself to resent you. I thought the Shark had parted you from me forever."

"He could never. Por Dios, I was gonna lose my *mind* hearing him blow that maldito whistle, knowing I could've . . ." My breath hitched. "Ay, amor, how can you forgive me?"

He gave me his most affectionate smile. "Your amends are complete," he said breathlessly. "The way you spoke tonight, my heart sings each time I think of it, my brave Benigno."

I reached my hand through the bars as Río's rose feebly out of the water. When his fingers grazed mine, they felt slick, as if he'd been dipped in grease. I was too grateful to touch him again to care. "Yeah, well. Houdini'll be spittin' mad 'cause, in a week, yours is gonna be the greatest disappearing act in Coney Island history," I said. "You can hang on 'til then, right?"

Río breathed out a laugh and bowed his head to gather himself. When he gazed back up at me, tears of hope and relief were running into the beads of water adorning cheeks. "I can try."

I lowered my face to the bars and surveyed the cloudy liquid. "Río, what's happening to your water?"

"I am mer," he said resignedly. "When we fall ill, the water follows."

"I'll adjust the pump then. I can probably get the boilers to—"

"It will not matter."

Halfway back onto my feet, I stilled. "Why not?"

"I am not a fish, Benigno," he explained. "I am spirit-bound to water. You can replace every drop in this tank, attach it to a dozen pumps, and it will still display my disease."

I cussed under my breath. "Then what else can I do?"

"Speak to me," he said. "Your voice is a balm to my ears."

"If your ears need a balm, then this might help." I dug into my pockets.

"¿Azúcar?" he asked.

"Less sweet and a lot more useful." I threaded an arm back through the bars and dropped earplugs into his palm where he examined them closely. "Courtesy of Lulu. You put them in your ears to protect them from the whistle. Try them on."

One at a time, he placed the plugs inside each ear.

"Well?"

"The sound does seem blunted," he called up loudly.

"Shhh," I hissed, grinning despite myself.

"Oh . . ." He took them out and held them to his breast. "Thank you. And thank . . . Lulu."

"You're welcome."

He shuddered. "I cannot tread the water for long, Benigno," he said. "I feel weak to my bones."

The grin slid off my lips. "Por supuesto. You should rest—"

"But, stay. Please?"

The only thing worse than Morgan's whistle was the sound of Río's pleading. "Oye," I murmured. "I ain't going anywhere. I'll make you so sick of me, you'll wish you'd got rid of me when you had the chance."

Relief loosened his shoulders, where the bones cut a sharp outline against his skin. But even in illness, staring down death, he was still as majestic and handsome as ever.

With a soft smile, he whispered, "Barnacle."

My makeshift bed was still in the wing. I pushed it against the tank where we resumed our routine positions, on opposite sides of a gulf made of four-inch-thick tempered glass. Only days ago, his cheek had found a home on my shoulder. Our hands had laid tracks on each other's skin I thought we'd get to ride again and again. Soon I'd have to learn to live without this view of Río, of his drowsy smile and steep nose and the ever-blue eyes where I always found my truest self reflected.

I tried hopelessly to brand him into my mind. Hopelessly, because, when it came to losing people, the more you tried to make them permanent on the shorelines of your recollection, the more time eroded them away. I wondered if he was doing the same, carving my face into his memory, sealing my voice between his sensitive ears.

He'd wanted me to speak to him. So I went with the truth. "I'd go with you, you know."

His eyebrows gathered in the middle, lips taking shape around words I couldn't hear before pinching shut.

"I would. I'd let you steal me away like the merfolk in the legends." I leaned my forehead against the glass. "You've ruined me for life on land anyway. It's your fault the world feels like boots that don't fit. I'd go with you, and it would be the beginning of my life."

He shifted closer until his forehead touched the glass too.

"Fíjate," I murmured. "I'd learn how to speak your native song. I'd call you by your true name, and you'd call me by whatever the word in your language for 'barnacle' is."

Río shook his head and chuckled noiselessly into the water.

I ran my fingers along the glass in a path around his face. "We could visit all the places you love so much. Those pretty reefs in Australia. The Pacific kelp forests and the Aegean—"

He lightly tapped the glass between my eyes.

"Fine. The Caribbean then. Pushy."

He smiled.

"That ain't a bad idea, actually. Ever been near Vieques? They say the tides there are magic because they light up blue at night, and no one knows why. In the shallows, where the water glows . . ." I skated my fingertips over the glass and imagined his hair threading between them. "That's where I'd make love to you."

His smile wavered then faded away. I worried I was making him sad, but then he gripped the glass.

"Keep talking?" I asked.

He nodded and closed his eyes.

"You would be well again," I whispered. "You would sleep in my arms, and I would kiss you without ever having to come up for air. I would make a hymn of both our names. It would make the most beautiful sound . . ."

I'd dropped my English because Spanish has so many words for declaring love, and I needed to use them all before it was too late. And though his tears were invisible in water, we both wept to the sound of promises whispered like prayers through the glass about a future where time couldn't chase us, where my heart would beat for him for as long as he wanted it—until the oceans boiled and the rivers dried.

Por los siglos de los siglos.

When his eyes opened, two halves of the same grief met in the glass between us. In the dark, you could almost forget which one of us was behind it.

THIRTY-ONE

ive days before previews, New York City's heat wave turned lethal. Temperatures reached 104 degrees in the shade while industry ground to a halt and young and old alike died of heat stroke in the poorly ventilated tenements. Not a soul in or outside the city could explain why the ocean breezes had mysteriously died, leaving boats to boil on the piers or sink in the harbors as the heat melted the pitch.

I had to believe Río's decline had something to do with it. As if the sea was retaliating on his behalf by refusing the entire American Northeast its cooling breath. Río's skin had paled so much his copper hair looked garish against it. His fins, once lush and sharp with fronds, looked feathered and frayed. He moved like los hambrientos in Puerto Rico, like a sheet left hanging in the breeze, a living ghost.

Lulu discovered a long-forgotten tarpaulin in a steamer trunk, a remnant of the show's traveling days. Painted against a faded red-and-white-striped backdrop was the voluptuous form of a scantily dressed woman holding a large hoop over her head in which letters read in bright golden script: "Queens County Menagerie." It made the perfect costume for the tank.

She'd need more fabric than just ten feet of canvas, so we all turned our bolsillos inside out to pay for more. Lulu and Igor, having both cleared their act revisions with Morgan, set about taking apart Saul's clothes, dragging tiny hooks through the seams until they had converted his costumes to strips of fabric they could bleach then patch together.

Then Navya came into the parlor dragging a mass of brightly colored satin behind her.

"Navya, nyet," whispered Igor, shaking his head. "Your favorite saris . . ."

Madam Navya raised her dignified chin. "I have enough for my personal uses," she said. "Once we return Mr. Benny's maahi to the sea, these clothes may never see a stage again anyway. I feel better knowing they will help to conceal the merman on his way to freedom."

I looked down at the rainbow pile with a lump in my throat. "I'd say your karma's looking pretty good right about now, madam."

She sniffed and quickly swiped at her eye. "Of course, it is," she said, then left the room.

As Lulu and Igor hurriedly worked at the tarp, the rest of the company took turns directing Morgan's eyes away from the treason happening right under his nose. Matthias and I scouted the path from the rear entrance of Luna Park through Dreamland while Eli and Emmett set upon Sam at his tent with a never-ending onslaught of bad jokes and bizarre ideas for new gags to impress the crowds.

The way Eli told it at the dinner table that night, Morgan tolerated this like a convict facing the firing squad without the benefit of a blindfold.

"Emmett goes, 'Hey Eli, whaddaya call a clock with too many ticks?' And I say, 'A metronome with the hiccups!' And *then* we start tap dancing! Get it? 'Cause of the ticks?"

Emmett's face took on the purple hue of repressed humiliation. "That's when Sam threw us out," he grumbled.

The most difficult task fell to Sonia and me. As players in the headlining act, we walked the tightrope between proving the Prince of Atlantis would be ready for previews and denying Morgan the chance to rehearse Río to exhaustion. I played extended versions of every song I'd ever learned until he started nodding off in his chair. Sonia's strategy was far more developed, a pattern that started with an especially tricky maneuver that required a new prop or costume change, followed by complaints of tenderness in her wrist or ankle, ending with demands for a different trick altogether.

Despite our best efforts, Morgan made sure he had time alone to bully his star attraction into quién sabe qué.

I stayed close to Río whenever I could. Despite the suspicion I'd seeded in Morgan's mind when I protested the whistle, he still relied on me to maintain the water, which had become a daily necessity now that it only took hours for it to cloud over. At least Río no longer winced when the whistle blew, which told me Lulu's earplugs were helping, but in a particular instance when Río and I shared the stage in Morgan's presence, I'd noticed a new problem—something anyone without asthma might have missed.

After his dozenth turn about the tank, Río faltered, gulping water. I noted his posture, the way his chest was heaving, and instantly recognized what was happening.

Río couldn't breathe.

Morgan took the pipe out of his mouth so he could blow the whistle. "No, no! Where is the power? Where is the drama? You are supposed to be the god of the ocean, Poseidon himself!" he hollered. "Again!"

I'd been hoisting a full moon into the rigging over the stage, a flat panel of wood and plaster I had spent the morning painting. As the mercury on my rage rose, I pulled it higher into the fly system over our heads until it had reached the catwalk.

Then I let go of the rope.

Sonia shrieked. The moon hit the stage with a hollow *crunch*—mere feet across from where Morgan stood.

He staggered back and shot a crazed look in my direction. "What the devil—"

"Sorry!" I ran over to pick up shards of splintered plaster. "My hands got too sweaty in the heat—it just slipped through my fingers."

Slowly, Morgan strode toward me, the pits of his shirt wet and his face slick with sweat.

"Sam," said Sonia in a small voice. "It was just an accident—"

He ignored her. "How exactly does *heat* make a *blacksmith* lose his grip on a bit of rope?"

I stood up with shards of the shattered set piece. "I'm only human."

Faster than someone courting heat exhaustion should move, he pulled the derringer out of his breast pocket. My arms instantly emptied, scattering splintered wood and plaster as he shoved it in my face.

"Sam!" gasped Sonia.

"You must think I'm an imbecile," he snarled. "You think I don't know what's going on here? That I haven't seen through your ruse since the day you burst in here shouting about whistles?" He jabbed the tip of the gun at my face. "How much was it? Come on, now, what did he pay you?"

Pay me? My heart was thundering, but this suggestion was even more shocking to me than his threat to shoot me. "What are you talking about?!"

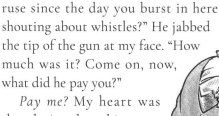

"Reynolds, Reynolds," he shouted, spit flying into my face. "You're in league with that grifting bastard, aren't you!"

My eyes pinned themselves on the business end of his roscoe. "I'm not in league with *anyone*! I couldn't tell Reynolds from Juan ni Pedro!"

"Liar!" He grabbed me roughly by my suspenders. "Tell me the truth, you greasy spic!"

There it was, right on cue. My entire character reduced to profanity as soon as some pendejo decided I needed reminding of where I stood. My eyes hardened as they stared into his, and for a moment, his expression wavered with something like fear. If he wanted the truth, I'd give it to him.

"I would *never* sabotage the show . . . *for Reynolds*."

Breathing hard through his nose, Morgan held me there for as long as it took for him to snap out of his tantrum. Finally, his hand unclenched around my suspenders, and he stepped back with a look that told me he'd been less unnerved by my "accident" than his explosive reaction to it.

"Fix that prop," he muttered. "You'll pay for it out of your wages." He smeared the sweat off his face. "Now get out of my sight."

By the end of the day, I'd rebuilt the moon, but I didn't do it for Morgan.

I did it for Río. I'd hoped the counterfeit version of the real thing hanging over his head at night would console him and, after the previews, never be needed again.

Gracias a Dios, I had help now when it came to lifting his spirits. The company's acts resumed their rightful place on the stage whenever Morgan saw no value in pushing a merman who had nothing left to give, so we'd leave the curtain open so Río could watch and be entertained.

Lulu debuted her new beard to the praise of everyone in the company. Igor and Madam Navya choreographed a dance together wearing their traditional garments, a spectacle that lacked all the absurdity they were going for and looked strangely beautiful instead. Eli and Emmett successfully fit into their shared set of trousers thanks to Lulu's handiwork and delivered a comedy set so terrible it succeeded in being hilarious. And when Vera took the stage, it was as the beguiling, flame-wielding Phoenix.

The Mighty Matthias, the final act and original headliner, swaggered onstage like a demigod. Effortlessly, he lifted his enormous barbels. Bent thick iron rods with his bare hands. Sonia balanced herself on her forearms atop a large weight marked in white numbers—"2,000 pounds," it read—and he hoisted them both into the air with vibrating arms while she arranged her legs in an elegant tower over her head.

Matthias never did tell me how much that thing actually weighed, but I decided to take the numbers at face value. Because as the company cheered and Río smiled at them from the floor of the tank, I realized that, just when I thought I'd lost my faith in everything, I believed in my family.

I hoped, when the time came, I would be strong enough to let them go too.

Thirty-Two

Against all odds, previews day had arrived. My housemates formed a dazed line to the bathtub to rinse off the night's sweat and ready themselves, greeting me with smiles haunted by the unspoken question no one could answer: Would the Menagerie live to see another day?

Would Río?

We arrived at Luna Park an hour before the gates opened. Though the rest of the city had shut down from the heat, the park had come alive. Fresh paint glowed under a potent sun, a cacophony of pipe organ music and outside talkers competed with the growl of roller coasters undergoing their final tests. Sprays of flowers now hung from the bright white archways and canopies overhead.

In the hall to the theater, the newest addition to the lineup of posters on the wall made me stop in my tracks—I'd completely missed it on the way out.

Beside the Prince of Atlantis painting was a shirtless and slighter version of *me* filling the center of an oval frame. He screamed extranjero, with his straw hat, small guitar, and the words "The Caribbean Balladeer" over his head in the same lavish font as everyone else's.

After I terminated my stage career to become a criminal, maybe Vera could light a match to it.

"Gosh, this place looks good enough to save us," Lulu mused as we passed through the theater. "We been so busy, I forgot to notice."

Madam Navya's admiring grin caught my eye. "Well done, Mr. Benny. The Menagerie is reborn," she said, and murmurs of agreement rippled through the company.

"Reborn to die," Matthias said through the side of his mouth.

Sonia scuffled gloomily toward the greenroom doors. "It's just as well. You're gonna have to scrape my melted remains off the stage today when I die standing on my head in this heat," she said.

"You don't gotta spend all day strapped to *this* gamey knucklehead," Eli said, which Emmett rewarded with a gentle thwap to his chest.

"Beggin' yer pardon, but you can all feck off," Vera snapped as she dug around in Sonia's handbag for lip rouge. "None o' you is breathing actual *fire*."

We dressed in amiable silence after that. Halfway through buttoning my vest, I got my first view of Lulu's handiwork on everyone at once. The costumes made a bright—and American— complement to my refinished facades. So much red, white, and blue.

I barely recognized myself in the mirror. Lulu resisted Sam's instructions to "accentuate my heritage" with a straw hat and unbuttoned linen shirt, though a part of me wished she hadn't now that I was boiling in sticky heat like a human sancocho. She dressed me in a billowing off-white satin thing with a drawstring collar over earthy-brown pantalones cinched at the waist by an ocean-blue sash.

I looked like a damn pirate.

Vera plucked Eli's pocket watch off the table and held it up. "Speech time, lads."

Waiting for us in the renovated museum, clean, pressed, and a little deranged in his lime-green suit, was Sam Morgan, who'd finally dropped the frayed scowl he'd worn all week in exchange for a toothy Steeplechase smile of his own. With the promise of mutiny on the literal horizon, everyone tried a little too hard to look excited—except Matthias, who stood on the edge of the circle like a man reliving his most boring memory.

"Gather round, everyone, gather round," said Morgan, hastily corralling Eli and Emmett who moved like molasses stuffed together in a single pair of pants.

"Prepare yourselves for an historic day," he began. "I am told that beyond the gates wait nearly two hundred spectators, braving sun and deadly heat to experience an attraction unlike any the world has ever seen—and you can rely on that number to *double* by the time the doors open!"

Everyone's eyes widened—even Matthias's—which I guessed boded well for Morgan's profits.

"Never again will anyone regard Morgan's Menagerie of Oddities as some common stick and rag show," he went on. "After today, we will forevermore be the standard-bearer for all sideshow amusements. After all"—he gave a slightly manic chuckle—"the future of this production depends on it."

Lulu caught my eye, inhaled deeply, then looked away, her anxiety safely hidden under the fuzzy peluca on her face.

"Now then. Who'd like to recite the code of conduct?" Sam continued.

Sonia raised her hand. "Smile wide, don't speak unless spoken to, and if someone gets handsy, it's no refunds."

"Capital. Today's schedule: You will be out on the promenade for the morning, exerting your world-renowned talents and appeal to ensure that all of Luna Park's patrons are reminded of the where and when of our show. Curtain goes up at two o'clock. The Menagerie act is first, followed by the Prince of Atlantis."

I tugged at my shirt and pulled out San Cristóbal. The later in the day Río had to perform, the worse his condition would be.

"Now then. Smile wide and keep them coming back for more! Our most esteemed patrons will be"—he tugged on his bow tie—"watching."

Everyone turned to head for the stage, where I was headed too before a gloved finger to my chest stopped me.

"*You* are not in the Menagerie performance," Morgan said. "Hence, while the rest of the company is advertising the show, you'll open all the theater windows to ventilate the space, and then it's back to the ticket counter. Fifty cents a head. Tear the tickets, place the stubs in the box. And don't forget to relocate that eyesore of a circulation pump outside the barn doors before the performance. Can you handle all that?"

My eyes bulged in my attempt to resist rolling them. "I can handle it."

"Good. Return the box to my tent for counting later. If for any reason the ticket stubs do not match the number inside the box, it will come out of your pay. Understood?"

From craftsman to hired hand to common thief. I was so goddamn *tired* of people deciding who I was.

"Yes, sir."

By the time I took my place at the front door, the line to enter had wrapped around the promenade. More surprising than the sheer count of people was the variety of them—ladies in plumed hats and white lingerie dresses next to working-class immigrants with giggling children clinging to their knees. Clusters of young men and women fanned themselves in the shade of their parasols, laughing and bochinchando in each other's ears. I wondered if they'd even known each other before they met at the—

Wait a second. I *knew* those faces.

That lemon-peel smile belonged to Farty Walsh. And across from him was Dan.

"Sea la madre," I cussed under my breath.

Already wheezing in the heat, I glanced down at the spectacle I made in my Caribbean pirata getup and growled another stream of profanity under my breath that Tití Luz would have sent me to church to repent for.

There was nothing to do but tear the tickets and pray Farty and Dan were still a couple of unobservant idiotas.

Which, apparently, they were. When I took their money, their eyes didn't so much as trip over my face, occupied as they were with the bosoms of the ladies they'd brought with them, those sinvergüenzas.

My nerves hadn't even begun to settle when I recognized another set of faces. Three men dressed neatly in three-piece linen suits, with matching bowler hats between them.

Frankie Agostinelli—Righty and Lefty beside him in their respective spots—had arrived.

"Fifty cents, please," I mumbled, holding out his ticket stub with my palm up for the change.

"Nah, kid." He reached over and plucked the ticket out of my fingers. "Morgan knows me and my brothers get in gratis."

He touched the rim of his bowler in salute. They disappeared into the museum.

Que Dios nos ayude.

Morgan's theater could seat three hundred and fifty people and hold four hundred with standing room open. I'd torn almost as many tickets before the light over my head started blinking and

I had to turn guests away. I locked the doors and made my way through the museum, the spectators packed like pickles in a very hot barrel as they scoured for open seats inside the auditorium. "Two quarters says the merman's a fake," came a deep voice from over my shoulder.

"It's *obviously* a fake," laughed the voice next to it. "I just wanna see 'em try to hoodwink us."

I gripped San Cristóbal all the way to the greenroom and tried to clear the whistle from my chest. Between trading words with mobsters and my near brush with Farty and Dan, my anxiety wasn't giving up its stranglehold on my windpipe any time soon.

At five minutes to start time, Morgan flashed the house lights. With the pump removed, the theater went deadly quiet as the company gathered in the wings. I poked my head behind the curtain hoping to see Río but couldn't make him out. The hopper window was shuttered, casting everything in darkness except for a thin band of yellow light where the red velvet met the stage.

The Menagerie performance would unfold in front of the curtain, preserving the surprise of Río's presence. From the proscenium, I watched Vera stride confidently onto the apron to a swell of applause holding an unlit torch and a tin cup, which she placed at her feet. Out of a pocket in her bustle came her lighter, which she flipped open with a flourish to produce a small flame, inviting the front row to touch it before snatching it away with a teasing grin.

Once she'd stirred up the audience's craving for a demonstration of her might, she took a swig from her tin cup, and *foom!* Fire blasted out over the cowering crowd, inciting a surge of cheers.

"Behold our fire-breathing phoenix, Miss Vera!" Morgan shouted. "Isn't she a marvel with a flame?"

The crowd answered with more whoops and clapping.

"Welcome, one and all, to Morgan's Menagerie of Oddities! And, speaking of marvels," he said ominously, "I know what you are all here to see. What lies beyond this curtain will do more than shock and astound you. It shall rend the fabric of reality as you come face-to-face with a creature of myth and legend: the very Prince of Atlantis himself!"

The words blew out a candle in my chest. Peeking around to the front side of the curtain, I saw Morgan on his podium, top hat in one hand and cane in the other, gesturing widely to an audience lavishing him with roaring cheers and laughter.

"But first! Here to delight and entertain you—your favorite and mine—the Menagerie of Oddities Shooooowwww!"

Lulu, who couldn't be on her feet for long in the heat, was next on the program, so she pulled her shoulders back, tilted up her bearded chin, and walked elegantly out onto the stage in her queenly attire. Timmy sat atop a stack of salt crates between Sonia and me, quiet as a mouse—or rather, quiet as a boy who'd been raised by sideshow performers and knew not to make a racket while his mother was working.

"Some folks wear scarves during the winter," she announced haughtily. "Me? I grew my own. Do you like it?"

She stroked her fake beard as laughter pealed through the crowd. My heart ached to hear it, but her smile didn't waver. She simply lifted her chin higher and strode about the stage until, as they'd rehearsed, she invited Morgan to give her beard a pull to prove it was real.

One by one, the company took the stage, putting on their respective máscaras before venturing in front of the crowd to be gawked, giggled, and pointed at. It's exactly what everyone on the stage had invited them to do—for fifty cents a head.

What a strange country America was.

After Matthias's final act ended the hour-long show with his signature feat of strength paired with Sonia's feat of flexibility, Morgan returned to his podium and Sonia and Matthias returned to the wings. There, Lulu, Vera, and Madam Navya hurried to help

Sonia into her next costume—a little red boat that hung from straps over her shoulders with a hole cut out for her stockinged legs.

"Thank you, thank you, mightiest of men," cried Morgan, "but! We're not done yet! Brooklyn may be hot, but I daresay the fun is *sizzling* here in Coney Island! Are you enjoying yourselves?"

Cheers. Always more cheers. Like a magician, Morgan put a finger to his lips and the sound ceased.

"Behind this curtain lies what you've all journeyed from the farthest reaches of New York to see. And I have one question! Are you ready to behold this wonder of the deep?"

Four hundred people screamed "Yes!" and my heart plummeted into my bare feet.

"Only at Morgan's Menagerie of Oddities will you witness this miracle of God's own creation: a living—breathing—*merman!*" bellowed Morgan, and the audience, ravenous for more, squealed with delight. "I give you, the *Prince of Atlantis!*"

Igor pulled on the rope. The curtain swung smoothly open.

Front-row spectators let out a collective gasp at the sight of Río in the tank. Behind me, Navya whispered, "God forgive us."

Río lay in a heap against the glass. His tail was limp, his back turned to the audience and heaving with the effort of breathing. I smothered my mouth with my fist to hold in a noise that would give away my horror.

The crowd gawked in silence with no idea what to make of what they saw in the cloudy water.

"Ladies and gentlemen, your eyes do not deceive you," Morgan called out grandly from the podium before stepping off with a flourish of his cane toward the tank. "He is flesh and blood—the rarest beast in the ocean—lured from the Caribbean Sea. Shall I tell you the tale?"

What would it take to break the glass? What would trying do to my fists?

"Benny. *Benny*," hissed Sonia, making panicked guitar-strumming gestures with her hands.

"Shall I *tell you the tale*?" Morgan repeated.

Coño, my cue! I dropped my hand from my mouth and placed it on the frets of my instrument. Morgan watched me out of the corner of his eye as I stepped numbly onto the stage.

Wooden as I was, standing there in a stupid pirate outfit with my cuatro, I found I had no stage fright; the audience had become a mass of faceless heads. I started playing "La Palomita," and Morgan's shoulders relaxed.

"Imagine palm trees. Golden sand. Not Long Island, but another island left to bake in the equator, the air oppressive and thick. You stand in the eye of Phoebus," he said in a voice dripping with drama. "If the young lady only knew she would never reach her destination!"

Behind me, I knew what was happening without turning to look. Sonia had stepped out in her barquito costume, her chest out and arms arching wide toward a crowd revived by her presence. Just like we rehearsed.

"On a stormy night, her steamship capsizes"—cue Sonia climbing the rungs to the roof of the tank—"and lo! She is adrift! Alone in the Devil's Triangle with no food, no water! No hope for return!"

Clinging to the iron bars with a single stockinged leg, she turned herself upside down, the back of her hand over her forehead in a swoon as the audience gasped.

I continued to play, but I was counting too. Each chord, each spoken line registered in my mind like a tick of the clock while Morgan laid the drama on thick under the full moon I'd built. Sonia made her way onto the lattice, pretended to call for help, and swooned some more. Morgan was about to say, "And then, she saw the creature."

That was Río's cue. He was meant to rise to the top of the tank. To swim in a wide circle before breaking the surface to reach toward Sonia, who would regard him with false terror.

"And *then*, she saw the creature!"

Still strumming my cuatro, my eyes flitted toward the tank. Río's back stayed turned to the audience.

Morgan tittered nervously. "Aha. Just like a prince. It wishes the lady would not disturb his slumber! Poor maiden!"

Sonia, ever the consummate show-woman, feigned impatience and tapped her foot, prompting trickles of laughter from the crowd. The rest of the company watched warily in the wings. My fingers played. My eyes scrutinized Río's back.

Still breathing . . .

"Hey, King o' Queens!" a man called out. "Are ya dead?"

Whispers and giggles swept through the audience like noisy spirits. Morgan laughed jovially along with the heckler, taking several steps backward until he was level with Río's tank and me. When he turned to face the glass, his face was lit with fury.

He knocked on the iron bars with his cane. "Look alive, merman," he growled under his breath. "Your public awaits."

The music stopped. I looked down at my hand and realized it had grabbed Sam's wrist.

More astonishingly, words were coming out of my mouth.

"Don't. Do. That."

Morgan's eyes flitted toward the crowd, then back to me. Panic or fury or both had reduced his pupils to tiny black points.

"Oi, that's Benny!"

No sooner had I registered the sound of Farty's voice than the sharp fin on Río's back flared out. Four hundred people gasped in unison.

Water burbled as Río pulled himself up on his arms, his shoulders hunched, eyes squeezed shut, and teeth gritted with effort.

"My God," breathed a tearful lady in the front, her hand at her throat. "He's real."

I let go of Morgan's wrist. "Let me," I whispered.

He said nothing but pulled his cane back. I knelt next to the tank and let my fingers move across the strings in their familiar dance.

And I began to sing: *"Llévame, Río, hasta el mar, sobre las olas de agua cristal . . ."*

Río turned his face toward me with deep shadows cut into his cheeks and eyes.

"Porque soy un muchacho al que le gusta cantar. Con tritones y sirenas, me gustaría bailar."

I had no assurances that he would perform as Morgan had hoped. That wasn't my goal. I simply sang to comfort mi amado. To remind him where he was going as soon as the path to his liberation was clear.

"'Acercate más, amante del mar,'" I sang. *"Dijo las olas de agua cristal . . ."*

With a strained breath of water, he pushed off the floor and began to rise toward the surface.

His body had lost its strength, yet somehow retained all its majesty and grace, leaving the entire theater frozen in the grip of awe as he moved. Slowly, slowly, his hand reached up toward Sonia.

"El ritmo que sientes, la tentación fluvial, el latido de mi corazón es tu cantal."

The moment his face broke through the water, Sonia's persona vanished. With wet eyes, she threw off the red barquito strapped to her shoulders and lowered onto her belly so she could thread both her arms through the bars.

As their hands touched, a wall of sound—applause and cheers—shook the stage under my feet. It wasn't done; there was more to the act, but even Morgan couldn't deny the impossibility

of expecting more from Río at that moment. It didn't matter anyway. By the deafening noise, it was clear enough that the Prince of
Atlantis debut act had already succeeded.

Sonia's tears fell through the bars into the cloudy water.
Morgan's lips curled in triumph.

And Río . . .

His head dipped back under, and he turned slowly toward the
crowd. Through the glass, he regarded them, not with judgment,
but with a distant sort of confusion in his eyes. This human crowd
could never think of him in terms of flesh and blood, thought and
feeling. His existence was wrapped in a story they could consume
far more easily than the truth of his enslavement.

Like every foreigner, Río seemed to become more imaginary
in person.

Ten minutes later, I found myself back outside the Menagerie,
blinded by sunlight and wheezing from the heat. Morgan, somehow both pleased and irritated with my role in engaging Río's
participation, had shoved me out the door to guard against loiter-
ers or folks trying to sneak back in for a closer look at the star
attraction. Already, a massive crowd had formed on the promenade to accost anyone who'd been lucky enough to get a ticket for
the preview.

"Please, I have to know—is it worth coming back tomorrow?"
one lady asked another on her way onto the promenade.

"Deary," she replied breathlessly, touching the other woman's
arm. "You've never seen anything more be-*yoo*-tee-ful in your life!"

At least I agreed with these yanquis on something.

"Well, if it ain't the Porto Rican pox," said a voice over my
shoulder. "How's it goin', Wheezy?"

I swiveled to discover Farty and Dan linked to a pair of

ruddy-faced girls about Sonia's age, all of them grinning like they were about to make a meal out of me.

"Didn't recognize you in them pirate togs. Thinkin' we should change your name to Black Beardless," Farty sniggered.

"Yeah, did you bury your treasure out there on Brighton Beach?" asked Dan. "Been donkey's years since we seen Wheezy, eh, Marty?"

"Seems like only yesterday he'd got hisself sacked for being sloppy on the furnace."

I gestured mechanically to the promenade. "Time to clear out. Show's over."

"What's the matter?" laughed Farty. "This here's a happy re-union! It's nice to see you embracing your true nature, Benny."

"Yeah, who'd've thought a manky freak show would suit him so well?"

Farty elbowed Dan in the side, sneering. "I did, ya eedjit."

Over a good-natured grin, my eyes narrowed to slits. "Shame Dreamland's closed today," I said. "They got a ride there called Hell Gate. Two dimes says you'll feel right at home."

The girls started sniggering, and Farty shook his arm free to stride into my face, leaving Dan scowling behind him.

"What was that Spanish tripe you was singing, Wheezy? A love song?" he sneered. "That thing in the tank your sweetheart? Did you lob the gob with the dolphin in there?" He grabbed my shirt and started making kissing noises in my face.

Without consulting my brain, my hand drew back, closed in a fist.

Then it buried itself in Farty's stomach.

The girls yelped as he doubled over, gasping, and crumpled to the floor. Between them and Farty stood Dan, his face slack with astonishment at what I'd done. I was pretty surprised, myself.

My first leveler.

"Come on, Dotty, let's scram," said Farty's compañera. Tugging on the other girl's arm, they hurried away while Dan called after them and looked like he couldn't tell whether sticking by his fallen friend was worth it if entertainment of the feminine persuasion was gonna split.

"Y-you . . . y-you're gonna pay f-f-for that," Farty gasped at my feet.

"Out of my way," shouted Madam Navya, who wove nimbly through the crowd to stand next to me. "What nonsense is occurring out here, Mr. Benny? Do you know these men?"

"I used to work with these two pendejos, or as you would call them"—I gestured down at Farty, then up at Dan—"two khoti'am da puttar blocking the damn door."

Beaming, Navya bumped her elbow into my knee. "Remind me to teach you more Hindi."

Dan wrinkled his nose. "What'd you call me?"

"Means sons o' donkeys." Matthias parted the crowd like Moses to join Navya and me.

He eyed Farty and Dan like they were stains on nice upholstery. "Or as I prefer to say, a couple o' meaters with dung for brains making their last stupid decision before I punt their asses back to Erin."

Farty and Dan's faces both went paper white. "Now, w-we don't want no t-trouble, strongman," stammered Dan, standing over his friend like a shield.

"We was just having some fun, f-for old time's sake," added Farty in a strangled voice. "Wasn't we, Benny?"

"I say we light up the little gobshites." Vera materialized on the other side of Matthias with a newly lit cigarillo. "That'd be fun for me."

She casually flicked it onto Farty's lap.

"Oi! *Argh!*" Farty and Dan flapped and flailed at the smoking thing, yelping like pups—just as an enormous figure engulfed them in shadow.

They gazed skyward and froze.

"Only *pridurki* will be making trouble where trouble is not welcome," growled Igor.

Caramba, I'd never seen Igor mad before. He bent at the waist, hands on his hips, and brought his long face down from its place in the clouds to glower in Russian at my old coworkers. "Vremya vesel'ya zakonchilos!"

"Allow me to translate." Vera got down on one knee and grabbed Farty by the collar. "If you want to keep your wee peckers in your pants, you'll bugger off. Or Igor here is gonna make borscht outta them."

Farty and Dan's necks retracted into their shirts. Without another word, Dan helped Farty to his feet and they stumbled off together, scowling daggers over their shoulders at me before disappearing into the crowd.

"That's right! Off with you, ya shite-hawks, and stop giving the Irish a bad name!" Vera shouted after them. "Go ndéana an diabhal dréimire de cnámh do dhroma ag piocadh úll i ngairdín Ifrinn!"

I gaped. "What'd you just say?"

"'May the devil make a ladder of your backbone while he picks apples in Hell's garden.' Don't worry. They got it, even if you didn't." Then she plucked the lit cigarillo off the ground and stuck it back between her teeth.

"Mr. Benny," said Madam Navya, suddenly standing at my feet, clutching the drape of her shawl. "The men in suits remain. Inside the house with Sonia. They seek Mr. Morgan."

My face fell. "You mean, they're not going back to the hotel?"

"That is why I came to find you! It seems they do not want to leave!"

"Miércoles, of course they don't," I muttered, scrubbing a hand over my sweaty face. "Where *is* Morgan?"

"He has already taken the earnings to the Albemarle," she said fretfully. "What are we to do? We cannot steal a merman in sight of the criminals who paid for him!"

"All right . . . I gotta think . . ." I stepped away, my head swimming in panic and perspiration. I heard Tití Luz's voice call from the edge of my memories. *Solo es un problema, Benigno. When you don't have solutions, pretend that you do.*

Claro. That was it.

I spun back. "Madam Navya, Igor, if I take care of the Agostinellis, do you think you can manage keeping Morgan away from the park?"

Their gazes met across the seven feet between them. Igor clapped his hands together as he rumbled, "Is how the Americans say: duck soup!"

Matthias took a step toward me. "Whaddaya got in mind, brother?"

I closed my eyes. Molded my throat around the sound I wanted to make. And when I opened my mouth, the voice that came out was genteel. Snobby. Tainted with an accent befitting a persona, not a person.

"I'm thinking it's time I put my hidden talents to good use. What say you all?"

Vera's rompepecho fell out of her mouth. Around her, three sets of eyes bulged in shock.

I grinned.

"Capital."

THIRTY-THREE

"Pardon, sirs, gotta sweep the house," I announced, striding down the aisle toward a still-costumed Sonia, Frankie, Righty, and Lefty. The latter two stood like boulders right where you'd expect them to be.

"Benny! Come meet our esteemed patrons," Sonia said too brightly. "I'm just keeping these gents company while they *wait for Sam*." Her toothy smile conveyed all the alarm her voice could not.

"Oh! Well, they can just follow me."

Dread flashed across Sonia's face before she reset it. "F-follow you? You mean to say Sam's come back?"

"He never left! He's in his tent," I said with what I hoped was a jaunty laugh.

Without turning his head, Frankie's eyes peered right at Righty, then left at Lefty. Whether or not Sonia understood what the hell I was trying to do, she relented quickly enough once she noticed how far up my forehead my eyebrows had risen.

She giggled loudly. "I suppose he must be then!"

All five of us filed out of the stage door onto the hot gravel walk to Morgan's tent, Sonia keeping up behind me as I led the way.

"*What the hell, Benny,*" she hissed through her teeth.

"Just go with it," I whispered back.

At the tent flap, I turned around and held out my hands to stop everyone. "Hey, Sam?" I called into the tent. "You've got some visitors!"

Predictably, there was no answer from inside the tent. Beside me, Sonia was a live wire, fidgeting with a ream of ribbon hanging off her costume while her eyeballs tried to generate electricity with nothing but her pupils.

"Sam, you all right in there?" I called again. I looked over my shoulder at the Agostinellis, whose faces were shiny and red in the heat. "Just give me a moment, would you?"

I pushed into the tent, closed the flap behind me, and quickly took stock of the room. The money box I'd brought in earlier was gone. On the desk was the open ledger, with today's date scrawled in neat cursive above the amount we'd raked in: 198 bucks and fifty cents. The room stank of pipe smoke, an aroma that always snagged in my lungs regardless of whether Sam's pipe was lit nearby.

In this instance, it would help.

"Sam, you look awful!" I said loudly.

I replied to myself in Morgan's voice but grimmer and slightly nauseated. "Mr. Caldera, you couldn't have come at a worse time!"

Me: "What happened?"

Me as Morgan: "What does it look like, you imbecile? Those sandwiches Eli brought over for lunch. I don't think they were—"

And then, bendito sea Dios, I started to retch. Or pretend to, anyway.

"Benny, what's going on in there?" came Sonia's baffled voice from the other side.

"You don't wanna know, Sonia! Looks like the salami from Salvatore's didn't agree with the boss," I shouted back, then retched some more.

"Ohhhh," I groaned (as Morgan). "Who in hell is outside the tent?"

Sonia's voice was wavering. "The Agostinellis are here to see you, Sam. Can they come in?"

I opened my mouth to say no, and heard Frankie Agostinelli say it instead. "Uh-uh. I ain't goin' in there if he's spewing his lunch," he snapped. "You can hear me just fine, can't you Sammy boy?"

Me as Morgan: "*Ughhhh.*"

Me as me: "Yeah, sure he can hear you."

"First thing's first," said Frankie uncomfortably. "Today was a full house, Sammy, and it's collection time. One third plus today's earnings. Where's the dough?"

"It's at . . . *hnngggghhh* . . . the Albemarle!"

"You just finished the show and now you're upchucking antipasto. How'd today's profits make it all the way down the street?" *¡Coño!*

"Ooohh, *oh,* yes . . ." Sam's smoky tent air was getting caught in my lungs; my wheezing was getting worse. When a cough pushed its way out, I tried to make it sound like one of Morgan's. "I had Benny run the—*uurrggh*—earnings to the front gate. I was going to pick it up on my way. Didn't want to risk keeping it in the theater with so many" (—a burp—) "folks around."

"I see," said Frankie, sounding more gravelly than usual. A pause. "Then we will go back to the Albemarle and wait for you there."

"No!" shouted Morgan-me. I'd just remembered: the Agostinellis couldn't go back to the Albemarle if that's where Navya and Igor were distracting a healthy and un-poisoned Sam Morgan! "The hotel is full of prying eyes, don't you think? We should go somewhere more private. Salvatore's?"

"Ain't that where you ate the rotten salami?" That was Righty.

Damn it, Benny, keep your story straight!

"They must've served that stuff to at least a few hundred folks today," I said as myself. "By the time you get there, the place'll be a ghost town! Right, Sam?"

Morgan-me groaned. "Good thinking, Benny."

Jesucristo, maybe I was actually *great* at acting.

"All right," said Frankie. "Tonight, when Luna's lights go out, bring the cash to Salvatore's. But I'm leaving Vincenzo here. I got some safety concerns about the Prince of Atlantis act now that the cat is out of the bag."

"Safety concerns?" I asked—in my own voice, before catching myself. Quickly, I switched: "What safety concerns?"

"Reynolds's stooges were in the audience today," said Frankie, sounding close to the canvas flap. "What are you doing to make sure our investment is protected, Sammy?"

"From what?" asked Sonia.

"Sabotatori."

That sounded a lot like "saboteadores." Meaning "saboteurs."

"The tank's practically indestructible," I said in my normal voice. "And if someone breaks into the theater, I'll be guarding it."

A snort sounded from the other side of the canvas. "You? The small brown pirate man with the violin?"

I seethed. Five-foot-nine wasn't small.

"Yes, me. I heard you got sway with the cops, why don't you ask them to keep an extra patrol on Luna Park if you're so worried?"

At this, Frankie laughed. "Yeah, I got connections. But that means *less* cops pokin' their noses in our business, not *more*."

"Well, I can tell you that the merman won't take kindly to strangers hanging around at night. He's been known to get"—Morgan-me gagged for good measure—"violent."

I heard a rustle outside the tent, then: "Vincenzo. Give the kid your roscoe."

"What? Why's it gotta be mine?"

"Because you're the figlio di puttana who ate my last cannoli. You really need a reason?"

With a scrape of metal against concrete, something skidded under the tent flap and stopped at my feet.

This gun was a lot bigger than a derringer.

"Can you fire one of these without taking off your own feet, kid?"

I gulped. "Uh, yeah. Definitely. Yes, sir."

"Good. You come across anyone trying to steal himself a merman, you have my permission to bump him off," he declared. "Sammy, I will see you at Salvatore's at nine o'clock—whether or not you are done puking your guts out."

With a last long groan, Morgan-me said, "I'll be there, Mr. Agostinelli."

"Make sure you bring the principessa," he mumbled, followed by the wet *smack* of a kiss. "I'd like to congratulate her on her performance in private."

For a moment, I thought I really might retch.

As their footsteps in the gravel faded away, the muscles in my legs nearly gave out in relief. Sonia threw open the tent flap and rushed into Morgan's tent right past me toward the screen partition. She poked her head behind it, looking for evidence that I wasn't alone before her wild eyes finally landed on my face.

"*You*," she gasped. In three steps, she reached me and threw her arms around my neck. "You are a goddamned freak of nature, Benny Caldera! I swear to God, I'da sworn Morgan was really in here spewing his lunch into a trash can, and no one coulda convinced me otherwise!"

I stepped out of her arms and picked up the gun with two fingers. "Come on. We gotta get the wheels back on that tank, and pronto."

Sonia and I met Matthias, Eli, Emmett, and Vera at the tank. They stood around it like the tabaqueros at Tití Luz's internment, Río's body the centerpiece of their dismay.

My beloved now lay on the tank floor, panting, shivering, and surrounded by sloughed scales.

I refused to grieve. Río was still here, and I had a promise to keep.

"Lulu left the coveralls in the greenroom," I said hoarsely. "If someone could grab the hose and circulation pump from outside—"

"I'll get it," said Eli.

"Thanks. Get dressed, then meet back here."

"You're the boss," said Vera grimly, and everyone turned to leave.

"Hang on, Em." I pulled out Lefty's gun and held it out to him, with the stock facing up. "I dunno how to fire one of these."

He leaned away like it might bite him. "Where in the nine circles of hell did you get that?"

"It's Vincenzo Agostinelli's. For saboteurs."

Emmett sighed and took it from my hand. "I'll do my best."

And he left too.

Alone with the tank once more, I crouched beside Río's head. "Mi cielo."

His muscles went taught under his thin skin as he rolled slowly toward me. The whites of his eyes had gone gray. His chest heaved. But then he smiled at me, and it fueled my courage like a shot of absinthe.

Slowly and with great effort, he shifted himself toward me until he reached the wall where I pressed my hand against the tank, then my lips. He kissed me through the glass.

And though my heart lay dying with him, I whispered, "Time to go home."

Río

The blaze dwells inside me now, Mother. I burn alive like those aboard the vessel we watched sink. It stings less now that I have accepted it.

Whatever comes next, be it salvation or death, I know I shall hear your song again soon.

THIRTY-FOUR

eturning Río to the water would make smithies of all of us. Like handling a glowing iron round over an anvil, one careless mistake would make us all burn.

Lulu had hidden the coveralls under the vanity. Across the greenroom, tucked behind a wall of empty salt crates underneath a paint-stained drop cloth, was the tarp. Sewn from canvas, Saul's silk costumes, and Madam Navya's saris, it barely took up space folded up. Unfolded, it was gigantic. I scooped it off the floor and threw it to Vera, who had used the black of a burned-up match-stick to draw herself a mustache.

In a separate crate was all the hardware Morgan retained from having disassembled the wheels back in March. Most of the tank's undercarriage was intact behind the wooden and steel platform that propped it up, but the braces would need to be reattached if there was any hope the ride wouldn't crush the wheels.

We had precious little time for it. Our diversion was flimsy at best; no one could say how long it would be before either Morgan or the Agostinellis caught on that they'd been duped.

I was carrying the tool crate to the tank when Eli showed up with the first snag of the evening.

"Looks like Reynolds's stooges have already been here." A stack of droopy rubber tubing was laid across Eli's arms, the very hose I'd used only yesterday to replace Río's water.

It was in pieces.

"No me digas," I breathed as Matthias hissed, "You gotta be kidding."

"Pump's been busted too," said Eli.

Emmett stomped his peg leg on the stage. "Those dirty bastards were trying to kill Río ahead of opening!"

"How'd you know it was them?" I asked feebly.

He tugged on his blond hair. "It's *always* them!"

I put down the crate, picked up a severed piece of hose, and felt a whole lot less conflicted about Emmett's intention to pin Río's disappearance on these Dreamland sons of bitches.

"Forget the pump then. We open the hatch at the bottom of the tank." I picked up a pry bar. "Pa'lante."

Vera, Eli, and Sonia rushed outside to corral the horses and move the basin, which would catch the water we drained from the tank. Meanwhile, Matthias, Eli, and I took our pry bars to the platform, releasing the tank from its side panels one at a time, each snap of splintering wood setting my teeth on edge.

When I raised my head to check on Río, he was flat on his back on the tank floor, his hand in a fist over his chest. Panting.

"Faster," I grunted, ripping into another wooden panel.

By the time we'd freed the tank of the platform, Eli was rolling open the barn door to the loading dock, where the Menagerie's horses towed the same wagon that had made the journey to Red Hook. Matthias rushed over to help Sonia and Eli lug the basin to the metal hatch I'd built into the tank side, all of them red-faced with heat. Vera alone seemed unperturbed. In the face of our collective tension, she dismounted the horse with the manner of a master grifter practiced in midnight escapes, an unlit rompepecho hanging casually from her lips.

I caught my breath. "Here's the tricky part."

"Whaddaya mean?" said Eli indignantly. "Wasn't *that* the tricky part?"

"That hatch got sealed from the outside," I explained. "We gotta break the seal to let the water out."

"Allow me." Matthias pushed past Eli and Emmett toward the hatch. "I just gotta twist this doodad here, right?"

"Well, yeah, but don't open it too wide," I said. It hadn't been opened since March and now held the pressure of hundreds of gallons of water—and one dying tritón—behind it. "It needs to close again, and we don't wanna flood the stage."

"Got it."

Matthias wrapped both hands around the bolt handle and pulled upward. His eyes narrowed, the cords of his forearms bulging against his shirt. His already wide neck widened further with strain. I gripped San Cristóbal.

"Nothing's happening. Something supposed to be happening?"

"Will you shut yer hole, Emmett," said Vera breathlessly.

Suddenly, near the strongman's hands came a groan of metal grinding against itself. I squinted at the iron frame surrounding the hatch; water was now dribbling from the corner.

"Yes," whispered Sonia. "It's working!"

"Almost," grunted Matthias. "Damn thing's . . . stuck tighter than . . . a flea's ass . . ."

He gave it another tug, rocking the whole tank. Water swished gently.

"Careful, big guy," said Eli, looking warily up at the tank. "This thing's standing on nothing but stilts."

Matthias let go and shot him a withering glare. "You wanna come over here and do it, simp?"

"Nah, you're already there."

Shaking out his hands, Matthias once more curled his palms around the bolt handle. "C'mon, mighty man. Soft hands . . ." He gave it another jerk.

This time, there was a hiss like a cap releasing from its bottle of soda water. Gradually, the hatch ground up the metal tracks that held it, and the trickle of water grew until it poured green and clouded with sand into the basin below like Matthias had opened a tap.

"Ha!" I let go of my chain and blew out a gust of air. "John Henry's got nothing on you, man!"

He stepped away, slapping the blood back into his hands. "They don't call me 'mighty' for nothin'. Brother, what are you *doing*?"

I'd laid down on my back and slid myself right under one of the reaches with a wrench in my hand. "Quick, hand me two pins, a reach brace, and a couple o' them axel clips," I ordered. "Someone get another set and take the opposite side. We gotta get the wheels on two at a time."

"This looks . . . not safe," Sonia said in a small voice.

From my spot under the tank, legs swayed, and feet shuffled in place. "Anyone?" I asked.

"Well now, don't all volunteer at once," grumbled Vera, who crouched down and plucked the materials off the ground.

To the set of feet next to Emmett's prosthetic leg, I said, "Eli, fit the jack in the middle between Vera and me and crank it so it's level."

Eli knelt next to my head with the jack and maneuvered it into place. "We only got one stinkin' jack?"

"Unless Emmett's willing to sacrifice his hardware below the knee for the cause," huffed Vera.

She got down on the ground beside me. I held up the wrench. "See that reach over your head? You're gonna—"

"Save your breath, Benny, I know what I'm doin'." She fit the brace against the reach and stuck a pin between her teeth like a cigarillo. "Used to fix undercarriages for Lord Sanger. Mind your own wheel."

So Vera and I went to work. Between us, Eli began cranking. I mentally ran through my list of actions in order: Brace. Pin. Clip. Fasten. Vera was moving faster than I was.

Suddenly, as the top of the jack met the iron, a tremor ran through the metal with a loud creak from behind our heads. Eli's hands flew off the jack.

The creak became a groan.

I looked at Vera, the whites of her panicked eyes glittering back at me, then whipped my head back the other way to find the stilts folding in like an invisible motorcar was grinding into them. "Get out of the way!" I shouted. "Matthias, shut the hatch! ¡Apúrate!"

Vera rolled sideways. Emmett yanked me out by my ankles. As soon as we were clear, Matthias slammed the hatch closed.

The tank listed, slowly at first, then faster as gravity redistributed water directly into the corner joint where iron met glass. Like a steamer hull on rough seas, a hollow groan echoed off the theater walls followed by an earthquaking *crunch* as the corner of the tank collided with the stage floor, nearly knocking us off our feet.

"Jesus, Mary, and Joseph," panted Vera. "Punched a hole right through the feckin' floorboards!"

I couldn't speak. The tank was tilted. Irreversibly. One rear swan spring was all that was keeping it from completely capsizing now that an entire corner of the cage was stuck *in the stage*.

My head aching with anxiety and shortness of breath, I scrambled over to the iron bracket now jammed in wood and knelt beside it with my hand against the pane. Río was wedged against the corner, his head back, eyes closed and mouth open, gulping water. "Amor, ¿cómo—?"

I never finished asking if he was all right. Numbly, I peeled my hand off the glass and rubbed my thumb across my fingertips.

"What is it?" ventured Sonia.

"The glass is wet."

"*What?*" said Emmett.

"The tank. It's leaking."

Emmett hurried over and ran his own fingers over the surface. "I thought you said this glass couldn't break!"

"It *didn't*. It's the pitch. The stuff that seals the glass to the iron. It probably loosened in the heat."

I stood back for a better look at what we were dealing with. Though the tank was otherwise intact, it would never stand upright again, that was for damn sure. For all I knew, the moment Matthias tried to tip it back up, water would burst through the seals, flooding the theater and trapping Río in his bulletproof cage.

Eli yanked off his cap and cowered. "God, Benny, I'm so sorry—"

"No, this was my mistake," I said. "The draining water pulled Río's body toward the hatch. I didn't consider what might happen if he set the weight off balance. *Coño.*"

I pointed to the basin. "Matthias and Vera—dump this water outside, then fill it back up with water from the hydrants, fast as you can."

As they crouched around the basin to lift it, I threw off my coveralls and started pulling off my shirt.

"What are you doing?" asked Eli.

I wrenched off one shoe, then the other. "The tank's dead. If we're gonna get him back to the ocean, we've gotta get him out of here in the basin."

"The *basin?*" Emmett balked. "His tail's five feet long all by itself! How's he gonna fit?"

Bending down to grab the hammer and a wrench, I yelled, "Dammit, Emmett, we'll figure it out! I'll bring Río up, I just need two extra sets of hands to help me!"

Sweat ran into my eyes and coated my hands, leaving me slipping on the rungs that led to the lattice as I tried to scale them at an angle carrying the tools. Sonia stripped off her skirt and shirtwaist before she and Eli made their precarious ascent up the rungs after me. Carefully, I lowered myself to my knees, propping my bare feet between the lattice gaps to keep from skidding off the roof.

With a smithy's might, I brought the hammer down onto the padlock, broke it off the shank, and threw open the creaky hatch. Sonia and Eli crouched behind me as I tossed my hammer away, sucked in a breath, and slid into the water.

The tank was bottomless tonight, the water hot and green with algae that stung my eyes as I swam down. My undergarments dragged at my limbs like shackles. When I finally reached Río, I touched his cheek and nearly forgot to keep air in my lungs when he turned up his face toward me and smiled in relief.

I gripped his hand. *Aquí estoy*, I thought fiercely at him. *I'm getting you out of here.* Then I gently pulled him upright, got an arm around his waist, and pushed off the floor, aiming for the side where the bars slanted toward the water. We burst through the surface where Sonia and Eli waited, stretched out on their stomachs, their arms reaching for us.

"It's too far," rasped Eli. "Can you lift him?"

Even with the tank tipped, draining the water had left too much distance between the hatch and the water's surface, and Río was a dead weight in my arms, slick as oil and burning with fever. "I—I can't," I grunted.

"What if we got a rope?" offered Eli.

My grip was slipping. "I don't wanna drop him—"

Sonia clapped her hands. "Forget the rope!"

She sat on the vaulted roof with her back toward the ledge and hooked both stockinged feet under the iron bars. Then, as if her spine were made of taffy, she hung upside down over the hatch with her arms outstretched. "Come on, time's a-wasting!"

Sonia Kutzler was a genius. "Río, can you grab her arms?" I gasped through my teeth.

Breath wheezed into his lungs before his voice came in a gravelly hiss. "I—I th-think s-so."

Everyone on the tank seemed to trip in their movements at the sound of Río's voice. Even I startled at hearing his speech so readily added to the mix of panic-laced Brooklynese. Three months ago, he would never have allowed it.

I gently unhooked his arm from my neck and turned him around. Frantically kicking my legs, I used the rest of my strength to raise him by the waist high enough for Sonia to catch him above his elbows.

"Aw, Christ, he's slipping!" Sonia cried. "Eli!"

Río's weight plunged me back underwater, but as I pushed him from below, Eli reached around Sonia to tow his body up until all three of them toppled over onto the bars. Río's head now lay dripping in Sonia's lap, while Eli clambered back on all fours to help me get out next.

As I found my footing on the lattice and caught my breath, Río gazed at the Fraülein through hooded eyes. She carefully smoothed his hair off his forehead and wrapped an arm across his chest to tame his shaking. "Hiya, angel," she whispered through trembling lips. "Bet there's a party waiting for you when you get home." She looked up at me. "Benny, he's boiling hot."

"I know." I slid myself next to Sonia and searched Río's body for injuries. His hand was still clamped in a fist over his chest. "¿Cómo te sientes, querido?"

"D-débil . . ."

"Emmett, throw me my shirt," I called down. "Where the hell are they with the basin?"

"They gotta be back any moment. Hydrant's on the corner, not in Queens," he called back. My shirt sailed up over the tank side. Sonia caught it and helped me drape it over Río's chest to cool him.

Suddenly, another loud groan sent vibrations through the metal holding us aloft.

"Guys," Emmett yelled, "I got some concerns about this hole in the stage!"

But before I could sort out our next step, the tank lurched again and my foot skidded out from under me. The world went topside down—I splashed backward into the water to the muffled sound of Sonia and Eli shrieking my name.

The gap between me and the lattice was a lot wider now. I burst through the surface to find Sonia and Eli's hands split between holding onto the grill and holding onto Río like passengers clinging to a sinking ship. More worryingly, my ears detected a new sound—the *shish* of running water. "I'm fine, what's happening out there?"

"The leak's worse," Sonia panted. "We gotta get you outta there, Benny!"

I waded across to the highest point of the tank. "Worry about me later," I shouted. "Get Río off the roof!"

"I'll catch him," Emmett said. "Just lower him down nice 'n' slow."

Sonia gently shifted out from under Río's body, threaded her legs back through the bars, and hung like a spider, over the wall this time. Río's tail went over the edge first.

"Ow! Watch his fins," Eli grunted. "They're sharp!"

Río's weak gaze met mine as he descended into Emmett's waiting arms. This must have been what it was like for him to see the rest of the world go by while he stayed trapped in here like a goldfish in a bowl.

Eli landed on the stage and had begun lifting Río's tail off the floor when the barn doors flew back open. Vera, Matthias, and the coverless wagon rolled through them, the basin loaded and splashing water in its bed.

Vera gasped in horror at the sight of us. "I thought we was getting Río *out*, not putting Benny *in*!"

"Gangway!" Matthias pushed past her and scooped Río's shaking body into his embrace. "Don't you worry 'bout a thing, your highness. I got you."

"Eli . . . grab a sack of salt from the greenroom . . . dump it in Río's water," I panted.

"What about you?" Sonia asked anxiously from her perch on the lattice.

"I'm thinking . . ."

Madre de Dios, to think McCoy had called this tank a head-smelter back when it had only been a charcoal sketch! I cussed myself for not bothering to leave a kink in the construction that might help break me out of it. If I hadn't been in such a rush to put the wheels on—if it hadn't been so goddamned *hot*—maybe bad leverage wouldn't have been enough to make this maldito tank sink like the *Slocum* and we'd already be halfway to— *Wait.*

That was it. *Heat.*

"Vera!" I yelped, and the Phoenix rushed over. "Light up a torch! Sonia, toss me a pry bar."

Eli nabbed it off the stage and lobbed it up where Sonia caught it, then let it drop into my hands. Meanwhile, Vera sprinted into the wing and emerged with a fresh torch and her lighter.

"And God said, 'Let there be Light,'" she murmured, and her torch licked to life.

Matthias joined her with a second crowbar in his hand. "What're we doing, Benny?"

"Gotta break the glass," I huffed.

"Won't that flood the stage?" Eli argued.

"Forget the goddamn stage!" spat Sonia as she leapt down from the rungs. "If we can't ditch the tank in Dreamland, we may as well ditch it here and blame them anyway! Now gimme another pry bar!"

I gulped air, ducked under the water, and jabbed the chisel at the glass. It struck with a low gong. So I swung again. Then again. *Again*. And everyone seemed to understand what I was doing, because Vera put the torch right against the part of the glass I was attacking, while Matthias and Sonia struck it from the other side.

We swung at it until a crack spiderwebbed across the pane. I brought my foot up and kicked at the break as hard as I could until a sound like splintering ice made us all freeze.

Sonia, Matthias, and Vera dove out of the way a split second before the entire viewing pane exploded, spilling a torrent of murky water, sand, glass—and me—out onto the stage. The spray soaked everything up to the third row.

Eli hooted in shock at the soggy aftermath. "Sam's gonna hit the roof when he sees this! Holy shit!"

I rolled over onto my knees, wheezing, my legs heavy and wob-

bling. Matthias stepped gingerly over the revolú and helped me to my feet; meanwhile, Vera was staring at me like I'd just earned my human oddity title. "He just held his breath for ten minutes! Did no one else notice that Benny just held his breath for ten bleedin' minutes?"

"I take back everything I ever said about

you bein' weak," Matthias said, slapping chunks of pebbled glass off my union suit. "You got dumbbells for balls, brother."

Grinning weakly, I croaked, "Put that on my next poster."

I staggered barefoot over to the mound of rainbow cloth. Now that the tank was dead, we didn't need the whole tarp—but Río's tail was still hanging bare off the edge of the basin and needed to be wrapped in something wet. I pushed the bundle into Vera's arms and directed her to tear the saris off while I climbed back into my coveralls.

Finally, blessedly, I reached Río's side. Eli and Emmett carefully leaned him forward so I could step into the chilled hydrant water behind him. Once I was sitting, they settled his burning body in my arms. Vera was ready with the reams of colorful silk, everyone plunging hands into the water to saturate them and drape them over Río's tail.

"*Benigno.*"

As if they instinctively understood the rare gift of hearing a merman speak, everyone fell silent. Tears instantly clouded my vision, and as his body quaked, he smiled and spoke in a voice softer than the beat of wings. "You have b-become an e-excellent s-swimmer."

I kissed him. Without thinking. Without caring that God and everyone could see us. I wrapped my arms around his chest and imagined the glow of relief in my heart bleeding into him to stop his shaking, knowing with crushing certainty that I'd never hold anything so precious ever again.

Eventually, Emmett cleared his throat, and we broke apart. My coconspirators stood soberly around the basin.

"We're so sorry," Sonia murmured, her head bowed over her algae-stained undergarments. "We should never've brought you here, and that's the truth."

"P-perhaps you d-did not bring me here," Río whispered, "b-but the C-Currents did."

Matthias and Emmett lifted the bows over our heads so Vera could fasten them to the wagon bed. Eli and Sonia spread out the remaining tarp and were about to fly it over us when a new voice echoed across the theater, high-pitched and panicked.

"Mr. Benny! Mr. Benny!"

Madam Navya's head was bobbing down the aisle in a full sprint toward us. Behind her lumbered Igor, his stride slower than Navya's but wider by a yard and a half, rolling Lulu in on her wheelchair. Timmy zipped past them, skidding to a stop as soon as his feet met puddles of murky water.

"Stay back, Timmy," I shouted. "What's going on?"

"Morgan and those bloody mobsters," panted Navya. "They've figured it out! They are coming this way!"

THIRTY-FIVE

"Jiminy Crickets, what do we gotta do to get rid of those dingbats?!" Sonia cried as she yanked her skirts back on. "How'd they figure it out?"

Navya was doubled over catching her breath, so Lulu cut in. "Morgan was getting all impatient, pacing the parlor like a cat in a cage, and he's all 'Where's Frankie? Why aren't they here yet?' He starts talking about coming back to the theater, so I poured him five Shandies just to stall him, but then, outta nowhere, Frankie and his men actually *do* show up!"

"Agostinelli boss demand answers from Morgan," continued Igor. "Is not understanding why Morgan tell him to go in other direction. Is accusing Morgan of being nechestnyy. Liar. Crooked. And then—"

"They solved it," pushed out Madam Navya. "The men know you tricked them, Mr. Morgan thinks you are working for Mr. Reynolds, and they will *be here* any moment and find out that— Haye mere rabba, what happened to the tank?"

"We fixed it," Matthias quipped.

"What are we waiting for, the Staten Island Ferry?" Emmett snapped. "Let's scram already!"

Río and I could do nothing but watch while the company moved in a blur around us, Sonia throwing her clothes back on while the others covered the bows with the remnants of Lulu's tarp. When Río was safely hidden, Matthias and Vera climbed into the driver's seat and everyone else piled in next to the basin. Only Lulu stayed behind, snatching Timmy up before he could climb in himself.

"But Mama, I wanna go too!"

"Say bye-bye, Timmy," she said, pulling her recalcitrant nene onto the seat of the wheelchair. "Mama's gotta go light some candles for our friends to come home safe."

Before she could roll Timmy away, I stopped her. "Lulu!"

"Yeah, Benny?"

"My cuatro's in the greenroom. Hold on to it for me, will you?"

"Your *cuatro*?" I stared intently at her as Lulu's expression wafted from confusion to understanding to, finally, a sad smile. Whatever she was thinking, she kept to herself, knowing I might not be ready for everyone to find out what I was trying to say without saying it.

"I'll take good care of it," she said, stoically clutching her chest. "I promise."

"Thanks, Lulu. For everything."

"You too, kid. Godspeed, Benny."

Water splashed over the basin's sides onto everyone's legs as the wagon jerked forward and sent nearly everyone toppling off their seats, inciting a round of cusses like convicts in a paddy wagon.

"Y'all are louder than Hell's bells," Matthias barked. "If we live through this, remind me to teach you knuckleheads the meaning of 'discreet'!"

Moments later, the lights filtered through the silk in brighter red. Río tucked his head against my chest. Maybe the extra jostling was to blame as the wagon traversed the uneven dirt path toward the rear gate of Luna Park, but his shaking seemed worse. "How long 'til we're at Dreamland?" I asked.

"Can't go faster than this," Vera answered. "That trough ain't tied to anything what can hold it."

The street might as well have been a canyon for how long it took to cross. Tourists we couldn't see bustled noisily around us in a hodgepodge of languages and moods and ages to either camouflage or expose us. I instantly recognized Officer Joey's voice yelling, "Move along, you're blocking the intersection!"

I held onto Río and tried to breathe. His hand found mine under the water and gripped it.

Navya scooted closer. She placed her fingers over our joined hands, where the water slapped at her shiny bangles, clinking them together like chimes. "Mr. Río," she said quietly. "Do you know the Chenab?"

"Asikni," he murmured.

The madam's eyes shone with emotion. "Yes! The river of Heer and Ranjha. East to west, it flows for those whose love must overcome great challenge. Tonight, a tremendous wrong will be righted, and God will reward us all with your safe passage and long life. But you must stay strong. Both of you."

As she said that last bit, she glanced at me. Like Lulu, she'd figured out what I hadn't yet said aloud—that, whether or not we succeeded, I wasn't returning to Luna Park.

"Dhanyavaad," he whispered, and Navya's entire face lit up in the dark at the sound of her native song on his tongue.

"Next stop, Dreamland," Matthias hissed over his shoulder. "You ready, Sonia?"

"Abso-tively."

The wagon rocked to a stop. Sonia leaned back against the sideboard to draw a calming breath before hauling her skirts off her seat and around Emmett to leave. With a foot out of the bed, she cast a crooked smile back over her shoulder.

"Good luck, you crazy kiddos."

And she was off.

"We're waiting here 'til we've got the all clear," said Vera.

"Benigno . . ." Río's head lolled against my shoulder.

I caught his cheek with one hand and felt my stomach drop when I realized he wasn't shivering anymore. His hair was drying, the copper waves beginning to curl. I scooped water onto his forehead. "Quédate conmigo. We're almost there."

His eyes were open just a crack, revealing a blue so bright it seemed to glow against his gray skin.

"Benigno . . . it is time I told you."

"Told me what?"

"How beautiful you are."

I shook my head. "Tell me later."

"No, now."

The fist he'd been holding to his chest opened. In his gray palm lay a small calico scallop shell upon which he'd etched a picture of an ocean breaker with a large circle carved out behind it. Held up to the light, it would look like the moon.

"When I look at you . . . I see the earthen reefs where I played as a child," he murmured between strained breaths. "When you hold me . . . I feel the shallows warm around me. I have collected your smiles, your laughter, your songs like precious pearls. When I was alone, I held them close"—his voice caught in his throat—"to guard against my nightmares."

"Por favor, no hables así—"

"And your eyes." He touched my chin meekly. "Never have I seen such eyes as yours. Dark as the night . . . Kind as your namesake . . ." His voice was quiet, private. "Benigno, eres hermoso. Keep this shell . . . that you might never forget it."

I stared at him. Like Morgan, Río had the power to speak realities into being—but unlike Morgan, there were no crafty illusions, no self-serving manipulations in the words Río chose.

I took the shell and kissed it. "If you think I am beautiful, then it must be so," I said in Spanish.

Careful not to jostle him, I reached behind my head with one hand to unhook my necklace, brought the chain around Río's neck, and redid the clasp.

"Your San Cristóbal?"

I nodded. "You're going to live. This way, the patron saint of travelers will always be with you," I said. "And so will I."

Río's soft smile opened a window in my heart to let the light in. He pressed closer to me as if granting me permission to resume running my wet palm across his burning forehead with my wrinkled fingertips.

A sniffle made me look up to find Eli wiping tears. "What the *hell* is taking so long?" he demanded.

"Morgan and the men in suits will soon be finding us," rumbled Igor worriedly. "I regret, I have no arms."

Navya looked skyward in a bid to heaven for patience. "You mean, you are not *armed*."

"It's jake, Igor." Emmett held up Lefty's gun. "I got the arms right here."

"I'll tell you who's got an arm," came Matthias's voice from behind me. "Sonia's got Georgie's!"

"Attagirl," Vera said.

The reins cracked, and the wagon rolled on. I tried not to fixate on Vera's smeared mustache or Matthias's complete lack of disguise, silently begging God to make everyone within a five-yard radius of our wagon temporarily blind as the light outside grew

brighter, the music louder. Eventually the sounds of Surf Avenue waned behind us. We'd made it through Dreamland's gate.

"Keep left of the towers," called up Emmett. "When you see the Canals of Venice ride, cut through to Sixth Street—"

Emmett never finished delivering his directions before the *crack* of a gunshot flared nearby, followed by a voice that crushed our collective bravado in only three words.

"*Where is it?!*"

Frankie's husky roar drove through the din of carnival music and frightened shouting like an Italian battering ram. "I'm gonna smell ya out, ya thieving little skunk! *Where is the merman?*"

"Time to dance," Matthias said.

Another crack—the reins, this time—launched the wagon forward at a speed that left everyone clinging to the side panels for dear life, their spare feet shoved against the basin so Río and I wouldn't skid out the back of the wagon. Frankie's shouts faded behind us.

"Ya great eejit, you just gave us away!" Vera yelled.

"I gave us a chance," Matthias fired back. "Why can't these donkeys go any faster?"

"They weren't counting on no race! And they're hauling the whole bloody company!"

A second bullet ricocheted close to the wagon. Dust and pebbles rained on the silk over our heads amidst a chorus of screams from outside.

"Find somewhere to let everyone off," I called up. "Frankie won't chase them if they don't have Río!"

"Where exactly is 'somewhere'?" Matthias called back.

"Take the access road behind the Fighting Flames attraction," shouted Emmett. "We'll lose the goons and get a straight shot to the bathhouse!"

Vera stuck her head in. "Everyone who ain't Porto Rican or a merman better get ready to make for the trees!"

"Is best if you hold tight to my neck, yes?" Igor said urgently to Navya, who instantaneously dropped all her old reservations about sitting on his shoulders to climb onto his back.

As we pulled onto gravel, the light dimmed and the wheels crunched to a halt. "Last stop!" hollered Matthias.

"Wait," I shouted, and everyone froze mid-exit. "*I* made you do this, all right? No one at Dreamland's gonna take the fall, and you know it. You have to blame me!"

"Mr. Benny—" protested Navya.

"The Menagerie can still survive!" I cried. "They'll jail you or kill you if you don't say I put you up to this. You know I'm right!"

It was Tití who'd taught me the value of brief farewells. She was awful at it, always drawing out the ends of conversations in case there was some tontería she'd forgotten to share that would only emerge if she held onto your ear a little longer. At the end of her life, she'd held on the same way, leaving only after she had passed on every last worry, hope, and expectation for me—a lifetime of counsel funneled into the space between slowing heartbeats.

It took all I had not to do the same. I wanted them to know everything. How much I loved and admired them. How they'd become my family when I thought my only family had died of tuberculosis in Puerto Rico. Between the heat and humidity and terror that had crowded out the air in my lungs, my throat had become too small a gap for all my feelings to pass through at once.

"Promise me!" I shouted.

"All right," Emmett said with a grim smile as Eli said, "We promise."

"We will meet again," added the madam, "in this life, or the next."

"Zhivy búdem—ne pomrëm, Mr. Benny," rumbled Igor. "All will be well."

The wagon bed pitched and swayed as bodies large and small escaped into the humid night air, their fast footsteps against the gravel soon disappearing. So much water had sloshed out of the basin in our rush to dodge the Agostinellis that Río was barely submerged anymore. I scooped the remaining dregs onto his chest and face while the wagon rocked back into motion.

A handful had just gone into his hair when he suddenly jerked to life in my arms and tried to sit up.

"I hear them," he rasped, staring wildly at nothing. "Benigno, can you hear them?"

There was nothing to hear but pipe organs and Matthias and Vera shouting about directions. "Hear what?"

When Río's face spun around to meet mine, his pupils were gone leaving two cobalt pools in their place. He groped for me, making a fist in my damp clothes. "They call . . ."

"Amor, you need to save your stren—"

"*You*," he gasped. "They are calling *you*! Benigno . . . what *are* you?"

Tití Luz had hallucinated just like this at the end. The worst night of her fever, she swore she heard voices and saw the dead. I gathered him back in my arms and tried to calm him.

Frankie's voice snarled in the distance. "That's them! Don't let 'em escape!"

More gunshots rang out, followed by a scream so pained it instantly unlocked a vision in my mind of a roaring river and a pewter sky.

"*Vera!*"

With a tooth-grinding *RRRRIIIPPP*, the silk dragged over the ribs of metal that sheltered us, exposing Río and me to the night. Matthias vaulted off the driver's seat, scooped up Vera who was cursing fit to summon demons, and laid her gently next to us. Blood bloomed dark and red on the leg of her coveralls.

"It's just a bloody scratch," she grunted. "I can still drive—"

"Shut your fire-breathing piehole," he said and leapt over our heads into the driver's seat.

And there—trapped in a Dreamland access road—Frankie fired the bullet that would change Coney Island forever.

Time seemed to slow as it carved a smoking path through the thick air toward Matthias. I shouted his name, but it was as if his self-preserving instincts had shoved him out of the way. The bullet soared past his shoulder toward a cluster of barrels that lined the fence—the ones Georgie had carted in through the gates of *Creation*—and it didn't take me a split second to recall a very specific detail about the contents they held.

Tar is flammable.

Heat exploded up my neck as they ignited. The horses reared, pitched hard to the side, and the wagon listed, nearly spilling us onto the gravel. I followed Matthias's frenzied gaze to find the Agostinellis staggering backward, shielding their eyes.

"We gotta get outta here!" I cried.

Back in the wagon bed, Matthias helped Vera to her feet and swung her onto the ground, returning in an instant to lift Río's body off me. Vera limped into a veritable wall of black smoke to settle the terrified mares; the picket fence was already ablaze.

Then something happened that hadn't in any of the days New York had been baking in deadly heat: A *breeze* blew inland from the ocean. It fanned the flames, sending sparks into our faces, advancing the fire along the fence until the flying embers landed like seeds to set new walls on fire. Dreamland's most famous scenic railway attraction—Hell Gate—was about to become a reality around us.

"Ain't nowhere left to go," shouted Frankie, his gun apparently reloaded and pointed at us. "Give us what's ours, and maybe we won't scatter your diced remains across Brooklyn."

I looked helplessly at Matthias and Vera and instantly wished I hadn't. Their faces had gone paralytic with fear.

A loud *POP* made us all jump, the Agostinellis included. They ducked and spun in the direction of the sound.

"*Get going, numbnuts!*" Emmett hollered from behind a storage shed, Lefty's gun in his hand. He pointed it over the mobsters' heads and, with a bright flash and another *pop*, scattered them like foulmouthed marbles, pistols flashing as they fired blindly back over their shoulders.

With the world's fastest prayer for Emmett's safety, I clambered out of the basin, splashing water across the wagon bed. Río's pupilless eyes still gazed at nothing, his head rolling as I hoisted him over my shoulder like a fallen soldier. My legs immediately started vibrating under me from the sheer weight of him.

"Jesus, Benny, lemme take him," Matthias insisted.

"No. Take Vera and make a break for it," I yelled, "before this whole place lights up like the sun."

He helped us onto the gravel. "Ain't no way—"

More popping—electric lamps and bulbs were exploding from the heat, inevitably lighting more fires as they went out one by one.

"*Please,*" I gasped. "We both know it's gotta be me. Matthias, they *need you.*"

The strongman's lips formed a thin line. For a moment, I thought he might force my hand. But then he reached down and arranged Río's silk-wrapped tail across my body and around my other shoulder.

"I don't care if it's a postcard, a telegram, or a goddamned message in a bottle, you find a way to tell me you two made it out alive. And Benny . . ."

His large hand wrapped around my bicep and squeezed.

"I believe you can lift two thousand pounds."

He pointed me toward a gap in the wall, and I bolted. No money. No cuatro. No plan beyond returning Río to the sea.

The fire routed me back onto the Dreamland promenade where I staggered into bedlam and tried to weave upstream past scrambling laborers, ride operators, and animal trainers dragging elephants and ponies by their leashes and chains. No one noticed me or the limp form over my shoulder; they were too occupied with the business of trying to escape with their lives through the only streetside exit in this stupid, grandote *shit* of an amusement park.

My throat and lungs were quickly lining with ash, leaving my breath too quick and too thin, like I was sucking in air through a clogged spigot from a place deep underground. I hid my mouth and nose in the crook of my elbow and tried to get my bearings. To my left, the Fighting Flames ride had already been swallowed up by the eponymous element, but if I could find the Sixth Street promenade, then I could make it to the bathing pavilion and out the other side to the beach.

"Hold your breath, Río."

I ran.

"Hey!" yelled a voice I didn't recognize and therefore didn't heed. "You're heading straight for the fire, you idiot!"

But I just held onto Río, my knees aching with the effort of trying not to shake him too roughly. His hair was completely dry now, the long copper waves flying up in the heat and sticking to my sweaty neck. A temperature more blistering than anything I'd ever felt as an ironworker licked at my bare feet. It had taken only minutes for Dreamland to become a monstrous crucible, and I was carrying Río through it.

The closer we got to the water, the more lucid he seemed to get. His tail shuddered and squeezed around my shoulder.

"Y-Ya estamos llegando . . ." The words disappeared in a fit of coughs. My windpipe was scalded; the pain went all the way down. "We're . . . we're almost . . . there."

All our worries about witnesses seemed ridiculous now. Anyone within a mile of the beach would have only one thing to look at: Dreamland's skyline devoured by fire. My feet stepped off the rough promenade stairs and sank into the soft sand where I fell to one knee and lowered Río into my arms.

"Río," I gasped. "¿Estás bien?"

His pupils had reopened. A dry hiss issued from his parched lips, and his hand went weakly to his throat. The smoke had stolen what was left of his voice.

"I know. Nos vamos." I gripped him behind his back and below his fin, then stood back up, teetering on the uneven powder under my raw feet.

The inferno was behind us, leaving me trudging through a firelit reinvention of my dreams; the same rolling waves, the same shade of night, except the distance to the water could've been miles. My chest seemed to feel heavier with every stinging footstep that led to being parted from Río forever, and though we'd somehow avoided getting singed, my limbs burned with exertion.

Maybe I was desperate for the distraction, but it got me thinking about the burn that started all this. "I never told you," I said in a soot-stripped voice, "what your mother d-did for me—the night she told me to s-save you."

Río lifted his dry, tired eyes to my face.

"I had a bandaged-up b-burn on my hand. She'd g-grabbed it. Got it all wet. Damn near b-blacked out from the pain—"

My foot sank too deep and, grunting, I caught myself before we both spilled onto the beach. I forced my eyes seaward. Just a few more yards.

"Thought she'd done it to h-hurt me. But that night, I took off the b-bandage, and the burn was g-gone. That's when I knew. . . I had to find you." Despite the impossibility of any water left in me for tears, one ran onto my cheek. "Wish I could've h-healed you

like she healed m-me, Río. She saved my life w-when she told me to save yours."

I felt Río's fingers searching for a grip on my shirt. I looked down to find his lips moving around silent words, his pink-rimmed eyes alert and wide. He looked like he was trying hard to say something but couldn't reach a place to touch me so he could say it in my mind.

"It's all right," I breathed. "Look. We're here."

My scalded soles met ocean water, and the sting was followed by almost instant relief. A few steps farther in, where the water was high enough to lap at my thighs and drag at my toes, Río tipped his chin toward me and wrapped his trembling fingers around San Cristóbal. The moment his fin grazed the water, his free hand grabbed my shoulder.

He was shaking his head. He didn't want to go.

Gritting my teeth, I lowered myself unsteadily onto one knee, submerging Río in the shallows up to his chin. Navya's garments lifted off his body like crimson clouds.

"I'll f-find you again," I whispered through tears. "Steal a boat from the pier every night if I h-have to. Río—you gotta let go."

Traces of his stubbornness reappeared as his eyes flitted from the ocean and back to me.

Suddenly, another wave rode inland that seemed to wash the indecision out of him. His grip loosened. He laid back into the waves, leaving me to watch breathlessly as he closed his eyes and sank below the surface.

It was if I'd laid him in a tomb. I placed my hand on his to send the only words that mattered into his mind. But no sooner had I touched him than the wave pulled back toward the open water it came from.

It pulled Río with it.

"Wait—"

I lunged for him, but a sudden breaker plowed into me, and I fell back. I couldn't even get a foothold before another wave lifted me up like a bundle of seaweed and deposited me on the sand, empty-handed but for a wide ream of red silk.

Coughing and spitting salt water, I clambered onto my hands and knees and whispered Río's true name to the wind.

Unexpectedly, the wind carried my name back to me.

"BENNY!"

Sonia?

Then Morgan's derringer fired.

Río

The Currents received me at the shore—as if, indeed, they had been waiting patiently for my deliverance. Thank the Seven Seas that the water embraced me in my moment of greatest need, Mother, for I had no voice left to tell Benigno what he unknowingly revealed when he said you had healed him! Could the Currents have known his truth all along?

It all became clear as the water pulled me away, the very moment my ears filled with a sound I had prayed never to hear again!

THIRTY-SIX

ónde está mi milagrito?"

Tití Luz was wearing her nicest nightdress. A relic of the life she lived before el Grito de Lares and San Ciriaco and tuberculosis. Her once tanned skin hung gray across the bones of her face, her hair whittled to straw. She rested on an embroidered pillow I'd given her with my first earnings at the Sobrinos de Portilla foundry—a fancy thing that had only ever decorated a parlor chair before, but which she wanted to use before she died.

With her, nothing ever went to waste, not even me.

I moved from the chair where I was keeping watch to her bed and wrapped my fingers gently around the fragile knobs of her hands. "Aquí estoy, Tití."

"Mijo," she said in a breath that rattled out of her.

Her hand slipped out from under mine and gestured toward the night table drawer where an envelope sat at the top of her stationery pile. I made to hand it to her, but her fingers came gently down on my wrist to stop me.

"You have been strong against life's many storms," she whispered in

Spanish, *"but I worry for the part of you that has hardened under all that strength. That accepts pain and injustice as your birthright."*

Though it was pointless to say it, I told her in our shared language, *"You don't have to worry about me."*

She pretended not to hear me.

"The things I've seen have hardened my heart as well," she went on. *"I lost my family. My country. The future I'd fought for. When you are as lonely and angry as I was, all you can do is pray that the light of God still shines upon you. Little did I know when I found you clinging to that riverbank that the Lord had delivered the answer to my prayers."*

Her eyes flitted to the envelope. *"And now, He answers another. A new beginning, Benigno. For you."*

I said nothing. Any strength she saw in me was just the mask I wore to hide my fear—of her illness, of the ways I wasn't like the other boys and men around me, of forces of nature like rivers and oceans and storms and love. And as I sat there, beside her dying body, I could feel the terror of who I'd become without her weave another knot into the net that held me. Why did new beginnings feel like the end of everything?

"Like the lagartijos that shed their skin many times before they die, every change strengthens us. But staying soft in here"—she pointed weakly to my chest—*"is up to you. When next you shed your skin, you must hold on to the love that lives in you and wants to be free, even if that love is . . . different."*

Even then, she knew.

My tití reached for my other hand and took it, clutching them both with the dregs of her strength. *"You are the blacksmith of your fate,"* she whispered. *"I will not have your spirit wither on an island of tragedies when you can go to New York and forge a life. Promise me."*

What else could I say? *"I promise."*

Tití's face relaxed, and she smiled. *"Now. Open it."*

Next to a wad of American dollars and an address to someplace I would never find was a string of pewter links. I pulled out the medallion by the chain and held it in the air.

"San Cristóbal protects . . . all who journey . . . my little Odiseo," she murmured, her breath turning labored. *"Make freedom your destination . . . and you will know what metal you are made of soon enough."*

"Goddamn you, Sam, what have you *done*?"

My face was in the sand. Grit was everywhere, in my hair, on my tongue. The bullet had entered my side with the disturbance of a wayward pebble before the burning spread from a root somewhere under my ribs, incinerating me like paper over a flame. I looked dimly in the direction of Sonia's weeping to find Morgan purple-faced and dragging her by the arm as he stalked toward me, his derringer still fixed on its target.

"Where. Is. My. MERMAN?"

My mouth opened to answer, but only a hiss came out.

He's gone.

"Get your meat hooks *off* me," Sonia shrieked, yanking against Morgan's grip before he pulled her face up to his and spat into it.

"Shut your traitorous mouth, you little— *Argh!*"

Sonia's free hand whipped up and dug its fingernails into Morgan's eyes. Howling, he dropped the gun and her arm. As he staggered in a blind circle, Sonia raced over and flung herself down beside me.

"Oh, please, God, help me . . ." She reached trembling fingers around my waist, pulled her hand away, and found it slick with dark red. "Benny, get up! *Please*, kiddo, you gotta get up!"

Morgan reappeared over her, blood beading along diagonal gouges that fractured his face. He made a fist in her bright red hair and heaved her out of my field of vision, where I heard a muffled *thwack* that stopped Sonia's whimpering.

He was back a moment later to yank me to my knees by my shirt. "Tell me where the beast is or I'll tear you apart!"

My voice was thinner than a cuatro string, but I found it none-theless. "*No.*"

He backhanded me across the face into wet sand. "You un-grateful *shit!*" he bellowed. "I opened my doors to you! Handed you a living! A goddamned poster in the hall! And this is how you thank me? By demolishing everything I've built?"

When his hand went for my collar, I grabbed it. "You d-did that yourself. When you sold us to Frankie and stole the m-merman."

"That's *it*, isn't it," he sneered with disgust. "Your perverse at-tachment to that watery *fiend*. You think ingratiating yourself to a scaly incubus makes you something special? That you're anything more than a worthless blight on the populace best left in a gutter to lick rats?" He barked a rabid laugh, and the tang of booze went up my nose. "Who in hell do you think you are?"

It was the same question McCoy had asked me the day I'd burned my hand. The day I'd turned over a tank with the bits of my Puerto Rican identity I hadn't already lost to assimilation baked right into the iron. I'd kept quiet back then because even after years locked in the pit of my own mind trying to puzzle it out, I was still too afraid to look myself in the eye in case I saw someone I wasn't allowed to be.

But I had an answer now. And I'd be damned if this murdering crook was going to decide anything for me ever again.

I grabbed a fistful of sand and whipped it into Morgan's face, sending him lurching backward, snarling like a wounded ani-mal. I used the rest of my strength to pull myself back onto my feet, a stone's throw from where Sonia was sprawled on her back, unconscious.

"S-soy boricua, pa' que lo sepas. I'm with it, for it, n-never against it," I croaked. "The company's my f-family—"

Morgan swung at me and missed.

"—and if you weren't a selfish, shit-eating bastard, they could've been yours too!"

He swung again, and this time, his punch launched me into the surf. I couldn't get off my back before Morgan was on top of me, pinning me to the sand with a heavy arm across my neck. Salt water ran into my mouth.

"Think I can't replace that tank? That I can't find another siren to fill it? That I can't get rid of you just like I got rid of old *Jack?*" Morgan spat. "No one will even bother riddling out how you died as long as there's one less immigrant mongrel in New York City!"

Samuel Morgan had killed his own mentor. Of course he had. That brazen declaration rang truer than anything that ever came out of his mouth, especially his petty insults.

There will always be yanquis calling you a mutt instead of a man.

I spat out salt water and blood so I could smile. "M-must eat you alive," I choked, "knowing I've heard the merman s-sing."

With a roar to shake the scales off his museum monsters, he slammed his knuckles into my open wound, the pain exploding across my body just like Dreamland Tower's electric bulbs. I'd barely gasped in any air before his thumb and fingers clamped around my jaw and pushed my face sideways into the water.

Tití Luz was wrong about me. I wasn't strong, not anymore. And even blacksmiths get burned—a weeping red stripe across my palm for daring to be free in a world where freedom was the exclusive province of people nothing like me.

But I held my breath anyway. Because if I was going to die on Manhattan Beach, then I would choose when. Despite everything, I wanted to live, even if I had only seconds left to do it. Time stretched long as I gazed beyond Morgan's blood-smeared, hate-filled face to a sky about to welcome the sunrise. To the vast tract of blue that touched every shore, ones I'd visited and ones I'd never get to see.

I was still *here*, and as I closed my eyes and let the pain and disappointment turn to sea foam, the only thing I couldn't understand was, *how* was I still here?

I put the question aside to make my last petitions to God. *May the Menagerie live on. May Río find his harmony. May Sonia be freed. And if the Currents are real . . .*

I sure hope they find me.

CRACK.

Morgan's hand lurched, then let go.

My eyes blinked open to find something dark dribbling into the water above my stomach from a small hole in the middle of Morgan's limey waistcoat. Dazed, he touched it, watched it run over his fingers, then looked up.

"S-Sonia . . ."

She limped into view, the sandy derringer in her hand, her bruised face dark with cold resolve. Through trembling lips, she whispered, "My name is Mary."

Then she lifted her skirt and, with the toe of her shoe, pushed him off me into the shallows.

Sonia—or rather, Mary—splashed down next to me. The water was ribboned with blood—mine and Morgan's. And though she knew I wasn't going anywhere, she tried to get a hand behind my shoulders. Pleaded through sobs for me to get up and go back to the skin I'd just finished shedding.

But Tití Luz said to never look back. Even if you left your keys . . .

"Dammit, Benny, *please*. You have to come with me—"

"He cannot!"

My heart quavered in my chest when I heard that musical voice. I peered at the water beyond my feet and wondered if I'd already died.

Río had never looked so glorious. The iridescence of his body was restored; the lush blue-greens and silvers gleamed in the growing sunlight. He sailed in on a breaker that seemed to obey his command, steering him toward us and seating him neatly at my side—like he'd actually been a prince of the deep this entire time and we just never knew.

He gathered me easily into his arms, San Cristobal still hanging from his neck. "*V-volviste*," I whispered through tears, trembling like a leaf in a storm.

"Mi luna." He kissed my forehead and covered my wound with a soft hand. "Nunca te abandonaría."

My eyes combed his features hungrily for evidence I wasn't dreaming. Even the scar across his brow was gone. "H-how . . . ?"

"Salt water's healing properties," he reminded me, wiping my eyes with a gentle fingertip. "It is why our tears are made of it."

A soft groan turned our heads. Morgan's breaths now gurgled wetly through the hole in his chest. Río held me closer and gazed upon his old captor with pitiless eyes as Morgan gaped back with an expression more like yearning than resentment. A moment before the gurgling ceased, his glassy eyes dropped back to look at me.

Not look. *See.*

Then a wave climbed up the shore, wrapped itself around Morgan's body, and dragged it into the Atlantic.

"Río, please," whispered Mary, "Benny needs a doctor—"

"No. Out of the ocean, his body will succumb." Río reached around me with both hands and widened the rip in my union suit where the bullet hit me. "Indeed, seawater is all that is sustaining him right now."

Mary spoke for us both: "What are you talking about?"

"You have liberated us all from the Shark's treachery. I live in gratitude for your courage, my friend," he said in lieu of an answer to her question, then turned back to me. "There is no time left to lose. One more breath of air, Benigno."

"C-can't . . ."

"You *must*," he insisted. "I beg you to try!"

I gulped in a dram of sea breeze, and as if I were no heavier than an empty conch shell, he lifted me to his chest.

"Wait!" Mary's hand flew out to grab Río's wrist. "Where are you taking him?"

Frothy waves rushed in around us. "Home."

The ocean's din gave way to silence as we dove into the surf. Río seemed to swim at the speed of a locomotive, leaving me blind in the wake of bubbles we left behind. Though my body was dead weight, a flimsy arrangement of busted human parts, only seconds passed before the shelf disappeared and open water stretched out around us as far as I could see. Río's swimming slowed, then stopped, delivering us to an undulating calm.

I was about to rattle right out of my skin, my heart hammering like a cogging machine against my rib cage, everything inside me overtaxed and starved for air. I thought Río might bring me back up for another breath.

He didn't.

Instead, he brought his face level with mine, and as the light above grew around him like the first rays of sun after a storm, I realized I'd been here before. In my dreams. The same liquid universe around us and nowhere to focus except deep into a piercing set of azure eyes.

Gracias a Dios. I could go peacefully if this was the last thing I saw before my lungs finally gave up.

Llévame, Río, hasta el mar.

As if he'd figured out how badly I wanted his kiss to escort me from this world to the next, he wrapped himself around me and brought his lips to mine. Lost in a swirl of copper hair, I felt him take hold of my chin and open my mouth while it was still pressed to his, his tail tightening around my legs.

And he inhaled.

My body was too wrecked to resist. Río drew all the air I had into himself, and when he couldn't take anymore, I watched with wide eyes as he turned his face away to cough dark clots of my blood into the water like he'd just drawn poison from a bite. With his hand firm on the skin of my neck, he made me look into his eyes again.

Now, he whispered to my mind, *breathe deep and live.*

The last of my breath was gone. We were sinking. I shook my head. *It's over, Río. I'll drown—*

You cannot drown, mi amado. You never could.

As soon as he'd said it, a strange sensation filtered into my skin and bones. Like my body had become sediment. It took quick command of my thoughts until one word repeated in my mind.

RESPIRA.

A finger at a time, I surrendered my frantic grip on his shoulders. Then, squeezing my eyes shut, I breathed in, the pain sharp and instant as water entered my lungs like a river of knives. I tried to make myself spacious, unlocking the corners of my chest to make room the way Río had taught me. Once I'd taken in all I could, Río's mouth fastened to mine again and forced the exhale from my lungs, the last of it escaping in a stream of warmth.

He turned and spat another bloody cloud into the sea.

In the pause before I inhaled again, I found myself desperate for the water, suffocating without it. Again, I drew ocean into my lungs, only this time, it was painless. *Easy.* Waves of relief rolled through my limbs and un-seized my muscles.

That's when I noticed the burning in my side had dulled. My headache was quieting too, soothed by rare strains of music that seemed to hum in my ears from every direction. Río pulled another exhale from my lips as every inch of me thrummed like ripples from a drop in still water, sealing my wound and stirring my cells as if from a long slumber.

Glimpses of my half-lived life began to zoetrope behind my eyes. The face in the Río Humacao. Coughing blood at the forge. A mermaid's dying wish and my flooded fantasies. Learning to love like learning to swim, until each night in the tank with Río felt like being consecrated by forty tons of holy water. I relived in rapid succession every night I'd ever stared across the Gowanus at Lady Liberty making silent prayers I didn't think anyone could hear until a head-smelter fell into my hands and ruined my life.

Only it hadn't. Though I'd had Río right as the person fate had bonded me to, I'd had everything else wrong.

All this time. I'd thought I was bringing *him* home.

The Currents are real. I feel them now, thundering through me like a silver rapid as the cords around my chest dissolve into the sea. Anyone might look at my body and think nothing has changed, but inside it, I am unbound.

Breathing more freely than I ever have in my life, I take Río's face between my sandpaper palms as he gazes back with all the wonder of having just witnessed his first miracle.

Are you my captor or my savior? I ask.

With Benigno's voice in my mind and his kiss on my lips, I impart the truth my soul has known since he first sang to me from across the iron bars.

Son of Neptune, I answer. *I am your harmony.*

EPILOGUE

Excerpt from <u>The Heaviest Weight: A Mighty Memoir</u>
by Matthias Martin

On May 27, 1911, Dreamland went the way of dreams. The blaze gobbled up several city blocks, the bathhouse, and the pier before four hundred firemen finally doused the last embers. *The Sun* blamed it on maintenance workers making electrical repairs on the Fighting Flames ride that night, but two jitneys says Frankie Agostinelli ghostwrote that bullshit.

After that, the scandal of Sam Morgan's and the Prince of Atlantis's disappearances swept through Coney Island faster than the fire did. Theories ranged from the mundane to the obscene, with an especially popular thumper claiming Sam had offed himself to escape conviction for setting the Dreamland fire. Those of a more dramatic persuasion started the rumor that Poseidon came ashore and killed Sam as retribution for holding a merman captive. In other, especially secretive circles along the waterfront, folks speculated he'd become obsessed with the merman and died of a busted heart.

Don't ask me what the true story is, but Sonia—who got to calling herself Mary again after we discovered her on the beach that morning looking rougher than an August pinecone—swears that last one hits closer to the mark than the rest.

The rumor mill didn't stop the papers from painting a pretty portrait of Sam, with long-winded reflections of his life as "the showman in green whose wit and style was a keystone in Luna Park's historical legacy." Only his familiars in the company knew the thorny bit where he'd sold his soul to win a war that had nothing to do with Dreamland in the end.

With his playground in ruins, Reynolds never did resume his mission to out-amuse Luna Park, which opened right on schedule to a crowd that saw the shuttered doors to Morgan's Menagerie of Oddities and got right on with living, as folks do. The immediate question to answer was, who among us was batty enough to steer our ship into uncharted waters if Sam wasn't around to do it himself? Personally, I was more interested in retiring after a few more seasons than running a show myself, nor were many of my fellow freaks keen to take up Sam's distinguished mantle—except for Mary. A year after the Prince of Atlantis act opened and closed on the same day, our establishment was resurrected under a new flag: Schneider's Wonders of the World. Mary's show was a near-instant success, though whispers on the boardwalk said a mutually beneficial arrangement with some folks of questionable character had given her a head start once she threatened to take her story to Tammany Hall.

As seasons passed and folks started asking themselves what enjoying a sideshow said about their morals, the crowds thinned, and Schneider's Wonders became a museum—a time capsule of the days we were gods and millions from all walks of life came for the entertainment and left with that savory taste of hope and possibility that still makes New York City run to this day. But before Thompson and Dundy's amusement haven went the way of Dreamland, our little company of born and self-made curiosities enjoyed our most fruitful years.

Vera's Phoenix persona reached immortal status when she chopped off her hair in the '20s and traded her bustle for a belt of torches and a candelabra hat. It was around that time Lulu finally ditched that fake beard and started spending the offseason devoting her talents to making fine dresses for women of rare size.

Igor and Madam Navya fell in love over a bottle of vodka. Their marriage, apart from prompting gasps from crowds who'd never seen a ten-foot-tall man married to a two-foot-tall woman, ensured they had someone to argue New York baseball with for the rest of their lives.

Meanwhile, Timmy stopped climbing Madam Navya's bookcases. Once he was big enough, he scratched that itch by joining Schneider's Wonders as an aerialist. And when science had decided all conjoined twin sets ought to be genetically identical, Eli and Emmett reinvented themselves as the famous juggling vaudeville-style comedy duo the Three-Legged Pants.

As for me, seems the only thing harder than lifting two thousand pounds is writing a goldang memoir nobody's gonna read. But I'm writing it anyway because when you get to my age, you find out memories are about the only things worth holding onto. And, to that end, I'll never forget my friend.

The last time I saw Benny Caldera, brother was running barefoot into Hell carrying one of nature's greatest mysteries on his shoulders, and I don't mean a merman.

You'd never guess by looking at him—that brown, Caribbean smithy who barely came up to my armpits and fiddled with his chain whenever his nerves got louder than his asthma—that he was made of stronger metal than the iron he hammered. Then again, things in this town are rarely the way they seem. Courage is a weight heavier than anything I've ever lifted, and you only had to watch Benny disappear behind that wall of flames to realize he had more of it than most people have need to carry for themselves.

But, wouldn't you know it, the kid kept his promise. A year after Sam's show sank, Oscar Barnes showed up bamboozled in his new coveralls at the stage door of Schneider's Wonders of the

World, a sandy absinthe bottle in his fist. Damp and worn inside it was my old flyer for Morgan's Menagerie of Human Oddities with the instructions written right across my chest: "Pls. deliver to Matthias Martin at Luna Park."

Dear Matthias,

It's just like you said. Ain't no being free on the outside unless you're free on the inside.

Tell the gang I've got no regrets. I'm more myself than I ever was, and I'm never alone.

But if you're the sort who needs to see to believe, come to the Iron Pier on a clear night when the tide is in, and the moon is full. Look for Río and me.

We'll be waves on the water.

Siempre,

Benigno

ACKNOWLEDGMENTS

Just as a sideshow can't go on without the efforts of manifold skilled players behind the curtain, this book owes its completion and success to the many generous people who have surrounded it since its humble inception on AO3.

My literary agent, font guru, and "ambassador of quan" Saritza Hernández regularly transcends her job description to help me see myself and my work more clearly, for which I'm deeply thankful. She packaged this book for submission with a set of my sketches because she believed a fully illustrated historical romantasy was a goal worth reaching for. Per usual, she was right.

It is a rare publisher that will hear a proposal for an illustrated book for adult readers and throw all their support behind it, but Erewhon Books and Kensington Publishing Corp. met the challenge with more enthusiasm than I could have ever hoped for. Endless thanks to "Team Tides" art director Cassandra Farrin whose creative oversight gave me space and freedom to bring my illustrative vision to life, to designer Leah Marsh who gave this book its stunning interior aesthetic, to Martin Cahill for his invaluable efforts to put this book in as many hands as possible, and to Viengsamai Fetters for being this project's exemplary wingman.

Above all, I am indebted to my peerless editor Diana Pho who gave my story a home and elevated it to Woolworth Building heights. Collaborating with her has been transformative to both my writing and my confidence, and just so joyful. Thank you, THANK YOU, Diana.

Tides was researched at the height of the COVID-19 lockdown, a feat made possible by the subject matter experts who generously donated their knowledge and resources via innumerable emails and Zoom meetings. Endless thanks to David Sharp, president of the Waterfront Museum, for the copious photos and references that made it possible to render 1910s Red Hook in words and pictures; to Virginia Sanchez-Korrol, professor emeritus of Puerto Rican & Latino Studies at CUNY Brooklyn, for immersing me in the Boricua history our schools never teach us; to Jamie Salen, David Favaloro, and Lana Rubin of the Tenement Museum for educating me on immigrant life and labor in New York City; and to Adam Realman, sword swallower and artistic director of the Coney Island Circus Sideshow, whose emotional insights into sideshow life—as well as his instruction to include the axiom "with it, for it, never against it"—gave Benny's Menagerie family its beautiful beating heart.

For all other facets of the story's integrity, I am incredibly thankful for the critical eyes of Anna Racine, Mark Duplane, Anna Sward, and Denise Morales Soto. For their valuable artistic input and frequent sanity checks, I owe my deep gratitude to artists Jeska Stowell and Alicia Mestre Bruce.

An unexpected reward of writing a merman romance was getting to mingle with the beautiful and beguiling members of the performing Mer community. Heartfelt thanks to Morgana Alba and the professional mermaids of the Circus Siren Pod, as well as professional mermen Andy Vargas, Joshua Michael Breaux, and Jack Laflin, all of whom offered their platforms to *Tides* and whose talents anchor Río's existence firmly in the real world. They are living proof that certain truly special humans can indeed hear the Currents' call.

Readers who have followed my artwork before this know that I might never have reached this milestone without the LGBTQ+/BIPOC book community that raised me from fan artist to author-illustrator. Mil gracias y abrazotes to my incredible queer/Latinx writer mentors through the Highlights Foundation, Alex Villasante, NoNieqa Ramos, and Mia Garcia, as well as the many other authors who have honored me with blurbs, paired my art with their books, shared resources, and encouraged and uplifted me, among them (alphabetically) Becky Albertalli, Andrea Beatriz Arango, Sarah Rees Brennan, Alison Cochrun, Lex Croucher, Camryn Garrett, Valerie Gomez, Sophie Gonzales, Alexis Hall, Zakiya N. Jamal, Jackie Kahlilieh, TJ Klune, Sher Lee, Freya Marske, Everina Maxwell, Alyssa Reynoso Morris, Bethany C. Morrow, Casey McQuiston, Rainbow Rowell, Eliot Schrefer, Dallas Smith, Fay and Karelia Stetz-Waters, Sera Taíno, Aiden Thomas, Marisel Vera, Sarah Wallace, MA Wardell, Jennifer Weiner, and Julian Winters. I am profoundly humbled by all your generosity.

There remains a special place in my heart for book-loving friends that have hyped up *Tides* all the years it has been in development. Notable shoutouts to my generous Patreon members; my lifelong cheerleader Heather Butler; Ai & Blue, who honored this story with its first underwater cosplay photoshoot; Molly McBride, for the gorgeous Benny & Río fan art that hangs in my office; Nunzi Pietrangelo, who gave Benny and Río their ship name ("Brío"); Kelly Shea and Jonathan Lawrence, who like to pretend they don't moonlight as my personal public relations team; Janna Tanner, who gave me my first author/illustrator DC Public Library event; and Sierra Reid of Novel Cookies, who made my cover reveal memorably delicious. From Bookstagrammers and BookTokers to Tumblr friends and public librarians, being in the orbit of so much kindness has blessed me and my work immeasurably, and I hope to continue paying it forward.

Benny is more than the hidden history he represents; he also stands in for my ancestors, aunts, uncles, cousins, grandparents, and parents, whose lives are woven into the diasporic tapestry. Thank you, Mom and Dad, for passing down your experiences as extranjeros who found a home—and each other—in Brooklyn, for your unending love and support, and for imbuing me with your relentless work ethic. To my sister Vidalia: Before I realized I could do this for a living, you were already pushing me to better my writing, teaching me about passive/active voice like you'd taught me long division when we were kids. Thank you, Big V, for being my greatest friend, protector, and ally. Thank you also to my extended family in Puerto Rico, whose love, hospitality, and insights into our shared history bless my writing each time we visit—especially Manuelita, Nelson, Cookie, Jenny, Benji, Wilma, Nino (the original Benigno), Tití Nydia, and Tití Ana. And to "Mr. VKelleyArt": Only one other person has read every draft of this book (and cried at the end every time), and I'm blessed to have married him. For single parenting when deadlines loomed, paying bills, and indulging countless late-night brainstorming sessions—for giving this book its beautiful title—you have my undying love and gratitude, Mike.

Though my children, Harrison and Colin, won't read this until they've matured, I owe them thanks for their patience with me when I was at my busiest, and for the core memories they helped create every time they looked over my shoulder and told me they liked what I was drawing. This book is for them too; their unconditional acceptance of what makes people different is a trait I pray they never lose, and if, like Benny, life's trials dampen their sense of inherent worthiness, I hope this story gives them a road map back to themselves.

$\mathcal{A}$UTHOR'S $\mathcal{N}$OTE

Puerto Rico, Colonialism, and Hybridity

In the tradition of mermaid tales (and tails!), Benny's story is about hybridity: when having a foot in multiple cultural worlds—racial, ethnic, geographic, or otherwise—presents challenges to identifying with any of them. Hybridity has specific historical relevance to colonialism, as Benny's "otherness" is a direct outcome of his homeland Puerto Rico's occupation, his geographic displacement, and his assimilation into New York City's labor force, all of which convolute Benny's ability to truly define or defend himself in his new reality. Further complicating his trajectory to self-actualization is his queerness, a quality seemingly at odds with both the culture he has left behind and the one he must now survive in.

Benny's character, inspired by the true accounts of teenage Afro–Puerto Ricans who made the steamship journey to Red Hook as stowaways, is culturally representative of Puerto Rico's conditions at the turn of the century when the island nation was in limbo. The 1898 Paris Treaty marked the end of the Spanish-American War and assigned formalized control of Puerto Rico, Cuba, Guam, and the Philippines to the United States. These agreements eventually gave Cuba autonomy in 1902 but detached Puerto Rico politically from its sister island, leaving its identity caught in the liminality between colony, commonwealth, and sovereign nation.

As the island changed hands from Spanish to American rule, immediate economic changes set the stage for Benny's migration. The American dollar supplanted the Spanish peso, and the island's agricultural profile whittled from coffee, tobacco, sugarcane, and cattle farming to predominantly sugarcane exports, advancing a preexisting job famine and bankrupting Puerto Rican farmers like Tití Luz as American mainlanders bought out the land.

The blaze for island sovereignty had remained lit until the San Ciriaco hurricane left a path of devastation that further steepened the climb for independence. By the time Puerto Ricans received US statutory citizenship via the Jones-Shafroth Act in 1917, the relationship between Puerto Rico and the United States had entered an era of cultural, economic, and racial exploitation that persists to this day.

Puerto Rican migration to New York City began as early as the mid-nineteenth century with a wave of affluent revolutionaries and political exiles who resisted Spanish rule. These "Pioneros" established enclaves in Manhattan and found work as merchants, skilled laborers, domestic workers, and most notably, tabaqueros—tobacco workers who rolled cigars and cultivated an educated, hardworking, politically minded community that organized against colonial occupation from afar. By the time we encounter Benny at the ironworks, there are roughly 1,600 Puerto Ricans living and working in Manhattan[1]—so why doesn't Benny seek them out?

In modern terms, Benny is a demisexual homo-romantic man, though the historical term for both homosexuality and transgender individuals at the turn of the century was "inverted." Despite

---

1   Matos-Rodriguez, Felix V. & Hernández, Pedro Juan. *Pioneros: Puerto Ricans in New York City, 1898-1948.* (South Carolina: Arcadia Publishing, 2001), 7.

a lack of documentation about LGBTQ+ migrants from the turn of the century, contemporary attitudes on the island and its mainland regime suggest queerness presented an additional layer of otherness to contend with. An early twentieth-century account of Puerto Rican perspectives toward homosexuality appears in Bernardo Vega's memoir when he notably threw his wristwatch into the ocean on his steamship voyage to New York in 1916 after a fellow traveler told him the jewelry might make Americans think he was "effeminate."[2] Though sodomy was officially criminalized in 1902 when Puerto Rico aligned its penal codes with America's, a culture of homophobic intolerance was already in place where Roman Catholic patriarchal traditions defined gender and sexuality in the narrowest terms, threatening outliers with censure, marginalization, and violence.[3] Someone like Benny, therefore, would likely have been closeted and found escaping persecution a valid reason to migrate, as did many other queer individuals who found refuge on the Brooklyn waterfront. There, they and other hybrids established subcultures much like the one Benny encounters in Coney Island where they could be accepted and protected.

Coney Island Sideshow Performers

Though the tradition of sideshows well precedes Luna Park, the performers that took the stage in Coney Island during its golden era embodied the excess and fantasy that defined Coney Island's culture. Per historian John F. Kasson, and in antiquated terms, "Midgets, giants, fat ladies, and ape-men were both stigmatized and honored," providing a visual counterpoint to the industrial

---

2   Iglesias, César Andreau. *Memoirs of Bernardo Vega: A Contribution to the History of the Puerto Rican Community in New York*. (New York: Monthly Review Press, 1984), 6.
3   La Fountain-Stokes, Lawrence. *Queer Ricans: Cultures & Sexualities in the Diaspora*. (Minneapolis: University of Minnesota Press, 2009), 1.

severity that existed beyond the parks.[4] For "born oddities"—individuals whose acts were tied to their biological or hereditary deformity or other disability—the alternatives to performing were predictably cruel, including poverty, abuse, institutionalization in an asylum, or imprisonment. This stood in contrast to sideshow performers who either cultivated rare talents (such as Vera's firebreathing), altered their physical presentation (with tattoos, piercings, or other surgical procedures), or "gaffed" their acts, which involved manipulating audience expectations to make them believe a falsehood (such as Eli and Emmett's fake conjoined twins act). Such self-made performers often sought the stage due to their other marginalities, making the sideshow an attractive refuge for LGBTQ+ and BIPOC individuals.

Performing not only offered marginalized individuals the freedom, autonomy, and notoriety many able-bodied people yearned for, it also enveloped them in a supportive community willing to protect them against social institutions constructed to punish them for their differences. For this reason, the words "with it, for it, never against it" function as both mantra and rallying cry among the Menagerie members, a reminder that, regardless of ability, race, class, sexuality, or gender, their sideshow family loves and values them unconditionally.

Historical Timeline

The historical events referenced throughout *When the Tides Held the Moon* occurred as documented with some liberties taken to better suit the fantastical elements of the story.

Benny's story begins during the 1899 San Ciriaco Hurricane, the longest-lived Atlantic hurricane and one of the deadliest in recorded history, which carved a path across the Antilles, killing

---

4   Kasson, John F. *Amusing the Million: Coney Island at the Turn of the Century*. (New York: Whill & Wang, 1978).

roughly 3,400 people in Puerto Rico alone and causing USD$35.8 million of damage. With twenty-eight straight days of rain and up to 100 mph winds, it decimated the island's agriculture and left 250,000 people without food, work, or shelter only a year after the Spanish-American War had already disrupted the island's society and economy. In Humacao, a town on the southeast coast of the island where Benny was first discovered, twenty-three inches of rain fell in twenty-four hours, causing rivers to rise to unprecedented levels. Between relentless rain and the storm surge, those who lost their lives in these areas and the surrounding coastal regions likely drowned.

Five years later, a tragedy on New York City's East River would leave a similar mark on one of its immigrant communities, Little Germany. The sinking of the *PS General Slocum* on June 15, 1904, was the worst disaster in New York maritime history, killing an estimated 1,021 out of its 1,358 passengers and crew. Most of the *Slocum*'s victims were German immigrant women and children, as the ship had been chartered by St. Mark's Evangelical Lutheran Church in Little Germany for its annual excursion. A discarded match or cigarette likely lit the fire that precipitated the side-wheel boat's demise. However, blame for the excessive death toll fell not to merpeople bystanders who failed to intervene, but to the Knickerbocker Steamship Company's neglect of the ship's safety equipment and procedures. These conditions made it impossible for the crew to put out the fire and left passengers reliant upon crumbling, cheaply made life vests that, upon contact with the water, didn't float. In the disaster's aftermath, state and federal passenger ship safety regulations were tightened, and Little Germany saw a steep population decline—an event young Mary Schneider would never forget, even after she became Sonia Kutzler.

Preventable tragedies like the *Slocum* disproportionately impacted New York City's lower-class immigrant communities, but none so greatly as the 1911 Triangle Shirtwaist Factory fire, the deadliest industrial disaster in the city's history. New York City garment district workers, like Igor and Lulu, were not the only citizens outraged by the catastrophe, which claimed the lives of 146 laborers—predominantly young women and girls. The fire exposed the dangerous inequities suffered by New York City's immigrant labor class to the entire country as details emerged of how workers' escape was impeded by obstructed exits and locked doors, nor was there a sprinkler system to put out the flames. The fire's victims jumped or fell to their deaths from the windows of the building's uppermost floors or otherwise succumbed to smoke inhalation. Reforms to factory safety regulations soon followed, along with a reenergized movement to improve working conditions for sweatshop laborers.

Two months later, on May 27, 1911, another famous fire destroyed Coney Island's Dreamland. Investigations revealed that tar was indeed responsible for setting the park ablaze, albeit not with the help of Frankie Agostinelli's bullet. The Hell Gate ride had been caulked earlier that night using hot pitch, and investigators suspected a tar spill at 1:30 a.m. likely exploded light bulbs within the ride or otherwise created an electrical short that ignited. Fanned by ocean breezes, the fire rapidly spread throughout the park until 5:00 a.m., when the FDNY extinguished the last flames.

Finally, the Northeastern heat wave was not caused by a captive merman's illness, but rather by dry air from the southern plains which had stifled the cooling ocean winds. This produced heat so oppressive that it reportedly warped railroad rails and melted the pitch that kept rowboats afloat, causing them to sink in the marinas. These conditions lasted for eleven days in mid-July—not late May, as the story implies—during which 211 New Yorkers died out of an estimated 2,000 deaths across the entire American Northeast. City residents were especially hard hit, as poor ventilation and crowded tenement living conditions made it difficult to find relief. Once again, minority and poorer class communities were disproportionately impacted.

In Brief

Though *Tides* only scratches the surface of the rarely told histories of postwar Puerto Rico and the Brooklyn waterfront, it is my deepest hope that readers will close this book with, if not an appreciation for the struggles of marginalized New Yorkers during the early 1900s, then empathy for those past and present who stride the line between identities and whose quest for freedom demands riding a different wave.

GLOSSARY

*All terms are Puerto Rican Spanish unless otherwise specified.

Aguacate—Avocado
Amor—Love
Amor mío—My love
Andiamo (Italian)—Let's go
¡Apúrate!—Hurry!
Aquí estoy—I'm here
Aquí vamos—Here we go
Aquí voy—Here I go
Arcángel Miguel—Archangel Michael
Arey, kya? (Hindi/Punjabi)—Hey, huh?
Atrevimiento—Daring
Atrocidades—Atrocities
¡Auxilio!—Help!
Ave María—Hail Mary
Aye Haye! (Hindi/Punjabi)—An expression of either irritation or amazement, depending on context.
Ayúdame—Help me
¡Ayúdano', Señor!—Help us, Lord!
Bacalao guisado—Codfish stew
Bahía—Bay

Banjaxed (Irish slang)—Ruined or broken
"Barco que no anda no llega a puerto."—(idiom) Literally translates as "the ship that does not move does not reach port" and means you get nowhere by standing still
Barquito—Little boat
Barullo—Ruckus
Beenastok (Hindi)—Beanstalk
Bendito—Literal meaning is "blessed" but used in vernacular as "aw, man" or "geez"
Bendito sea Dios—Blessed be God, similar usage to "bendito"
Bigote—Mustache
Bobo—Stupid or daft
Bochinchando—Gossipping
Bolsillo—Pocket
Borínquen/borinqueños—Name for Puerto Rico and Puerto Ricans derived from the island's indigenous name, Boriken

Boricua—A Puerto Rican or person of Puerto Rican descent, derived from the island's indigenous name, Borikén

Brujería—Witchcraft

Buen provecho—Enjoy the meal

Buenas noches—Good evening

Bueno—"Well" or "well, then"

Cabello—Head of hair

Cabeza—Head

Cabras—Goats

Cabrón(es)—Bastard(s)

Café (con leche)—Coffee (with milk)

Cafecito—Coffee (diminutive)

Cafetera—Coffeepot

Caffler (UK slang)—An impertinent young boy

Camarero—Waiter

Camarón—Shrimp

Carajo—Dammit

Caramba—Expression of dismay

Casa de la alcaldía—City hall

Chavo—Cash

Chayote—Type of green squash

Chillón—Gaudy

Chiquitín/chiquitines—Small child/children

Cigarillos ("rompepechos")—Cigarettes ("chest breakers")

Claro—Of course

Claro que no—Of course not

Comemierda—Shit-eater

¿Cómo?—"How's that?" or "come again?"

¿Cómo se dice . . . ?—How do you say . . . ?

¿Cómo te sientes, querido?—How do you feel, dear?

Comodito—Comfortably

Compañero/a—Companion

Confía en mí—Trust me

Confundido—Confused

¡Coño!—Rude term for female genitalia but in Puerto Rican vernacular translates more closely as "holy shit!"

Coquí—A small tree frog indigenous to Puerto Rico, so named for the sound of its chirp

Corazón—Heart

Corona—Crown

Cosa—Thing

Cristo—Christ

Cuatro—An instrument unique to Puerto Rico, derived from the Spanish guitar, often with four or five double-strings

Daddle (UK slang)—Hand

Dale consuelo al tritón, Señor—Give comfort to the merman, Lord

Dame un momento—Give me a moment

Débil—Weak

De nada—You're welcome

Dhanyavaad (Hindi/Punjabi)—Thank you

Diablo—Devil

Dios mío—My God

Dios misericordioso—Merciful God

Dios purísimo—God most pure

Dios tiene su plan—God has his plan

Dolor de cabeza—Headache

¿Dónde está mi milagrito?—Where is my little miracle?

Dur fitteh muh! (Hindi/Punjabi)—Expression of annoyed outrage in response to something absurd, terrible, or both

Eejit (Irish slang)—Idiot

El cuco—The boogeyman

El Leviatán—The Leviathan

"**El pez muere por la boca.**"—(idiom) Literally translates to "the fish dies by its mouth" and means what you say can surely get you in trouble if you're not careful

El Tiburón—The Shark

El tritón—The merman

Embusteros—Tricksters or liars

En el nombre del Padre, el Hijo, y el Espíritu Santo—In the name of the Father, the Son, and the Holy Spirit

Eres hermoso—You are beautiful

Erin (Irish)—Term taken from the Hiberno-English word for Ireland, Éirinn

Escabeche—In Puerto Rico, this dish is often presented as green bananas in a vinegar marinade

Escúchame bien—Listen to me closely

¿Estás bien?—Are you all right?

Estupido/estupidez—Stupid/stupidity

Extranjero—Foreigner

Familia—Family

Feck (Irish slang)—Euphemistic version of "fuck"

Figlio di puttana (Italian)—Son of a bitch

Fíjate—In context, this means "Imagine it"

Flaquito—Skinny person

Gato estresa'o—Stressed cat

Ghanta! (Hindi/Punjabi)—Slang expression of dismay, anger, or disbelief

Git (Irish slang)—An annoying or stupid person (usually a man)

Goldbrick (English)—Someone who doesn't do their fair share of work

Golpetazo—A violent hit or punch

"**Go ndéana an diabhal dréimire de cnámh do dhroma ag piocadh úll i ngairdín Ifrinn.**" (Gaelic)—Insult that translates as "May the devil make a ladder of your backbone while he picks apples in Hell's garden."

Gobshite(s) (Irish slang)—Stupid, incompetent, or contemptible person(s)

Gombeen (Irish slang)—Shady, corrupt person, often of higher rank, looking to exploit others for a quick profit

Goop(s) (US slang)—Idiot(s)

Gracias a Dios—Thank God

Grandote—Gigantic

Gringo—White English speakers (derogatory)

Grito de Lares—The first of two failed Puerto Rican uprisings against Spanish rule in 1868

Guayabera —A staple of Caribbean menswear—a smocklike shirt with large pockets

Guten Tag (German)—Greeting: "good day"

Habichuelas—A type of bean

Hamaca—Hammock

"**Hay una infección sobre la humanidad.**"—"There is an infection on humanity."

Haye mere rabba (Hindi/Punjabi)—Oh my Lord

Heer and Ranjha (Punjabi)—The protagonists of the eponymous tragic romance from Punjab

Hep (US slang)—Being on top of the latest developments in popular culture

Hermoso—Beautiful

Homero—The classic poet Homer

Ich bin zuhause, mein Lieben (German)—I'm home, my dears

Iguaca—Green bird indigenous to Puerto Rico

Increíble—Incredible

Invert/inverted (English)—Term from the late nineteenth/early twentieth century for homosexuality and transgender individuals

Jefe—Boss

Jesucristo—Jesus Christ

Jíbaros—Refers to lower class subsistence farmers from the mountain regions of Puerto Rico, used in context like the English word "hick"

Jitney (English)—A nickel (five cents)

Juan Bobo—Folkloric character, the Puerto Rican "everyman"

Khoti'am da puttar (Hindi/Punjabi)—Sons of donkeys

Krasivaya (Russian)—Beautiful

Kulich (Russian)—Classic Easter bread

La consumición—Consumption, referring to tuberculosis

La danza—A type of ballroom dancing that flourished in Puerto Rico during the second half of the nineteenth century

Lagartijos—Small lizards found in Puerto Rico

La Playa del Condado—Condado Beach

La Sagrada Biblia—The Sacred Bible

La sirena—The mermaid

La sirena me habló en español—The mermaid spoke to me in Spanish

Lambón—Suck-up, creep, or freeloader

La tisis—Shorthand term for tuberculosis

Lector(a)—The person in a tabaquería or tobacco factory with the designated job of reading aloud for the entertainment of the tobacco workers

Llévame—Take me

Locura—Madness

"Lo que no se dice, no se sabe."—(idiom) "What is not spoken is never known."

Los hambrientos—The starving

Maahi (Hindi/Punjabi)—Beloved

Madre de Dios—Mother of God

Maicena—Creamed cornmeal breakfast food

Malas mañas—Bad habits

Malcriado(s)—Spoiled kid(s)

Maldito—Damned

Manganzón—Lazy, rascally, or immature person

Manos a Dios—Hands to God

Marineros—Sailors

Máscaras—Masks

Meaters (Irish slang)—Cowards

¡Me cago en ná!—(profanity) A euphemism for a worse cuss that literally means "I shit on God" and functions like a stronger form of "Goddammit"

Mein Freund (German)—My friend

'Metido—Abbreviation of "entremetido," meaning "nosy" or "meddling"

Me voy a morir—I'm going to die

Mi amado—My beloved

Mi cielo—Common term of endearment meaning "my heaven" or "my sky"

Mijo—Term of endearment meaning

"my son"

Mi luna—My moon

Miércoles—Literally means "Wednesday" but is an oft-used euphemism for "mierda"

Mierda—Shit

Milagrito—Little miracle

Mírate—Look at yourself

Molodoy chelovyek (Russian)— Young man

Monstruos—Monsters

Moreno—Person of brown complexion

Mot (Irish slang)—Girl or girlfriend

Muchachito—Kid (masculine)

Nechestnyy (Russian)—Liar

Nene—Little boy

Ni macho ni hembra—Neither male nor female

No digas nada—Say nothing

"No hay mal que por bien no venga."—(idiom) "There is nothing bad through which good does not follow," but used in context as "Every cloud has a silver lining."

No lo merezco—I don't deserve it

No me digas—Don't tell me

No me importa—I don't care

No pares—Don't stop

No puede ser—It can't be

No puedo—I can't

No te alcanzo—I cannot reach you

No te preocupes—Don't worry

Nos vamos—We're going

Nunca te abandonaría—I would never abandon you

Odiseo—Odysseus

Olvídate—Forget it

Oye—Listen

Pa'lante—Abbreviated form of "para alante" meaning "onward"

Pantalones—Pants

Pashka (Russian)—Russian Easter dessert

Pedacitos—Bits/pieces

Pelirroja—Red-haired woman

Pendejo(s)—Asshole(s)

'Pérate—Puerto Rican abbreviation of "espérate" meaning "wait a sec," or "hold up"

Perdóname—Forgive me

¿Perdóname?—Beg your pardon?

Pero, ¿qué?—But, what?

Pero, ¿qué demonio . . . ?—But, what in the devil?

Perrito—Puppy

Perro ahoga'o—Drowned dog

Pezzo di merda (Italian)—Piece of shit

Piragua—Shaved ice dessert

Pirata—Pirate

Por Dios—By God

Por favor—Please

Por favor, no hables así—Please don't talk like that

Por los siglos de los siglos—Forever and ever

Por supuesto—Of course

¿Por qué?—Why?

Pridurki (Russian)—Assholes

Principessa (Italian)—Princess

Pulmones—Lungs

Puttana (Italian)—Whore

Qual è la tua opinione? (Italian)— What is your opinion?

¿Qué dijiste?—What did you say?

Que Dios nos ayude—May God help us

Que Dios te perdone—God forgive you

¿**Qué sé yo?**—What do I know?

¿**Qué significa eso?**—What does that mean?

Quédate conmigo—Stay with me

Querido—Beloved

Queso blanco—White cheese

Quién sabe qué—Who knows what

Respira—Breathe

Río—River

Rubio—Blond-haired

Sabor—Flavor

Sabotatori (Italian)—Saboteurs

Sálvalo—"Save him" or "save it"

San Ciriaco—The saint for which the hurricane of 1899 was named, as it made landfall on August 8th, the day of the Roman Catholic feast of Saint Cyriacus

San Cristóbal—Saint Christopher

San Miguel—Saint Michael

Sancocho—Stew

Sankt-Petersburg—Saint Petersburg

Santa María—Holy Mary

Sea la madre—(profanity) "Be the mother"

Shararti ladka (Hindi/Punjabi)—Naughty boy

Si te digo la verdad . . .—To tell you the truth . . .

Sinvergüenza—Shameless person

Solo es un problema—It's just a problem

Sonrisa—Smile

Tabaquero/a—Tobacco farmer

Te lo prometo—I promise you

Te quiero—I love you

Ternura—Tenderness

Tierra de oportunidad—Land of opportunity

Todo es posible—Everything is possible

"**Todo lo prieto no e' morcilla.**"—(idiom) "Not everything black is blood sausage," but used as "Don't believe everything you hear."

Tonterías—Nonsense

Tosineta—Bacon

Traje—Dress

Ven a la isla—Come to the island

Vestido—Suit

Vieja—old woman

Vodyanoy (Russian)—Merman

Volviste—You came back

Vremya vesel'ya zakonchilos (Russian)—Fun time is over

¿**Y pa' qué?**—And for what?

Ya estamos llegando—We're almost there

Yanquis—Yankees

"**Zhivy búdem—ne pomrëm**" (Russian)—Literally translates to "We will live—not die." A Russian saying which, in context, means everything will be all right.

Lyrics to Palomita Blanca

Palomita blanca del piquito azul,
Llévame en tus alas a ver a Jesús.

Little white dove with the little blue bill,
Take me on your wings to see Jesus.

Si niñito es bueno yo te llevaré
Porque con mamita te has portado
bien.

If you, little boy, are good, I'll take you
Because with your mother you've
behaved well.

Ella no comía ni un grano de arroz
Y se mantenía con el corazón.

It wouldn't even eat a grain of rice
And only by its heart would it survive.

Ola, ola, ola,
Ola de la mar,
¡Qué bonita ola para navegar!

Wave, wave, wave,
Wave of the sea,
What a lovely wave to sail upon!

Lyrics to Llevame Río

Llevame, río, hasta el mar,
Sobre olas azules de agua cristal.
Por que soy un muchacho al que le
gusta cantar.
Con tritones y sirenas me gustaría
bailar.

Take me, river, to the sea,
Over blue waves of crystal water.
Because I'm a boy who loves to
sing.
With mermen and mermaids, I would
like to dance.

"Acercate más, amante del mar,"
Dijo las olas de agua cristal.
El ritmo que sientes, la tentación
fluvial,
El latido de mi corazón es tu cantal.

"Come closer, lover of the sea,"
Said the waves of crystal water.
The rhythm you feel, the river's
temptation,
The beating of my heart is your song.